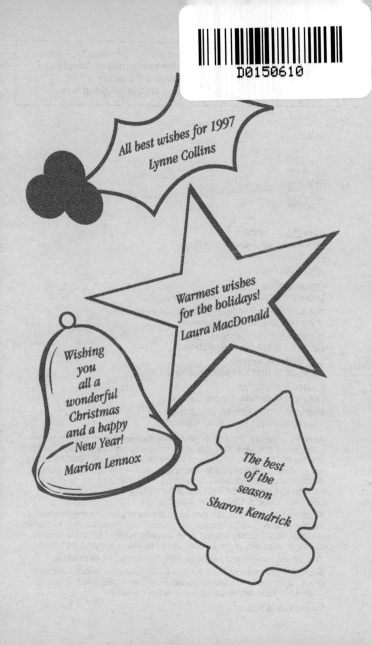

All best wishes for 1997
Lynne Collins

Warmest wishes
for the holidays!
Laura MacDonald

Wishing
you
all a
wonderful
Christmas
and a happy
New Year!

Marion Lennox

The best
of the
season
Sharon Kendrick

HARLEQUIN BOOKS
225 Duncan Mill Road, Don Mills,
Ontario, Canada M3B 3K9

ISBN 0-373-15266-3

COMFORT AND JOY
Copyright © 1997 by Harlequin Books S.A.

The publisher acknowledges the copyright holders
of the individual works as follows:

CHRISTMAS PRESENT
Copyright © 1991 by Lynne Collins

THE WAY WE WERE
Copyright © 1991 by Laura MacDonald

A MIRACLE OR TWO
Copyright © 1991 by Marion Lennox

THE REAL CHRISTMAS MESSAGE
Copyright © 1991 by Sharon Kendrick

Comfort and Joy

LYNNE COLLINS

MARION LENNOX

LAURA MACDONALD

SHARON KENDRICK

Harlequin Books

TORONTO • NEW YORK • LONDON
AMSTERDAM • PARIS • SYDNEY • HAMBURG
STOCKHOLM • ATHENS • TOKYO • MILAN
MADRID • WARSAW • BUDAPEST • AUCKLAND

CONTENTS

CHRISTMAS PRESENT

Lynne Collins

CHAPTER ONE

IT WAS just one of a number of cards from friends and colleagues that greeted Carola's arrival at the hospital that morning, a traditional card with a cheerful portrayal of a plump partridge in a pear tree and simple Christmas greetings. But the inscription lingered in Carola's mind long after she had stored the card in her bag with the rest and hurried to help with the usual routines of the busy unit.

Remember me? I remember you. Noel.

The name didn't ring any bells but she had the vague feeling that it should. She had met so many people during her years at Hartlake that it was obviously impossible to remember them all. By name or face. Yet there seemed an oddly disturbing hint of intimacy about those boldly scrawled words on a Christmas card.

Carola didn't welcome any of the traditional reminders of the festive season this year and couldn't help a growing heartache as it drew nearer. For she should have been preparing to be a Christmas bride, just as she and Jeff had planned, to commemorate their very first meeting. Without him in her life, it was just a time for painful memories and thoughts of the might-have-been.

Which, being a level-headed and strong-minded girl, she pushed firmly to the back of her mind as she tenderly bathed the tiny limbs and frail body of a sleepy infant and wrapped her in a blanket to cuddle her close. It was a time for loving these little ones and for giving them the best possible Christmas, the first of their lives in many cases, she told herself firmly.

Carola loved her work in the Special Care Unit that looked after the prems and the delicate new-borns, and she enjoyed nursing as much now as when she had first begun her training. A pretty girl, slender and shapely in the old-fashioned but much-respected uniform of a Hartiake nurse, dark hair curling about the crisp cap and dark blue eyes set deep in a heart-shaped face, with the hint of a sunny smile in the curve of her warm mouth, she softly crooned a lullaby to the baby she cradled in loving arms, stealing a few extra moments from a busy morning.

Since her first-year days when she'd met a good-looking houseman with flaming red hair and an Irish charm and fallen headlong into love, she had dreamed of combining a nursing career with the joys of marriage and motherhood. That dream had been shattered about this time last year when Jeff had chosen the night of the traditional staff dance to tell her that he'd met someone else. From that night on, convinced that no one could ever take his place in her heart, she had felt that she was destined to spend her life caring for patients like the little Leanne. And what could be more worthwhile?

'I wish I had a camera with me. . .'

Startled out of her wistful reverie, Carola glanced round at the speaker, a tall and handsome stranger who wore the long white coat of a senior doctor over powerful shoulders, a stethoscope bulging one of the deep pockets. 'Sorry. . .?'

He smiled. 'That was a moment to capture and now it's gone for ever,' he said regretfully, the warm voice with its attractive timbre sending a sudden tingling shiver down her spine. He bent over her as she sat in the low nursing chair with the baby in her arms and touched a long, strong finger to Leanne's soft cheek. 'How is she?'

'Doing very well. She gained another three ounces this week. She'll be going home soon. After Christmas. . .' Carola heard herself speaking too quickly, almost disjointedly, and knew she was unaccountably disconcerted by his nearness, the waft of expensive aftershave and the unmistakably masculine aura that threatened to trigger almost forgotten and certainly unwelcome feelings. She got to her feet to put the sleeping baby back into her cot, laying her gently on the warming pad and re-connecting her to the machine that monitored her still uncertain heartbeat. 'Were you looking for Sister?' Her tone was deliberately brisk. 'She's off duty this morning.'

He took Leanne's chart from its hook and scanned it with a professional eye. "I was looking for you, actually.'

He said it softly, with an implication that brought sudden warmth to her face and a query to her sapphire eyes. She glanced at him, tensing, and then mocked a foolish readiness to read more than he had meant into the lightly spoken words. As the senior staff nurse on duty that morning, she was responsible for the routine running of the unit in Sister Paine's absence and no doubt he had been directed to the side-ward by one of the junior nurses.

With the thought, her expressive face cleared. 'You must be Mr Buchan's new registrar!'

He nodded. 'That's right. The name's Partridge.' A wing of thickly waving dark auburn hair fell across his brow as he turned his head to smile.

For a startled second, Carola stared at him as a colourful scene from a Christmas card flashed into her mind. Then, telling herself that it could only be a coincidence, she took the hand he was holding out to her with unexpectedly informal friendliness and felt the warm, reassuring strength of his clasp of her slender fingers. 'I'm Staff Nurse Bailey... Carola Bailey.'

'Yes, I know. We've met before,' he reminded her gently.

She looked up at him, into warmly smiling grey eyes, and felt a slight shock of wholly feminine reaction to the magnetism of a very attractive man. Then things fell abruptly into place and the mystery of the Christmas card was solved.

'It's *Noel*, isn't it?' she exclaimed, slightly taken aback as the memories came flooding.

Jeff's cousin. Unwittingly caught up in the maelstrom of that dreadful evening, blundering upon an emotional scene that it still shamed her to recall and thankfully bringing it to an end with his arrival. Then, as Jeff stalked from the shadowed terrace and she fought back tears, doing his best to ease the situation for her and to cover up for the obvious humiliation of a girl he'd only met for the first time at that Christmas dance.

He nodded, his smile deepening. 'I was just beginning to feel that I must have been totally forgettable,' he drawled.

Carola frowned, remembering. 'You said I mustn't cry because it was your birthday and it would bring you bad luck for the coming year...' It was strange, the things she recalled when so much else about that night was a muddled blur. For instance, she had forgotten this man's face, but she remembered his warm, lilting voice uttering the light words in a kindly attempt to bring a smile of sorts to her eyes.

'Did I?' He looked down at her with a wry gleam in the grey eyes. 'I dare say I was saying the first thing that came into my head, most of the time.'

She smiled up at him with sudden warmth, knowing how embarrassed he must have been that night. But so kind and so understanding, whisking her off to dance so that she didn't have to face the others right away with heartbreak written all over her. She recalled the comfort of his arms, holding her securely as she stumbled about the dance-floor to a dreamy melody that she had always associated with Jeff and their lasting love-affair. Except that it *hadn't* lasted, after all...

'I was very grateful. Thanks to you, I don't think anyone else realised that my world had just fallen apart.' She found it a relief to speak frankly and freely about the worst thing that had ever happened to her. For too long, she had been pretending to family and friends and colleagues that it had been an amicable parting of the ways, daring any one of them to suspect or sympathise with her persisting pain.

'You seem to have picked up the pieces and put it together again,' he said approvingly.

'Oh, yes!' Not really, but he couldn't want to hear that Jeff was still very much on her mind and in her heart and that she would never get over the sudden, undeserved shattering of all her hopes and dreams.

Noel studied her thoughtfully. 'I didn't like leaving you that night. You were shocked, very upset. But you were on duty on the ward the next day so I knew you were coping.'

Carola warmed to him even more. He'd been really concerned, had cared enough to check that she had turned up for work and would no doubt have called at the flat to see if she was all right if she'd stayed home to lick her wounds. He had more heart than his cousin! Jeff hadn't even phoned her!

'Nurses are trained to cope with most things, aren't they? And I'm pretty resilient,' she assured him brightly. 'But it was nice of you to worry about me...'

He *was* nice, she thought, remembering that he'd given her time to put on a brave face before taking her back to their table and explaining Jeff's sudden departure by saying that he'd been called to an emergency, an occupational hazard for most doctors. He'd talked a great deal to hide the fact that she was stunned into a despairing silence by the dreadful things that Jeff had said to her and after a while he'd got her away and taken her home in his own fast car. She'd fled from him then, too near to tears even to thank him, and she hadn't seen or heard anything of him since, not surprisingly.

Noel shrugged. 'I suppose I felt responsible, in a way. Jeff's family—and I'd heard so much about you that you didn't seem like a stranger. Anyway, I liked you. I thought you were a lovely girl.'

The simply spoken words with their ring of sincerity were balm for hurt pride, the agony of feeling all these months that she must have failed Jeff in a number of ways that she had never suspected, and Carola threw him a grateful glance.

'When I got this job with Buchan, I knew it meant I'd see you again, perhaps even be working with you on occasions,' he went on. 'I hoped you wouldn't mind too much.'

'Mind?' She frowned. Surgeons came and went all the time in the unit. Some she knew as friends but most were merely colleagues and none of them impinged on her life outside the hospital walls.

'I'm still Jeff's cousin,' he said quietly.

A constant reminder, he meant, she realised, touched by his consideration. 'A lot of water has passed under the bridge since last year and nursing doesn't leave much time for fretting about the past. Besides, that isn't my style,' she assured him firmly. She smiled at him brightly. 'How *is* Jeff these days, anyway?' It wasn't quite as casual as she'd hoped to make it sound.

'I thought you might not ask. I suppose it was inevitable that you *would*.' His smile was rueful. 'He's fine. Doing great things at Sandy's and ear-marked for an early consultancy, apparently.'

'That's good. He was always ambitious,' Carola

said as warmly as she could, having expected to share in Jeff's eventual success. She still felt that if he hadn't gone to work at Hartlake's most respected rival because it offered more opportunities in his specialist field of renal surgery he wouldn't have met the girl who'd taken him from her. 'And his wife?' The words almost stuck in her throat.

It had always been hard for her to accept that Jeff had actually married someone else after all they had shared and the promises he'd made her for the future. It had happened so quickly, too, within weeks of the worst Christmas that she'd ever known.

'Very pregnant. The baby's due any day.'

'A Christmas baby? That's nice.' Her smile wavered only slightly. 'Perhaps you'll pass on my good wishes.' She turned to the other cot in the small side ward. 'Let me introduce you to Adam. He's Mr Buchan's latest success...born with a seriously damaged heart and one of the youngest patients to have a transplant. He's getting on wonderfully well.'

Having admired the healthy colour and the sturdily kicking limbs of the bright-eyed baby boy whose steady progress since life-saving surgery was recorded in the file he had studied before coming to the unit that morning, Noel settled down to examine the patient who had become his responsibility since he had joined David Buchan's team of cardiac surgeons.

Tucking both hands inside the wide bib of her apron, Carola studied him thoughtfully, thankful to note that he bore very little resemblance to his cousin. The auburn hair, toned down considerably in his case, was possibly the only pointer to the family connection.

He was very good-looking, in a totally different way from Jeff. She liked the lean, humorous features and the warm mouth and the intelligence in the kindly grey eyes. She liked the way he handled Adam, talking softly to the tiny boy while strong, finely sculpted hands moved expertly over the delicate frame. She liked his hands, the set of his broad shoulders, the quiet but impressive confidence.

He was already a talking point among the juniors, she realised, as first one and then another found cause to pass the open door and steal a glance at the new registrar. He was bound to capture a few hearts with his warm smile and easy charm, Carola felt.

At least she could be sure that her own wouldn't be among them. . .

CHAPTER TWO

CAROLA waited while Noel completed his examination and entered his findings on Adam's chart in the bold, definitive hand that was already becoming familiar. As she restored the chart to its hook, Noel took a slip of paper from the breast pocket of his white coat and consulted it briefly.

He turned to her with a smile. 'Master Wainwright. ..?'

'Oh, that's Ashley. He's on the main ward. Not very well today, I'm afraid.' It was understating the case, for the infant was on the critically ill list and there was very little that could be done for him.

'Then I'd better have a look at him.'

Carola led the way along the corridor, ticking off those of David Buchan's patients who were currently being cared for in the unit. 'You've met Adam. Ashley isn't strong enough to undergo surgery but desperately needs a new heart. Josh is listed for hole-in-the-heart repair tomorrow morning—I expect you'll be assisting with that one, won't you?' She flashed a smile at the surgeon as she spoke. 'And this is Angela.' She paused by a cot just inside the door of the main ward. 'She's really well enough to go home, but we're keeping her a little longer as she's the star of the nativity play that the nurses are putting on for the Children's ward.

We aren't supposed to have favourites but Angela is everyone's pet. Aren't you, sweetie?'

She hung over the cot to stroke the jet-black curls and the plump brown cheek, the warm tenderness in her expression transforming mere prettiness to a rare beauty that transfixed the surgeon's gaze. The baby girl gurgled happily, huge black eyes intent on Carola's face and small brown hand instantly curling about her finger in response to her touch and the sound of her voice.

Suddenly aware that Noel was studying her rather than the baby in the cot, she felt a shock of dismay as she saw a very special warmth in his eyes. For a startled moment, she thought of it as the look of love. Then, as he smiled at her blandly and turned his attention to Angela, she realised that she had foolishly imagined a particular meaning in his gaze.

'She's totally blind—but you knew that from her notes, of course,' she said matter-of-factly as they continued down the ward. 'An excess of oxygen at birth damaged the optic nerves. Apparently her heart was failing and it was a choice between losing her and the risk of brain damage. She was very ill when she came to us. Mr Buchan operated right away but she wasn't expected to live. As you saw, she's a credit to his surgical skill.'

'And excellent nursing care. My new boss was singing your praises only this morning,' Noel told her with a smile.

'We've some very good nurses on the unit,' Carola agreed, promptly passing on the compliment. 'And Sue is one of the best...' She put an affectionate hand on the slim shoulder of the nurse

who sat beside Ashley, monitoring his condition.
'Sue Allen—Noel Partridge, Mr Buchan's new
registrar. . .'

Making the introduction, she saw the swift gleam
of interest in her friend's sparkling eyes above the
mask and wondered how long it would be before
Sue chalked up yet another conquest. Attractive,
outgoing and very popular, she took life and love
very lightly, and at times Carola wished that she had
adopted a similar policy instead of devoting all her
spare time to loving Jeff and making plans for a
future that they hadn't been meant to share, after
all.

However, at the moment, the new registrar was
obviously much more interested in Ashley than in
any nurse. Not the kind to be easily distracted from
his work, Carola decided approvingly, noting the
rush of concern to his expressive eyes as he observed
the waxy pallor of the infant's face and the laboured
rise and fall of the tiny chest even with the aid of a
ventilator. Ashley had an ailing heart and poorly
developed lungs due to prematurity and there
seemed little likelihood that he would live to see
Christmas Day. A number of early presents, cuddly
toys and colourful mobiles, surrounded him as he
lay in his cot.

Sadly, death was a fact of life for the unit staff in
spite of their combined efforts. Such experiences
didn't harden a genuinely caring nurse and, along
with many of her colleagues, Carola found it particularly upsetting to lose one of the small, vulnerable babies in their care.

'Can you take a call, Staff? It's Mrs Burgess and

it sounds urgent. . .' A junior nurse put her pertly capped head into the ward with the message.

'Yes, I'll come. . .' With a murmur of apology that she doubted the surgeon even heard as he bent over the cot, Carola hurried away to the office, leaving him to do what he could to make Ashley more comfortable, with Sue's experienced assistance.

She had just replaced the receiver after reassuring the anxious mother of a successful liver transplant patient who had been discharged the previous day when Pharmacy rang through to query the amount of a drug she had ordered on the daily stock replacement list. Carola dealt with that just in time to take charge of a new admission from Accident and Emergency and abruptly became much too busy to return to the guided tour of the unit and his newly acquired patients with Noel Partridge.

However, she had an excellent deputy in Sue and she knew her friend must be looking after the new registrar just as well as *she* could—and probably getting better acquainted with him by the minute. And why not?

She was setting up a drip for the baby girl who had been badly injured in a car accident when she saw the surgeon pass the open door with his long, confident stride and a swirl of white coat, apparently too deep in thought or in too much of a hurry to notice her busy figure in the side-ward. Carola didn't call after him, for they were sure to see a great deal of each other now that chance had brought him not only to Hartlake but also to work closely with her on many occasions in the coming months.

Rather pleased that their paths had crossed again so unexpectedly, she had no intention of dwelling too much on his relationship to Jeff. It could have no bearing on her instinctive liking for a man who had been so kind and so supportive at a difficult time, and she was glad of the opportunity to repay him in some small measure by welcoming him to Hartlake as a potential friend rather than as Jeff's cousin. . .

'Nice, isn't he?' Sue commented as they queued together in the staff cafeteria at lunchtime.

'Who?' It was a genuine query, accompanied by a rapid survey of their immediate neighbours, for Carola had spent most of the morning in such a flurry of activity that she had virtually forgotten the arrival on the scene of a new registrar.

Her friend threw her a sceptical glance. 'Now who could I mean, Miss Innocent? Your secret admirer, of course!'

For a moment, she continued to look blank. Then light dawned and she laughed, shook her head. 'I suppose you mean Noel Partridge? Don't be daft, Sue. I hardly know the man!'

'That isn't the way he tells it,' Sue said slyly.

'Oh?' Carola felt a stir of alarm. 'What has he been saying?'

'Divulging all your guilty secrets.' It was teasing. Then she smiled reassurance. 'Not really. But he did say that you two are old friends.'

'Not exactly friends.' Carola helped herself to a limp-looking salad and a more appetising dish of trifle with fresh cream.

'But you *do* know each other?'

'Very slightly.'

'Well, that gives you a head start over the rest of us, doesn't it? Plus the fact that he likes you a lot. Oh, he didn't say that, but I've an instinct for these things.'

Carola carried her tray to a vacant table, followed by her friend. 'I'm really not interested, Sue,' she said firmly. 'He *is* nice and I suppose you *could* say that we're friends, but that's all there is to it. So, if you fancy him, don't let me stand in your way.'

Sue hesitated, toying with her own meat and two veg. 'Sometimes angels rush in where even fools fear to tread,' she misquoted, smiling. 'But don't you think it's time to stop hankering after your ex and realise that there are other fish in the sea?'

Carola knew the words were prompted by genuine concern and affection, but she still resented the absurd implication that one man was much like another and that it was possible for her to be happy with someone who wasn't Jeff or anything like him. 'I'm quite happy as I am, Sue,' she said stiffly.

'Well, it's Christmas and soon it will be New Year. A time for new beginnings. Promise me that you'll think about finding yourself a new man, at least!'

'Oh, I'll think about it,' she agreed brightly. It was easy to promise. Thinking wasn't doing, after all. She knew it must be hard for fickle Sue to appreciate that she really wasn't interested in replacing Jeff. Deep down, regardless of pride or lost causes or any other consideration, she knew she could never, ever love anyone else.

That evening, arriving home at the end of a day

filled with interest and event and much talk of the approaching festivities, Carola took the stack of Christmas cards from her bag and looked through them more carefully, pleased and touched by the warmth of the messages from her many friends at Hartlake.

Coming across Noel's card, she impulsively put it to the forefront of the others on the shelf above the old-fashioned fireplace in her small sitting-room. A partridge in a pear tree...wasn't that supposed to be a promise for a happy Christmas?

He couldn't have known that this was the Christmas that she and Jeff had planned for their wedding and so wasn't likely to be a very happy one for her in spite of his good wishes. Still, it had been nice of him to send the card.

'I thought you were a lovely girl...'

The soft-spoken and simply said words echoed in her thoughts. Carola found herself softly humming the words of the traditional Christmas song that had been triggered by the picture on his card as she began the preparations for her evening meal.

There was another card from Noel the next morning. Recognising his bold scrawl on the square-shaped envelope that Sister handed to her with some others, Carola felt a flicker of surprise. Curious, she opened it immediately and then marvelled at the trouble he must have taken to secure just the right card to follow the first...a pair of plump turtle doves cooing fondly at each other above a steaming Christmas pudding.

How about dinner tonight? Please. Noel.

She smiled at the absurd card and the surgeon's unconventional approach. But it was a totally unexpected invitation and she wasn't at all sure that she wanted to accept.

He was only being friendly, of course. He was a newcomer to Hartlake and she was the only familiar face in a sea of unknowns. He was so nice and so understanding that she could be sure he didn't expect anything from her but friendship—and didn't he already feel like a friend? So where was the harm in going out with him, just this once?

She saw Noel briefly when he came to the unit to run the routine rule over Josh before he went down to Theatres, but she had no chance to speak to him for it was the busiest time of the morning. He was in Theatres until she was about to go to lunch and then he accompanied Josh on his return from hole-in-the-heart surgery and she caught a glimpse of his tall figure in the distance, wearing theatre greens and boots and with his distinctive hair almost hidden beneath the surgeon's cap.

She hesitated and then sped down the corridor to the main ward where she found him connecting Josh to various pieces of monitoring equipment. 'How is he?' The sick baby looked very frail with tubes and wires sprouting all over his small body, but he had a good colour and his heartbeat seemed to be reassuringly regular.

'He'll do,' Noel said briefly. It was the traditional term for those patients who were expected to make a good recovery from surgery or sickness.

'I got your card,' Carola murmured, conscious that a martinet of a Sister was only a few feet from them, attending to another of the seriously ill infants.

Noel glanced up. 'Do I get an answer?'

'Shall we say seven-thirty?'

He had such a swift, sweet smile, she thought inconsequentially, wondering if he knew its devastating impact. Oh, not on herself! She was immune to its charm. But she could well imagine its effect on someone with a heart to lose!

'I'll call for you,' he agreed.

He obviously remembered where she lived, Carola realised as she hurried away. He was the kind who didn't forget anything. She fancied that he would be a comfortable and considerate companion, making no demands of any kind on her emotions.

That was good. She didn't want excitement any more. . .

CHAPTER THREE

How could Carola have forgotten the disturbing reaction to Noel's maleness that she had experienced so strongly only the day before? It came back to her in a sudden, swamping tide as their eyes met across the table in the intimate setting of the small Italian restaurant and Noel raised his wine glass to her in smiling salute.

It must be the wine, she decided, as the warmth in those grey eyes threatened the cool of her determined defences and the touch of his hand, sliding to clasp her own so naturally, triggered a startling awareness of his very physical attractions. Feelings that had lain dormant for months abruptly surged to the surface.

Studying his handsome face, Carola found herself fantasising about the taste and the feel of that sensual mouth, the brush of his lean cheek against her skin, the hardness of his powerful frame crushing her close and the stirring caress of those strong but sensitive hands on her body.

'I'd like to make it a happy Christmas for you, Carola. . .'

The light words drifted across an erotic image of bodies entwined in a tumble of excitement and ecstasy and euphoria, mouths and arms locked and flesh enjoined. With racing pulses and a soft flush to her face, she dragged her wandering, wanton

thoughts from dangerous paths and clamped a rein
on quickened senses, hoping that her clouded gaze
hadn't betrayed the alarming reaction to a very
potent sexuality.

'I haven't been looking forward to it this year, I
must admit. But there will be so much going on and
so many other things—and people—to think about
that I doubt if I'll have much time to dwell on my
problems.'

A frown flickered in Noel's eyes. 'But Jeff isn't a
problem any more, surely?'

Like everyone else, he thought that a year was
quite long enough for her to get over heartbreak,
Carola realised wryly. No doubt it ought to be. . .

'No, he isn't,' she said firmly. 'It took time to get
used to the idea of a future that didn't include him,
of course. But now I've accepted that things have
changed. He's married—and I'm getting on with my
own life.'

'And you no longer love him.'

Carola studied the hand that lay across her own
in such friendly, inoffensive intimacy, the hand of a
surgeon with its shapeliness and sensitivity, the hand
of a man who could wield a scalpel or caress a
woman into weak and willing submission with
equally perceptive skill. She liked its strength, the
well-kept nails and the faint sheen of golden hairs
that gleamed in the muted light from an overhead
lamp.

She looked up to meet his thoughtful gaze. 'I
didn't say that, Noel.'

'No. You didn't say that,' he agreed flatly and
removed his hand to brush back the wing of thick

auburn hair that seemed to have a tendency to spill across his brow.

'Five years of loving someone isn't wiped out so easily.' For some reason, she was slightly on the defensive, although there could be no wrong in long and loyal loving or in clinging to the memories that were all she had left of those years with his cousin.

'I know about loving,' Noel said abruptly, a harshness tinging the deep voice. 'It can take over your whole life and get in the way of everything else. It can make your decisions for you, for good or bad. It can ask far too much of a man, in fact.'

Carola felt a rush of sympathy for him as she saw the throb of a pulse in the lean cheek and the burn of an intense emotion in the grey eyes. His expression and the brusqueness of the words gave her a sudden insight into his understanding of the way she felt about Jeff. It seemed that he had been badly hurt at some time, had loved and lost like herself, and that he needed the comfort and companionship of an undemanding relationship just as much as she did.

'And there's no getting over it, is there?' she sympathised wryly. 'No remedy—except hard work, perhaps...'

'And the company of someone who accepts that you only have so much to give and can make that enough.' he suggested quietly.

Carola was swift to interpret his meaning. He was so attractive, so personable, that women were probably a problem, casting out lures and making emotional demands that he couldn't meet, and he was reaching out to her because he knew she wasn't looking for someone to take Jeff's place in her life. Understanding the acute loneliness and the sense of loss and the total lack of interest in a new commitment, Carola didn't have the heart to turn down his suggestion. Besides, she was sure that they had a lot to give each other apart from friendship.

'I think we must have been meant to meet again,' she said impulsively. 'The way you've turned up at Hartlake — out of the blue! And just at this particular time when I most needed cheering up. . .' She smiled at him with grateful warmth.

'Seems like destiny, doesn't it?' Noel agreed, with just the faintest gleam of amusement lurking at the back of his grey eyes. He refilled her glass with more of the sparkling wine. 'Let's drink to destiny. . .'

Carola drank the toast, rather doubtfully, vaguely troubled by a certain something in his smile, an elusive quality in his light tone. Was it possible that he had taken the job at Hartlake so that they could meet again? Had he remembered her so vividly because he had found her attractive at the time of their first meeting? Had it already occurred to him that they might console each other to some extent?

She shook off the doubts. It just didn't seem likely that he could be so devious. But in any case, much as she liked him, nice though he was, an affair with Noel Partridge was out of the question. She was a one-man woman — even though her man had married someone else and forgotten all about her.

Mind and heart clung stubbornly to the thought of Jeff and insisted that no one could ever take his place, but her treacherous body surprised her with a craving for physical contact with his very attractive cousin as those warm grey eyes smiled into her own. Carola was shocked by the stir of her senses and a sudden hunger for his touch, his kiss, his enfolding arms.

Once more, she was inclined to blame the wine. . .

However, her head was perfectly clear when he drove her home after a stroll by the river in the cool of the night at the end of a very pleasant evening. So she had absolutely no excuse for responding to his obligatory goodnight kiss with such misleading fervour. His lips were cool and firm and surprisingly sweet as he took renewed possession of her mouth with an assurance that swept away any hesitation or inhibition she might have been feeling. His arms were just as strong and as comforting as she remembered.

With a murmuring sigh, Carola drew away from his warmly reassuring embrace, although she was terribly tempted to linger. It was a long time since she had been held so tenderly and she liked his nearness, his body-warmth, the pleasantly male scent of him and the security that seemed to surround her as she stood in his arms. But she was acutely aware of his arousal and its effect upon herself, and it was a shock to realise that it would be disastrously easy to tumble into bed with him and forget everything in the voluptuous tumult and togetherness of lovemaking.

She had never felt such a fierce degree of desire for any man, not even Jeff, and it was alarming. She wasn't sure that she could trust those violent waves of wanting or where they might lead her. Yet she knew instinctively that she could trust Noel to take care of her in all things. He was that kind of man.

She looked up at him with a smile that softened her withdrawal. 'I've really enjoyed this evening. . .'

'Does it have to end just yet?' He tilted her chin to look deep into her eyes, the real question behind the soft-spoken words burning in his gaze.

Carola fought the strong stir of temptation. 'I'm afraid so. We both have to work tomorrow,' she reminded him lightly. It was mundane, matter-of-fact, and they both knew that it was a very lame excuse for cold feet.

'That's true. But tonight is a kind of celebration, isn't it? Getting the job with Buchan. Meeting you again. The season of goodwill. What better way to celebrate?' His smile was warm with persuasion.

Weakly, she inserted her key in the lock and opened the door of her apartment. She led the way into the sitting-room and switched on the tall standard lamp beside the sofa. 'Make yourself at home while I make some coffee. . .do you mind instant?'

She glanced back at him from the doorway of her tiny kitchen. Long legs stretched out before him, head thrown back, he was already relaxing against the deep cushions of the comfortable couch, the light from the lamp falling on his handsome profile and throwing its shadow across the opposite wall.

He looked very much at home, having taken her at her word, and as the raging in her blood began to subside Carola wondered if it had been wise to bring him into the aparment. Would she be able to send him away once he had drunk the coffee she was about to make for him? Or would he be so persistently persuasive that it became embarrassing?

As Noel sent her a warm, lazy smile, her doubts fled. There was something so reassuring about him that she felt as if she had known him all her life. Of course he would leave without protest as soon as she asked it. It might be more of a problem to *want* him to leave, she admitted ruefully. . .

There was certainly no problem finding things to talk about over their coffee, and the intended ten minutes stretched imperceptibly to forty. Noel had been working abroad for much of the year and had several interesting or amusing anecdotes to relate about his experiences. Carola was fascinated and appalled to hear that hospital conditions and medical supplies and equipment were still so poor in the Third World.

He had contracted a mild form of tropical fever that was likely to trouble him intermittently for the rest of his life and had been advised to return to the more temperate climate of England. The job as Buchan's senior registrar had been on offer on his return and he had applied for it.

'You look to me like a man who's never suffered from anything worse than toothache in his life,' Carola teased, seeing the ripple of muscles beneath the thin shirt as he moved and admiring the tan he had acquired during those months in Africa.

Noel showed an excellent set of teeth with a dazzling smile. 'Not even that, I must admit. I'm perfectly fit at the moment and now that I'm home again I'll probably never have another attack.'

'It must have been a blow, having to give up a job that you obviously enjoyed?'

'It was something I'd always wanted to do. But I'm not sorry to be back. My future lies here—and Hartlake has the prettiest nurses in the world,' he added lightly. 'It would be churlish to complain about my lot when I'm sitting next to one of them right now.'

Carola laughed, but a pleased blush swept into her pretty face. Noel smiled down at her and then he took her face in both strong hands and brushed the soft dark curls that sprang from her temples, her brow, the tip of her shapely nose and the curve of her cheek with a succession of feathery kisses that left her weak with delight and wanting more—she turned her mouth to his on a little gasp of eager welcome and melted against him.

She wasn't thinking of Jeff in that moment. She wasn't thinking of anything but that tidal flood of long-suppressed need, the sizzle of ice-cold fire in her veins and a soaring excitement in response to his seeking, sensual kiss.

It was hard for her to resist the power and the passion she sensed in his ardent embrace when it promised to ease the loneliness and longing that had haunted her ever since last Christmas. But it was the thought of Christmas come again that suddenly brought Jeff vividly to mind and crushed the wild impulse to betray the continuing love for him in another man's arms.

As she froze, closing her mouth against his persuasive kiss, Noel let her go, rueful understanding in his smiling eyes.

'Too soon? I expect you're right. But we aren't exactly strangers, are we? I've thought about you a lot, Carola. Perhaps that's why I feel that ordinary conventions ought not to count where you and I are concerned. But I won't rush you. We've plenty of time to get better acquainted and I guess I still have to exorcise one or two ghosts.'

The ghost of his lost love, Carola supposed. And, in her case, the ghost of Christmas past. . .

CHAPTER FOUR

No ONE could doubt that it was almost Christmas.
The unit was festooned with colourful streamers and
bunches of bright balloons were pinned above each
cot, just where they would catch the eye of a
wakeful infant. Strings of cards adorned each cot or
incubator and a small tree in the main ward had
been dressed with tinsel, glittering balls and a fairy
doll, and already a number of presents for the babies
lay around its base. On Christmas Day, they would
be handed out by a doctor in the guise of Santa
Claus.

Snatches of familiar carols drifted constantly
along corridors as the staff became infected with the
spirit of the season and it seemed to Carola that the
juniors could think and talk of nothing else.
Bunches of mistletoe had been slyly fixed at strategic
points by hopeful housemen and cards that were
addressed to all the staff were pinned to notice-
boards that advertised seasonal events such as the
bazaar that was organised each year by the hospital's
League of Friends.

Passing a huge poster that invited staff to the
traditional dance on Christmas Eve, she found that
the reminder didn't hurt as much as she'd expected.
In any case, it was impossible to be down-hearted
for long amid so much excitement.

She was surprised and pleased to receive a few

early gifts during the course of the day. Chocolates from grateful parents who were taking their baby home in time for Christmas, fit and well after by-pass surgery. Perfume from a friend who was going to Wales for the holiday and handing round gifts before she left. A couple of theatre tickets from a houseman who couldn't use them himself—should she ask Noel if he'd like to go with her? she wondered. Or would that seem as if she was running after him? After all, he hadn't said anything about seeing her again when they'd parted last night.

Why would he? she asked herself sensibly. He'd obviously expected to run into her during the day. In fact, she hadn't seen him at all and she felt vaguely disappointed. However, Christmas might be looming but Outpatients was still busy and it had been a cardiac clinic day. No doubt he had been up to his eyebrows in patients.

She had been busy herself but she'd still found time in the midst of dressings and drips and drug rounds to think about Noel. She realised that he was growing on her. He could never take Jeff's place, of course. But he seemed to have slotted into a place in her life that had been waiting for him.

Carola went off duty late that afternoon with an indefinable sense of something missing or something forgotten. She was just about to step into the lift when a junior nurse rushed along the corridor, calling her name.

'I'm glad I caught you!' The breathless girl produced a crumpled, slightly stained envelope from the deep pocket of her uniform skirt. 'I was supposed to give this to you ages ago but I forgot all about it. . .sorry! I hope it isn't important.'

'Just a Christmas card, I expect.' Carola didn't have the heart to scold the forgetful junior, her spirits having unaccountably lifted at the sight of the envelope she had been half expecting throughout the day. She didn't need to glance at it to know that it was inscribed with her name in Noel's strong handwriting.

As the lift doors closed, concealing her from the nurse's curious gaze, she tore it open with impatient fingers. Not a card, after all, she saw, but a single sheet of notepaper on which he had drawn, rather skilfully, three jolly hens in flouncy skirts and high heels doing a leggy can-can beneath a theatre bill that advertised the Folies Bergere. Three French hens! And there was a message beneath the cartoon.

One of these little birds told me that you've been given theatre tickets for this evening. I doubt if you need an escort but I am available.

She loved his sense of humour and his knack of striking just the right note. But how had he known about the tickets that Yussif had passed on to her? It seemed impossible to keep anything to oneself in a large general hospital!

Her face was wreathed in smiles as she paused by the big reception desk in the main hall that was presided over by the bulky head porter who never seemed to be off duty. After thirty years at Hartlake, Jimmy was as much of an institution to the people in the district as the hospital itself, a familiar figure to staff and patients.

An avid reader of medical textbooks, he liked to discuss theoretical cases with the young doctors and students and he prided himself on having a talent for instant diagnosis of any new patient entering the portals of Hartlake. Somehow, he was seldom mistaken. He was also the main root of the very efficient grapevine, Carola suspected, knowing his penchant for harmless gossip and his delight in the romances that struck up between members of the staff from time to time. It was said that Jimmy knew an engagement was in the offing long before the couple concerned!

'Nice to see you looking so happy, Staff... Christmas and all,' he said with a satisfaction that told the surprised Carola that he knew all about the heartache she thought she had hidden from the world. He beamed at her, having followed with avuncular interest her progress from apprehensive first year to present-day staff nurse with a responsible job in the Special Care Unit. 'What can I do for you?'

'I'd like to leave a message for Mr Partridge, Mr Buchan's registrar. Could you be a dear and see that he gets it before he goes home, Jimmy?'

'Too late, I'm afraid.' He indicated the empty gap on the board where Noel's nameplate had been slotted earlier in the day. 'He's already gone...'

Carola's heart sank. He must have waited all day for some response to his note and then left believing that she wasn't interested in going out with him again. He wouldn't push himself, she realised—that wasn't his way. His suggestions were always tentative, leaving her with a get-out if she wanted one—and that was something she liked in him.

'Oh dear! I particularly wanted to contact him,' she said impulsively.

'I could let you have his telephone number, if you like.' Jimmy lowered his voice conspiratorially. 'I'm not supposed to give it out, mind. But I know I can trust you to keep it to yourself.'

'That would be a great help!'

He slid a piece of paper across the desk towards her. 'There you are, Staff. Don't forget to eat it later!' He guffawed at his own joke.

Smiling, Carola turned away to head for the row of telephone kiosks at the other side of the main hall. Waiting for a vacant box, she wondered if she would find Noel at home or if he'd made other plans for the evening when he hadn't heard from her during the day.

She rushed into speech at the sound of his deep voice. 'Noel? It's me—Carola! I've only just got your note. Are you still free for the theatre this evening?'

'It means disappointing six other girls, but I expect I can make it.'

Carola smiled at the drollery in his tone. 'The show starts at seven-thirty so we're a bit rushed for time. Shall I meet you in the foyer?'

It wasn't until she stepped out of the taxi, having known it would be impossible to find a parking space for her car in the heart of London's theatre-land, that she realised that she hadn't named the theatre or the show they were going to see! She forgot to pay the cabby in her panic and he called her back in irate tones as she made a dash for the foyer in a seemingly vain hope that she would see Noel waiting for her.

Rather more slowly, she mounted the few marble steps and pushed through the entrance doors into the crowded foyer—and felt her heart lift with relief as she saw him, towering over everyone around him with his distinctive height and powerful build. He was so strikingly handsome in the fashionable grey suit that Carola saw a few envious glances from other women out of the corner of her eye as Noel moved to greet her and felt a little glow of feminine satisfaction that he was *her* date.

'Did another little bird tell you the name of the theatre?' she teased. 'I completely forgot to say.'

Noel smiled down at her. 'There *were* three of them,' he reminded her lightly.

Carola's fingers folded over the piece of paper that she had impulsively tucked into the pocket of her bright cherry jacket, worn over a simply cut floral dress of cherry flowers on a beige background and matching her high-heeled shoes and leather bag. It was a new outfit, her Christmas present to herself, and she felt good in it. She knew that she looked good, too, as she saw the gleam of admiration in his grey eyes.

She nodded, smiling back at him. 'Fifi, Mimi and La Belle. . . I remember!'

She liked the way he laughed, the way the warm grey eyes crinkled and his handsome face lit up with merriment in response to her impulsive, flippant christening of the cartooned hens. She liked the way he hugged her, too, in swift appreciation of a sense of humour that complemented his own.

She glanced at his good-looking profile as they sat in the darkened auditorium, waiting for the curtain to go up, and warmed to his air of expectancy. He was a man who enjoyed most things, she felt. Sometimes Jeff had been very bored and allowed it to show, and that had marred her own enjoyment of an evening at a theatre or restaurant. So it was rather nice to feel that Noel would not only enjoy whatever he undertook but also take pleasure in her enjoyment of it, too.

The show was excellent, the latest in a long line of musical successes for a famous impressario, and they emerged from the theatre with Carola hugging Noel's arm and humming the catchy number that had recently topped the charts.

'Hungry? I've booked a table for supper at the Flamingo.'

She was surprised. 'How on earth did you manage that at such short notice?' The Flamingo was London's newest cabaret club, graced nightly by young royals and the stars of stage and screen.

'Influence.'

There was a twinkle in the grey eyes that struck Carola as strangely familiar and she stared at him suspiciously. 'Did you plan this?'

He met the challenge with a bland smile. 'I had to make one or two telephone calls, obviously.'

That wasn't what she'd meant, but she didn't pursue it. Somehow, he seemed so open that it was hard to think of him as devious—and surely it would take a very devious mind to arrange for a medical colleague to pass on theatre tickets to a certain staff nurse and then ensure that he was the one who took her to see the show? It would need a surfeit of conceit, too—and Noel didn't seem to be *that* sure of her!

'This is quite a week,' she breathed, as an attentive waiter drew out her chair and then handed her a gold-embossed menu card with a bow and a flourish. Carola looked about her, slightly awed by the glitz of their surroundings and the expensive elegance of the other diners, glad that she was wearing the new outfit which had cost her rather more than she usually paid for her clothes. She must have had a premonition that it would be needed for such an occasion! 'I haven't been out two nights in a row for longer than I care to remember!'

Since last Christmas, actually. Then she and Jeff had been caught up in night after night of festive fun with their friends, culminating in the staff dance, and she hadn't had the least suspicion that he was secretly longing to be with that other girl. She'd put his occasional snappiness and spells of moodiness down to overwork.

'I hope you're prepared to make it three in a row? I'm giving a small party tomorrow night and I'd like you to be there,' Noel told her warmly.

Carola looked doubtful. Tomorrow was Christmas Eve and there was very little time left for last-minute preparations. Not that she had much to do, she admitted, for she had volunteered to work through the holiday, partly because it was a wonderful time of the year in the hospital and she wanted to be with the babies and partly to free those of her colleagues who had families needing them to cook the turkey, help unwrap the presents and entertain the in-laws.

'I'm not sure that I can make it, Noel. . .'

'I've been looking up old friends and making new ones in the last few days, and I thought it would be nice to get them together. I know it's short notice but do come, Carola. If only for half an hour or so,' he urged with his most persuasive smile.

'It's the nativity play in the afternoon and I've promised to go round the wards with the carol-singers in the evening. It's a Hartlake tradition. Some of us dress up in the original Victorian uniforms and carry Nightingale lamps and sing a different carol on each of the wards. It's fun——' She broke off abruptly, putting an impulsive hand on his arm as she was struck by a sudden thought. 'It's your birthday. . .!'

CHAPTER FIVE

THEY were interrupted by the return of the waiter who had been assigned to take care of them. Carola agonised over the magnificent choice of tempting dishes and finally settled for chicken in a cream and mushroom sauce. Noel beckoned the hovering wine waiter and ordered champagne.

'We'll celebrate now in case you don't get to the party,' he said in response to her raised eyebrow.

'It really *is* your birthday tomorrow, I suppose? It wasn't just a joke?'

'No joke. I really was born on Christmas Eve. Hence the name.' He smiled wryly. 'I wasn't going to mention it,' he added gently.

He hadn't wanted to remind her of the painful circumstances surrounding his last birthday, Carola realised gratefully. Automatically, her thoughts shied from that Christmas Eve and her last memory of Jeff, flushed with embarrassment and guilt and with something like scorn in his blue eyes as she humbly pleaded with him not to break her heart.

Now, all these months later, she could still squirm at the memory of a humiliation that had stung far more than the discovery that Jeff no longer wanted her, a humiliation she had made worse for herself by letting him see how dependent she was on him for her happiness.

Well, she had learned to live without him,

although it hadn't been easy. It had taken time to realise that her heart had been badly cracked rather than totally shattered, time and the unexpected discovery that another man's smiling friendliness could melt some of the ice that she had packed about it to protect her from the risk of being hurt again. . .

'I suppose I scarcely need to tell you that my parents live in a house they've called Pear Tree Cottage,' Noel went on lightly, attempting to distract her thoughts from the past.

Carola smiled at him. 'I think that's rather nice,' she said warmly.

He nodded. 'They're nice people. Rather predictable and a little old-fashioned in their attitudes, but nice. Maybe you'll meet them one of these days.'

The arrival of the champagne saved her from making any reply to the tentative words. She liked him enormously but she was a very long way from making any plans for the future or any promise of commitment.

She looked around the crowded nightclub with eager interest. 'Surely that's Don Hathaway in that corner,' she said, lowering her voice, discreetly indicating the table where sat the well-known film star.

It was fun to play 'spot the celebrity' and there were a fair amount of them sprinkling the room. Noel entered into the game with gusto, putting names to faces much more quickly than she could, making her laugh by putting some very famous names to the most unlikely faces. The thought of Jeff was driven completely from her mind by the charismatic reality of his cousin's company, and Carola glowed from the delight of an evening spent with him by the time they emerged from the Flamingo, well after midnight.

She didn't know that it was so late and it was only as they drove past Big Ben on their way through Westminster that she realised that Christmas Eve had sneaked up on them without warning. Sitting next to Noel in his big, comfortable car, cocooned in a content that she hadn't felt for a very long time, admiring the twinkling string of street-lights along the dark ribbon of river as they drove along the Embankment, she sent up a silent prayer of thanks to the guardian angel who had arranged for someone so nice, so undemanding and so reliable to walk back into her life at just the right moment.

When the car came to a halt outside the tall building that housed her apartment, Carola put her hand over Noel's as it rested squarely on the steering-wheel and smiled at him with her heart in her eyes.

'Happy birthday,' she said softly, and reached to kiss the lean, slightly beard-roughened cheek.

'I hope that isn't all I'm getting,' he drawled, a spark of meaningful mischief in the grey eyes that smiled back at her.

'I'm afraid I haven't got a card for you,' she murmured in mock regret, her own eyes dancing with a provocative amusement as she pretended to misunderstand him.

'I was thinking of something much more exciting than a birthday card.' Noel bent his auburn head to kiss her, very lightly, the merest breath of a kiss that ought not to have seared her to the soul with its promise of an all-consuming passion.

Carola caught her breath on a sudden shock of desire. The tension in his powerful frame hinted at urgent arousal, although he held back from touching her except with those light lips. As her own pulses quickened and leaped, she was filled with an unbearable ache of longing. Perhaps it was madness, but she put an arm about his neck and leaned against him, lifting her face to be kissed once more, inviting the caress of strong, sure hands with the sighing swell of her breasts.

He crushed her to him on a groan and then released her, almost too abruptly, causing her to wonder on a surge of dismay if he was rejecting her impulsive implication of surrender.

'Is it all right to leave the car here?' He indicated the spookily silent, dimly lit square with its edging of elderly houses and tall apartment buildings. 'Or will it be minus its wheels in the morning?'

Carola smiled at him and began to look for her keys in her handbag. 'It's a fairly respectable neighbourhood,' she assured him. 'I think you can safely take a chance on leaving it overnight.'

Between them, they had dealt with question and answer in very satisfactory fashion. Yet, once in her apartment with the front door securely fastened, he kept his distance, giving her time to change her mind if she wished. He wasn't the kind to rush her into anything, Carola thought gratefully, and he didn't yet know her well enough to realise that once she felt committed to a certain course she didn't lightly turn back from it.

Loving Jeff as she did, she would probably love him for the rest of her life. But he was lost to her and there was really no good reason to go on denying his caring and considerate cousin—or herself—the warm delight to be found in each other's arms.

Christmas was a time for giving, after all. . .

With a fluttering heart in spite of her calm resolve, she turned into the strong sanctuary of his embrace and put her arms up and about his neck, reaching to kiss him with lips that spoke of willing surrender to the desire that she sensed in his powerful frame.

Arms tightening instantly about her, Noel looked deep into the starry sapphire eyes. 'Sweetheart, I want you so much,' he said huskily.

She nodded. 'I want you, too.' He was so nice, already dearer than she had believed any man could be again, and her body was responding to his nearness with a flame that left her breathless.

Carola liked his leisurely approach that heightened rather than lessened the importance of their lovemaking. She liked the way he undressed her, without haste, admiring appreciation of her firm, peaked breasts and handspan waist and slender, rounded hips glowing in his grey eyes. She liked the homage he paid to her body with warm lips that followed the trail of gentle, reverent hands with a succession of quick, light, almost light-hearted kisses that lulled any last-minute apprehensions that she might have felt.

Shortly, Noel's clothes joined her own in a tousled heap beside the bed and he stretched at her side to take her into his arms. Then, for the first time since he had begun to make serious and single-minded love to her, he sought her warm and willing mouth.

His kiss began softly, so sweetly that her heart tilted and only gradually did it become urgent, insisting on a response to the increasing need in the powerful frame that lay so close to hers, touching but not yet urging itself upon her.

As his deepening kiss demanded the rising tide of a desire to match the throbbing tumult in his blood and his trembling hands swept her body with clever, intimate caresses, Carola clung to him, weak with wanting, unable to refuse him anything he might ask of her as her senses swam and her flesh clamoured for even closer contact. She was convinced that their coming together in such wild and joyous abandon must lead to a greater ecstasy than she had ever known even in the days when Jeff's arms had been about her and her heart had welled with love for him.

Slowly but surely, their bodies drew closer to merge in an instinctive, rhythmic union that was sweet and unhurried insurance of a mutual fulfil-ment that would leave them both glowing and content.

Oh, but he was the kind of lover a woman dreamed about, Carola thought joyfully, as each sure thrust and slow withdrawal sent a delicious shock of excitement along quivering nerve-endings and swamped her with eager anticipation of the next. His body was a powerful shaft of sheer physi-cal sensation that she wanted never to end even while her fevered instincts urged her inexorably towards the ultimate peaks of pleasure and the final crescendo.

Dark waters crashed slowly and pleasurably over her head and she felt herself drowning in a sea of delight that was the nearest thing to heaven that mere mortals could know. It was wonderful, wonderful, and her whole being was fired by that thrilling wave upon wave of pleasure that left her beached with Noel in the afterglow of a stupendously satisfying climax to those golden moments.

'Oh, *wonderful...!*' she murmured happily, still holding him to her, reluctant to lose any of the magic.

Noel kissed the tip of her nose, the tilt of her chin and finally the soft, quivering mouth that quickened involuntarily beneath the touch of his lips. 'So are you...' He stroked the mass of dark, silky curls from her brow with tender hands that went on to frame her lovely, ecstatic face. 'What more could any man want on his birthday?' he said softly.

The teasing smile in the deep-set eyes caught at Carola's heart, because she sensed a sadness behind the words, a sadness that she thought she understood only too well.

It *was* possible for him to want more, in spite of the disclaimer, Carola knew. She was not the lover he really ached to hold in his arms. Like Noel himself, she was second best. They had shared a brief and magical enchantment but, deep down, he still wanted his lost love.

Just as she still wanted Jeff...

Seeing the shadow that crossed her face, Noel quickly kissed it away and the fleeting thought of another man was driven from her mind as he began to make love to her once more, with a fierce and almost angry ardour this time as if he was intent on exorcising his own ghost from the past. Her body rose to him at a touch and her heart moved within her on a surge of warm compassion for a lingering pain so like her own.

Afterwards, they slept, bodies still linked like the lovers they had become. . .

Carola almost danced across the main hall on her way to the unit the next morning, happier than she had been all year but sensible enough to accept that her euphoria sprang from a purely physical satisfaction and the knowledge that she was admired and desired by a very attractive man whom she liked more than any man she had ever known. But liking wasn't loving and she wasn't likely to confuse the two emotions. In any case, she didn't want to fall in love. Noel wasn't looking for a lasting commitment, either, so they were well suited with an easy, undemanding and comfortable relationship for the time being.

They really *were*, and would remain, just good friends with a special understanding of each other's needs. . .

'Good morning, Staff. You're looking very bonny, if I may say so. Did you manage to get hold of Mr Partridge last night, by the way?' It was a slightly sly query, for Jimmy's wise old eyes had taken in the warm glow in her cheeks and the shine in her eyes and the smiling curve to her mouth that told its own story.

Unaccountably, Carola felt herself blushing. Then

she laughed, nodded. 'Oh, yes. I got hold of him,' she agreed demurely, amused that Jimmy was scenting romance where none existed, in his usual hopeful fashion. 'Thanks very much for your help. . .'

She walked on to the lifts, her excited heart hugging the memory of a sweet and sensual and so satisfying encounter with Mr Buchan's new registrar. Waking that morning with a lingering glow of content, she had found Noel bending over her with a smile and a breakfast tray and an easy acceptance of their altered relationship that had swept away the last of her doubts.

Meeting him again and welcoming him into her life as friend and lover had eased a number of bitter memories just in time for Carola to enjoy the advent of Christmas, after all. . .

CHAPTER SIX

As she came out of the clinical room with a syringe that held a pain-killing injection for Josh, Carola paused, frowning, heart leaping wildly in her startled breast.

It had been the merest glimpse but surely she had just seen *Jeff*, crossing the corridor from Sister's office to the main ward! A gleam of bright hair, the unmistakable swing of broad shoulders combined with a lithe stride. . .she shook her head. Impossible! He had no reason to be here, in the Special Care Unit at Hartlake. He was on the other side of London, working at Sandy's or relaxing with his heavily pregnant wife.

It had been simply a trick of the light. Or a trick of her imagination, fostered by an absurd guilt because she had spent the night with Noel. She had no cause to feel so guilty, she scolded herself sensibly. Jeff was married—and she was a free agent. That blissful interlude with another man wasn't a betrayal because her heart wasn't involved—and surely that was what counted!

It could only have been a confusion of two vaguely look-alike cousins, she decided. It must have been Noel, making his way into the ward, his richly auburn hair brightened by a wayward shaft of most unseasonal sunshine.

It was a mild December and the experts said it

was unlikely to be a white Christmas. No one but the children minded, for the best place for snow was on the Christmas cards when doctors and nurses had to get to their essential jobs on time. There was plenty of the artificial kind adorning the doors and windows of the wards to provide atmosphere.

Clutching at such irrelevant thoughts to stifle a fierce disappointment and steady the foolish beating of her heart, Carola continued along the quiet corridor with the covered kidney dish—and almost dropped it as Noel suddenly appeared at the swing doors leading into the main ward and grabbed her by the arm.

'Don't go in just yet, Carola. I'd like a word...'

He sounded so brusque, so unlike the man who had held and cherished her so tenderly throughout the night that she was alarmed. 'Yes, of course. What is it?'

He thrust her into the nearby sluice and shut the door behind him with a decisive snap. Carola looked up at the tall surgeon with the beginning of a smile that faded as she saw the grim set to his sensual mouth, the strain in his handsome face. Her heart sank.

Only a few hours before, he had parted from her with a last tender kiss before she left for Hartlake and he shot home for a change of clothing. Now he was about to tell her that last night had been a one-off and she wasn't to waste her time dreaming about future encounters. Obviously, he regretted everything.

Squaring her shoulders, she faced him with her

warmest smile. 'There's no need to spare my feelings,' she said lightly as he appeared to hesitate, to be groping for the right words. 'I'm not seventeen any more. . .'

'Christine had her baby last night.'

It took a few seconds to readjust her thinking and to make sense of the abrupt announcement. Then, as light dawned, she exclaimed, 'Oh, do you mean Jeff's wife? I don't think I ever heard her name. . .'

She ought to be feeling a wave of hurt, she thought, surprised by her lack of reaction to the words. Jeff's baby. The child that might have been hers as well if he hadn't fallen out of love with her. She was puzzled by the tautness in Noel's powerful frame, the concern in the grey eyes that held her own. If he cared so much about causing her pain, why hadn't he broken the news more gently?

Then she realised that the concern was not for her. 'Something's wrong with the baby, isn't it?' she ventured.

Noel nodded. 'He's been rushed across from Sandy's with a serious heart defect. He's going to need a transplant and we just don't have a heart for him at the moment. We're waiting for Buchan to decide if it's viable to do an emergency repair to keep the boy alive until we can locate a donor heart. . .he's a good weight and full term and ought to be able to tolerate major surgery.' He paused. 'I just wanted to warn you that Jeff's in the ward, with his son. Shattered, naturally. . .'

'Thanks. But I *can* cope, Noel.' Carola didn't mean to sound so sharply defensive. But, perhaps unreasonably, she resented the implication that she was still so vulnerable that a chance meeting with Jeff could break her up. A year ago, she had been devastated by what he'd done to her. A year ago, she couldn't have faced him with any degree of equanimity, she admitted. But she'd come to terms with humiliation and heartache even if the falter of her pulses and the tremble of her limbs at that brief glimpse of him in the corridor proved that she hadn't stopped loving him.

'I'm sure you can. He'll want to talk to you, Carola. You knew each other for a long time and you've nursed enough sick babies to know just what to say to him at this time. Go and give him a little comfort,' Noel urged.

'Reassurance, you mean,' she said firmly. 'David Buchan is a great surgeon and he's just about due for another miracle. We'll find a heart for Jeff's boy from somewhere. . .'

At the expense of someone else's grief, of course, she thought ruefully as she hurried from the sluice, reminded that Josh was overdue for his injection.

That was an aspect of transplant surgery that had to be faced, but most grieving relatives were willing to donate the organs of loved ones when asked, feeling that he or she lived on in that way and that death wasn't a complete waste. Carola was always moved by such generosity at a very difficult time.

But new babies needed tiny hearts of equally new babies who hadn't survived, and new mothers found it understandably hard to agree to the quiet request that they should help someone else's baby to live. Carola's heart went out to women in such circumstances.

Jeff sat by the cot that held his newborn son, seemingly unaware of the unhurried bustle about him as nurses came and went in the routine tasks of caring for the seriously ill infants on the ward. As she gave Josh the injection to ease his post-operative discomfort and lingered to make him comfortable, Carola glanced at the slumped shoulders, the bowed head and anxious profile as he gazed at the mass of tubes and electrodes and wiring that connected his son to a number of drips and monitors as well as a ventilator that assisted his breathing.

She couldn't find it in her heart to go on being bitter and angry with him for what he'd done to her, she realised. There were many kinds of pain and hers couldn't possibly be compared with what he was going through, the anxiety and the terrible anguish of not knowing. She ached to put her arms about him and hold him close and comfort him in the old way. But that had only helped in the days when Jeff cared about her, needed her and depended on her to see him through the bad times when a young doctor was hurried and harassed and overworked. He no longer wanted her love or her tender loving now that he had Christine — and she had no right to offer it.

But there was nothing to prevent her from offering affection and heartfelt sympathy to an old friend. Having settled Josh, Carola crossed the ward to lay a tender hand on the shoulder of the man who had once played such an important part in her life. 'I'm so sorry that your baby isn't well,' she said gently.

Jeff showed no surprise at her touch, the sound

of her voice, and she realised that he had been aware of her and simply hadn't bothered to turn and acknowledge her, too concerned with the painful present to give a thought to the past.

'Just one of those things, I suppose.' He spoke flatly, without expression, not looking at her.

'He's like you,' Carola murmured, unable to suppress a slight smile as she saw the flame of red hair surmounting the pale face — with its classic blue tinge of the cardiac patient — although it was obvious to her experienced eye that the baby was very poorly indeed. 'Very good-looking.' The light tone endeavoured to lift his spirits.

He didn't smile. 'I don't think I can handle this, Carola,' he said tensely, hunching forward over arms that locked across his body to contain his pain. 'I'm a doctor, qualified to diagnose and treat the sick. I'm used to feeling that I'm doing some good for people. But to sit here, like this, feeling so useless, just watching my son die. . .' The harsh voice broke.

'He isn't going to die.' She rallied him stoutly. 'I don't need to tell *you* about David Buchan's skill — or his reputation! If anyone can save your little boy, he can. And *will*!' She didn't mention the problem of finding a donor heart in time to a man who knew all the difficulties. She looked down at him with a reassuring glow of confidence in her sapphire eyes. 'Of course you're anxious. Who wouldn't be? But come away for a few minutes, Jeff. I'll make some tea and sit with you while you drink it.' She glanced round the ward and caught the eye of her friend, who nodded tacit agreement and promptly left what she was doing to approach the cot with its critically ill occupant. 'Sue will keep an eye on young Jeffrey...'

'Jerome. We've called him Jerome. Christine likes the name.' Almost too weary to protest, he let her steer him from the ward and along to Sister's room, deserted at that busy hour of the day. He sank into a chair as she switched on the electric kettle and hunted for mugs and tea-bags, watching her listlessly, with sombre eyes. 'Pretty feeble, aren't I? Going to pieces like this. It must be the shock. We had no idea that anything was wrong, you see. Christine's been so well, had such a good pregnancy and nothing showed on scans or pre-natal checks. I ought to get a message to her. The poor girl must be half out of her mind with worry, not knowing what's happening here...'

But he made no move to get out of his chair and Carola realised that he was utterly exhausted by events. More than anything else, he couldn't like the feeling that things were beyond his control, she knew. Jeff had never been very flexible when faced with the unexpected. 'I'll see to it,' she promised.

'She's at Sandy's. She had a difficult labour and they want to keep her in for a few days. But she ought to be here—with Jerome...' He sighed.

'I'm sure something can be arranged,' Carola soothed. 'I'll have a word with Sister.'

She put his mug of steaming, sweetened tea on a table by his side. As she turned away to fetch her own, Jeff reached out for her blindly and buried his despairing face in the soft warmth of her body.

'You're such a caring girl, Carola. You always were,' he mumbled. 'I've missed you. . .'

She felt the shock of his embrace start in her heart and ripple all the way to the roots of her hair and the very tip of her toes. Frozen by surprise, she stood very still with Jeff's arms tight about her slender hips, and wondered why she felt like thrusting him away when she ought to be thrilling to his continuing need of her. Did she want to punish him for falling in love with someone else? He couldn't have wanted to hurt her so badly. No one could help the dictates of a heart that insisted on its happiness, wherever it lay—and she'd forgiven him, hadn't she?

Carola didn't feel very comfortable in his arms, although she'd longed and longed to know them about her once more. Her heart beat wildly, not with love or excitement but with the fear that the strictly conventional Sister Paine would walk in on them and misinterpret the emotional moment. Life played some odd tricks, she thought ruefully. Just a year ago, Jeff had stormed out of her life in a rage because she hadn't made it easy for him to end their relationship. Now, he was clutching at her for comfort as if nothing had changed between them.

On a stir of compassion, she stroked the bright blaze of his unruly hair. 'I can't help caring, can I? Haven't I always cared about you——?' She broke off, startled, as the door swung open. Seeing Noel on the threshold, a wave of heat surged into her face, although he was the one person who would surely understand more than most just why Jeff had needed to reach out to her.

'Buchan's here and he wants to talk to you, Jeff. Feel up to it?' Genuine concern for his cousin brushed aside the impact of that tender scene and the overheard assurance for the time being, but his face darkened.

Unceremoniously bundled aside, Carola hastily rescued the untouched mug of tea that had been almost swept to the floor as the anxious young father hurtled from the room. 'You were right,' she said wryly. 'He *is* shattered. Poor Jeff.'

Noel looked at her with a steady, searching gaze that seemed to penetrate deep into her heart and mind. 'You were doing a very good job of helping him through the trauma,' he said quietly, and turned on his heel to follow Jeff back to the ward.

There hadn't been condemnation in the grey eyes or the level tone, but Carola had sensed his dismay and his dislike of finding her in Jeff's arms when the bed they had so recently shared was scarcely cold. She was swamped with anxiety at the thought that she might have lost his respect and his liking and, even more important, the friendship that had already come to mean so much. . .

CHAPTER SEVEN

IT MIGHT be Christmas Eve but it was a day like any other in the Special Care Unit. Except for the increasing silliness of junior nurses and the growing excitement of those convalescent patients who were old enough to anticipate the coming of Father Christmas and the handing out of toys, Carola thought with some asperity as she scattered a group of giggling girls in the corridor and hurried on to the playroom to separate a couple of militant little boys before the bedecked tree crashed to the floor.

She hadn't forgotten that it was also Noel's birthday—*still!*—and she had rushed out in her lunch hour to buy a suitable card and the compact disc of the show they had seen together as a present for him. He had given her so much in the last few days that she felt it was the least she could do in return—and perhaps it would serve to show him that she desperately wanted their newfound relationship to survive.

It was unusual for Carola to feel so divorced from her surroundings and the small patients who depended on her nursing skills, but she found herself constantly thinking about the look in Noel's eyes and all it implied.

Walking in on them just as she put a loving hand to Jeff's head on a rush of forgiving acceptance, Noel had totally misinterpreted the gesture and their

61

closeness — and who could blame him when she had made no secret of the fact that she still loved Jeff? Indeed, she had stressed it to such an extent that she might almost have wanted to convince herself that Noel's charm hadn't weakened the strength of her feeling for his cousin.

It *had*, of course. Or she couldn't have gone so readily and with such delight into the arms of a man she hardly knew. She wasn't in love with Noel. No one could mistake *that* feeling! But he had lifted her out of the slough of despond into which she had fallen on losing Jeff, and she was grateful. He had shown her that it might be possible to find a new happiness in time, not necessarily with him but with someone who wasn't Jeff, and she was even more grateful for that.

At the same time, he had made it clear that he still cared deeply for the girl in his own past and was no more ready to love again than herself, Carola recalled with an unexpected tremor of jealousy.

As the telephone buzzed in Sister's office, she hurried to answer it, telling herself to take care not to become too fond of Noel or she might end up being hurt again!

It was Theatre Sister on the line, letting her know that Jerome was on his way back to the unit after remedial surgery designed to keep him going until a new heart could be found for him. To take his mind off what was happening in Theatres, Jeff had gone to see his wife at Sandy's and arrange for her removal to Hartlake so that she could be near their sick son. A private room was being prepared for her along the corridor.

Amid the bustle of the baby's return and the setting up of drips and monitors, Carola found time to study the crest of red-gold hair, the tiny features and the chubby frame of a miniature Jeff and to marvel that she'd had no part in his being for all the long-cherished dream of marrying Jeff and having his children.

The absence of any real pain or jealousy in her breast assured her that she had finally accepted the way things had turned out for them. It hadn't been easy; it had taken a long time and it might never have come about at all if she hadn't met Noel again.

Thinking about the instant rapport between herself and Noel, the strong and mysterious sense of belonging that had overwhelmed her and the way she had melted into the warm welcome of his embrace, Carola understood at last that a force greater than anything he had ever felt for her had catapulted Jeff into another woman's arms.

She didn't care to call it love. But she found it possible to believe that love might eventually grow from the seed of an irresistible physical attraction, given time and the right encouragement. . .

Carola was on her way from the main ward with Angela in her arms, the baby newly bathed, sweetly scented and swaddled in a blue blanket to play her part in the nativity play, when Noel arrived to check on Jerome's condition that afternoon. He looked tired and rather drawn after a long session in Theatres and she felt an odd little catch at her heart.

He paused, a tenderness in the grey eyes for the

picture they presented, lovely nurse in the becoming Hartlake uniform with her soft, dark curls teasing the starched demurity of her cap and the baby girl with her beaming brown face and gurgling contentment.

'Hello, gorgeous.' The greeting might have been meant for either, and his smile embraced them both.

'Isn't she?' Carola's enthusiastic response directed the compliment away from herself to the baby but the hint of rose in her face betrayed relief at the warm friendliness of his tone, his easy manner. Nothing had changed, after all, she thought thankfully. 'I'm sorry to rush away, but this young lady mustn't keep her public waiting,' she went on lightly. 'The curtain's about to go up. . .'

As she laughed up at him with a dancing light in her sapphire eyes, the glow of happiness in her pretty face was unmistakable—and so was its cause, Noel decided, even as his heart turned over at her beauty.

He was furious with his cousin for stirring the embers of an almost forgotten flame after all his efforts to extinguish it in Carola's heart and mind. Married and with a newborn son to think about, Jeff had no right to raise her hopes again so foolishly. As for himself, his own hopes were dashed, abruptly appearing so absurd that he wondered that he had entertained them for so long.

'Off you go, then,' he said, releasing her from any kind of commitment with the seemingly casual words. 'I just wanted to tell you that there's a change of plan. The party's off, for obvious reasons.

A few of us are just meeting for a drink in the Kingfisher, that's all.'

He sounded so offhand, so unlike the caring man who had held her close through the night, that Carola looked after him in dismay as he strode down the ward, apparently too rushed or too indifferent to explain further. It seemed to her suddenly sensitive mind that she wasn't included in the new plan for the celebration of his birthday but she had no time to pursue her disappointment. She hurried on to the children's ward with the star of the nativity play held to her bewildered breast.

Mary had spina bifida and Joseph was getting over surgery to remove a bone cancer. One of the small shepherds was Nigerian and, of the three kings, one was Chinese and another Asian, for Hartlake was in a part of London that had a community of many races and colours.

It was a nativity play like so many others throughout the country that Christmas and every other, some of the cast forgetting their lines and arguments breaking out and many interruptions from the watching children. But the essential message of love and goodwill to all men shone through it all and Carola wasn't the only adult in the audience with tears in her eyes at the end.

Angela had behaved beautifully, although Carola had been standing by to comfort the blind baby if she suddenly took fright or felt bewildered by all that was going on around her. She had crowed with delight as the childish voices piped the traditional carols and she had lain placidly in Mary's arms as the kings and shepherds paid homage to Baby Jesus beneath a lop-sided tinsel star. Carola rewarded her with an extra-loving cuddle as she carried her back to the Special Care Unit.

Having handed Angela over to a nurse, she paused to appraise the condition of the baby boy who had undergone delicate heart surgery earlier in the day. Jerome looked too bonny to be so seriously ill, but she knew that he had a long way to go before a healthy prognosis could be assured. He slept peacefully, surrounded by monitors and linked to a drip.

Due to go off duty with some time to spare before joining the group of nurses and young medics for the watch-night carols now that the party was cancelled, Carola collected her things and looked doubtfully at the neat little package in her bag, wondering if she would have an opportunity to give it to Noel. He hadn't said anything reassuring about seeing her again that evening and tomorrow would spoil the surprise, she thought wryly.

In any case, tomorrow was Christmas — and it was a rather special birthday gift for a rather special man. Perhaps she should drop it off at his home on her way to or from Hartlake. But she was absurdly shy of seeming to pursue him for, like a number of men, he might have lost interest in her now that they had been to bed.

'I suppose you've no idea if Noel Partridge is still in the hospital?' she asked Sue, in such a diffidently negative fashion that her friend stared in surprise at the usually confident staff nurse.

'He was here half an hour ago, talking to his

cousin. Jerome's mum has been admitted, by the way. He might be in her room,' Sue volunteered helpfully.

Carola knocked and put her head round the half-open door of the small private room, her heart beating a little faster at the thought of coming face to face with Jeff's wife for the first time.

Christine was propped against a mound of pillows, surrounded by a mass of flowers, magazines and the usual paraphernalia of a stay in hospital. Carola felt a shock of surprise. So this was the temptress who had lured Jeff away from her, not the raving beauty she had assumed but a wee mouse of a girl with soft, flyaway fair hair and freckles and a rather shy smile.

'Oh, Nurse. . . I'm sorry to be a nuisance and I promise not to buzz every five minutes as a rule. But I need my handbag and I'm not allowed to get out of bed, I'm afraid.' The apologetic words made it clear that she thought Carola had arrived in answer to a summons.

She lifted the bag from the windowsill where some thoughtless person had left it out of reach and laid it on the bed. 'How are you feeling?' she asked gently, unexpectedly warming to the sweet-faced girl whose baby lay so critically ill in a crib at the end of the corridor. 'I'm Carola Barnes. I dare say Jeff's mentioned me. . .'

Christine's eyes widened. 'And you've come to see how I am? I thought you'd hate me,' she said frankly.

Carola smiled. 'I thought I would, too,' she admitted. 'But it all seems a long time ago and I can't bear a grudge. Besides, life has a way of making up for disappointments.' She was thinking of Noel as she spoke and realising how much it mattered that she was free to welcome his interest with all its golden promise for the future. He was so nice and she liked him so much and she thrilled to the memory of a tender, sensual lovemaking that had transported her to a new and wonderful world.

Perhaps something of those thoughts showed in her expressive eyes. For Christine ventured shyly, 'Does that mean you've found someone else?'

She hesitated. 'It isn't serious. . .well, not at the moment, anyway,' she temporised. 'But I'm over Jeff.' There was the ring of newly discovered truth behind the firm words and she felt as if a great weight had lifted from her heart.

'I'm glad. I've felt so guilty,' Christine confessed impulsively. 'Because you and Jeff were engaged, weren't you?'

'It was more of an understanding. I didn't have a ring. But we had talked about getting married.' Carola didn't enlarge on the hopes and dreams and plans that she and Jeff had shared for five years. She had put them all behind her along with a loving that belonged in the past. Automatically, she straightened sheets, adjusted pillows and tidied the array of articles on the bedside locker. 'Are you comfortable, Christine? Is there anything you want?'

'Just my baby.' The words were wistful, like her smile.

'You'll be able to see him soon,' Carola comforted, knowing that the ache and the anxiety must be almost unbearable. 'He's still sleepy from the anaesthetic but he's a beautiful boy and I'm sure he'll be fine.'

'Jeff says he needs further surgery.'

'Yes, I believe so, but then he shouldn't have any more problems. Where *is* Jeff? I thought he'd be here...'

'I sent him to get something to eat. He looked dreadful—and Noel promised to see that he got a decent meal and some rest.'

Remembering an obstinate streak in his nature, Carola was surprised that someone who seemed so gentle and so self-effacing could compel Jeff in any way at all. But appearances could be deceptive and a man in love would do anything to please his woman. She smiled at the girl that Jeff loved, happily relinquishing all claim to any part of his heart or his life. 'That was sensible. And you can trust Noel to take good care of him,' she said, unaware of a betraying warmth in her tone as she spoke of the surgeon.

'You and Noel are very close, aren't you? He was telling me what a difference it's made to everything meeting you again. He's very fond of you, I know.'

The innocent words warmed Carola's heart, allaying the vague apprehension that she would never take the place of the girl in Noel's past. For, if he had talked so freely about his feeling for her to the girl who seemed to invite confidences with her sweet smile, then perhaps he already cared more seriously than she had supposed.

And perhaps she could begin to care for him now that the last strands of the bondage that had been her love for Jeff for so long had finally parted without causing even a pang. . .

CHAPTER EIGHT

CAROLA's heart banged in her breast as she recognised the tall figure in theatre greens who emerged from Sister's office just as she left Christine's room.

Carola quickened her step to catch up with him. At the sound of her voice calling his name, he turned with a reassuring readiness.

'I thought I'd missed you——'

'I've been trying to find you——'

Both spoke at the same moment and both broke off, laughing. Noel was seized with an irresistible longing to sweep her into his arms, but he contented himself with smiling down at her.

'I'm glad I ran into you, Noel. I've something for you.' Flustered by the unexpected encounter and the warmth in his smiling eyes, pink with a foolish embarrassment as she recalled her recent thoughts about him and the dawn of a new and joyous hope, Carola began to rummage in her handbag for the small package that had become annoyingly elusive. 'Just a minute...oh, here it is! It's been Christmas-wrapped by the shop but it's actually for your birthday!'

'*Another* present?' The lurk of mischief danced in the grey eyes. She blushed. His expression softened to an amused tenderness as the warm colour spread in her pretty face, heightening the sparkle of her sapphire eyes. 'I shouldn't tease you,' he repented.

'Thanks very much, Carola. I'll open it later, if you don't mind. I'm on my way to look at Ashley.'

'It isn't much,' Carola warned as he turned away. 'Just a small memento. . .'

Continuing on his way to the main ward in response to an urgent call from Sister Paine, Noel felt his heart plummeting at the seeming finality of the words. A memento? Something to remember her by? An indication that something that had scarcely begun was already over as far as Carola was concerned?

He had hoped to drive Jeff from her heart and mind with an apparently light-hearted courtship that would allow her all the time she needed to realise that he could make her happy. But the glow of rekindled love in her beautiful face and the tenderness of her touch as she'd cradled Jeff's head had told him that it was useless to anticipate any kind of future with the girl whose image he had carried about with him ever since that first meeting.

With a heavy weight bearing down on his usually optimistic spirits, Noel wondered why he had chosen to continue with the parade of loving and giving that suddenly seemed to have become a charade. . .

There was a neat parcel sitting in the middle of Sister's desk when Carola went into the office to say goodnight to Sue, who was busily entering facts and figures into the computer's memory. 'It looks as if Father Christmas has come early for Sister,' she said lightly, indicating the square-shaped package.

Sue glanced up. 'Oh, that's for you. . . Noel Partridge left it when I said you hadn't gone home yet.' Her tone was tinged with feminine curiosity.

'I've just seen him and he didn't mention it. . .' Carola tore off the red and gold Christmassy wrapping to reveal a square-shaped box. It contained a humming top adorned with four brightly painted birds on its gleaming sides and, as usual, he had enclosed a note.

Too old for toys? Never mind. Put it on the tree for one of the infants and leave it to me to make Christmas hum for you. Love, Noel.

Four calling birds. Her face lit up at his thoughtful ingenuity and the meaningful humour of the accompanying message. It was the first time that he had given any hint of his feelings in writing, too, and she savoured the assurance in a simple word.

Having been vaguely hurt by his casual acceptance of the compact disc and the way he had walked off without a mention of seeing her again, she was heartened by the gift with its continuing Christmas theme. It might be only fun but it was making this Christmas really one to remember, she thought warmly.

'That's a strange thing for him to give you, isn't it?' Sue stared at the child's toy in astonishment. Unaware as she was of the earlier symbolic tokens, the implication of the top with its colourful painted birds escaped her.

A little shyly, Carola explained about the two Christmas cards, the cartoon hens, and added with almost defensive lightness that she had taken her friend's advice and begun to date the new registrar.

'I knew he fancied you! And he's sending you all the things in the carol?' Sue demanded, visibly impressed. 'The partridge, the turtle doves, the french hens—and now the calling birds!'

Carola nodded. 'It looks that way.'

'Well, I must say he's going to a lot of trouble for you. He certainly knows how to make a girl feel special!' Sue sounded quite envious.

'Yes. Yes, he does.' She smiled softly to herself, hugging memories, knowing she was fortunate to be embraced by Noel's warmth of heart and sense of fun and generous good nature. 'He's a good friend. . .'

Sue snorted. '*Friends* don't go to those lengths, Christmas or no Christmas! The man loves you, Carola—and I don't see how he could put it any plainer!'

Carola stared, her heart giving a shocked leap. 'Oh, no! It isn't like that at all! You've got it all wrong, Sue,' she protested with a strangled laugh. 'It's just a joke. . .'

Her friend shot her a sceptical glance. 'Think about it, ducky,' she advised. 'What does the carol say. . . "*my true love sent to me*"? *I'd* say that's how he sees himself and he wants you to know it! I think it's jolly romantic.' She crowed with delight.

Carola's heart was beating so hard and so fast that she felt faint. Could Sue possibly be right? *Was* Noel courting her with the meaningful if amusing tokens? Was it his own original way of declaring his feelings and promising that he would be her true love for always?

How could he be so sure, so soon?

She knew in her bones and in her blood and in the very heart of her that he would be truer than

Jeff had proved, if he did indeed love her. The man was as steadfast as a rock and would devote his life to keeping her content. She could certainly trust Noel with her life.

But with her heart, too. . .?

'I'll just put this under the tree,' she said and fled with the humming-top, needing time to think, to question the totally unexpected turn-around of all her deepest feelings.

Could she have tumbled out of love with one man and into love with another at almost the same moment in her life? Or had her feeling for Jeff only been a pale promise of the real thing that had blossomed with Noel's second advent? Perhaps Jeff had done her a favour by falling out of love with her!

It was much too soon for her to be sure how she felt about Noel, but she knew that since meeting him again she had felt a strange glow of content, a conviction that she was half of a predestined whole. Being with him was so right and so natural, completing an inevitable circle that encompassed them both in a private world. Perhaps it wasn't love, but she could no longer envisage a future without Noel to warm her with his smile and keep her safe in his strong arms. . .

Entering the main ward, Carola walked into a crisis. A monitor began to bleep an urgent warning and Ashley's small chest laboured furiously with the onset of sudden heart failure. Dropping the top among the pile of toys beneath the Christmas tree, she ran to help as Noel started emergency treatment.

With the instinct of experience, Sister Paine had trundled the resuscitation trolley to the side of the cot when Ashley first showed signs of the distress that had prompted her to send for the registrar. Now, she was reaching for ampoules of vital drugs and filling syringes with deft hands, getting ready to respond instantly to his urgently voiced instructions.

For several minutes, they worked as a team to save the tiny boy who'd had such a precarious hold on life for the past week. At last, their combined efforts were rewarded and, as Ashley's heartbeat fluttered and then steadied and his breathing became easier, Carola allowed herself to relax and register the fact that Angela was crying loudly in her cot at the end of the ward.

'Panic over, thank God...' Breathing a sigh of satisfaction, Noel moved aside to make way for Sister Paine to give yet another injection to sustain the infant's frail but determined battle to survive.

No one else was free at that moment, so Carola hurried to quieten Angela, who was instantly soothed by the sound of her voice, the comforting touch of her hand. She realised that the baby girl had sensed the emergency and reacted instinctively to the heightened tension in the ward.

There were beads of perspiration on Noel's brow and upper lip as he passed her on his way from the ward, throwing her a smile and a brief word of thanks for her prompt and useful assistance.

She hurried after him and caught him up by the swing doors that led from the unit. 'You just worked a miracle, Noel,' she said quietly.

He shook his green-capped head with a hint of impatience. 'Teamwork.'

'I didn't think Ashley was going to make it,' she admitted ruefully. Carola hesitated and then remembered that she could say anything at all to this caring, kindly man and know that he understood her feelings and her motives for them. 'I was praying for him like mad but at the same time, I couldn't help thinking. . .a possible heart for Jerome?'

Noel sighed, knowing it was inevitable that her thoughts should constantly turn to Jeff and his current anxiety. She couldn't let go, he thought wearily, and he could do nothing but accept the hopelessness of his own situation.

'There's no way it would have been suitable. Too badly damaged. Ashley needs a new heart himself, poor mite.' The pain of a frustrated desire to help in a hopeless case touched his deep-set eyes and sensual mouth. 'I'm afraid we've only postponed the inevitable, Carola. Maybe we should have let him go, but instinct and training—and the Hippocratic Oath—demands that we do our damnedest to hold on to a patient while there's the faintest spark of life in him.'

'I'd like to believe that Ashley has a future,' Carola said with wistful regret.

'He's more of a fighter than we thought. If we can just keep him going long enough to get some flesh on him and get those lungs working a little better, he may have a chance of surviving a transplant. Provided we can locate a heart for him when it's needed,' he added grimly. 'Damn it, that's the biggest problem we face! Kidneys, corneas, even livers—they all come easier than hearts.' Broad shoulders sagged with resignation.

'It's so hard for relatives to accept that it's just an organ like all the others,' Carola agreed.

'I know I'd feel exactly the same if it was my child, my wife.' If it were *you*, sweet love, heart of my heart. . . The betraying words rushed to Noel's lips, longing for life, but he held them back, tortured by a too-vivid image of Jeff's arms about her and the look of love in her beautiful eyes. 'But I hope I'd have the courage to admit that sentiment shouldn't come before somebody else's life. However. . .' He straightened with a wry smile. 'Heaven forbid that I should ever be faced with such a difficult decision. It's going to be hard enough playing God with these infants, deciding which of them should have a donor heart when one does become available.'

Warming to the dedication of a man who had just breathed life back into the small, struggling body of a sick baby, Carola smiled at him and reached to kiss the lean, tanned cheek, ignoring their clinical surroundings and ward etiquette and the risk of being caught in a most unprofessional encounter with a senior surgeon. 'I like you so much, Noel!' she exclaimed with genuine feeling.

Predictably, he greeted her words and light kiss with an amused arch of an eyebrow. 'What was that for?'

She was totally unaware that the light-hearted mockery of his tone concealed dismay at the confirmation of his fear that she could never offer him anything more than her liking, her friendship. Too shy and too unsure to confess that her kiss was partly because she trembled on the threshold of loving him with all her heart, Carola laughed up at him. 'It's still your birthday, isn't it?'

With the light words, she scurried for the sanctuary of a shared humour whose healing powers had begun their work just a year ago when this warmly generous man had done his best to bring a smile to her woebegone face.

His compassion and his practical way of showing it had stayed in her mind. The thought of him had lingered too, all unsuspected, deep in her heart. . .

CHAPTER NINE

IN EACH of the hushed wards, appreciative faces turned towards the group of nurses in the long skirts and the beribboned caps of the original Hartlake young ladies who had tended the sick of the district with lamps held high. The trill of girlish voices blended nicely with the mellow baritones of young doctors in Victorian frock coats and top hats, offering up the familiar and much-loved carols, and for a few moments perhaps some of the pain and anxiety of the listening patients was eased by the age-old magic of Christmas.

Carola felt touched by its magic, too, as lined faces softened and young faces brightened and busy nurses paused in the middle of routine chores to listen and smile. Her heart felt lighter than it had been for a very long time with the advent of Christmas and the promise of a New Year that might bring her a new and true happiness.

She thought that Sue had exaggerated, as usual. Noel was a long way from loving her, his heart and mind still turning to the past and the girl who had mattered so much to him. But, like herself, he felt that they had some kind of future with each other, given time, and so he was courting her gently with daily proofs of his liking and interest, underlined by the sense of fun that she loved in him. Laughter could be an effective way to a girl's heart — and it had already worked to some extent, hadn't it?

Tomorrow was the fifth day of Christmas. The words of the traditional carol promised five gold rings, Carola recalled, smiling to herself. Knowing his light touch, he would probably send her five brass curtain rings!

It was nearly ten o'clock when the final carol was sung in the last of the selected wards and the singers were free to change back to their own, modern-day clothes. Sue and her boyfriend were hurrying off to the staff dance. Carola shook her head to the well-meant invitation to join them. She might be over Jeff and able to reflect on that last Christmas Eve without a lingering bitterness, but it would still be poignant with painful memories.

It was sleeting when she emerged into the night, the first hint of winter, and she wondered if it would be a white Christmas after all as she drew her coat about her shoulders, huddling within its warmth. On the other side of the busy High Street, lights blazed in the Kingfisher, the local pub that was a favourite haunt of off-duty doctors and nurses, and she caught the drift of music as doors opened and closed on noisy revellers.

Carola stood irresolute between hospital steps and car park for a few moments, wondering if Noel was still in the Kingfisher with his friends. He hadn't exactly issued an invitation but she had sensed from his later manner that she was welcome to join them if she wished.

Going home to spend what remained of Christmas Eve on her own didn't appeal. She couldn't afford to be too late as she was due back on duty at eight in the morning, but perhaps one drink. . .?

Entering the pub, she was met by a blast of sound and warm air and stale beer. The bar seemed to be a swarming mass of people and she couldn't see Noel or anyone else that she knew at first. Then, as someone crossed the room with a brimming glass in each hand, the crowd shifted to give her a clear view of a corner table where Noel sat with an arm draped about the shoulders of a pretty, laughing girl with a mane of blonde hair. His long, strong fingers were twined in the trailing curls and their heads were close together as he looked into her animated face. He was smiling at whatever she was saying to him, the slow, sweet smile that never failed to tilt her heart, and Carola felt a searing shaft of jealousy.

She had no claim on Noel, of course. Handsome, strongly sensual and generous with his affections, he was bound to be much admired by other women, and she had no right to resent the way he looked and smiled at the girl within his embracing arm. But the heart that had begun to love him felt as if it were being torn into tiny shreds all over again.

Only last night, she had lain in his loving arms, trusting him with her happiness and her peace of mind. Would he take this other, unknown girl to bed before Christmas Day dawned? A choke of emotion rose in her throat and she turned to leave the smoky, stifling atmosphere of the pub, thrusting blindly at the block of high-spirited young men who stood in her path.

An arm snaked about her waist, holding her fast. Carola spun, ready to rebuff a half-drunk stranger, and looked into Noel's warmly smiling eyes. She hardened her heart against their treacherous charm, telling herself that she hadn't fallen a lasting victim to it and regretting the need for comfort and consolation at this harrowing time of the year that had swept her into the surgeon's embrace.

'I'd almost given you up, sweetheart. . .'

She answered the soft, pleased words with a tight, cool smile. 'Oh, hello, Noel. Enjoying the evening? It's a dreadful crush, isn't it? I'm trying to fight my way to the door. . .'

'You aren't leaving, surely? I thought you were going to have a drink with me. . .?'

'I daren't have another. I'm driving.'

Noel frowned. 'Another?' Having watched and waited for her all evening, he was puzzled by the words that implied she had been in the Kingfisher for some time.

'Oh, didn't you see me at the bar? I've just had a drink with Tom Beacon.' Compounding the impulsive lie, Carola nodded at the broad back of a houseman they both knew who was propping up the bar.

The airy brightness of her tone convinced Noel that her presence in the pub was unconnected with his expectation of seeing her that evening. Struggling with his disappointment, he smiled down at her. 'Oh, I see. Well, have a soft drink, Carola. My friends have been looking forward to meeting you. . .'

She looked past him to the corner table. Her first glance had only comprehended Noel and his pretty companion. Now, she saw the group contained another, darker woman and three other men. Only the blonde was looking in their direction with any interest. Her obvious concern was unnecessary, however, for Carola had no intention of playing turn and turn about with any woman just to please a sensual surgeon! Her chin tilted.

'Denise particularly wants to meet you,' Noel added with a smiling glance for the watching girl.

'Another time,' she said carelessly. 'I'm dead on my feet and I'm on duty tomorrow. I really must go home. Oh, by the way—Happy Christmas!' Breaking free, she pushed through a sudden gap in the pressing throng, a smile pinned to frozen lips and pride hugged to her dismayed breast.

She hadn't been blind to the special smile in his grey eyes or deaf to the tender softening of his deep voice as he spoke the girl's name. Denise obviously meant something to him. Maybe she was the love he still carried in his heart and maybe it wasn't such a lost cause, after all. So where did that leave *her*? On the threshold of making a fool of herself, she suspected bitterly. She had loved once and suffered as a result. She wasn't going to do it again! She needed to know where she stood and she couldn't bear the possibility of losing out to another woman all over again.

Carola lay awake for much of that night, fretting and fuming because she had allowed her jealousy to show, sore at heart and mind filled with foolish dreams and body craving for the soothing, satisfying comfort of Noel's arms about her. She had never felt so desperate with longing in all her life, she admitted ruefully. Even her love for Jeff, at its height in the early days of their relationship, couldn't compare with the intensity of her feeling for Noel, her need to retain the security and warmth and humour of their friendship. By the time she rose to get ready for the day, she had been compelled to admit that, whether she liked it or not, Noel was firmly entrenched in her heart.

Christmas Day was for the children, and she suppressed her own wishes and desires to ensure that it was as happy as possible for those in the Special Care Unit at Hartlake. In Sister Paine's absence, she was in charge, and so the day would be a busy one for her. David Buchan was officially off duty, like most of the surgeons and consultants, but he came in to deputise for the most essential visitor on this one day of the year.

Carola's heart warmed to the delight and wonder in small faces as a jolly Father Christmas took toddlers on his knee or within the embrace of his arm to hand out their gifts. Only essential routines were carried out that morning, for most of the nurses were busily helping to open presents, admiring the contents and playing with the children. Even the tiniest of the convalescent babies responded to the spirit of the day, little legs kicking and arms flailing with excitement, eager hands stretching out for crackly, colourful wrapping paper or the cotton-wool balls that hung above their cots, just out of reach.

In the main ward, few of the seriously ill infants were aware that it was Christmas, however. Gifts were tucked into corners of cots, cuddly toys and bright plastic balls and picture books contrasting with the grim paraphernalia of medical care. Here, in this section of the unit, there could be no relaxation of routines, but the steady monitoring of progess or deterioration, the checking of drips and the giving of injections and the regular dressing of surgical wounds.

By mid-morning, it was apparent that the baby girl with serious head injuries from a road accident was dying in spite of the immediate surgery she had undergone and the concentrated care she had been receiving, and all the staff were saddened. On this day of all days, it hurt to lose one of the babies.

There was some small compensation in Ashley's noticeable improvement since the crisis of the previous day, recorded on his chart. Jerome was 'as well as could be expected', but everyone knew that his chances for the future were very slim unless he could be given a new heart. The desperate hope was stamped on both parents as they kept a vigil beside his cot. Carola gave them what comfort she could, spending a little time with them in the course of her busy morning.

A highlight was Angela's departure for home in time to join her family's Christmas celebrations. Before her beaming, thankful parents carried her off, Carola held her close for a few moments, her cheek resting against the silk crest of black curls, her heart very full, for the baby girl had become special to her in the past weeks. Every nurse accepted that patients came and went but there were always a memorable few and Angela was one of them, she thought warmly.

The loving expression on her pretty face tore at

Noel's confused heart as he walked into the ward and the look in her eyes seemed to linger as they met his own, giving him new hope, until surprise took its place.

'Noel! What are *you* doing here?' Carola demanded unguardedly, unable to conceal the rush of warm delight that effectively betrayed her feeling that his unexpected arrival completed the day.

'I couldn't let Angela leave without a Christmas kiss, could I?' The surgeon put a tender hand to the small head and bent to brush his lips across a smooth brown cheek. Angela gurgled happily, revelling in the affection and the attention, and her mother held out eager arms to take her.

'I didn't expect to see you today,' Carola said with revealing warmth as Mrs Lennox moved away with her baby to thank the nurse who had specialled Angela for much of her stay in hospital.

Noel smiled at the girl whose cool, competent professionalism seemed suddenly shattered by his presence. 'I couldn't let the day go by without giving you a Christmas kiss, could I?' With a mischievous flourish, he whisked a sprig of mistletoe from the pocket of his white coat and, holding it high above her head, bent to kiss her, lightly and yet so meaningfully that Carola's heart shook.

She backed away, colour storming into her cheeks as the nurses about them beamed approval of the new registrar's boldness. Fortunately, Sister Paine wasn't around to disapprove. Besides, it was Christmas, and rigid hospital rules occasionally went by the board on this one day of the year.

'Do be serious, Noel!' she said sternly but the

dance of her eyes belied the reproach. Her dancing heart wanted to believe that he had given up the day to be with her and the babies that he so obviously cared about as a dedicated healer.

'Buchan sent out an emergency call for me. Apparently there's a possibility of a heart for Jerome becoming available and he wants me standing by to assist with the transplant.'

'Saving lives in your own time? How dedicated can you get?' Carola teased warmly, wondering why it hadn't occurred to her that David Buchan would beg for the dying baby's heart to ensure the survival of another baby. She caught and held Noel's gaze. 'Do you heal hearts in your off-duty moments, too?'

Noel searched the sapphire eyes that looked up at him with such seeming innocence in their limpid depths. 'What else have I been trying to do ever since I met you?' he said quietly.

The brief touch of his hand on her slim shoulder before he walked on was a caress. . .

CHAPTER TEN

As EXPECTED, the little girl died shortly after midday. David Buchan was an eminent surgeon, noted for his work of transplanting new hearts for old, and he had a very persuasive approach. So it came as no surprise to Carola to hear that he had gained permission to use the dead child's heart for another baby.

He had left the grieving parents to comfort each other while he instructed Carola to prepare the critically ill Jerome for immediate surgery and he prepared the parents whose child was likely to benefit from their loss. 'Thank God that's over...the part that any surgeon hates,' he said heavily. 'But it was less of an ordeal than I expected. The parents knew what I wanted before I said a word. They're intelligent, caring people and I imagine they had discussed the donor position in advance. A brave couple. We're getting the heart. John Cromer has two kidneys and a liver that he didn't expect—and if Angela's sight could have been supplied by surgery she might have had the child's eyes.'

'That's wonderful,' Carola said warmly.

He nodded. ' A minor miracle, don't you think? By the end of the day, at least three lives may be transformed for the sake of one little life lost. Say a prayer for the parents, Staff.'

'Of course I will!' She could feel genuine compassion for the couple even in the midst of her welling delight for Jeff and Christine.

Christine burst into tears on hearing the news. Jeff promptly put his arms about the girl who had been so calm, so controlled, until she learned that their son's delicately balanced future might be assured by an immediate transplant.

'It's a miracle!' she sobbed.

David Buchan shook his head. 'Not yet, I'm afraid,' he warned cautiously. 'Your little boy has already undergone major surgery and isn't yet recovered from that trauma. At this stage, I'm not prepared to guarantee how things will turn out. But I think it's a chance we ought to take, if you agree.'

'Oh, *please*!' Christine's response was fervent.

As a medical man, Jeff appreciated all that the consultant had left unsaid. He knew his son's condition was critical and that there was a considerable risk that he wouldn't come through further surgery. Installing a new heart in such a tiny frame was always a risky business, even for someone as skilled and experienced as Buchan. But, like his wife, he felt that they had no choice but to consent. At least then they would both feel that they had done their best for their baby.

'Go ahead,' he said quietly. 'He's in your hands.'

The consultant was a deeply religious man. 'He's in God's hands,' he amended, smiling. 'I'm just a humble healer.'

'Jerome will make it,' Noel firmly assured his cousin and Christine as his boss left to scrub up for surgery. 'Buchan knows what he's doing. If he's prepared to carry out the transplant then there isn't much doubt that he thinks he's on a winner.'

Carola smiled at the surgeon in his green, V-necked tunic and loose-fitting theatre trousers, cap barely concealing the dark auburn of the thick, tumbling hair that she longed to stroke. 'Noel's right,' she agreed brightly. 'Buchan doesn't back losers.'

Christine bent over the cot that held her baby as if she wanted to scoop him up and run off with him before he could be whisked away from her for yet more surgery. 'He doesn't look so ill,' she said piteously, as if the sheer force of longing could alter the situation.

Jeff had crumbled on the previous day, clung to his former girlfriend for comfort, despaired. Now he was in control, strong enough to support his anxious wife and cope with the prospect of losing his much-wanted son. At a nod from Carola, he led Christine away from the cot with a loving arm about her shoulders, her face turned to hide her tears against his chest.

Staff nurse and registrar immediately began to prepare Jerome for Theatre. 'Why did you run away last night, Carola?' Noel asked quietly, as clever hands began the routine examination of Jerome's small body. 'I had such plans for us.'

The warm intimacy that surrounded the soft, linking word touched and thrilled her, sent hope soaring, although she still wasn't taking anything for granted. She had known him well for too short a time and she knew what it meant to be hurt through loving and trusting too blindly. 'It was late,' she defended.

He shot her a glance. 'It was more than that.'

His tone compelled honesty, but she was reluctant to admit that seeing him with that other woman had provoked a storm of jealousy and a desperate desire to escape the possibility of further hurt. It would be tantamount to admitting that she had fallen in love with him. . . 'I'll get the pre-med,' she said hastily and hurried away.

When she returned from the clinical room with the prepared hypodermic syringe in a kidney dish, Noel smiled at her encouragingly. 'Well?' he prompted.

Expertly, Carola slid the needle into the tender flesh of the tiny buttock, withdrew it. Even with time to formulate an answer, she hadn't been able to think of a convincing one. 'You were with your friends and I didn't like to intrude. You seemed to be having a good time.'

'Denise,' he said baldly. It wasn't a question. Noel sighed, marvelling that Carola could still be so unaware of the way he felt about her and how little any other woman could mean to him while she was in the world, possessing him heart and soul. 'We were at university together. She's a paediatrician and we met up again at Queen's a couple of years ago.' He named a famous hospital on the south side of the city. 'She's marrying another old friend in the New Year and I'm very pleased for both of them,' he added firmly to allay the absurd suspicion that Denise could be a contender for the wealth of love for her in his heart.

It seemed to Carola that things had fallen into place. 'Is she the girl you talked about?' She kept her tone light, hoping he wouldn't resent her touching on a possibly still sensitive wound.

Noel looked puzzled. 'Did I talk about a girl?'

'The other evening. You said you understood how I felt about losing Jeff because you'd been through it yourself.'

His handsome face lost its frown. 'I recall the conversation but I don't think I used those exact words, Carola. I was talking about love and the way it takes control and affects everything in life, but that had nothing to do with Denise. I'm not in love with Denise. Never have been, never will be. There's only one woman I want and that's why I'm here at Hartlake, working with Buchan and hopefully making myself indispensable all round.' He smiled down at her wryly. 'I thought I'd made that almost ridiculously obvious in the last few days.'

'*Me*, do you mean?' Carola's heart leaped wildly in her breast and she raised an astounded, rosily incredulous face to the smiling surgeon.

'Well, I don't kiss *every* girl I meet on Christmas Day—and Angela is a little too young for me, don't you think?' he said softly, warm and reassuring laughter kindling the grey eyes. He shook his head at her wondering face and resisted the urge to kiss the soft lips that had parted on a breathless 'O' of surprise. 'You didn't have a clue,' he teased gently. 'Sweetheart, what did you think it was all about?'

'The cards?' she stumbled.

'Everything.'

'Oh, Noel! I didn't dare to think. I just *hoped*—

more than I even knew,' she admitted on a rush of impulsive confession. She glanced around the room with its monitors and drip stands and clinical efficiency, its busy nurses and sick babies and its air of quiet drama that seemed such an unlikely background to romance but was exactly right for a blossoming love between surgeon and staff nurse both dedicated to their essential work. 'I wish I could kiss you,' she murmured regretfully.

'Later,' he drawled, with a look in his eyes that promised so much more than a kiss. 'Right now, this little lad's new heart is on the agenda. What's gone wrong with your sense of priorities, Nurse?'

Carola laughed at the mock scold. 'The Christmas spirit seems to have gone to my head!'

It had certainly affected her heart, she thought joyously, a new confidence in the future enriching the day in spite of the anxiety she shared with Jeff and Christine during the tense hours while Jerome was in Theatres. She supported them as best she could in the brief intervals between the heavy demands of her work in the unit. When she went off duty, much later than was really required of her, Jerome was in Recovery, far from stable with a possibility that he might need more surgery, and Carola knew that he was unlikely to survive another such ordeal.

There was no point in hanging about at the hospital. Jeff and Christine only really needed each other at such a time and she was unlikely to see Noel while he might be needed in Theatres. She could only hope that '*later*' had meant what it said. But his first concern must be for Jerome and she

wouldn't want it any other way, she told herself
stoutly. Noel's compassion and dedication to his
small patients made him the man that she knew she
loved with all her heart.

Once home, she wallowed in a luxuriously hot
bath with one ear perked for the telephone and
then, in a comfortable peach-coloured track-suit,
settled down with a tray to watch a Christmas
spectacular on TV. It was scarcely how she had
expected to spend the evening but she was content
as long as Noel eventually telephoned her at least.
It was hard to believe that he'd let the day end
without speaking to her, confirming the incredible
truth that he'd touched on so lightly but so
convincingly.

Disappointed, she went on hoping for word from
him until twenty to twelve and then decided that
she might just as well go to bed. Noel wouldn't
come now, although she had rung the unit and
learned that Jerome had left Recovery with a much
better prognosis than earlier in the evening and that
both David Buchan and his senior registrar had
gone home.

When the intercom buzzed, startling her, Carola
thought it must be a mistake. At sight of Noel's tall
figure and handsome face and endearing smile, she
almost cast herself on his broad chest in sheer relief
and glad delight. He was so nice and she loved him
so much—if he really did care for her then it would
be the best Christmas present that a girl could have!
The precious gift of his love could erase the shadow
of Christmas past for ever and brighten the prospect
of Christmas future beyond belief.

His kiss of greeting was warm and sweet and she felt its promise steal into every part of her being. Going into his arms was like going home, knowing that she was welcome to stay for the rest of her life.

'I'd given you up!' she declared in quite shameless warmth of pleasure in his arrival, however late. 'It's nearly midnight!'

'But not quite. It's still Christmas Day. I had to make sure that you got this, Carola. . .' He fished a velvet-covered jewel case from his jacket pocket and offered it to her. 'I'm sorry, darling—I just haven't had time to wrap it for you. . .'

'That doesn't matter! Oh, what is it, Noel?' She was like an excited child, eyes sparkling and lovely face aglow, staring at the box in her hand, almost not daring to open it and certainly not daring to believe that it could contain what a girl in love desired more than anything else from the man in her life.

'I had to take a chance on it being as applicable as I've hoped from the first night we met,' Noel said quietly.

Her eyes widened at the meaningful words. But it was a jewel-case, not a ring-box! With a flurried heart, she lifted the lid. Inside lay the five gold rings that the carol promised. . .a gleaming pair of gold hoops for her ears, a delicate gold bracelet and, most important of all for its unmistakable promise for a shared future, a square-shaped sapphire to match her eyes and a gold wedding ring. How could she doubt that they came from the heart of a true love?

'They're beautiful,' Carola murmured, breathless

with love and wonder and delight. 'I don't deserve anything so beautiful. . .'

'You deserve all the happiness in the world and I mean to see that you get it,' Noel said firmly, the ardent glow in his grey eyes supporting the determined words. 'It's Christmas, sweetheart—and the real miracle of Christmas is the love it generates and the exchanging of gifts to show it.'

She looked down at the five golden symbols of his love and his wish to marry her, greatest compliment that a man could pay the woman in his life, and then she looked up at him with regretful eyes. 'I didn't give you anything,' she mourned.

Noel drew her into his strong, sure arms and touched his cheek to her soft, sweet-scented hair. 'You gave me the one thing I wanted more than anything in the world, Carola. You gave me your heart.'

And it was true.

THE WAY WE WERE

Laura MacDonald

CHAPTER ONE

'I'M GOING to England to ask my husband for a divorce.'

'Your husband? But I didn't even know you were married!'

Dr Elizabeth Brent gave a wry smile as she gazed out of the train window and recalled the conversation she'd had earlier in the week with one of her colleagues at the Morrison Memorial Hospital in New York. The woman had been astonished to learn that she was married, but that hadn't really been surprising, for Elizabeth had never imparted much information about her personal life while she had been working there.

The Gloucestershire countryside flashed past and Elizabeth marvelled at how mild the weather was considering it was nearly Christmas. Her timing was bad, she knew that, just as she knew that Callum would be none too pleased at her turning up unannounced, but it had been unavoidable.

She was on a flying visit before returning to the States to take up her new appointment on the paediatric unit. It had been when the question of her marital status had needed confirming for her new job that she knew the time had come to sort out her future and her marriage.

She had fully intended ringing Callum from the home of a friend in London where she had been staying for a couple of days but in the end she'd decided it might be better if she just turned up, told him what she wanted then continued her journey to Bristol, where she planned to spend Christmas with her sister.

As the train drew into the Cotswold village of Ashwood, Elizabeth tightened the belt of her cream trenchcoat and lifted her bag down from the luggage rack, then stepped out on to the platform. It had been by train from this very station that she had left after that final appalling row with Callum when she had come to the conclusion that their marriage was over.

Outside the station she set her bag down for a moment, smoothing back her thick red-gold hair and adjusting the silk scarf she wore around her neck. Elizabeth was tall for a woman, slender, and with the deep smoky eyes and fine alabaster complexion so characteristic of redheads.

A quick glance at her watch revealed that it was only four o'clock, probably a good time to catch Callum as he finished afternoon surgery. Picking up her bag again, she made her way up the main village street, between shop fronts packed with festive fare and mellow cottages of Cotswold stone, their windows bright with decorated Christmas trees.

With each step Elizabeth found her apprehension growing, for, now that she'd actually arrived and everything looked so achingly familiar, she found herself wondering if she could go through with what she had set out to do.

She knew she could have written to Callum about

the question of a divorce, but some instinct told her that she needed to see him—just once more.

The surgery where Callum was in partnership with his father, Edward Brent, was in Dunster House, a fine old building of the same sandy-coloured stone as the cottages, set on the far side of the green beside the church. It was almost dusk as Elizabeth turned into the drive, her boots scrunching noisily on the loose gravel. She noticed that the coach lamps on either side of the black panelled front door had been switched on and she bit her lip when she caught sight of the japonica bush that she had planted in a stone urn beside the entrance.

As she stretched out her gloved hand she suddenly hesitated, then, squaring her shoulders, she firmly pressed the doorbell. It had, after all, been her idea to come; no one had forced her to do so.

As the chimes of the bell sounded inside the house her heart began to beat very fast and at the sound of approaching footsteps her mouth suddenly went dry. Would Callum have changed, or would he still have the effect on her that he'd had when they'd first met? On the other hand, maybe it would be her mother-in-law who answered the door, and Elizabeth was in no doubt what her reception would be from her.

When the door opened, however, it wasn't Callum who stood there, or his mother, but Ivy Potter, the housekeeper.

'Hello, Ivy. Is Dr Callum at home?' asked Elizabeth quietly.

Ivy, a small wiry woman in her late sixties, stared at Elizabeth in astonishment.

'Why, Mrs Brent. . .bless my soul! Well!' She continued to stare in open-mouthed amazement and Elizabeth, although she'd guessed her sudden arrival might cause a certain amount of consternation, began to feel uncomfortable.

'May I come in, Ivy?'

'Oh, yes, yes, of course.' The older woman finally stood aside to allow Elizabeth to enter the hall. 'I'm sorry, I'm quite forgetting my manners, it's just that we were only saying. . .the doctor and I. . .and well, you're just like the answer to a prayer and that's a fact.'

'Well, I'm not sure that Dr Brent will see it like that,' replied Elizabeth with a wry smile as she set her bag down and gazed around the hall. 'I'm afraid he doesn't know I'm coming. Could you tell him that I'm here please, Ivy?'

Before the housekeeper had a chance to move, however, the door behind her suddenly opened.

'Who is it, Ivy?' As Callum Brent appeared in the doorway he caught sight of Elizabeth and stopped dead.

For a single moment their eyes met; they stared at each other and it was as if they were alone, not only as if Ivy weren't there, but as if the rest of the world had ceased to exist.

It was Elizabeth who found her voice first; she swallowed, trying to ignore the fact that he hadn't changed at all, that he was still as devastatingly handsome as he had always been, but at the same time reminding herself that he was probably still as proud and stubborn as ever.

'Hello, Callum. How are you?'

'Elizabeth. You always were full of surprises.' He spoke lightly, but she knew she had disturbed him by her unexpected appearance, and she'd noted the immediate look of concerned alarm in his dark eyes when he'd first caught sight of her.

She was vaguely aware of the ringing of the telephone in the room behind him, of Ivy's muttered apology, followed by her disappearance, before Callum spoke again.

'You're looking well.'

'So are you.' Suddenly she was stuck for words; she couldn't just blurt out why she had come. The clock in the corner behind him suddenly chimed the hour and in an involuntary gesture he glanced at his watch then his eyes flickered to her bag.

'Have you come to stay?'

'I just wanted to talk to you, Callum.'

'I see.' He turned as Ivy appeared again.

'I'm sorry, Doctor, that was the cottage hospital. They want you to go down right away, it's old Mr Parsons.'

'Very well, Ivy, thank you.'

Elizabeth thought she detected a weariness in his tone as he said, 'Ivy, will dinner stretch tonight, do you think?'

'I'm sure it will, Doctor.' She beamed at Elizabeth and bustled off to the kitchen.

'I'm sorry, but I shall have to go,' said Callum. 'Do you mind waiting?' His manner was polite, his emotions firmly under control.

'There was no need to invite me for dinner,' she said. 'I do want to talk to you, but I can wait while you do your call.'

'Not at all.' He held up his hand and she knew the matter was closed. 'Would you like to wait in the morning-room? The fire's lit in there.'

'Thank you.' Wordlessly she followed him across the hall. She wanted to tell him that she didn't have much time, that she wanted to catch the eight o'clock train to Bristol, but suddenly she felt tongue-tied like some gauche schoolgirl. He opened the door of the small morning-room and stood back for her to enter.

The room was bright and cheerful, the lamps lit and the fire crackling in the hearth. Elizabeth walked into the centre then paused as Callum said, 'Let me take your coat.'

She fumbled with the buttons, only too aware that he was standing very close behind her, then she stiffened as she felt him lift the coat from her shoulders. She turned sharply, catching her breath as a wave of nostalgia flooded over her. Briefly their eyes met again, then he said quietly, 'I must go; I'll see you later.'

She watched him as he strode from the room, his case in one hand, her coat over his arm, calling to Ivy as he went that he was carrying a pager. His hair was as dark as it had always been and although he was thick-set and muscular there wasn't an ounce of spare flesh on his body. The only difference she could see in him was that he looked tired, with fine lines around his dark eyes.

It had been his eyes that had first attracted her, at a party at the hospital where they had both been working. She'd walked into the room and it had happened, just the way it did in films, eyes meeting across a crowded room—instant attraction.

She gave herself a little shake. There was no point remembering things like that, not now when she had come to ask him to end their marriage. In an effort to change her mood she sat down in an armchair beside the fire and stretched her hands out to the blaze. The house seemed very quiet and she wondered where Callum's parents were—not that she was in any hurry to renew her acquaintance with his mother, but Edward Brent was a kind man and she knew he had been fond of her.

She heard Callum's car draw away from the house and she sighed and gazed into the fire. In spite of his cool manner he must be wondering why she had come back. A year was a long time, during which they'd had no contact. While she'd been in the States she'd been engaged in locum work and had been moving around continuously.

Could he now be thinking that she wanted to come back to him? That she wanted to try again? And if he was thinking that, what was his reaction? Elizabeth was under no illusions that Callum's fierce pride would play a large part in his feelings. She had, after all, left him, no doubt wounding his pride to such an extent that he would be only too ready to agree to a divorce. Apart, however, from the almost imperceptible look of surprise followed by that brief flicker of concern when he'd first seen her, he'd shown no emotion whatsoever, but then, she thought as she listened to the sound of his car receding into the distance, Callum Brent had always been a cool customer.

Moments later Ivy appeared with a tray of tea and Elizabeth realised that she was very thirsty.

'There you are, Mrs Brent, I expect you could do with that,' said the housekeeper kindly as she set the tray down on a small table and drew the blinds, shutting out the darkening December afternoon before bustling from the room again.

As Elizabeth sipped her tea she was momentarily reminded of another time she'd taken tea in the same room. That had been on her first visit to Ashwood just after she and Callum had met. She sighed and replaced the cup in its delicate bone china saucer. Maybe if they'd never returned to Ashwood after that first time they might still have been together, because until they'd taken up residence at Dunster House everything had been quite wonderful.

Not that they hadn't had their differences, of course; that had been inevitable with the two strong-minded characters they both were, but they had always resolved those differences in the most blissful manner.

Theirs had been a whirlwind courtship after that first meeting of glances when time had stood still, and the impossible—love at first sight—had happened. Callum's demanding, ardent attentions had left her breathless and by the end of the first week, after they'd made love so many times that she'd lost count, she knew without a doubt that he was the man for her.

By the end of the second week he'd asked her to marry him and they had married a month later in London. They had planned a quiet wedding, but

their friends at the clinic where they were both
working had decided otherwise and it had been a
glorious affair with a hired Rolls-Royce and, at the
reception, a jazz band.

She'd become so lost in her thoughts that she
hadn't heard Ivy come back into the room and she
jumped when she suddenly spoke.

'I'm so glad you've come back, Mrs Brent, and
that's a fact,' she said.

'And why is that Ivy?' Elizabeth looked up
sharply.

'Well, it's the doctor; he needs help. I was really
worried about him. It's been chaos since we had the
call about Dr Jessop's accident three days ago. We
had a locum while he was on holiday, but Dr Brent
hasn't been able to get one since, and it doesn't look
as if he will either, not until after Christmas. I'm off
to my daughter's later this evening, I was all set to
cancel it, but Dr Brent insisted I went, said I
couldn't disappoint my grandchildren. But I feel
much better now that you're here, Mrs Brent. As I
said, it's almost the answer to a prayer.'

Elizabeth gazed blankly at the housekeeper, wondering what on earth she was talking about. 'I'm
sorry, Ivy, but who is Dr Jessop?'

Ivy stared at her. 'Dr Jessop? Oh, he's Dr Brent's
partner. . . I thought you knew.'

Elizabeth shook her head. 'No, Ivy, I didn't. . .'

'Well, he's had this dreadful accident, skiing he
was in Switzerland, anyway he's broken his leg and
there's no way the doctor is going to manage on his
own.

'Just a minute, Ivy,' Elizabeth interrupted her,

'let me get this straight—how long has Dr Brent had this Dr Jessop as a partner?'

'Let me see now, it must be about six months.' She frowned. 'Well it must be since. . .since. . .'

'Since what, Ivy?'

'Well, since Dr Brent's father retired.'

Elizabeth stared at Ivy, hardly able to believe what she was hearing. The main cause of the arguments between herself and Callum had been over his father's reluctance to retire.

'Well, as I was saying, Mrs Brent, I'm just so pleased you're here. I can tell you I was feeling guilty about going to my daughter's but now that you're here. . .maybe at least you could give the doctor a hand with Dr Jessop's patients.' Ivy turned to leave the room again, but Elizabeth called her back.

'Just a minute, Ivy—why can't Dr Brent's father help out with locum work?'

'Well, I dare say he would if he was here. . .' The housekeeper trailed off and began to look uncomfortable.

'So where is he?'

Ivy cleared her throat. 'They live in Norwich now, I'm sorry, Mrs Brent, but I thought you would have known.' She drew her mouth into a firm line then, as if she'd said quite enough.

Elizabeth took a deep breath. She now understood Ivy's remarks about her being the answer to a prayer. She didn't, however, want to disillusion the housekeeper by telling her that she had no intention of spending her Christmas playing locum.

'What time is dinner, Ivy?'

'Seven o'clock, Mrs Brent.'

Elizabeth bit her lip; at this rate there would be no way she would be catching the eight o'clock train so she would need to find somewhere to stay the night—she could hardly stay here at Dunster House. 'Could I use the telephone, please, Ivy?' she said standing up.

'Of course you can, Mrs Brent.' The housekeeper turned to leave the room and Elizabeth followed her into the hall.

As Ivy disappeared down the passage to the kitchen Elizabeth glanced up the stairs. She simply couldn't believe the irony in the fact that Callum's parents no longer lived there.

She looked quickly through the telephone directory on the hall table and dialled the number of the Feathers Hotel in the village. Moments later she replaced the receiver, after being told that the hotel was fully booked until after the Christmas period and that, as far as they knew, the other establishments in the village were full as well.

She was still deliberating on what she should do when the doorbell rang. After only a moment's hesitation she opened the door and found two middle-aged women on the step.

'The door was locked,' said one indignantly. 'It's time for surgery, isn't it?'

Elizabeth's heart sank. She had been hoping to talk to Callum on his return, but if he had another surgery to take that evening there seemed little chance now of that. She stood aside to let the women pass and they headed for the waiting-room.

Several more patients arrived and then, when

Callum returned, he put his head round the morning-room door. He gave Elizabeth an apologetic smile. 'I'll see you at dinner—if I get through.'

'Just a moment, Callum.' She called him back as he would have headed for his consulting-room. 'I was hoping to catch a train this evening.'

He paused then shrugged and spread his hands. 'Well, I'm sorry, but you can see the chaos here. Look, why don't you stay the night?' He must have seen her indecision for he added cryptically, 'Don't worry, we've converted the back of the house into a flat for Tim Jessop—I'll stay there. OK?'

'I suppose so...'

At that moment Ivy appeared again just as another group of patients arrived.

'My word, Doctor, you have got a full surgery tonight,' she said. 'I was only saying earlier how lucky it is that Mrs Brent is here to give you a hand.'

'Ivy...' began Elizabeth warningly.

'I say, Elizabeth, are you going to help? I hardly dared to ask.' Callum's face suddenly brightened and lost its hunted look while Ivy beamed at the pair of them.

Elizabeth sighed. She suddenly found she hadn't the heart to refuse. This, after all, was a crisis situation and her professional instincts began to take over. 'You'd better show me what you want me to do,' she said.

'Well, perhaps you'd like to use Tim's room, oh, and Ivy...' Callum turned to the housekeeper '...before you go to your daughter's, would you change the linen on my bed? Mrs Brent has decided to stay the night.'

'Oh, I am pleased,' replied Ivy. 'It'll be just like old times.'

Elizabeth had no time for further speculation, for Callum ushered her into Tim Jessop's consulting-room, showed her where the basic essentials were to conduct a surgery, and, almost before she had time to draw breath, had called her first patient.

Luckily her first two patients were quite straightforward, one a routine blood-pressure check for which she issued the patient's usual hypertensive drug, and the second a teenage girl who'd been suffering from persistent sore throats and had recently been to the hopsital for a test for glandular fever.

The test was negative and Elizabeth carefully examined the girl's throat, ears and glands, then prescribed a further course of antibiotics.

'Come back to surgery in a week's time when you've finished the tablets,' she said as she handed the prescription to the girl.

'Yes, thank you, Doctor. Will I be seeing you again?'

Elizabeth smiled and shook her head. 'No, I'm afraid not.'

'Then who will it be? Will Dr Jessop be back?' The girl looked anxious and Elizabeth realised there might be a danger of her not following up her treatment.

'No, it won't be Dr Jessop, but I would think by then Dr Brent will have managed to get a locum to take Dr Jessop's place. But you must come back, Lucy. Do you understand?'

The girl nodded. 'I liked Dr Jessop, but it's been

nice talking to a lady doctor.' She smiled then and left the room, leaving Elizabeth reflecting that if everything had gone according to plan the girl would probably have been registered with her anyway. But that had been before, when their dreams had been intact, hers and Callum's, before everything had gone so disastrously wrong.

To her surprise she managed to get through the remainder of the surgery without too many problems; she had imagined that she would be hopelessly out of touch after her year in the States but not much seemed to have changed in the problems that presented themselves in a pre-Christmas evening surgery in a village practice. She finished before Callum and went through to the morning-room again, where she found Ivy had set a table for two before the fire. She frowned. A cosy tête-á-tête was the last thing she had planned.

CHAPTER TWO

CALLUM joined her almost immediately. 'How did it go?' he asked, as he crossed to the sideboard and poured them both a drink.

Elizabeth shrugged. 'Not too bad.' She noticed he'd removed his jacket and tie, loosened his collar and turned back his cuffs.

'Well, I'm grateful to you, thank you. God knows what time I would have finished.' He handed her a drink, then paused with his back to the fire, his own drink in his hand. 'Ivy said it was just like old times. Shall we drink to that?' Callum raised his glass with a quizzical smile. Then, not waiting for her reply, he repeated, 'To old times.'

Elizabeth took a sip of her drink but didn't reply. There might be some old times she would drink to, but there were others which were best left forgotten.

Later, after they'd eaten and Ivy had left to go to her daughter's, Callum leaned back in his chair and surveyed her thoughtfully across the table.

'You really are looking very well, Elizabeth,' he observed.

'Thank you,' she murmured, suddenly embarrassed by the undisguised look of admiration in his eyes. She still hadn't found the right moment to tell him why she was there and with each passing hour it became more difficult.

'So what have you been doing?' he asked casually.

When she didn't immediately answer, he added, 'I gather you've been working abroad.'

She threw him a sharp glance, wondering how he knew that. 'Yes, I've been working in the States.'

'Really? In what capacity?'

'Locum work mainly. I... I've been moving around quite a bit but lately I've been at the Morrison Memorial.'

He gave a low whistle. 'Have you, indeed? New York, I'm impressed. What field?'

'Rheumatology.' Now would surely be a good time to tell him of the new job she'd been offered on the paediatric unit, but before she had chance to speak Callum said, 'So what are your immediate plans?'

'I'm going on to Bristol for Christmas, to my sister's.'

'Ah, your sister.'

She glanced up sharply, something in the tone of his voice goading her into retaliation.

'What's the matter with my sister?' It came out indignantly.

'Nothing, nothing,' he said hastily, raising his hands as if to fend her off. He was silent for a moment and a log crackled in the hearth, then nonchalantly he asked, 'I suppose she still has those children?'

'Of course she does,' Elizabeth replied, more sharply than she had intended. 'What do you think she's done with them?'

He raised his eyebrows. 'I can't imagine...' he said innocently.

She stared at him angrily, then suddenly she saw

the funny side, her shoulders sagged and she laughed. 'They were pretty awful, weren't they?'

He grinned, then joined in her laughter as, inevitably, they both silently recalled a disastrous holiday they'd once spent in Snowdonia with Elizabeth's sister Janet, her husband Walter and their three children.

As he leaned across the table and filled her coffee-cup he said seriously, 'And you fully intend spending Christmas with them? I didn't know you had masochistic tendencies.'

Elizabeth shrugged lightly. 'Well, Christmas always was for families, wasn't it?'

'When do you intend going?'

'Tomorrow morning,' she replied firmly.

He sighed. 'And there was me beginning to think you might consider spending some time with me.'

'We do need to talk, Callum,' she said, then paused as the telephone rang and he stood up.

'Excuse me,' he said, and walked out of the room to take the call in the hall.

While he was gone Elizabeth sipped her coffee and looked around the cosy morning-room. Nothing seemed to have changed in this room; everything was exactly as it had been when Margaret Brent had been mistress at Dunster House.

She sighed and focused her thoughts for a moment, trying to pinpoint the exact time when things had begun to go wrong. It hadn't been very long after they'd arrived at Dunster House, she was quite sure of that.

But it had even been before that, very soon after they were married to be exact, when Callum had told her that it had always been accepted that he would one day join his father in his practice in Ashwood. Elizabeth remembered that at the time she had remarked that it might have been nice if he'd told her before they were married.

'Why?' he had asked with his most charming smile. 'Would it have made any difference if I had?'

She had laughed. 'Of course not.' But she had felt uneasy. Her career was tremendously important to her and, much as she loved Callum and had wanted to marry him, she also wanted to continue with her work. Then, when Callum had gone on to say that his father was planning early retirement as the pressure of work had been affecting his health, and that she would then be able to join him as a partner in the Ashwood practice, her happiness was complete.

The nightmare had begun after they had moved into Dunster House and her in-laws had failed to recognise Elizabeth's strong need to continue with her career. Callum's mother had firm ideas on what constituted the perfect GP's wife and they didn't include being his professional equal.

To add to Elizabeth's growing frustration, the more her father-in-law's workload had eased with his son's help, the less he was inclined to bring forward his retirement.

Suddenly she looked up, startled to find that Callum had come back into the room and was standing watching her.

'Oh, I didn't hear you come back,' she said.

'I was watching the firelight on your hair,' he said

quietly. 'I thought I'd remembered its exact shade, but I hadn't.'

She coloured slightly and in an effort to change the subject said. 'Do you have to go out?'

He shook his head. 'No, the call was from people staying in the village. They have a baby who is sick; they're going to bring him in by car in a few minutes' time.'

'How are you going to cope, with your partner away?'

'I've no idea. Double surgeries for the next two days I suppose. . .unless, of course, you would be prepared to——'

'No, Callum, I'm sorry,' she interrupted quickly.

'No? Ah, well, it was worth a try.'

She hesitated, then said, 'Ivy told me about your parents.'

'I thought she might.'

'Norwich, is it?'

He nodded. 'Yes, they've bought a bungalow very near Mother's sister.'

Sudden anger flared inside her, twisting her heart. Why, oh, why, couldn't that have happened before? Why couldn't they have gone and left her and Callum alone to run the practice and Dunster House?

She glanced at him and wondered if he was thinking the same thing.

'Oh, damn, there goes that phone again.' With a rueful smile he disappeared into the hall once more, leaving Elizabeth beginning to feel guilty about his workload in spite of her earlier resolution not to get involved any further.

Within minutes he was back and she saw he was carrying his case.

'I'm afraid I have to go this time, a suspected CVA.' He glanced anxiously at his watch. 'That child will be here in a moment. . .'

'Go on, Callum.' Elizabeth sighed. 'I'll see the baby.'

'Would you really? That's very good of you. Use my consulting-room, and Elizabeth, if I'm a long time, make yourself at home, won't you? I'll see you later.'

With that he was gone. Moments later she heard the scrunch of his car tyres on the drive and she was alone in Dunster House.

Slowly she stood up and began to clear the dishes from the table and with an increasing feeling of *déjà vu* she carried them through to the kitchen and loaded the dishwasher. She had barely finished before the doorbell rang.

She hurried into the hall and opened the front door. An anxious-looking couple stood on the doorstep, the man with a young baby wrapped in a blanket in his arms.

'We've come to see the doctor,' said the woman breathlessly. 'We did phone. . .'

'Yes, I know,' replied Elizabeth stepping aside for them to enter the hall. 'Bring the baby into the surgery.'

She opened the door of Callum's consulting-room then wondered how she was going to explain who she was.

'I understand you're staying in the area?' she said

as she walked behind the desk and began searching for a temporary resident's form.

'Yes, we're staying with my parents for Christmas,' explained the woman. 'They live in the village,' she added.

'Well, if you would like to fill in this form on behalf of the baby, I'll take a look at him,' said Elizabeth. 'We need a few details, like your home address and the name of your GP,' she added, taking Callum's spare stethoscope from a drawer in the desk. In the surprised silence that followed, Elizabeth glanced up and when she saw their expressions, she said, 'It's quite all right, I am a doctor.'

'Oh, I thought we were seeing Dr Brent,' said the woman. 'My parents are registered with him.'

'Dr Brent has been called out on an emergency,' said Elizabeth firmly, indicating for the man to sit on a chair with the baby on his knee. 'I'm his. . .partner,' she said.

The baby's father sat on the chair and had already unwrapped the baby so that Elizabeth could examine him, but his wife still seemed anxious.

'My father told me that Dr Brent's partner had had an accident,' she said dubiously.

'That's quite correct, he has.' Elizabeth smiled. 'You could say I'm just standing in for him for the time being.'

The woman seemed to relax and turned her attentions to the reason why they had brought the child.

He appeared very hot and flushed and Elizabeth

confirmed the fact that he was running a temperature. His lungs however were clear and there was
no signs of a head cold or a cough. There was a
slight rash across his cheeks and she established the
fact that he was in fact cutting two back teeth. She
knew there was no point in writing a prescription at
that time of night and a quick search in one of
Callum's cupboards revealed a sample bottle of
Calpol.

She told the couple to bring the baby back the
following morning if they were still worried about
him but that she believed he was suffering from
nothing worse than troublesome teething.

'We're sorry to have bothered you, Doctor,' said
the baby's father as Elizabeth showed them to the
door.

'Not at all,' she replied firmly. 'Teething can be
very painful and the poor little mites really do
suffer.'

After they'd left she walked back into the consulting-room and sat in Callum's chair behind his desk.
She looked round the room, which had been converted to suit a doctor's needs but which still
retained its elegant Adam fireplace, decorative cov-
ings and high arched windows. She'd always liked
this room and she found herself wondering, if she'd
stayed, whether this would have been her consulting-room or the one across the hall which Tim
Jessop used.

How could it all have gone so drastically wrong?
She stood up and began to wander round the room,
touching various objects: the computer on the desk,

a row of medical textbooks, the sphygmomano-
meter. When they had first arrived, six months after
their wedding, she had known and accepted the fact
that she wouldn't be able to be a full partner until
after her father-in-law retired, but it had been
decided that she would gradually become incorpo-
rated into the practice by doing various clinics.
There had been talk of a family planning clinic, a
clinic for cervical smears and diabetic and antenatal
clinics.

Elizabeth had been reasonably happy to bide her
time for a short while in spite of the fact that she
was keenly looking forward to the day when she had
her own list.

Her mother-in-law, however, had had other
ideas. Margaret Brent had been constantly indulged
by her adoring husband and throughout her married
life she had been used to getting her own way. She
loved her life at Dunster House and saw little reason
why it should change. At first Elizabeth hadn't
minded too much when her mother-in-law had
involved her in one charity or committee after
another but as the weeks slipped by and turned to
months and there was no sign of Elizabeth's being
included in the running of the surgery she began to
get edgy. She'd mentioned the matter to Callum on
many occasions and each time he'd begged her to
be patient, saying that if they appeared too insistent
it would seem as if they were trying to force his
parents out and that it was only a matter of time
before his father retired, then they would be able to
do as they pleased.

It was after they'd been in Ashwood for six

months that Margaret Brent began to drop subtle little hints about grandchildren.

'You can put her straight on that score,' Elizabeth had told Callum firmly. 'Of course I want children, but not yet; I have a career to think of first and I certainly haven't done all those years' training to give it up now.'

'Don't get cross with her,' he'd replied in an irritatingly calm way. 'It's only natural she should want grandchildren. Come to think of it, I wouldn't mind the sound of children around the place myself. . .in fact, I was wondering if now might not be a good time while we're waiting. . .'

She'd stared at him in exasperation. She knew this was something else they should have discussed more thoroughly before they had married, but there had been no time. They had hurtled headlong into marriage and there had been many times since when she had wondered if she was paying the price for their haste.

With a last glance round the surgery she flicked off the light switch and, stepping out into the hall, closed the door behind her. She stood for a while wondering what she should do next. Callum had indicated that he might be some time. He had also told her to make herself at home, but still she hesitated.

Nothing seemed to be working out quite as she had intended and she felt dubious not only about staying at Dunster House, but about sleeping in her old room.

At last, with a sigh, she picked up her bag from where it still lay in the hall. She was probably being unreasonable, for, after all, Callum had said he would be staying in his partner's flat.

Curiously she looked down the corridor which led to the sitting-room and on a sudden impulse she walked down and tried the door. It was locked, and she guessed that the flat consisted of the sitting-room, a back staircase and one of the bedrooms at the rear of the large house. Why, oh, why couldn't they have done that conversion when she and Callum had first arrived? she thought as she slowly walked back into the hall and began to climb the staircase. As it was, they had been expected to live in the house with his parents, taking meals with them and spending most of their free time with them.

Their only hours of privacy had been in the large guest bedroom at the front of the house and it wasn't without a pang that Elizabeth now opened the bedroom door and flicked on the light.

She stood on the threshold looking round the room and her breath caught in her throat as memories flooded back. It looked exactly the same as it had before with its Regency striped wallpaper and matching curtains and bedcovers.

There was, however, little evidence of Callum's personal possessions; his shaving gear on the shelf above the washbasin in the corner, a pair of shoes beneath the chest of drawers and a biography beside his radio on the bedside cabinet.

For a moment Elizabeth allowed her eyes to flicker to the bed and her thoughts to go back to the way they had once been. It was hard to believe now that they had once made such passionate love in

that very bed. Sex had never been the problem
between them, she thought ruefully, as she walked
slowly into the room and placed her bag on the bed.
The problems had come from other quarters.

She unpacked her nightdress, intending to leave
the clothes she had brought to wear over the
Christmas period in the bag, then she changed her
mind, deciding she might as well hang them up to
shake the creases out of them.

When she opened the wardrobe door she caught
a subtle whiff of the aftershave that Callum always
wore and another wave of nostalgia swept over her.
Quickly she hung up the dress and two skirts she'd
brought, then, taking her sponge-bag to the washbasin, she took out her toothbrush and put it in the
rack beside Callum's. She stared at it for a long
moment then almost angrily she snatched it out
again and returned it to the bag.

After she'd finished, she glanced anxiously at her
watch. If Callum didn't come back soon they
wouldn't have time to talk that evening. She was
just wondering if she could extend her visit by a few
hours in the morning when the telephone beside the
bed rang.

It was Callum.

'Elizabeth? Look, I'm sorry, but ambulance control have just paged me. I have two more calls to
make. God knows what time I shall get home.
You'd better go on to bed.'

She took a deep breath. 'Yes, all right, but
Callum. . .?'

'Yes?'

'When are we going to be able to talk? I had intended leaving first thing in the morning.'

'Yes, of course you had. I *am* sorry, Elizabeth.'

'Could we talk before I go?'

'Well, as I told you I do have a double surgery to take. . .' He trailed off and she felt a sudden pang of guilt.

There was silence for a moment then incredibly Elizabeth heard herself saying, 'Would it help if I were to do your partner's surgery?'

'But I couldn't expect you to do that. Surely that would upset all your plans?' His voice sounded smooth.

'I didn't say exactly when I would be arriving at my sister's,' she said. 'Then maybe after surgery we can talk before you go out on your house calls?'

'Of course. That really is most kind of you. Now I'm afraid I must dash. See you in the morning, and Elizabeth. . .?'

'Yes, Callum?'

'Sleep well.'

She stared at the receiver before slowly replacing it, then she sank down on the bed as she realised that at the sound of his voice, deep and slightly husky, her knees had started to shake.

After she'd undressed she slipped between the crisp clean sheets, but as she stretched out her legs in an attempt to relax she suddenly felt very strange. It was almost as if the clock had been wound back and at any moment Callum would appear in the doorway in his bathrobe, his hair wet from the shower. He would smile to see she was already in bed, then he would slip off his robe. He would be naked, and she felt herself tense as she recalled his powerfully built body, the broad shoulders and chest, the flat belly, the long lean thighs and the covering of dark hair over his legs, arms and chest.

He would cross the room in a couple of strides then slip into bed beside her, turning towards her, reaching out for her instantly, his need as great as her own.

Their lovemaking had been perfect, his desire to please her equally matched her own wish to satisfy him.

It had, however, always amused Elizabeth to wonder what his parents would have thought of the nightly passion played out in the bedroom near to theirs. But she was never to know, for very gradually, over a period of months, what had started as little niggles between herself and Callum had progressed to arguments, then to full-scale rows. At first, the making-up after these fights had made them seem almost worthwhile, but later even that hadn't compensated for the bitterness and frustration that had crept into their relationship.

The situation hadn't been easy for Callum, that much Elizabeth was prepared to admit, for he had virtually been caught in the middle, but as their rows had become more frequent she had accused him time and again of taking his parents' side against her and not demanding an end to the situation.

As her thoughts turned once again to Callum she shifted uneasily in the bed, his bed, and she felt an ache deep inside, an ache she hadn't felt for a long time, an ache that she knew could only be satisfied by Callum. Restlessly she ran her hands down her body over her breasts and her hips, covered only by the flimsy silk nightdress she wore.

Suddenly in spite of all her earlier resolves she longed for him. Seeing him again had awakened all kinds of memories and desires she had thought long gone. She sighed and arched her body beneath the sheets; at that moment, although she hated herself for even thinking it, all she wanted was for him to take her on one of their unforgettable journeys of love and exploration.

Then she jumped as a door closed downstairs, her body tensed and she lay rigid, straining her ears for the sound of Callum's footsteps on the stairs.

CHAPTER THREE

THERE was no lock on the bedroom door, and as Elizabeth lay waiting for the handle to turn she cursed herself for allowing herself to be put in such a vulnerable position. Callum had a very persuasive brand of charm, and she was only too aware that she had fallen victim to it many times in the past.

He did have the courtesy to knock, however, before opening the door just wide enough to put his head round.

'Oh, good, you're still awake,' he said. 'I didn't have a chance to get my gear before I went out.' He came right into the room, crossing to the wardrobe and taking out a clean shirt, rummaging in the chest of drawers then collecting his washing and shaving things from the washbasin.

Elizabeth lay with her nerves stretched to breaking point as she watched him. At least he wasn't in his bathrobe, she thought grimly, although she wouldn't have put that past him. As he finished collecting the items he wanted, he turned towards the bed, and she found herself holding her breath. What would she do if he attempted anything? Would she react angrily and tell him to get out, or would she helplessly give in?

He paused and his eyes met hers. Just for a moment she thought she detected a glint of amusement in their dark depths as he allowed his gaze to wander over her: her red-gold hair spread across his pillow, her creamy shoulders and the swell of her breasts above her nightdress, and the outline of her slim figure and long legs beneath the bedclothes.

'Goodnight,' he said softly, and there was something in the slightly husky tone of his voice that made her heart stand still. 'Sleep well.'

Then he was gone, leaving Elizabeth uncertain whether she was relieved or disappointed, but as she reached out to switch off the bedside light there was one thing she couldn't deny: the ache of longing was still inside her, unsatisfied and unfulfilled.

Surprisingly she slept well and when she awoke for a moment her brain didn't question her surroundings. Everything felt right, and it was as if she'd once again slipped back in time to the way things had been.

The house sounded very quiet, then she remembered that Ivy had gone to her daughter's for Christmas and she and Callum would have to fend for themselves.

After she'd showered and dressed she made her way down to the kitchen and put the kettle on. She was just wondering whether Callum had made his own breakfast in the flat when she heard the sound of a car outside followed by the slamming of a door before he appeared in the doorway. He looked tired and drawn.

'Bad night?' she asked sympathetically.

'You could say that.' He drew a hand across the dark stubble on his chin, hiding a yawn.

'You haven't had breakfast, have you?'

He smiled wearily. 'No, I was hoping you might

be going to cook me one of your specials before surgery. You know, one of those forbidden ones with fried bread, sausages and mushrooms.'

She hesitated only momentarily. 'All right.' She smiled, recognising the devastating Brent charm at work again. Even when he was so exhausted he had the knack of getting what he wanted. 'You go and shower and change and I'll start cooking. I presume there's plenty of everything in the fridge?'

'Yes, Ivy's stocked me up beautifully for Christmas; I'm sure you'll find everything you need.' He walked to the kitchen door then stopped and looked back over his shoulder. 'Oh, did you sleep well?'

'Very well, thank you,' she replied, avoiding his gaze.

For the next half-hour Elizabeth busied herself cooking bacon and eggs and all the trimmings Callum had requested. She was just pouring fresh orange juice for them both as the coffee bubbled nicely in the percolator when Callum returned with the morning papers under his arm.

He stopped in the doorway sniffing the aroma of the cooked bacon. 'Well, this is all very civilised,' he remarked. 'Quite like old times, in fact.'

Elizabeth took a seat opposite him at the large oak table but she declined to comment on his observation. She knew he wasn't referring to the time they had spent at Dunster House; in those days the kitchen had been very much Margaret Brent's domain, with Ivy to assist her, and there had been little room for Elizabeth. Callum's remarks alluded to the time they'd spent in their flat in the few

months immediately after their wedding, those blissful few months before the intervention of outside
forces.

As Callum tucked into his breakfast he suddenly
paused and looked approvingly at her own plate.
'I'm glad to see you're joining me; I seem to
remember your breakfast used to consist of toast
and coffee.'

'It still does usually. I have to watch my weight
these days.'

'Oh, surely not?' He paused, his fork halfway to
his mouth and stared at her. 'Your figure's as lovely
as it always was.'

She felt the inevitable flush touch her cheeks at
his words and, hating herself for it, she attempted
to ignore his remark and change the subject.

'I decided today was an exception,' she went on
almost as if he hadn't spoken. 'I am, after all,
supposed to be on holiday.'

He grimaced. 'And here I am getting you to
work.'

She shrugged. 'Well, I suppose it is a bit of a
crisis. I imagine your partner will be away for some
time if he's fractured his femur. Will you get a
locum?'

'I shall have to; the list has grown in the last year
as I'm sure you've realised. It's far too much now
for one to handle.'

'You'd better fill me in on a few details about
your partner if I'm to be seeing his patients,' said
Elizabeth as she poured the coffee.

'Well, his name's Tim, Timothy Jessop; he trained
at Sheffield and actually he isn't my partner.'

'Oh?' She looked up, interested. 'But I thought you said. . .?'

'I know. Somehow it's easier to refer to Tim as my partner but in actual fact he didn't want a partnership as he only proposes to be with me for a short time. He wants ultimately to work in Third World countries.'

'I see.' Elizabeth found herself wondering if that meant that Callum would shortly be looking for another partner, then, ruthlessly, she dismissed the thought. It was far too late for that.

Callum stood up. 'Ready to face the onslaught? I'll ring the FPC to tell them you're taking surgery and the local chemist to warn him they'll be a different signature on the prescriptions,' he said as he followed her through the hall to the consulting-rooms. 'If there's anything you need, please don't be afraid to ask. I really am most grateful to you for this,' he added quietly. 'I had resigned myself to two days of sheer hell.'

She was about to remind him that she was only staying to take one surgery, when they heard the sound of the telephone ringing in the hall and Callum excused himself and left the room.

With a sigh she sat down. She had been about to ask him about patients' records and whether people were booked in on appointments or whether they ran open surgeries where patients waited their turn. She knew the latter had been the procedure in Callum's father's day but she also knew that Callum had intended making changes.

As she was wondering what to do next she suddenly remembered that through the waiting-room door she had glimpsed a section of shelving filled with sets of records and she decided to investigate. In the hall she paused and listened; she could hear Callum's voice and it was obvious he was still talking on the telephone.

The waiting-room was empty, the chairs neatly lining the walls and the tables stacked with magazines and leaflets. She noted with interest the shelves filled from floor to ceiling with patients' records then her eye was caught by a desk situated below the window. On its top was a computer and electronic typewriter. Elizabeth was just marvelling on the apparent changes that had been made in the practice when the door that led to the conservatory opened and a woman appeared.

She appeared to be about thirty, her dark hair was cut into a short fashionable bob and she was wearing a suede sheepskin coat. In one hand she carried a green watering-can, the type for watering indoor plants. She stopped when she saw Elizabeth, her expressive dark eyes narrowing slightly.

'We aren't open yet. . .' she began, then trailed off as Elizabeth stepped forward.

'It's all right, I'm not a patient. I'm here to help out. I'm taking Dr Jessop's surgery this morning and I was just wondering about patient records.'

The woman's face had lost its suspicious look. 'Oh, I see. I'm sorry. Well, it'll be a relief to have some help. Poor Dr Brent, I really didn't know how he was going to manage. These two days before Christmas can be the busiest in the year.'

Again Elizabeth felt prompted to put the record straight by saying she was only staying for one morning and again she was prevented, this time by the arrival of Callum.

He glanced quickly from Elizabeth to the dark-haired woman. 'I'd come to do some introductions,' he said. 'Am I too late?'

'Not really,' replied Elizabeth. 'We hadn't got as far as names.' She smiled and the woman set down the watering-can on the desk and smiled back.

'Elizabeth, this is Hilary Young, our secretary-receptionist. She's an absolute treasure and will give you any assistance you require. Hilary, this is Elizabeth, who will be helping us out briefly.' The two women shook hands and murmured pleasantries then Callum glanced at Hilary again and added, 'Elizabeth also happens to be my wife.'

Hilary Young's expression froze a second after the smile slipped from her carefully made-up face, and in that same moment Elizabeth summed up the situation.

Callum, however, didn't seem to have noticed anything untoward, and he continued speaking. 'She has agreed to take this morning's surgery and I'm hoping we might persuade her to stay to help us out over Christmas Eve.'

Again Elizabeth found it impossible to contradict him. Somehow it just didn't seem the right moment, especially with Hilary Young no doubt hoping she was going to say she wouldn't be staying, even though, only moments ago, she'd implied they desperately needed help right up until Christmas. That, however, had been before she'd known that Elizabeth was Callum's wife, and now Elizabeth knew with all the certainty of a woman's intuition that Hilary Young wouldn't be wanting her around for long.

In spite of Elizabeth's earlier misgivings, the morning surgery went well. For the most part she found the only explanation necessary to Tim Jessop's patients was that she was standing in for him. As the majority of his list were newly registered patients Elizabeth found that thankfully she went unrecognised.

The list was varied; the usual assortment of blood-pressure checks, monthly prescriptions and sickness certificates to take people over the Christmas and New Year period, several children with heavy colds and sore throats, an elderly man with emphysema who wanted his medication changed and then, just when she was congratulating herself on not getting into any awkward situations, a patient entered whom she immediately recognised.

From the look on Audrey Summers' face as she stood in the doorway and stared at Elizabeth it was only too obvious that she remembered her as well. Audrey had been one of the ladies who had seemed to serve on every committee in Ashwood, a stalwart of the Mother's Union, a member of the church choir and a reliable source of information on just about every resident in the village. She had also been a close confidante of Margaret Brent's, and Elizabeth's heart sank as she stood up to greet her.

'Why, Mrs Summers, how very nice to see you again,' she said as briskly as she could. 'Please come and sit down.'

'Well this is a surprise, I must say; when Hilary said I would be seeing Dr Brent, I imagined she meant your...your...' She floundered. 'I imagined she meant Dr Callum Brent,' she managed at last.

'I'm simply helping...my husband out,' replied Elizabeth firmly, disliking the inquisitive, slightly hostile approach of the other woman.

'I see...'

Before she had the chance to ask any further questions Elizabeth stepped in smartly. 'Now, Mrs Summers, how can I help you?.'

Audrey Summers went on to give a history of gastric pain and dyspepsia after eating. Elizabeth asked her to undress then when she was lying on the couch conducted a thorough examination of her abdomen.

'What is your height, Mrs Summers?' she asked as she washed her hands.

'Five feet four,' replied the woman.

'And your weight?'

'Oh, I don't know, just over eleven stone, I think,' she said as she struggled to get off the couch.

'Let's just check, shall we? If you would just step on to the scales. Hm, yes, twelve stone, four, Mrs Summers. Now that, quite frankly, is far too much for your height.' Elizabeth walked back to the desk, 'I'll give you an antacid,' she said, as she wrote out a prescription for aluminium hydroxide, 'and I'll also give you a diet sheet that I would like you to follow.'

'I can't see that'll do much good,' said Audrey Summers indignantly. 'I don't eat enough to keep a fly alive as it is.'

'Well, you compare what is on that sheet to what

you eat and I'm sure you'll see a difference,' said Elizabeth firmly.

All the while she had been conducting the consultation she was aware that the patient was anxious to find out as much as she could about the situation at Dunster House, no doubt so that she could relate any choice titbits of gossip to her friends in the village. Elizabeth was equally determined she would find out nothing from her, but as the woman finished buttoning her coat and she handed her the prescription Mrs Summers had one final attempt.

'So are you in residence again at Dunster House, Mrs Brent?' she asked.

'It's Dr Brent, Mrs Summers,' replied Elizabeth firmly as she walked her to the door.

'Oh, of course, how silly of me. I always think of you as Mrs Brent. So does this mean we shall be seeing something of you again?'

'That depends, Mrs Summers,' Eliizabeth carefully parried the question. 'If the medicine works, I shouldn't think you'll have to come to the surgery again. If it doesn't, then yes, we will want to see you again in surgery and we'll arrange for you to have a barium meal test. Now be very careful what you eat over Christmas, won't you?'

With a sigh of relief she closed the door behind the woman and leaned against it for a moment. That was just the sort of thing she had been hoping to avoid.

A few moments later she opened the door and walked across to the waiting-room to see if she had any more patients. She found Mrs Summers and Hilary Young in close conversation.

'Do you have anyone else for me, Hilary?' Elizabeth asked quietly.

Hilary looked up sharply and had the grace to look shamefaced, for it was perfectly obvious they had been discussing her.

'No, Dr Brent,' she replied swiftly, in an attempt to cover up. 'That's all for this morning, thank you.'

Mrs Summers, however, seemed in no hurry to go. 'What's happened to the Christmas tree this year?' she asked looking round the waiting-room door into the hall beyond, where every year for as long as anyone could remember there had stood a beautifully decorated tree at the foot of the stairs.

'There just hasn't been time, what with Dr Jessop's accident and everything,' Hilary said. 'Actually the tree is outside in the conservatory, but Dr Brent couldn't remember where the decorations were. Apparently it was always his mother's task to decorate the tree.'

'I know where they are,' said Elizabeth impulsively. 'In fact,' she went on, 'I'll go and get them now. We can't have Christmas without a tree, can we?' She smiled sweetly at the two women, then swept past them and ran lightly up the stairs.

The Christmas decorations were in two large cardboard boxes in a tiny attic room at the top of the house. Elizabeth knew that that was where they were stored because she had helped Margaret Brent to put them away. And the reason she remembered the occasion so clearly was because it was the day her father-in-law had announced at dinner that because he was feeling so much better he'd decided not to take early retirement after all. After dinner she and Callum had had their last row, then she had walked out.

It was cold in the attic room and she shivered slightly as she looked round, at the trunks and suitcases, discarded items of furniture, a dress-maker's dummy, an old rocking-horse and all the other paraphernalia to be found in anyone's attic.

The cardboard boxes were stacked beneath the small sloping window, and a quick glance inside confirmed that they contained the decorations. Elizabeth dragged one outside on to the small landing and had gone back for the other when another box suddenly caught her eye. It was perched on the saddle of the rocking-horse and somehow it seemed familiar. Brushing aside the cobwebs that festooned the horse's ears, Elizabeth blew the dust from the box before carefully lifting the lid. At first glance it appeared to contain books but a closer look revealed a stack of photograph albums. One in particular she recognised immediately and with a smothered cry she began turning the dark pages each interfaced with thin gossamer leaves.

There had been many times she had wondered what had happened to her wedding photographs. There had also been times she'd wished she'd taken them with her, but she'd left in a hurry. With a growing feeling of hopelessness she slowly turned the pages.

Their faces, hers and Callum's, smiled up at her, both radiant and full of hope for the future. What had happened to all their hopes and dreams? How could they have just let them go? As she turned the pages a photograph fluttered to the floor. She picked it up, turned it over then as she stared at it, it felt as if a knife twisted in her heart. It had been taken of her and Callum in Paris on their honeymoon, the morning after their wedding night. They were standing on the balcony of their hotel bedroom; she was gazing up into his face and he was smiling down at her.

Her daydreams were suddenly interrupted by a sound behind her and turning sharply she found Callum standing in the doorway watching her.

They stared at each other for a moment without speaking then his gaze flickered to the album in her hands.

'So that's where it got to,' he said. 'I wondered where it was.'

A sudden spark of anger flared in her grey eyes and, before she could help herself, she said bitterly, 'Yes, Callum, that's where it got to, up here tucked away with all the rubbish. . .because that's obviously all it ever meant to you.'

CHAPTER FOUR

'AT LEAST I kept it.' Callum's retaliation was swift. 'You couldn't even be bothered to take it with you.'

'But you didn't know where it was, did you? You've just admitted that. It couldn't have meant that much to you.'

'Are you referring to the album or our marriage?' His voice had a dangerous edge to it. 'Because if it's our marriage you really should think again, Elizabeth. After all, it was you who walked out, not me.'

She caught her breath, then she straightened her shoulders and faced him unflinchingly across the rocking-horse. 'I walked out on a situation that had become intolerable,' she said, trying hard to keep her tone even but aware that her pent-up anger was seething beneath the surface.

'That is your opinion,' replied Callum tightly. 'I believe it could have been worked out.'

They glared at each other, the tension between them like some tangible force generated by the unexpected flaring of their tempers.

Elizabeth was shocked by the strength of her emotions and appalled that she had reacted so strongly to him. This was the last thing she had planned, a display of temper from them both that looked as if it could escalate into a full-scale row.

Still they eyed each other, like two adversaries drawn up for combat, then Callum's shoulders sagged slightly and he seemed to relax a little as he glanced at his watch.

'We have to talk,' he said grimly. 'I know that, but now is neither the time nor the place. I have several house calls to make.'

Elizabeth too felt the tension ebb out of her and she nodded. 'Is there anything else you would like me to do?'

He hesitated. 'How long do you intend staying?'

'How long do you need me to stay?' Her eyes met his and for a moment she saw some expression she couldn't read in their dark depths.

'If I'm honest I would like you to help out over Christmas,' he said. 'But Hilary didn't seem to think you'd be staying very long at all.'

'Oh, didn't she?' Elizabeth felt herself bristle. What right had the secretary to make assumptions like that? 'Well, I'll stay for the time being and help out. Would you like me to do Tim's house calls?'

'No, I can handle those, but there'll be another surgery after lunch. In the meantime do you think you could do something with that damn Christmas tree. . .? If I hear another person ask where it is this year. . .'

'Yes, all right, I've found the decorations.' Elizabeth pointed to the two cardboard boxes. 'Perhaps you could help me carry them down.'

With a last glance round the attic room she followed Callum down both flights of stairs to the hall where she saw he had already carried in the tree from the conservatory.

For the next hour Elizabeth amused herself with decorating the tree. She had always been artistic and this was the sort of task she enjoyed. When she had finished even Hilary Young admitted that it looked beautiful with its red bows, imitation snow and gold candles.

'Have you worked here long, Hilary?' asked Elizabeth as she cleared away the bits of tinsel and the pine needles that had fallen from the tree when Callum had carried it in to the hall.

'About six months,' replied the other woman. 'Dr Brent employed me when Dr Jessop joined him.'

'So you weren't here when his parents lived here.' Elizabeth stood back to survey the tree as she was speaking, then she added, 'His mother always dressed the tree, it was a sort of ritual, carried out on the Sunday before Christmas.'

'So I believe,' replied Hilary, her voice betraying no emotion. 'I haven't actually met Mrs Brent but I have heard. . .'

Elizabeth looked up sharply, wondering just what she had heard, gossip no doubt from Ivy or the village people.

'I have heard she could be difficult,' finished the secretary and for a brief moment her dark eyes met Elizabeth's and Elizabeth knew for certain that she had heard stories concerning herself and her mother-in-law.

'She is a very strong-minded lady,' said Elizabeth briskly, then, in an endeavour to change the subject, for she had no intention of discussing her private life with Hilary, she said, 'What time is afternoon surgery?'

There was an almost imperceptible pause before the secretary answered and Elizabeth sensed that

Hilary had thought she wouldn't be staying any longer.

'It's at two-thirty,' she replied. 'Will you be seeing Dr Jessop's patients again?'

Elizabeth nodded and, irritated by something in the other woman's manner, she found herself saying, 'Yes, and I'll be taking his surgeries tomorrow as well, so you can book appointments for them.' With that she walked briskly through to the kitchen, where she disposed of the rubbish she was carrying, then she leaned on the table for a moment and wondered just what the hell she had done.

She had now committed herself to staying at Dunster House until late on Christmas Eve. She would have to ring her sister and let her know what was happening. Already Janet must be wondering where she had got to, for although she hadn't given any definite time when she would arrive she had indicated that it would be well before Christmas.

She wasn't certain exactly why she had agreed to stay but she knew it had something to do with Hilary Young's attitude. She wasn't sure yet if there was any relationship betwen Callum and Hilary other than a professional one, but the secretary certainly seemed possessive of Callum and eager for Elizabeth to go.

Elizabeth sighed and looked out of the kitchen window at the herb garden that Margaret Brent had tended so meticulously. What was it about Dunster House, that there always seemed to be the influence of another woman at work?

She knew that if Callum was involved she really

didn't have cause to complain, for, as he had pointed out, she had been the one to leave. So why did she now feel so peculiar? What had prompted her to say she would stay? It surely couldn't be jealousy? How could she be jealous of Callum being with another woman when she had come to ask him for a divorce because she believed their marriage was over?

Resolutely she straightened her shoulders. Some-where along the line she had lost sight of the reason for her visit. A wonderful new future beckoned; a chance of a completely fresh start. Now was surely the time to be casting off the trappings of her old life and looking forward to better things.

Her life with Callum hadn't worked out, she'd had to accept that. Or at least she thought she'd accepted it, for when she'd left Dunster House she had been convinced that her marriage was over.

She'd felt hurt and betrayed that Callum had appeared to take his parents' side against her and had failed to recognise her needs. In an endeavour to put as much distance between herself and Dunster House as possible she had left for the States almost immediately after hearing of a temporary job in Boston from an old friend with whom she'd been at medical school. She'd thrown herself into work in the year she'd been away, working longer and longer hours, anything to ease the pain of missing Callum and anything to prevent her from thinking too much.

She hadn't been naïve enough to imagine that it would be easy coming back, especially to discuss divorce, but on the other hand she hadn't visualised its being quite so difficult either. She hadn't allowed for the overwhelming emotions that had assailed her almost from the moment she'd set foot in Dunster House.

Nothing had been quite as she had thought it would be. For a start she had braced herself to cope with Margaret Brent again, and it had come as a shock to find that her parents-in-law had actually moved away.

Secondly had come the unforeseen situation created by Tim Jessop's accident, which had meant that Callum needed help, something she would have found it difficult to ignore in any circumstances, and lastly there had been her tangled, unpredictable feelings for Callum himself.

Whether these had been revived simply by nostalgia or whether the presence of Hilary Young had anything to do with them Elizabeth didn't know, but she decided that the best thing she could do was to get these feelings firmly under control.

She'd committed herself now to staying another night and the following day, but during that time she had to set her mind on sorting out the reason for her visit. Then, once again, she had to walk away, and this time it had to be final.

She felt better once she had clarified these points in her mind, and as there was no sign of Callum she made a sandwich for her lunch then prepared herself for another busy surgery.

Her first task of the afternoon, together with the community midwife, was to take an antenatal clinic. The midwife, a pleasant-faced woman in her forties, had been in the district for many years.

Together they examined and chatted with the mums-to-be, checking their blood-pressure, weighing them, testing their urine, checking foetal hearts and generally discussing any worries or problems they were experiencing with their pregnancies. Some of the women seemed pleased to talk to a lady doctor and gradually Elizabeth felt herself relax and enjoy the surgery. One woman in particular, Vanessa Lee, who was very near her time, seemed very anxious.

'I see this is your first baby,' said Elizabeth as she helped her down from the couch.

'Yes, I shall be an elderly mum at thirty-eight, won't I?'

'Don't worry, you'll be taken good care of.'

'We've waited a very long time for this baby and we've had lots of disappointments,' said Vanessa. 'I couldn't bear it if anything went wrong. The trouble was, I think we left it rather late before we got around to trying for a family. I'm a solicitor, you see,' she explained, 'and my husband's a barrister and our work always came first. When we did decide the time had come, Mother Nature wasn't as obliging as we thought she'd be.'

Callum made no comment when he saw that Elizabeth was still there after antenatal clinic, but she could tell by his manner that he was relieved and grateful for her help. She in turn was surprised and pleased when he asked her advice concerning one of his patients whom he had been treating with non-steroidal anti-inflammatory drugs for his osteoarthritis.

'He needs a different drug as he's suffering gastric

disturbances,' he explained as they took an afternoon cup of tea together in his consulting-room. 'I
wonder if you have any ideas as you've been working on rheumatology.'

'What has he been having?'

'All the usual ones. I took him off Piroxicam six
months ago and he's now on Diclofenac.'

'I see,' she said slowly, 'Let me think, there is
something new. I'm pretty certain it's just become
available over here. One of the big pharmaceutical
houses is manufacturing it. It's had excellent results
in the States. I'll check up on the name of it, Callum,
and let you know.'

General surgery followed the antenatal clinic and,
whereas before Elizabeth had been apprehensive
about being recognised, this time she positively
glowed when one elderly man remembered her.

The man had come to the surgery suffering from
depression. His wife had died last Christmas and he
had been finding it difficult coping as the anniversary
of her death approached. This much Elizabeth
gleaned from his records before he came into the
room and she prepared herself to cope with his
depression as she noted that Dr Jessop had been
treating him with Dothiepin. She had, however, not
allowed for his reaction when he saw her.

His face, lined and grey, brightened immediately.
'Why, Mrs Brent,' he said. 'How nice to see you
again.'

Elizabeth stood up and shook hands with him.
Although his face was vaguely familiar she couldn't
remember where she had seen him before. As they
talked, however, she subtly drew it out of him.

'My wife always said how kind you were to her,' he said, his hands trembling.

'She did?'

'Yes, all those visits you made to the hospice; she really looked forward to them, you know.'

So that was where she had met this man, and his wife, thought Elizabeth, on one of those endless visits to the local hospice. Maybe all that charity work with Margaret Brent had done some good after all.

They talked for a while longer then gradually Elizabeth got round to asking him about his plans for Christmas.

He hesitated, twisting his cap in his hands. 'Well, my son and his wife want me to go over to them. They farm over Cirencester way but... I don't think I'll go...'

'I think you should,' said Elizabeth quietly but firmly.

'Do you...?' He looked up quickly then shook his head. 'I don't know... I'd made up my mind this morning not to, but seeing you and talking about Millie...somehow I feel a bit better...'

'I think your son and his family would be very disappointed if you didn't go,' said Elizabeth, then, before he had a chance to reply, she said, 'Did you all spend your Christmases together before your wife died?'

'Oh, yes.' He suddenly brightened at the memory. 'More often than not they'd all come to us...the grandchildren, you know? My wife was a wonderful cook...'

'In that case you really must go to them.'

'Yes?'

'Yes, just stop and think for a moment. They must miss your wife as well; their mother, and the children's granny, and Christmas must be especially difficult. How do you think they'll feel if you're not there either? You must go, and while you're there talk about your wife if you want to, talk about other Christmases and the way things used to be.'

Her patient left the surgery a far happier man than when he had come in, and after he had gone Elizabeth sat reflecting for a moment, hoping the advice she had given him had been right. Somehow giving advice was so much easier than finding solutions to one's own problems.

But telling him to remember Christmases past had triggered off her own memories, and she found herself recalling the Christmas she and Callum had spent in their flat, soon after they were married.

So many of their friends had asked them to spend Christmas with them that in the end, spoilt for choice, they had told each set of friends they were going elsewhere and then had spent the entire holiday alone.

It had been bliss, that much she had no difficulty remembering. Presents and breakfast in bed on Christmas morning, a turkey lunch prepared and cooked by them both followed by a long walk on the heath, then the evening in front of the fire making love on the rug in the flickering light of the flames.

She felt a thrill shoot through her at the memory, for in spite of what had followed in the months to come that was a night she would remember for the rest of her life.

So lost had she become in her thoughts that she jumped as Callum suddenly opened the door.

She blinked and looked up at him, bewildered for a moment by the intensity of her thoughts while he, obviously sensing something of her mood, refrained from what he was going to say, came right into the room and shut the door behind him.

'Are you all right?' She was struck by his look of concern.

She nodded. 'Yes, why?'

'You looked. . .' he hesitated '. . .pensive.'

She sighed and toyed with a pen on the desk before her. 'Did I? Yes, I suppose I did. I've just seen a patient of Tim's who not only recognised me but told me that his late wife had often spoken of the times I visited her in the hospice.'

'There you are, you see, I was always telling you that the time you spent getting to know the locals wouldn't be wasted.' He smiled.

'Don't you believe it,' she replied darkly. 'The natives aren't all friendly by any means.'

He frowned. 'What do you mean?'

'I had Audrey Summers in this morning and I knew she just couldn't wait to get down to the village to tell her cronies that that nice Dr Brent's wayward wife was back at Dunster House.'

He laughed then said, 'Well, that's just about what you'd expect from Audrey, isn't it? But among the rest there were plenty who had grown to like and respect you, but you wouldn't believe me, would you?'

'It wasn't that I didn't believe you, Callum, it was that it all went on for too long. . .and it just wasn't enough. I couldn't bear the frustration, I was beginning to vegetate.'

'I asked you to be patient.'

'I know you did, Callum, and I consider I was patient, but when your father informed us that he'd decided not to take early retirement after all I'm afraid that was the last straw.'

He stared at her for a moment then he glanced at his watch. 'I was going to suggest that we carry a pager with us and go to the Feathers for a meal, but, seeing the nature of this conversation, might it be better if we were to dine privately?'

Elizabeth took a deep breath; the idea of the Feathers sounded attractive but she knew she couldn't put off serious discussion with Callum any longer. 'Very well, I'll find something for us both in the freezer,' she said briskly.

While she prepared lamp chops and vegetables Callum lit a fire in the small morning-room where they had dined the night before. Mercifully the phone had only rung twice since the evening surgery that Callum had taken while she had prepared dinner, and neither call had required a visit.

Elizabeth changed into one of the skirts and blouses she had brought to wear at her sister's, a full, patterned skirt in bright jewel colours and a black silk shirt, a perfect foil for the flame-coloured hair which framed her face.

They both kept to small talk for the main part of the meal as if each was wary of broaching the subject they had earlier postponed. Callum seemed especially interested in what work she had been doing in New York.

'Have you enjoyed travelling around and working in different places?' He glanced curiously at her.

She nodded. 'Yes, it's all been very good experience for. . .' She trailed off awkwardly. She'd been about to say very good experience for the job she was going to, but he didn't know about that yet.

Callum, however, must have picked up her reticence, for he raised his eyebrows quizzically. 'For what?' he asked quietly.

'I'm sorry?'

'You were saying you'd gained good experience, but you didn't say what for.' He paused significantly, then when she didn't answer, he said, 'Can it be that you thought it would be good experience for when you become a GP?'

She caught her breath sharply. Surely he didn't think she'd come back just to pick up where she'd left off?

'Callum, I —' she began desperately, then she stopped as he held up his hand.

'No, wait a moment, let's make ourselves comfortable. We'll move this table out of the way and I'll pour a brandy to go with our coffee.'

Helplessly she watched as he pulled the sofa in front of the fire, turned down the lights, handed her a glass of brandy then sat down beside her.

This wasn't what she'd planned at all, for while they'd been eating she had made up her mind that the moment had finally come when she would tell him the real reason for her visit.

But now, suddenly, the evening was beginning to feel suspiciously like another evening; that too had been at Christmas, and then, like now, they'd sat together sipping brandy in front of a log fire.

CHAPTER FIVE

THEY were silent for a long time, staring into the flames, each busy with their own thoughts, then Callum said quietly, 'Why did you leave, Elizabeth?'

She threw him a startled glance, but he was still concentrating on the fire with only his profile visible.

She swallowed. 'You know why I left, Callum. The situation here had become impossible. I married you because I loved you; I also wanted to be with you, but at the same time my career was very important to me. I had slogged long and hard to get where I was and when we came here you led me to believe that it wouldn't be long before your father retired and I would take my place as your partner in the practice. I was even prepared to wait for that to happen, but from the moment we arrived things started to go wrong.'

'Surely you're exaggerating?'

'No, Callum, I'm not.'

'Well, what things?'

'The interference from your mother for a start——'

'Ah, my mother, I wondered when you'd start blaming her——'

'And why shouldn't I?' Elizabeth set down her glass and stared at him angrily. 'Because, believe me, a lot of the blame rests with her.' When he remained silent she went on, 'From the start she

157

had very firm ideas about the role of a GP's wife and it didn't include being his professional equal, I can assure you. She believed my place was one pace behind you, Callum, bearing your children, answering your phone, arranging your social life and playing Lady Bountiful to your patients, just as she had spent her life doing for your father. When I made it plain that life wasn't for me, she did her utmost to change me, to mould me into what she thought I should be. I had no real role here, Callum, and I could see myself slipping into a life of babies and domesticity. I wasn't ready for that—I'd worked too hard to let it all just drift away. We never even had any privacy, damn it, Callum, but now I find you've had a flat converted for Tim Jessop. Why couldn't that have been done for us?'

'There was a reason for that. I thought that if the house was converted before my father retired they might have wanted to stay on here afterwards. I didn't want that and I didn't think you would.'

'Too right I wouldn't,' she replied bitterly.

'I still think we could have worked things out if you had stayed,' he replied with that hint of stubborness in his tone that she recognised only too well. 'I thought,' he went on and his tone had changed now, it was softer, with almost a touch of tenderness, 'that what you and I had was special. . .so special that we could weather any storms.'

When she didn't reply he leaned forward and lifted her hand from where it lay in her lap. At the touch of his fingers her heart leapt as if an electric current had passed through her. 'It was special, wasn't it?' he asked urgently, his voice slightly husky now.

For a moment she couldn't bring herself to meet those dark eyes then eventually she gave in and, with a sigh, she said, 'Yes, Callum it was special. I can't deny that.'

The shadow of a smile touched his lips at her words. 'I was devastated when you left,' he said softly, and somehow she found herself mesmerised by his mouth, which suddenly seemed very close.

'I would never have known,' she replied bitterly. 'You didn't come after me. . .'

'Ah. . .' he breathed. 'Were you expecting me to?'

'Not necessarily.' She shrugged. 'Callum, I. . .there's something you ought to know. . .' The rest of her sentence was stifled as his lips covered hers.

Momentarily she felt intoxicated by his power, the gentle exploration of his kiss, then, returning briefly to her senses, she lifted her free hand and ineffectually tried to push him away but there was something about the familiarity created by his near-ness that stopped her. The touch of his hands, the smell of him, the feel of his skin and the taste of his lips and tongue evoked such memories, rekindling such desires, that within moments she was helpless with longing.

Even while he held her imprisoned in the circle of his arms he unbuttoned her blouse. Slipping the silky material from her shoulders, which glowed golden in the light from the fire, he dropped light butterfly kisses along the line of her throat, then, entwining his hands in the wild mass of her red-gold hair, he lowered his mouth to her breast, gently teasing with his lips and tongue until every nerve in her body pulsated with desire.

Swiftly and expertly he undressed first her, then himself, then gently drew her down beside him on to the rug.

'I have the strangest feeling, my love,' he murmured against her ear, 'that we've lived this moment before, but in a different place, during another Christmas and before a different fire. . .'

'Callum. . . I. . .' But any protest she might have been about to make was lost as he lowered himself on to her and took her in an instant of piercing sweetness. Only for the briefest of moments did she resist, then she gave herself up to the inevitability of their reconciliation. Her body quickly found and matched the familiar rhythm of his and they moved together in perfect accord, reaching almost simultaneous fulfilment as they had done so many times in the past.

Later, as she lay drowsy and contented in his arms in the aftermath of their love, she refused to allow her thoughts to wander beyond the magic circle they had created around themselves, refused to allow herself to consider the implications of what had just happened or to question her own motives or response.

Even when much later he thwarted her half-hearted attempts to get dressed and again reached out for her, she did little to resist him, her arousal matching his as he caressed her again to fever-pitch, their passion exploding once more in mutual abandon.

And, afterwards, she watched dreamily as he reached out and threw another log on to the fire. The wood crackled and the flames flared, bringing a glow to his naked body and as the muscles rippled across his shoulders and down his back she shivered slightly, for the first time wondering just what she had done.

Their lovemaking had been every bit as wonderful as it had in the past, a fact which did little to help as she attempted to bring some sense of order to her chaotic thoughts. How could she have allowed this to happen just when she had mentally prepared herself to bring their marriage to an end? As her tangled thoughts chased each other, the telephone on the bureau behind them suddenly rang. Callum sighed and reached over the back of the sofa to answer it.

She watched him as he gave the surgery number; his hard muscular body, the proud set of his head, the short dark hair and the strong line of his aquiline nose and firm jaw, and momentarily her determination wavered. Was she mad ending her marriage to this man who had just made love to her with such tenderness? On the other hand she knew the proud almost arrogant streak that lay below the surface and this, together with a stubbornness they both shared, caused her to question whether they could ever make a go of things.

She was jerked from her daydreaming as she suddenly heard him say, 'Yes, she's here.' She glanced up as he handed her the receiver. 'It's your sister.'

'Oh!' Guiltily she took the phone from him. 'Hello, Janet? I'm sorry, I've been meaning to ring you.'

'Elizabeth?' Her sister's voice sounded shrill and she winced. 'Are you all right?'

'Yes, yes, I'm fine——'

'We've been expecting you. We thought you'd had an accident; Walter says the roads are icy tonight. Why are you still at Ashwood?' she went on in the same shrill, accusing tone. 'You said you weren't going to stay there very long.'

'Yes, Janet, I know, that's what I said, but circumstances have changed rather...'

'What do you mean, they've changed?'

'Well, Callum's partner has had an accident——'

'What's that got to do with you?'

'I've been helping him with his surgeries.'

'You've been what?'

'I had to Janet.'

'What for, for God's sake?' Her sister sounded exasperated, and Elizabeth swallowed before answering.

'You don't understand; it's virtually impossible to get a locum at Christmas.'

'Even so...but surely you've finished surgery now, it's past nine o'clock.'

'Well, yes, actually...' Elizabeth threw a glance in Callum's direction then, seeing the amused expression on his face as he sprawled on the sofa, she flushed then turned her head away.

'So when can we expect you? Elizabeth...' The

tone of her sister's voice suddenly changed. 'I hope you're not staying there tonight.'

'Well, actually, I——' mumbled Elizabeth, desperately wishing her sister would hang up as she wasn't sure just how much Callum could hear. She got no further, however, for Janet interrupted sharply.

'I hope you haven't forgotten the reason why you're there.'

'Of course I haven't,' replied Elizabeth quickly, conscious out of the corner of her eye that Callum had stood up and was getting dressed.

'Well I sincerely hope you haven't. Callum Brent has caused quite enough havoc in your life. This is your opportunity to sort things out once and for all, so just make sure you don't blow it. From what you've told me you have the chance of a fantastic job in the States. As I was saying to Walter, there can't be many people who have a second chance like that in their lives.'

'No, Janet.'

'So have you told him yet?'

'Er—no, not exactly.'

'So when are you going to tell him?'

'I think that's my business, Janet.' Elizabeth began to feel her anger rising. Her sister usually had that effect on her.

'What? Yes, well, I suppose it is, but I know how soft you can be, especially where Callum Brent is concerned. You were besotted with him from the moment you set eyes on him.'

'Was I?'

'You know damn well you were. No one could

get any sense out of you. Now what time can we expect you?'

'Well, actually, Janet, I've said I'll take a couple of surgeries tomorrow. . .'

'Oh, for heaven's sake. I suppose next you'll tell me you intend spending Christmas there?'

Elizabeth felt her hackles rise even further at her sister's tone. 'Now that you mention it, I may just have to. It's a very large practice area, too much for one doctor to cope with,' she retorted.

'You're making a rod for your own back, Elizabeth,' said Janet sharply. 'You'll live to regret it, just you see if I'm not right. And you needn't think you can come running to me when it all goes wrong again.'

With that she hung up, leaving Elizabeth staring indignantly at the receiver. 'For God's sake,' she said angrily, 'I'm only doing a few surgeries for you, after all.'

'Is that so?' asked Callum quietly. He was struggling into his trousers as he spoke and he looked down at her as she half sat and half lay on the sofa.

She glanced down at herself, then she flushed and grabbed her blouse just as the phone rang again. Thinking it was Janet ringing back, she grabbed the receiver. 'Hello?' she snapped.

There was a silence on the other end of the line then a voice said, 'Is that Ashwood 236543?'

'It is.'

'Who is that?'

'Elizabeth Brent,' she said crisply, vaguely aware that the voice seemed familiar.

Another silence followed, then the voice said sharply, 'Is Callum there?'

Slowly Elizabeth lowered the receiver then, staring at Callum, she wordlessly handed it to him.

He raised his eyebrows.

'It's your mother,' she said. Then, standing up, with as much dignity as she could she gathered up her clothes and left the room.

As she hurried to the bedroom she had difficulty in repressing a chuckle, for it must have come as a shock to Margaret Brent to hear her voice. Elizabeth was only too aware that when she had left Callum, in his mother's eyes, she had committed the ultimate sin and at that moment her mother-in-law must be wondering just what she was doing back at Dunster House.

And a little later as she lay back and soaked in a hot scented bath Elizabeth found herself wondering exactly that. Making love with her estranged husband certainly hadn't been on her agenda when she'd left the States to sort out the details of her divorce. The trouble was, the word 'divorce' hadn't once been mentioned between herself and Callum during the entire time she'd been at Ashwood. And where once she had imagined that his pride would have been so injured by her leaving him that he too would want a divorce, now she wasn't so sure.

She sighed and absentmindedly began soaping her legs. She had been so sure before she'd arrived, but almost from the moment she'd stepped over the threshold doubts had crept in. Her feelings towards Callum had been tangled and confused but at the same time she was surprised at the strength of her emotions. Now their lovemaking seemed to have destroyed her final defences. She would be the first to admit that sex had always been good between them; adventurous and passionate, it had been a fusion of minds as well as bodies. Callum had taught her how to relax, how to let go and relinquish her inhibitions. She'd almost forgotten that, but he'd reminded her of it as they'd lain on the rug in front of the fire and he'd taken her to forgotten heights of ecstasy. She felt her cheeks grow hot at the memory. How could she have appeared so eager, wanton almost in her abandonment? Then a voice inside told her it was because she'd missed him so much and had been longing for his touch.

But what was to happen next? she asked herself in desperation. Her sister had accused her of being besotted with Callum; well, maybe she had been, maybe she still was, but what did it have to do with Janet anyway?

Her sister had always been envious of her, Elizabeth knew that much; she'd been jealous when Elizabeth had gone to medical school while she had failed her law examinations and got married instead. Elizabeth had always suspected that her sister's marriage was not particularly happy. Walter was a dull, pompous man and when Elizabeth had first met Callum she had again suspected her sister's envy. Callum, however, had seen through Janet right from the star; she in turn recognised the fact, and had been hostile towards him ever since he and Elizabeth had married.

When Elizabeth had left Callum, Janet had had difficulty in restraining her 'told you so' attitude, and from the recent telephone conversation Elizabeth concluded that her sister was none too pleased with the latest turn of events. Still, it was her life and nothing to do with her sister. . .or with her mother-in-law come to that—but she couldn't help wondering what Margaret Brent had said to Callum.

As her thoughts turned to Callum again she found herself wondering how he felt about what had happened. Apart from the fact that she knew he'd wanted and desired her sexually, he'd given little away about his actual feelings.

She shifted uneasily in the bath. The water had grown cool and impulsively she sat up, and turning on the hot tap topped up the water level.

She herself hadn't become involved with anyone else in the time she had been away, but Callum was a red-blooded male with an undeniable charm and a high sex drive, and somehow she couldn't imagine him going for very long without female company. Slowly she ran her hands down her body, over her firm high breasts, the curve of her waist and across her flat tummy. Callum had said her figure was as lovely as ever; had he really meant that?

She was still chasing unanswered questions in her head when there suddenly came a light knock on the bathroom door.

She froze.

'Elizabeth?'

'Yes?' she called.

The door opened and Callum came into the room. Suddenly, ridiculously, she felt embarrassed, and slid down as far as she could into the bubbly water. She was only too conscious however that the tips of

her breasts were clearly visible through the bubbles.
Callum, however, seemed quite matter-of-fact, as if
catching her in the bath was an every day event. He
perched on the side of the bath and looked down at
her.

'I have to go out,' he said. 'But don't worry, I'll
take the pager with me.'

'Very well, I was just going to get out anyway,'
she paused. 'Callum, what did your mother say?'

He pulled a face. 'She was surprised to hear your
voice, to say the least.'

'I'll bet she was.' She hesitated, then, when he
didn't say any more, haltingly, she asked. 'Will they
be coming to you for Christmas?'

He grinned, then he shook his head. 'No they're
going to her sister's.'

'I couldn't believe it when Ivy said they didn't live
here any more. I never thought they'd want to leave
Dunster House.'

'Mother didn't,' he replied abruptly. 'That was
my father's doing.' He stood up then and, picking
up a large fluffy bath towel, he held it open for her.
After only a moment's hesitation she stood up and,
only too conscious of his eyes on her as the water
streamed from her body, she stepped from the bath.

'I'd forgotten just how beautiful you are,' he said
softly as she turned and he wrapped the towel
around her. He didn't release her immediately,
holding her against him until she became aware of
the hardening response from his own body to her
nearness.

'Did she want to know why I'm here?' she murmured, leaning against him.

'Of course she did.' He lowered his head and kissed the nape of her neck and although it was less than an hour since they had made love she felt the familiar throb of desire deep inside.

'And what did you tell her?' she whispered, holding her breath as she awaited his reply.

'What could I tell her?' Briefly he tightened his hold then abruptly he released her. 'I don't yet know the answer to that myself.' He'd left her then as if he was finding difficulty in controlling himself.

Slowly, thoughtfully, she dried herself then slipped on her bathrobe. Could it be that Callum wanted her to go back to him? Was he waiting for her to say that was why she had returned, to seek a reconciliation? Or was she merely deluding herself? Was it all too late and had their passionate reunion simply been an impulsive recreating of the past? She left the bathroom and was just crossing the landing when she heard the sound of voices in the hall below followed by the closing of a door. The landing was in darkness, for she hadn't bothered to switch on the light, but the hallway below was brightly lit. She peered over the banisters and for a moment all she could see was the tree she had decorated earlier in the day. Then she heard Callum's voice and the lighter tones of a woman just before the front door closed behind them.

Swiftly she ran through to the bedroom and from the darkened window she could look down to the forecourt. Callum's car was visible directly below and even as she watched he appeared, followed by the unmistakable figure of Hilary Young. He opened the passenger door for her and she looked up at him before she stepped into the car. As he closed the door he glanced up at the window and Elizabeth shrank back into the shadows so that he wouldn't see her. Then he slid into the driver's seat and with a slight scrunching noise on the gravel the car pulled out on to the main road.

With a sinking feeling Elizabeth turned away from the window.

CHAPTER SIX

How could she have been so foolish to have imagined that things could have stood still in Callum's life during the time she had been away? And how could she have been so naïve to think, even for a moment, that he might want her back? Callum still had his pride. With her eyes blinded by sudden angry tears and with a pain deep inside which she now could no longer deny as being jealousy, Elizabeth listened as the sound of his car receded into the distance. He'd said he was going out, but he hadn't said where. He'd already eaten, so he couldn't be taking Hilary for a meal at the Feathers. Ashwood offered little else in the way of late night entertainment, and, as Callum was on call and couldn't go out of the district, Elizabeth finally concluded that he was going to his secretary's home.

She'd had her suspicions regarding a relationship between the two of them from the moment Hilary Young had learnt she was his wife. There had been something in her manner to suggest that she resented Elizabeth and didn't want her to stay.

Slowly Elizabeth slipped off her bathrobe and drew her nightdress over her head, and still the speculations went round in her head. If Callum really was involved with Hilary, why had he made love to her, Elizabeth? Had it indeed been a purely impulsive act and one which he was now bitterly regretting? He must have known he was going out with Hilary and yet still he had encouraged a return of the old intimacy between them. How could he have done so?

Suddenly she was angry. No doubt he would return very late from some little love-nest and expect to come up to the bedroom and spend what was left of the rest of the night with her. Well, if that was the case, he could think again.

Wildly she looked around, knowing there was no key to the door, then, grabbing a chair, she yanked it across the room and wedged the back firmly under the doorknob.

'That will fix you, Callum Casanova Brent,' she said aloud as she marched to the large double bed they had once shared and for the second night running she climbed between the sheets.

Later, however, when she had cooled down, she shed bitter tears of hopelessness into the pillow; tears for a dream, hardly formed, that had just been cruelly shattered.

For hours she tossed and turned but she didn't hear him come home for finally, exhausted, she must have slept, and when she awoke pale sunlight flooded the room and the chair was still in position beneath the door-handle. With a groan she turned over, then she remembered it was Christmas Eve.

He didn't appear for breakfast and she was glad because she didn't particularly want a repeat of the previous morning's cosy domestic scene. She had agreed to help him that day and she wouldn't go back on her word, but she now fully intended to get away as soon as she possibly could.

When she went through to the surgery not only was there no sign of Callum but Hilary hadn't put in an appearance either.

No doubt it had been a very late night, thought Elizabeth grimly as she picked up the large bundle of morning post and unlocked the front door.

The first patients had already begun to arrive for morning surgery before Callum came through from the flat. She noticed he looked tired, then she quickly stifled a pang of sympathy as she recalled why he probably was tired.

If he noticed the coolness of her manner he didn't comment, neither did he attempt any form of intimacy in front of the patients. She was just about to go into Tim's consulting-room when he called to her.

'Oh, Elizabeth, would you come with me later for the traditional Christmas Eve visit to the hospice?'

She hesitated fractionally, then nodded, thinking it would appear mean if she were to refuse such a simple request.

'Oh, and there's one other thing; you'll have to collect your own patient records this morning. Hilary won't be in. I'll explain why later,' he added with a glance at the waiting patients.

Huh! thought Elizabeth angrily as she began to collect the records she required from the files—the woman obviously has no stamina.

The surgery was frantic, setting the pace for the remainder of the day, and by the end of the morning they had seen more than double the usual number of patients. Most were last-minute panic situations;

temporary residents who had come away for Christmas without their medication or locals who had suddenly developed some condition that required immediate treatment.

In between were a series of house calls and in the end even Elizabeth did her share of these to ease the load on Callum. Throughout it all, however, she was aware of a leaden feeling; a feeling of acute disappointment. Surely now there were no complications, she could finally approach Callum, tell him the reason for her visit, leave Ashwood once and for all and get on with the rest of her life?

So if that was that easy, she asked herself, why did her sense of misery increase as the day went on?

It was late afternoon before they finally loaded themselves with parcels and set off for the local hospice. Somehow Elizabeth had managed to maintain her aloof air towards Callum. He must have noticed her coolness after their closeness of the day before, but still he made no comment.

The door of the hospice was decorated with a holly wreath and a brightly lit Christmas tree stood in the porch. Some of the more mobile patients were in the lounge with Sister Martin, who was in charge of the hospice. Hot mince pies and spiced punch was being served while a visitor was playing a selection of Christmas carols on the piano. Sister Martin hurried forward to greet them, her face lighting up as she recognised Elizabeth.

'Why, Mrs Brent, how lovely to have you home again,' she said, as if Elizabeth had only been away for a couple of weeks instead of a year. 'We've all missed your visits and when we heard you were taking Dr Jessop's place we hoped you'd come in to see us.' She turned to Callum. 'Hello, Dr Brent, they've all been looking forward to seeing you.'

He smiled and handed her the large bag of presents. 'Perhaps you'd like to put these under the tree for tomorrow,' he said quietly.

'Of course, and thank you.' Sister Martin's face softened. 'You're so kind to them. By the way, Doctor, how is Hilary?'

Elizabeth stiffened and threw Callum a quick glance, but his expression remained impassive.

'She'll be all right,' he replied briefly. 'I'll go and see her later.'

'Will you stay and have a glass of punch with us?' Sister Martin beamed at them both.

'Of course,' Callum nodded. 'And one of your delicious mince pies, please, Sister. I don't know what you put in them, but I've come to the conclusion that Christmas just wouldn't be the same without them.' He laughed and moved into the room to chat to the patients, who, Elizabeth noticed, all seemed to be gazing up at him with adoration.

She wondered grimly what they would think if they knew what he had been up to. Then she tried to dismiss the thought along with the fact that he'd just openly said that he would be going to see Hilary later. Instead she tried to concentrate on chatting to the patients.

Later they moved to the wards where the very sick cancer patients were, and they stopped to have a word with each one. Some had been undergoing courses of radiation and chemotherapy, some had lost their hair and others were battling with the effects of nausea and exhaustion. Again Elizabeth was struck by the esteem in which Callum seemed to be held, but it bothered her intensely when he insisted on introducing her to them as his wife, for all the world as if she would be staying with him.

It was dusk by the time they left the hospice and there was a decided chill in the air as they walked the short distance through the village to Dunster House for the evening surgery.

'It feels as if there's going to be a frost,' commented Callum, as he paused on the doorstep and looked up into the clear sky. 'The next best thing to snow, I suppose.' He grinned suddenly. 'Remember how you always longed for white Christmases? Do you still do that?'

She shook her head. 'Not any more; I guess I've grown up since then.' She walked slowly into Tim's consulting-room and without taking off her coat she sat down behind the desk. She had already decided she would speak to Callum after surgery and leave immediately after that. She just hoped she'd be able to get a train to Bristol that night. There was now no way she wanted to be trapped at Ashwood over the Christmas holiday.

She was so lost in her thoughts that she hardly noticed the door open, then with a start she looked up and found Hilary Young standing in the doorway. For a moment she simply stared at her, wondering what she was doing there when Callum had said she wouldn't be in that day, then gradually she became aware of the other woman's appearance. She looked drawn and tired with dark circles beneath her eyes. Her usually carefully-made-up features were now devoid of make-up and her dark hair was pulled back off her face.

Elizabeth half rose to her feet then sank back into her chair again, uncertain what to say.

'Hello.' Hilary hovered uncertainly. 'Callum told me not to come in today, but I thought you might be busy this evening.'

'Are you ill?' asked Elizabeth.

Hilary stared at her for a moment without replying, then slowly she said. 'You don't know, do you? I thought Callum might have told you.'

Elizabeth frowned and shook her head, a sinking feeling in her stomach as she braced herself for what she might be about to hear.

'My mother died last night.' Hilary's lip trembled. 'She had cancer, she was in the hospice. Callum took me there and stayed with me to the end. My husband had to stay at home. We have a little girl, you see—he was looking after her.'

Elizabeth stared at her, hardly able to believe what she was hearing.

Slowly she rose to her feet. 'Oh, Hilary,' she said at last. 'I'm so sorry. I had no idea. Here, come and sit down for a moment.' She indicated the chair in front of the desk and the other woman sat on the edge of it. 'You really didn't need to come in though, we can manage.'

'He's been wonderful, you know, Mrs Brent,' she said, twisting a silk scarf in her hands as she spoke, 'Dr Brent, I mean. He's been so kind to me and my family since my mother was diagnosed. It was breast cancer. She had a mastectomy followed by chemotherapy, we thought everything was all right but she developed secondaries. . .' Tears filled her eyes as she spoke. 'I really don't know how I would have got through it all if it hadn't been for your husband. . .'

Elizabeth swallowed and lowered her eyes. Oh, how she had misjudged this woman.

'I don't want to speak out of turn, Mrs Brent, but there's something I want to ask you,' said Hilary nervously.

'Yes?' said Elizabeth, then had to clear her throat and repeat the question when her voice came out as barely more than a whisper.

'I was wondering if you'd intended staying?'

'You mean over Christmas?'

'Well, yes, but I was thinking on a more permanent basis.' She looked anxious for a moment, as if she was afraid she'd said too much.

'Why do you ask?' said Elizabeth quietly.

'I'm sorry, I know it isn't any of my business, but since all this trouble with my mother, my family and I have got to know Dr Brent quite well. . .' She hesitated.

'Go on,' said Elizabeth.

'Well, I couldn't bear to see him hurt again. There, I've said it now. . .'

'What makes you think he was hurt before?'

'Oh, I know he was. Ivy told me he was absolutely devastated when you left. He lost a lot of weight and everyone was really worried about him. At first when you arrived I thought there was going to be more trouble.'

'So that's why you weren't too happy when you found out who I was,' said Elizabeth wryly.

'Did it show?' Hilary looked faintly alarmed, then gave a shy smile. 'You turned out to be nothing like the person I'd assumed you were and...and since you've been here he seems so happy; honestly, Mrs Brent, I've never seen him so happy.'

Elizabeth was suddenly aware that her heart had begun to beat very fast. She picked up a paper-knife from the desk and began toying with it. 'Don't you think it might cause a lot of complications if I were to stay?' she asked.

Hilary frowned. 'I don't understand.'

'Well, what about Dr Jessop?'

'From what Dr Brent has told me, Dr Jessop will be out of action for a very long time, and it was his intention to go abroad to work anyway. No, Mrs Brent, I can't see that would cause any problems but, even if it did, that isn't what's important. It's you and the doctor that count, and, as I just said, I've never seen him so happy as he's been the last two days.'

Before Elizabeth had the chance to answer there came a tap on the door and Callum looked into the room. He looked surprised to see Hilary and, pushing open the door, he came right into the room.

'Why, Hilary, what are you doing here?' The concern on his face was only too obvious and Elizabeth found herself thinking that, if she had misjudged Hilary, how much more had she misjudged her husband?

'Hilary came to see if we needed any help,' she

said, then added quickly, 'I told her we could manage.'

'Of course we can; you get on home, Hilary—you need to be with your family tonight.'

Hilary smiled bleakly. 'Thank you, we are trying to keep things as normal as possible for Melanie. After all, to a child Christmas is still Christmas, isn't it?' She stood up and walked to the door, then paused and looked back at Elizabeth. 'Will I be seeing you after the holiday, Mrs Brent?' she asked. The question seemed innocent enough, but Elizabeth was aware that Callum had stiffened as he waited for her reply.

She took a deep breath. 'Yes, Hilary,' she said softly. 'I shall be here.'

Callum took her to the front door, then returned and stood looking at Elizabeth with an indefinable expression on his handsome features.

'I meant to tell you about Hilary,' he said simply, 'but we've been so busy that I never got around to it.'

Their eyes met then and Elizabeth smiled.

'Let's get this surgery over, then I think perhaps we could chance a meal at the Feathers, don't you?' he said.

'Why not? We'll take the pager with us and if there are any calls we'll go together.'

He turned then and stepped out into the hall but before he closed the door he glanced back at her. 'Don't you think you ought to phone your sister?' he asked innocently, and when she pulled a face at him by way of reply he laughed and closed the door.

There were several locals dining in the hotel

restaurant when Callum and Elizabeth arrived at the Feathers, and one or two acknowledged them with nods and smiles.

The manager showed them to an alcove table and Elizabeth was content to let Callum order for them both. A quiet sense of contentment had crept over her and she was taken unawares when Callum, on finishing his meal, set down his knife and fork and looked steadily at her across the table.

'Did you mean what you said to Hilary about staying?' he asked softly.

'Do you want me to stay, Callum?'

'Of course I do. I never wanted you to go in the first place, and I blame myself that you did.'

She stared at him. 'What do you mean?'

'I should have clarified the position here at Ashwood before I asked you to marry me, then when you were so obviously unhappy I should have done something about it. I was totally insensitive to your needs and I left it too late before making my parents aware of what was happening.'

'Callum, what exactly happened after I left?'

He was silent for a moment, then, obviously choosing his words with care, he said, 'Would you believe an almighty showdown?'

Her eyes widened in amazement.

'Honestly, Elizabeth, I don't think any of us had actually realised the pitch you had reached.'

She remained silent, lowering her gaze.

'In fairness to my parents, they are of the old school,' he went on, 'and they simply didn't understand how important your career is to you. Deep down my father really was ready to retire—he'd had enough of general practice — but my mother was quite happy here, so to please her he pretended he wanted to carry on. In my own defence, I would say that I hesitated in demanding too much too soon for fear of it seeming as if I was pushing them out. I am very fond of them and they've done a lot for me. When they knew you had gone my father was horrified and he immediately made plans to retire. My mother still wasn't keen to go but he put his foot down and I think for the first time in his life he stood up to her. He thought that if they actually went you would come back and go into partnership with me. Since then even my mother has had battles with her conscience; every time she phones she asks if I've heard from you. The problem was, I couldn't find you.'

She looked up sharply. 'You mean you tried?'

'Of course I tried. But you seemed to have vanished off the face of the earth. Finally I contacted the medical council but all they could tell me was that you were abroad. In desperation I even rang your sister. . .'

'And what did she say?'

'That you were travelling around and that she didn't have an address for you. . .was that true?'

'Not entirely. . .'

'I thought not. . .but then I never was Janet's favourite person, was I?'

'Oh, Callum.' She stared helplessly at him. 'I should have trusted you. . .'

'Elizabeth, just answer me one thing; could you love me again?'

'I don't believe I ever stopped loving you, but I

didn't think you'd want me back. . .when I arrived I was going to——'

Leaning across the table, he took her hand and gripped it hard. 'I don't want to know, Elizabeth. Hell, why do you think I've spent this last couple of days using every trick in the book just to keep you here? I was terrified you were going to disappear again.' He gave her his old heart-stopping smile, the one that melted her bones. 'Now it's enough that we've found each other again. . .' He broke off as his pager suddenly sounded.

He sighed and stood up, then, looking down at her, he said, 'You know something, Mrs Brent? This could be the story of our lives from now on.'

She waited patiently in the holly-decked foyer while he used the hotel telephone and when he returned he pulled a face.

'I'm afraid I have a call to make,' he said as he took her arm and they stepped out into the crisp frosty night.

'Correction,' she murmured softly as she snuggled against him on the way to the car, 'we have a call. I said if you were called out I'd come with you.'

He smiled. 'I think it's a call you might enjoy. Vanessa Lee, the lady you saw in antenatal, has gone into labour. She's in the maternity ward at the private hospital. I told her I'd deliver her baby.'

'Are there likely to be complications?'

'I shouldn't think so, but they've waited so long for this baby and I don't want to take any chances.'

They found Vanessa well into the second stage of her labour; her husband was with her and she seemed happy and relaxed in the capable care of the midwife. She was pleased to see Elizabeth again, and between contractions which were barely three minutes apart and very strong they spoke briefly, while Elizabeth rubbed her back and helped administer gas and air.

The labour progressed without incident then the midwife announced that the cervix was ten centimetres dilated.

'Not long now,' said Elizabeth, gripping Vanessa's hand as the strong bearing-down pains began.

Callum prepared himself for the delivery, pulling on latex gloves and donning gown and mask while joking and placing bets on the sex of the baby with Vanessa's husband, Adam.

'We've waited so long,' gasped Vanessa to Elizabeth between bouts of pushing. 'I can't believe it's nearly over.'

Everyone's waiting was finally rewarded as the baby's head, crowned with a thatch of thick dark hair, was born and with a lump in her throat Elizabeth watched as her husband gently guided the tiny body into the world.

'There's nothing wrong with his lungs,' said Callum as he cut the umbilical cord and presented Vanessa with her baby for immediate bonding.

Briefly Elizabeth found herself part of the couple's joy, the laughter and the tears as they delighted in their son, and when she looked up her eyes met Callum's mistily above his mask. She knew what he was thinking and she found herself realising that perhaps a career and a family were not so incompatible as she had always thought.

Later as they left the hospital, Callum suddenly

stopped and took her arm. 'Listen,' he said, lifting his head and looking up into the wide starlit sky. 'The church bells are ringing, it must be after midnight. Happy Christmas, darling.'

Hand in hand they strolled back to the car, then Elizabeth said softly. 'Do you have any plans for today?'

He smiled. 'Well, I've been invited to several different places for dinner. . .'

'And. . .?' she asked questioningly when he paused.

'I've refused them all; I thought we could spend Christmas Day in front of the fire, the two of us. . .just as we did once before. What do you think?'

'I can't think of anything I'd like better,' she said softly, as she lifted her face for her husband's kiss.

A MIRACLE OR TWO

Marion Lennox

CHAPTER ONE

THE history of Mrs Rolands' headaches had been interrupted three times already when the phone rang. Dr Reiss sighed, but with an apologetic smile to Mrs Rolands she answered it. Becky, her receptionist, would have blocked the call unless it was urgent.

'Jana?' There was no mistaking the gruff voice of the local fire chief. 'I'm in your office,' he told her. 'Can you spare a minute?'

Jana glanced at her watch. Already she was an hour and a half behind, but if the fire chief wanted to see her she knew there would be a good reason. For the last five days fires had been burning out of control in the mountains behind Carrabookna, and the situation was worsening.

'I'll be there in two minutes,' she told him. With a brief explanation to Mrs Rolands she rose to leave.

The waiting-room was crowded. Every chair was full and there were children sitting on the floor by the Christmas tree in the corner of the room. As Jana emerged, all eyes turned to her and Jana sighed again. Their waiting time was going to be extended even further. She apologised briefly, explaining the likely delay. As she spoke, a tall man in rough bush gear stood up and came towards her.

'Are you the doctor in charge here?'

He sounded unsure. This diminutive, white-coated girl with her clear green eyes and flawless complexion was obviously not what he had expected.

The man's accent was decidedly English. His face was sporting a few days' growth of blond beard and his rugged, unkempt appearance told Jana as much as the backpack propped nearby. Backpackers were common in the national park around Carrabookna.

'I am,' Jana agreed. She looked up to meet his eyes and was caught momentarily by the intensity of their colour. The deep blue eyes set in the lean, tanned face were watching her with unashamed interest, touched with a trace of humour.

To her annoyance Jana felt herself flushing. His gaze told her that he found her attractive. She caught herself. The thought was nonsense. With her black hair caught back into a severe knot, her sensible clothes and her dark-framed glasses, Jana declared to the world that she had no time for romantic 'nonsense', as she termed it. Barry approved of her attitude and she was content to have it so.

'I'd like to speak to you, if it's convenient,' the man continued. Jana wasn't imagining it; the trace of humour was still evident in his soft-spoken words. His eyes held hers.

With an effort Jana broke her gaze and gestured to the rest of the room. 'As you can see, it's excessively inconvenient, Mr...' She broke off.

'Carisbrook,' he supplied helpfully. 'And it's——'

'Mr Carisbrook, is your problem urgent?' Jana interrupted.

'Well. . .' A smile was lurking behind the blue of his eyes. 'You might say it needs your attention.'

Jana gestured towards the seated patients. 'Some of these people have been waiting for an hour and a half already,' she said sharply. 'Is your need more urgent than theirs?'

By this time every eye in the waiting-room was on the backpacker. He looked around, his slow smile intensifying, and held up a hand in defeat.

'No,' he conceded.

'Then I suggest you wait your turn like everyone else,' Jana said with finality. 'If you'll take your seat again, I'll be with you as soon as possible.'

He sat.

The gaze of the big man followed Jana as she left the room, and her colour remained heightened as she made her way through the hospital corridor. She frowned to herself. The man had unsettled her for some reason. 'Arrogant tourist,' she thought angrily, pushing the memory of piercing blue eyes to the back of her mind. She had enough to cope with without his imperious demands.

The fire chief, for instance. She pushed an errant tendril of hair back from her forehead in a gesture of fatigue and increased her pace.

Ten minutes later Jana was looking with dismay at a mass of red dots on the Fire Authority map, all other thoughts driven from her mind. The scale of the fire was massive.

She dragged her gaze from the map and turned her attention to the haggard face of the fire chief beside her.

'It's so close,' she said in an awed voice. 'Shouldn't we start evacuating the town?'

Charlie Simpkin shook his head, rubbing his smoke-stained face wearily.

'No,' he told her. 'I've been out along the ridge all morning.' He motioned to the map. 'It's all through the valley in here, burning through the range at the back. It's got thousands of hectares to burn before there's a problem. My men are back-burning along the ridge to stop it extending towards us. We can evacuate by sea if we must, but I don't think it's going to be necessary.'

Jana nodded. 'It must be hard on you,' she said sadly. 'Watching all this lovely forest burn.'

The grizzled fire chief looked across at Jana. The more he had to do with Dr Reiss, the more he liked her. She was twenty-eight, but looked older with her severe hairstyle and her diminutive figure clad in a plain skirt, blouse and sensible white coat. The fire chief spent his life bemoaning his 'flibbertigibbet' daughters with their frivolous clothes and constantly changing boyfriends, but he would have liked to see Dr Reiss with just a little of the same light-hearted approach to life.

And now local gossip had it that she intended marrying Barry Fitzsimmons, the local pharmacist. Barry might be a worthy citizen, but any spark of fun Jana had left in her would be lost forever in the company of Barry and his domineering mother. What a waste, he thought sadly. Catching himself, he pulled his attention back to what Jana was saying.

'It doesn't do the forest any harm to have a burn,' he told her, pushing his errant thoughts aside. 'It's been fifty years since this section's gone up, and a lot of the trees have to burn to regenerate.'

Jana frowned in enquiry.

'It's true,' he told her. 'A lot of Australian native trees drop seed-pods that won't grow unless they've been subjected to intense heat.' He smiled. 'It's Mother Nature's own peculiar plan. Not meant for the convenience of us humans.'

'You can say that again,' Jana said with asperity. 'So where does that leave us?'

'Right where we are,' the fire chief grinned. 'All the roads through the valley are cut. Carrabookna is isolated from the rest of the country and looks like staying that way, at least until after Christmas.'

Jana nodded. By the look of the red dots she had assumed as much. Carrabookna was on a spit of land on Australia's south-east coast. Between the township and the rest of the country lay a vast wilderness of national park, now in flames.

'You're in for a rough few days,' she told the fire chief.

'You too,' he said sympathetically. 'That's why I dropped in to see you. The town's full of trapped holidaymakers here for the Christmas vacation. There'll be work for you from them and my men out on the ridges are going to need you. Also, we just had a radio message from Dr Howard.'

'Oh?' Even before she asked, Jana knew what was coming. Frank Howard was the second doctor at the Carrabookna hospital. He had taken a few days off to take his family to Melbourne for Christmas shopping, and the agreement was that he would return in time to relieve Jana for Christmas.

For Frank, the fire would provide a glorious opportunity to have a few more days off. 'He doesn't think he'll come back by boat?' Jana asked, knowing the answer before she voiced the question.

The fire chief met her look and smiled ruefully. He shared Jana's views of her colleague's attitude to work.

'He can't risk his family,' he said quietly.

'And he can't possibly come back without them.' Jana shook her head tiredly and walked over to hold the door of her office open for the elderly fire chief. 'Thanks for taking the time to fill me in,' she told him. She looked up at the man before her. Charlie Simpkin was past retirement age. With the load on his shoulders he should be standing aside to let a younger man take on the strain. The previous night, when he had come in to Casualty to check his men, she had tried to suggest it to him, only to have her head bitten off for her pains.

'Go home and have two hours' rest before you stir again,' she said firmly. 'You'll be doing the town no service if you run yourself into the ground.'

The chief raised his hand in acknowledgement. 'The same could be said for you, young lady,' he told her. He knew Jana had been doing the work of two for the last few days, and knew also that the work would only increase. Given a heavy demand, Dr Howard would simply refuse to see all but the most urgent of cases. Jana would just keep silently working.

He didn't envy her the job in front of her. He almost preferred his own.

* * *

After the fire chief departed Jana gave herself a couple of moments to get her thoughts back in order and then made her way back to the outpatient clinic at the rear of the building. The Christmas wreaths on every door and the gay decorations painted on the windows seemed out of place. It didn't seem like Christmas. She had intended to be in Melbourne with her family. With the phone links cut to the rest of the country it now seemed as if she wouldn't even be able to phone them.

She glanced at her watch and grimaced, pushing the thought of her lost festivities to one side. At least she was going to be too busy to miss them. Today she would be working until well into the evening just to finish afternoon surgery. After that there was a long ward-round, and finally the fire engines, with any firefighters needing attention.

The waiting-room was now even more crowded. The big backpacker was still there. Across the room Jana was aware of blue eyes in a tanned face, silently watching. She averted her gaze deliberately and crossed to Becky.

'You'd better ring any patients who are still due to come in and let them know of the delay,' Jana told Becky wearily.

'Dr Reiss, I believe you should see me. Now.' It was the backpacker again. He had pushed himself to his feet and was speaking with an air of calm authority.

Jana turned to look at him. Her fatigue and the mounting pressure of a mountain of waiting work swelled within her and she felt anger surge and surface. She took a deep breath and confronted him.

'You can wait your turn like everybody else,' she snapped. 'Now sit down and be quiet.'

It was two hours later before she finally reached the man's card. Every time she had emerged to usher in another patient she had been aware of his eyes on her, sardonically watching. It was almost a relief to finally pick up his card.

'Iain Carisbrook. Age thirty-two.' The card contained no other details and Jana frowned. She liked to have a comprehensive picture of her patients, even the itinerant ones as this man so obviously was. She stood at the door of the consulting-room and ushered him in.

'Now,' she said firmly, closing the door as he entered, 'what can I do for you?' Despite his arrogance she was determined to be pleasant.

He glanced at his watch. 'You've kept me waiting for over two hours,' he said pointedly.

Jana bit her lip. 'Mr Carisbrook, this hospital normally has two doctors. My colleague is unable to return because of the fires. Normally we are both busy. As well as the workload of two doctors I'm treating firefighters and I still have a stream of tourists who haven't got the sense to avoid sunburn in this heat. Now, if you're going to whinge about queue length. . .'

'Feeling under pressure, Dr Reiss?' The gentle undercurrent of laughter was back in his voice. His watchful eyes didn't leave her face.

'Yes,' she said harshly. 'Now, if you'd like to tell

me what your problem is, then perhaps I can get on with my work.'

'Perhaps *we* could get on with your work,' he suggested, the humour in his eyes surfacing at the look of startled enquiry on her face. 'Dr Reiss, for the last two hours I have been trying to tell you and your efficient receptionist out there that I'm a qualified doctor. I'm here on holiday from England and, like most of the holidaymakers here, I'm trapped by the fires. Unlike the majority, however, I don't intend to spend the next few days getting sunburnt. The locals tell me you could use a hand, and that's what I'm offering.'

Jana sat back in her chair and gaped.

'Close your mouth,' he told her kindly. 'You'll swallow a fly.'

'A doctor. . .'

'A doctor,' Iain agreed. 'A real live people-doctor with all the appropriate qualifications. Now, do you need me or not?'

With difficulty Jana closed her mouth and swallowed. The remnants of anger were still with her.

'Why didn't you say. . .?'

'Do you think I didn't try to?'

'You could have told Becky.'

'I did,' Iain said grimly. 'You've obviously trained her well in the art of avoiding salesmen. "I'm Dr Carisbrook and I'd like to see the doctor here," I told her. "Fine," she said. "She can see you at five-thirty and not before." And no further than that could I get.'

Despite herself, Jana found herself smiling. It

sounded like Becky. She was fiercely protective of the doctors 'in her charge'.

'I'm sorry,' she managed to say. She sat back and looked at the man opposite her. If he really was a doctor. . .

'I really am,' he smiled, guessing her thoughts.

'But you haven't Australian registration.'

'I have,' he said firmly. 'To be honest, this holiday is more than just relaxation. I've been practising in London. I've had enough of the city and decided to look for a country practice. When I thought of which part of England I'd like to live in I started thinking further afield. I took the precaution of obtaining provisional Australian registration before I came.'

Jana shook her head in wonder. 'You realise you're the answer to a prayer.'

'I knew I would be some day,' he smiled. 'The answer to a maiden's prayer.'

Jana flushed and laughed. 'If you're serious, then your offer of help would be very much appreciated. When can you start?'

'Now.' At Jana's startled look he surveyed himself ruefully. 'Well, perhaps after a bath. I've been living out of a pack for the last few days. I only came into town today when the bush started getting excessively unfriendly.'

Jana nodded. The last of the campers in the outlying areas had been accounted for that afternoon.

'There's an apartment at the rear of the hospital you can use for the duration,' she told him. 'I'll get

Becky to show you where it is. I'll try to finish up here and then show you around.'

When the last of the afternoon patients had been seen Jana filled in the final summary with a sense of relief. She was finished, and now the huge workload which had been hanging over her would be halved.

She emerged to find Iain waiting. He had been relaxing beside the Christmas tree in one of the waiting-room's easy-chairs, but stood as she appeared. Jana caught her breath at the sight of him. Unshaven and grubby, he had been an imposing figure, muscled and innately masculine. Now, freshly shaven in clean shirt and trousers, his fair hair glistening in clean, soft waves, he was almost awesomely good-looking. Jana had not believed that a man's physical presence could have such an effect on her. To her fury she found her colour mounting, and forced herself into efficient speech.

'Is your accommodation adequate? Would you like to join me on a ward-round?'

His eyes were on her, warm with understanding. Jana flushed again. It was almost as if this man guessed her thoughts.

'Thank you,' he said quietly. 'Yes, on both counts.'

Jana nodded and led the way to the door. As she did, it opened and Barry appeared.

She had forgotten Barry. Wednesday was her night for having dinner with Barry and his mother. It would have occurred to neither of them that a minor inconvenience such as a bushfire would prevent her coming.

She introduced the men briefly, aware of the comparison between the two of them. They were both large men, but Barry was dark-haired and thick-set as opposed to Iain's fairness and more muscular but lighter frame. Barry's eyes were serious. They were always serious, Jana thought reflectively. For Barry, life was a serious business.

'I'm very glad to meet you,' Barry was saying, shaking the other man's hand warmly. 'Jana's got too much to do here. Twice this week she's been late for lunch and today I don't think she had any at all.' It was Jana's routine to meet Barry for lunch whenever she could. That and her weekly meal with his mother were their sole commitment to each other, but it was enough for them to know that the other was 'serious'.

'That's dreadful,' Iain said, his voice an exact imitation of Barry's earnest tones. Jana cast him a suspicious look, but he was innocence personified. 'Of course I'll do anything in my power to remedy the situation.'

'We'd be exceedingly grateful,' Barry said briefly. He turned to Jana. 'Are you ready? Mother rang to say dinner was a quarter of an hour away.'

Jana shook her head. 'I'm sorry, Barry. I should have rung you before but I've had so much else on my mind I completely forgot. The fire engines will be coming down from the ridge in the next hour or so and I told Charlie I'd be ready to check his men.'

'There are no casualties?' Barry enquired, and Jana shook her head.

'Not that I know of, but after a full day backburning there are bound to be eyes that need washing and minor burns.'

'Couldn't Dr Carisbrook do that?' Barry asked.

'No.' Jana looked at Barry in annoyance. 'It wouldn't be fair.'

'I'm sure I can manage,' Iain broke in. 'I'd hate to be the cause of keeping you and Barry apart. And Barry's mother,' he added as an afterthought. Still his eyes maintained their innocence, and Jana bit her lip.

'It's out of the question,' she said curtly. She fought for and managed a smile. 'I'm sorry, Barry, but you'll have to apologise for me. I can't come tonight.'

Barry nodded. 'OK, my love.' He spread his hands expressively. 'I know when I'm beaten. Mother will be disappointed, but she'll be seeing you on Saturday, after all.'

'Saturday?' Jana said blankly.

'Christmas Day.' Barry smiled. 'Surely you haven't forgotten?'

'I. . .' Jana broke off. She had been trying to block out the thought of Christmas since it had become clear that she wouldn't be able to spend it with her family. She was fond of Barry, in fact she was almost certain that she was going to marry him, but somehow the thought of spending Christmas with him left her cold. She tried to imbue her voice with enthusiasm, though, as she replied.

'Of course,' she said. 'Tell her I'll look forward to Saturday.'

Barry turned and left. For a long moment there was silence in the room.

'Are you going to marry him?' Iain asked conversationally.

'Probably.' Jana turned abruptly. 'If he asks me. Now, if you'll come to the sisters' station we'll start our ward-round.'

'What on earth do you see in him?'

Jana wheeled on him. 'That is none of your business, Dr Carisbrook. Your offer of assistance is gratefully accepted and appreciated, but get one thing clear: my private life is none of your concern.'

The silence stretched out between them. The blue eyes watched her, lazily mocking.

'As you wish it, Dr Reiss,' he said finally. 'As you wish it.'

CHAPTER TWO

By THE time a ward-round had been accomplished Jana was beginning to relax. Iain walked at her side, chatting easily to the patients and asking questions which clearly displayed his competence. As they again approached the sisters' station Jana was sure that this man would be of immense assistance in the days ahead.

'We can get a meal in the kitchen,' she told him. 'Hospital dinner was about two hours ago, but Cook will have left what we need to make a sandwich.'

'Did you have lunch?' Iain asked curiously.

'Yes.'

'A sandwich?'

Jana furrowed her brow. 'I think so,' she said. 'I forget.'

He nodded. 'And for breakfast?'

Jana shook her head. 'My ward-round took ages this morning. I don't think I had any.' As they talked they entered the hospital kitchen. It was deserted, its stark cleanliness ready for the preparation of the following morning's breakfast. On one of the big tables was a plastic-wrapped plate, containing bread, cold meat, lettuce and cheese. Iain looked at it with disdain.

'If this is what this town feeds its doctors I'll resign forthwith,' he said. 'Have we got much more to do tonight?'

'The fire engines are on their way down from the ridge now,' Jana said. 'There are bound to be a few of them needing attention. If it's anything like last night we'll have a couple of hours' work.'

'So we can't go and find ourselves a pub?'

Jana smiled and shook her head. 'This is it, I'm afraid.'

'No, it's not.' Iain had opened the big refrigerator and was peering into its recesses. 'Hmm. Sausages, bacon, eggs, tomatoes. . . We can do all right here.'

'That's for the patients tomorrow,' Jana protested.

'The kitchen staff can worry about the patients.' Iain reached up to pull a large frying pan from its hook. 'It seems to me that this community is dependent for its health on you, Dr Reiss, and its first concern should be for *your* health. And starving you is going to do nobody any good.'

'I have an assistant now,' Jana reminded him. 'I'm not so essential.'

'Well, take it from me that your assistant is definitely essential,' Iain retorted. 'And your assistant intends to eat four sausages, two eggs and as much tomato and bacon as he can fit on the plate. He's going to top it off with bread fried in butter and strong black coffee, and if you can sit by and eat a sandwich while I scoff my load of calories, caffeine and cholesterol, then more fool you.'

The meal was delicious. Jana had not realised how hungry she was. Since Dr Howard had left she had been eating on the run.

'Why have you had enough of London?' she asked

the man beside her curiously as they ate. 'It seems a huge step, to leave practice in England and come here on the off-chance that you'll find something you'll like.'

Iain was silent, and for a while Jana didn't think he was going to answer. She frowned. Perhaps it had been an impertinence to enquire too closely. It wasn't as if this man was wanting a permanent job here — he had simply offered to help.

Iain stood up and took their dishes to the sink, poured coffee and brought it back to the table. His eyes were, for the first time, serious.

'I never wanted to practise in London,' he said finally. 'I was caught.'

'Caught?'

'My parents lived there. Just as I finished my training, my father died. My mother was a chronic invalid, totally dependent on my father. I had either to put her in a nursing home or stay in London.' He shrugged. 'I loved my mother,' he said simply. 'She died three months ago.'

Jana looked thoughtfully across the table. 'So you're off to see the world.'

'And sow my wild oats,' he agreed equably. His blue eyes regained their soft smile. Jana looked up at the warmth in his face, the wide, generous mouth and the fine cheekbones. For a moment she was caught, like a small animal caught in the brightness of a car light. There was just such a feeling of inexorable fate.

The sound of a heavy engine and the scrunching of gravel came to her aid. She brought herself sharply back to earth.

'The fire trucks are here. We're going to have to come back later and clean up.' She looked ruefully at the dishes stacked in the once pristine sink. Iain shook his head.

'Not us,' he said firmly. 'It's late now. Let Cook think she's got mice. Mice who use knives and forks,' he added.

Jana fought to suppress a grin, but it broke out into a delighted chuckle. Iain looked down curiously at her.

'That's better,' he said slowly. 'Tell me, Dr Reiss, why is life such a serious business?'

Jana shook her head. 'I don't know what you mean.' The breathless feeling of things being out of her control was back. She looked up, trying to meet his eyes. The top of her head hardly reached his chin.

He stayed looking down at her. His fingers came up and lightly touched her hair. 'This, for instance,' he said. 'I'll bet this hairstyle conceals ten years of your youth.' Before Jana could stop him he had pulled the pins holding the tight knot at the back of her head. Deep black waves of hair cascaded down on to her shoulders. She gasped and reached to reknot it.

'I thought so,' Iain said in satisfaction. 'Now, why do you have to reknot it?'

'I like it that way,' Jana said tightly, holding her hand out in demand for the pins.

He reached and loosened Jana's fingers from her hair, running his hand through the soft waves. He laughed lightly into her angry eyes and returned the pins.

'What a waste!'

Jana was speechless. She shoved the pins hard into her hair and stalked out of the room.

Despite her anger, Jana's belief in Iain's competence was borne out almost at once. By the time they reached Casualty the first of the fire engines had dropped off the men who required attention. Iain donned a white coat and worked with Jana, treating minor burns and sore eyes.

Busy herself, Jana was aware of his presence in the crowded room, talking easily to the smoke-stained men and getting to know the nurses as he worked. The nurses responded with pleasure to his presence. From where he worked there was a constant ripple of laughter. Her anger eased. Jana caught herself responding to the atmosphere he created.

The burden of her heavy workload evaporated, making her feel almost light-headed with relief. She had suffered a run of interrupted nights; Iain seemed rested and eager to work. Despite his personal arrogance, his presence would mean that perhaps tonight she could get some sleep. She looked up at the clock on the wall as the last batch of men entered the room. Nine o'clock. A couple more eye-washes and she could find her bed.

It wasn't to be. With the last truckload came Ron Harvey. He ran the local hardware shop and, like many of the men in the town, had volunteered to help in the firefighting. Jana frowned as he came into the room. He was nearly sixty. For a man who saw very little manual work, a full day backburning on the ridge was risking trouble.

And Ron had trouble. He was walking stiffly, his face reflecting pain. Somehow he lowered himself into a chair and sat waiting his turn, his face white and drawn.

Jana left what she was doing and walked across to where he sat. He didn't respond to her presence. His eyes were dull with pain, inward-looking. Jana dropped to her knees in front of his chair and gripped his hands.

'What is it, Ron?' she asked gently.

With an effort he focused his gaze on the girl in front of him.

'My groin,' he muttered. 'It's been getting worse all day.' He closed his eyes as another spasm hit.

Jana motioned to the sister assisting. Together they moved the man into an examination cubicle. Iain looked an enquiry but she motioned him to continue with what he was doing. She didn't know whether she needed him yet.

It took only seconds to find the cause of Ron's problems.

'How long have you had the hernia?' she asked Ron quietly.

'About three years, I reckon.'

Jana nodded. As she moved to administer morphine she considered the inevitability of Ron's trouble. He was unfit, and a heavy smoker. The hernia would have caused him pain only after exertion for the last few years and, by the look of Ron, he had done little of that. Now the loop of bowel had protruded further and was obviously twisting.

She looked down at the fist-sized lump. Ron was going to be very lucky if she could return it to position without operating.

It was too soon yet to know whether she could manipulate it. An hour of absolute stillness and perhaps she could ease it back. She waited with him until the injection had taken effect and then returned to the remaining firefighters.

An hour later she and Iain were scrubbing for Theatre. There was no way that the loop of bowel would be pushed back. If they waited any longer there was a chance that the section of bowel would die, requiring a resection. Jana sent up a silent prayer of thankfulness that Iain was here. Without him Ron would have had to be evacuated to Bairnsdale, and the chances of permanent damage to the bowel would be much greater with the increased time involved.

She was quiet during her time at the sink. She had done little surgery. Normally she gave the anaesthetic while Dr Howard operated. Still, she could hardly leave this operation to Iain, a doctor whose skill she knew nothing of.

'Would you like me to do it?' Iain asked. He was watching her thoughtfully. Jana bit her lip.

'I should be fine,' she said defensively.

'I did my first part of surgery in England,' he told her, guessing her qualms. 'I had thoughts of doing surgery before I settled on general practice. I've done this operation many times.'

Jana let her breath out and looked up gratefully. 'Thank you,' she said simply. 'I can operate if I have to, but I'm not as experienced as I'd like to be.'

'They really do need a surgeon in a place like this,' Iain said.

'A place like this is grateful for what it can get,' Jana said quietly. 'Dr Howard is only here until he can find a suitable city practice. When he goes we're going to have trouble finding a replacement. It's just as well for the town that I look like being permanent.'

'Because you're going to marry Barry.'

'Because I'm going to marry Barry.'

'But he hasn't asked you yet?'

Jana shook her head. 'It's something that we've both assumed,' she said simply. 'We suit each other.'

He nodded. 'I can see that.' Laughter was back in his voice. Jana cast him a look of dislike and turned to give instructions to the nurses.

Iain operated swiftly and competently. Once again Jana was forced to acknowledge how thankful she was to have him. He might be odiously arrogant, but the man was skilled.

He cut carefully, allowing them to see the angry purple of the twisted bowel. The small gap through which it protruded was extended, easing the constriction. Jana winced at the sight of the deep purple, hoping that the damage was not irreparable.

Carefully Iain manoeuvred the section, positioning it against warm saline packs. With the pressure eased, now it was just a matter of waiting, seeing if the section of bowel was still viable.

Slowly, slowly the purple faded. At first Jana thought it was her imagination but then she was sure. The dark purple faded to light and then, slowly, to its normal healthy pink. Jana let out her breath with relief. Ron had been lucky.

Iain painstakingly repacked the bowel into its correct position and stitched the area from where it had protruded.

'He's going to be more comfortable than he has been for quite some time,' he commented. 'Why on earth didn't he do something before this?'

'It wouldn't have been worrying him at all,' Jana said smiling. 'Ron spends his day leaning on the cash register absorbing local gossip. He's got an assistant to do any lifting required.'

As the last stitch was put into place, a dressing applied and the patient wheeled from the room, Jana looked up at the clock. It was nearly midnight.

'I need to find my bed,' she said quietly. 'Is there anything you need?'

Iain shook his head. 'My apartment is fine,' he said. 'How come it's empty?'

'Dr Howard prefers to live away from the hospital,' Jana said. 'His wife doesn't like the nursing staff constantly coming to find him.'

'So during the night they find you?' Iain looked thoughtfully at Jana. 'It seems to me that you've got a bit of an unequal partnership going.'

'If we don't keep Dr Howard happy then he'll leave,' Jana said. 'And then the town would be in real trouble.'

Iain didn't answer. For a moment he stayed looking down at the girl beside him. Jana thought he would speak and then he appeared to think better of it. They stood for a moment, silent in the now deserted Theatre.

'Goodnight, then,' Jana finally forced herself to say.

He was no longer smiling. The silence stretched out between them. Jana moved backwards and turned, but his hand reached out to grasp her and pull her back.

'Goodnight, Dr Reiss,' he said roughly, his hand still on her shoulder. 'Get some sleep.' Then he slackened his grip and was gone, striding swiftly down the corridor. Jana stood gazing after him for a long moment before she too made her way to her bed.

Despite Jana's bone-weariness, sleep was a long time coming. She lay with her hands under her head, staring unseeingly into the dark.

Iain Carisbrook was like no man she had met before. She touched the tangle of curls on the soft pillow, remembering the feel of his fingers running through her hair. The remembered touch sent a shiver of sensation through her, causing her to stir uneasily in the bed.

'You're being a fool,' she told herself angrily. 'You're behaving like a silly schoolgirl with a crush. Just because he's good-looking and smiles like. . .'

Smiles like what? She couldn't answer her own question. The blue eyes were before her, their remembered humour almost a caress.

She swore and threw back the cotton sheet, her only cover in the oppressive heat. Crossing to the window, she stared out at the dark ridge of mountains behind the hospital. The horizon was tinged with an eerie orange glow. The moon was shrouded by a smoke-filled haze.

I'm marrying Barry, she told herself fiercely. It's not right that I should be thinking of another man like this.

It's your last chance to do so, a little voice reminded her. After you marry, you won't be able to look at anyone like this.

I won't want to, she answered herself. I'll have Barry.

And he's never going to set your nerve-endings alight, the voice came back sarcastically.

He wasn't. Jana acknowledged the truth to herself with her accustomed honesty. Barry, though, was safe, a solid, dependable partner with whom to spend the rest of her life.

Jana remembered her father as having one ambition, and that was to avoid debt-collectors. At fifteen, as her family was evicted from the third house in as many months, she had vowed that such a life was not for her. She wanted security. Barry could give it to her.

On Jana's bedside table was a picture-frame, holding a photo of Jana and Barry at the last hospital ball. Jana flicked on the light and stood looking down at the two of them, Jana smiling into the camera and Barry with his eyes on Jana, fondly proprietorial.

Finally, as if satisfied, Jana turned the light back off and climbed into bed. She took the frame with her and lay clutching it in the dark. It was almost as if she was using it as a talisman, she thought grimly. The thought stayed with her until at last sleep overcame her.

CHAPTER THREE

AT SIX A.M. Jana was dressed and ready to face another day. The hospital was full to bursting. With no let-up in either the heat or the smoke envisaged for the next few days, it was beginning to look as if the hospital would be packed for Christmas.

The intense heat was causing many of the town's elderly people to have problems, and the smoke-filled air meant that any of the population with breathing difficulties were in trouble. The old people and the children were the worst affected. The children's ward was overcrowded.

Jana started off at the children's ward. As she pushed open the doors of the gaily decorated ward she discovered she had been beaten to her round. Iain was sitting on the bed of a small asthmatic boy, good-naturedly bullying him into tackling his corn-flakes. In his casual trousers and a short-sleeved, open-necked shirt he looked relaxed and ready for whatever the day might bring. He smiled welcomingly at Jana, then turned back to the little boy.

'Here she is,' he warned, in dire accents. 'Hurry.'

Jana looked around in amazement. The usually sleepy ward was full of giggling children, all virtuously polishing off their breakfasts. The sister in charge raised her eyes expressively to Jana.

'He's told them you'll prescribe pink ice-cream for anyone finished with their breakfast by the time you reach their bed.' She laughed. 'I haven't seen such efficient demolition of breakfast for years.'

Jana shook her head in wonder. Despite the mass of Christmas decorations and the efforts of the overworked staff it was hard to keep this ward cheerful at the moment, especially as most of the children were starting to realise that they would still be here for Christmas.

'Pink ice-cream when?' she queried dubiously.

'For morning tea.' The little boy at Iain's side was bursting with news. 'Dr Carisbrook said you'd write it on our charts.'

'He did, did he?' Jana fought for a straight face and failed. She walked over and sternly inspected the little boy's cereal bowl. Satisfied, she picked up the chart on the end of the child's bed and wrote,

'One dose of pink ice-cream, to be taken orally.'

'What's "orally"?' The little boy was shining with excitement and Jana smiled. His asthma had kept him in bed for the last three days, most of which time he had spent staring listlessly at the wall waiting for his mother to visit.

'It means,' she told him, 'that you have to hold your nose, close your eyes and force yourself to spoon it into your mouth.' She grinned down at him. 'Even though I know that the food you hate most in the world is pink ice-cream.'

With breakfast over, the ward-round was done in double-quick time. By the time they left Iain even had the dour ward-maid smiling. Jana looked up at him as they left, her eyes warm with laughter.

'It's fine making edicts,' she said, trying to sound

severe, 'but I hope you checked with Cook that she's got some pink ice-cream.'

He shook his head. 'She hasn't.'

'Iain!' The exclamation was out before she could help herself and he laughed down into her horrified eyes.

'Don't worry,' he told her. 'I discovered Thomas, your little asthmatic, in the night. He was very distressed. I managed to kid him back to sleep but before I went in this morning I rang the local milk-bar owner and checked on the pink ice-cream situation.'

Jana looked at her watch. It was still not yet seven. Iain must have phoned at. . .

'Five-thirty,' he concurred, reading her thoughts.

'Mr Lanzo must have thought you were out of your mind,' Jana exclaimed, visions of the voluble milk-bar owner making her shake her head in stunned amazement.

'In a time like this the town just has to pull together,' Iain said sagely. 'Mr Lanzo will personally deliver two drums of strawberry ice-cream before ten this morning and there will be no charge.'

Jana stared. When she finally got her voice back she thought of something else.

'Why were you up in the night?' she demanded.

'Because the night staff were under instructions to call me,' he said blandly. 'You, Dr Reiss, were in need of your sleep.'

Jana was lost for words. This man showed every inclination of taking over the entire hospital.

* * *

The rest of the morning passed quickly. The hernia patient of the night before was recovering nicely, his major concern being whether he could be out of hospital in time to rejoin the firefighters.

'You have to be joking,' Jana told him severely. 'It's back to leaning on the cash register for you for at least the next few weeks.'

Morning outpatients, a nightmare for the past two mornings with Jana trying to see far too many patients, was again a pleasure. Iain split the patients into those who asked specifically for Jana and those he could see himself. They were both busy, but not oppressively so. Without Iain, though, it would have been a disaster.

All morning Jana was conscious of his presence in the next room. There was an intercom between the rooms, and often Iain was forced to interrupt with a query regarding prescriptions. Dosages and brand names in this country were new to him. He was good, though, Jana acknowledged to herself, wondering how *she* would manage thrown into an unfamiliar environment the way he had been.

There was the sound of laughter from the next room and she smiled. The hospital had been very lucky.

Her next consultation drove away all thoughts of the man in the next room.

As she came out to usher in the next patient, Nick Lanzo, the milk-bar owner, was standing next to Becky's desk, talking seriously to the young receptionist. Jana took the next card from Becky and turned to talk to him. He was in his early forties, short and stocky and, despite having been born in Australia, still speaking with a heavy Italian accent.

'Mr Lanzo.' She held out a hand to grasp his. 'I gather we have two drums of pink ice-cream to thank you for.' She smiled warmly. 'I'm so sorry Dr Carisbrook woke you up.'

'That's nothing.' He spread his hands expressively. 'Sophie and me were awake anyway.' He hesitated. 'Dr Reiss, I. . . I need to talk to you.'

The words were said slowly, as if he was having difficulty finding courage to speak.

Jana looked at the man in front of her. There were three patients in front of him in the queue. She glanced around at the waiting patients and then back to Nick. His face showed the faint sheen of perspiration normally associated with distress. Jana put back the card she had just picked up and motioned him into her consulting-room.

'What is it?' she asked gently.

'It's Sophie.'

Jana nodded. She knew Nick's wife. The couple were an institution in the town. Although childless, they seemed to be on every committee and involved in every fund-raising activity going, their cheerful good humour and boundless energy making them universally liked.

'I haven't seen Sophie lately,' Jana said, thinking back. 'Is something wrong?'

Nick nodded. 'Sophie's mother died when she was forty-three, of cancer,' he said shortly.

'And?' Jana prodded.

'Sophie is forty.' Nick sat down heavily in the

chair opposite Jana and put his head in his hands. 'She believes she also has the cancer.'

Jana was silent for a moment, thinking back to the last time she had seen the big-boned, robust woman.

'What makes her think that?' she asked quietly.

Nick's reply was muffled in his hands and Jana had to lean forward to hear. 'She has been not well for months,' he said. 'Sick. Everything makes her sick. And she has cramps, and a few days ago I force her to tell me and she says there is a lump in her stomach.' He hesitated, then raised his eyes fearfully to look at Jana. 'I felt it,' he said simply. 'It is very big.'

Silence filled the room. Jana shook her head, trying to find words of comfort or reassurance. There were none.

'Why hasn't she come to see me?' she asked finally.

Nick shook his head. 'Sophie's mother died slowly,' he said. 'For the last weeks the doctor put her on a drip and kept her alive. Her pain was very bad and still they kept her alive.' He put his hands back to his face. 'My Sophie doesn't want doctors.'

Jana nodded. 'So why are you coming to see me now?' she asked softly.

Once again he met her look. 'I told Sophie I wouldn't,' he said harshly. 'But this morning we were awake because Sophie had bad pain, and I had to bring the ice-cream and I thought. . .' His eyes were a desperate cry for help. 'She's hurting,' he said. 'I can't bear it.'

'You love her very much,' Jana said quietly.

'She is my life,' he said simply. For a moment he was silent, and then he continued. 'Sophie and I never had children. We wanted them but they never came. Now there is only each other, but... It's enough,' he said finally. 'Each other is enough. And to watch her die and do nothing... I can't bear it,' he repeated. His voice broke on a sob.

Jana stood up and came around to put a hand on his shoulder.

'Nick, I can't do anything unless Sophie will see me,' she said quietly. 'You're going to have to persuade her to come.' She hesitated. 'You know, if she has got cancer then we can help, at least with the pain. I can promise you that. And maybe, just maybe it's not cancer. There are other things that cause lumps. Ovarian cysts, for example.'

'She won't come.' He stood up, his face red and blotched with weeping. 'Dr Reiss, will you come to her? Will you just drop in to...to thank us for the ice-cream or something? And see if she'll talk?'

Jana nodded slowly. 'I can do that,' she agreed.

'When?'

'I'll come around at about one-thirty,' she told him. She'd miss lunch with Barry again but it couldn't be helped.

'I'll be out then,' the milk-bar owner said. 'That way she'll have to come into the shop. She won't go into the shop unless she has to,' he explained. 'She thinks people will notice something's wrong.'

The rest of the morning passed swiftly. Towards lunchtime Barry called and Jana explained she wouldn't be able to have lunch with him.

'Can I see you tonight, then?' he asked.

There was no reason why not. With Iain's help she should be finished by six and have a couple of hours before the fire trucks came down.

'Not with your mother, though,' she asked him. She was fond of Barry but found his mother oppressive.

'No,' he agreed. 'I think it's about time we had some time to ourselves. I'll pick you up at six.'

Jana put the phone down, sighing as she did so. She would have liked a couple of hours to herself. It had been days since she had sat and done nothing for two minutes at a time. The need was almost overwhelming. She fought the urge to ring Barry back. If she was going to marry him it was unfair never to spend time with him.

When she finished her morning list of patients she went through to the hospital kitchens and found Iain already there. She sat down beside him and he pushed the central plate of sandwiches towards her.

'Have a sandwich for a change,' he smiled. Then his smile faded as he saw her face. 'What's wrong?'

Briefly she told him of Sophie Lanzo. She glanced down at her watch. 'I said I'd be there in twenty minutes,' she told him.

He nodded thoughtfully. 'How are you going to approach it?'

'I don't know. I can't force her to ask for help. I can't even tell her Nick's told me about her illness.'

'So you'll just hope she'll tell you?'

Jana nodded. 'It's all I can do.'

He was silent. Jana took a sandwich and ate it without enthusiasm.

'If it is a tumour it'll be too late to operate,' she said listlessly. 'If it's so big that it's noticeable then it'll have done all sorts of damage, even if it hasn't spread.'

'So our role will be palliation, if she'll let us near,' Iain said. He stood up and fetched coffee for them both. 'She must be terrified.'

Jana sighed. 'She must have gone through a bad experience with her mother to make her like this.' She hesitated. 'It's hard,' she said. 'When I was just out of college I might have done exactly the same thing. I remember thinking that the most important thing was to extend life, no matter what.'

'And now you're starting to realise that sometimes the cost is too high,' Iain said gently.

Jana drank her coffee slowly, thinking of what was before her. Iain seemed to sense her need for silence. Finally she glanced at her watch and rose.

'I have to go.'

He looked up, his eyes giving a message of strength and reassurance. 'Go to it, Dr Reiss,' he said.

The little milk-bar was around the headland, by the caravan park near the town beach. Jana parked her car on the gravel at the front of the shop and walked in. The shop was deserted.

On the counter was a bell. As Jana pushed the button she could hear the ring sounding out through the living-quarters at the back.

'Nick?' It was Sophie's voice. 'Are you there?'

Jana rang the bell again and waited. Finally Sophie came through, wiping her hands on her apron as she entered the shop. She was a big woman, bigger than her husband, with soft blonde hair caught into a bun at the back and wide blue eyes.

'Hi, Sophie,' Jana smiled.

Sophie made an attempt to return the smile but it didn't quite come off. Her eyes were frightened.

'I came in to thank you for the ice-cream,' Jana said warmly. 'And to apologise for Dr Carisbrook's waking you this morning.'

Sophie nodded, her eyes still wary. And pain-filled, Jana thought. Sophie's hand was on her stomach under the loose-fitting apron.

'It was a pleasure,' Sophie said quietly. 'It was good to be able to do something for the children.' A spasm caught her and she winced and tightened her hold under the apron.

'Is something wrong?' Jana asked. The look on Sophie's face made the question almost compulsory.

'No.' Sophie caught herself. 'Nothing is wrong, Dr Reiss. I have a touch of indigestion, that's all.'

'To have indigestion before Christmas is no fun,' Jana smiled. Then, at the closed look on Sophie's face, she changed her approach. 'Are you having family for Christmas?'

'Nick and I have no family in Carrabookna,' Sophie said tightly. 'Nick's family is in Melbourne and they can't get through with the fires. We'll be having Christmas by ourselves. Is there anything you would like, Dr Reiss?' She clearly wanted Jana to go.

Jana shook her head. 'I'd better get back,' she said slowly. 'The hospital's busy.' She hesitated, trying to find the right words. 'Sophie, if that indigestion gets too painful, please come and see me. It's obvious that it's worrying you. I'd really like to be given the opportunity to help. On your terms,' she added.

'Thank you, I do not need help,' Sophie said shortly. Jana was dismissed.

'So?' Iain was waiting when she walked back into the hospital.

Jana shook her head. 'Whatever it is, she won't let me near her.'

'But she is ill?'

'Mmm.' Jana frowned. 'But she doesn't look as if she has advanced cancer.'

'She's not emaciated?'

'No.' Jana thought back, trying to get a clear picture of the frightened woman. 'She's lost some weight in the face, but not an enormous amount. She's still big.'

'Could you see the lump Nick was talking about?'

'No. She held her apron out from her body. I couldn't see.'

'So there's a chance it could just be an ovarian cyst?'

'I wish I could think so. Nick says she's been ill, though. A cyst doesn't usually cause nausea.'

'It does if it's big enough to be putting pressure on other organs,' Iain said. 'And if it's twisting then the pain's explained.'

'Nick says she's been unwell for months.'

They fell silent, each going over the probabilities in their minds. A tumour untreated for months...

'There's nothing we can do,' Iain said finally. 'Jana, unless she asks for our help, I'm afraid it's none of our business.'

The afternoon was quieter than it had been for days. Iain took over the trickle of patients coming through casualty, and Jana took herself into her office and tackled the mound of paperwork that had accumulated. With only one doctor in the town everything that was not absolutely urgent had been shelved.

She worked steadily, grateful for Iain's presence buffering her from the stream of interruptions. As it was, she was only called out a couple of times for the afternoon, to talk to a relative and to reinsert a drip.

As she worked she found herself thinking back to Sophie. Her pen would stop of its own volition and she found herself staring into space, racking her brains to find an approach that could help. Nothing.

At about five-thirty Iain came to find her.

'How goes it?'

Jana smiled, gesturing to the pile before her. 'Half done,' she said.

'You've been thinking of Sophie?'

'Yes.'

He nodded. 'I don't think professional detachment is your speciality, Dr Reiss.'

Jana flushed. 'It's hard in a community as small as this,' she said defensively.

Iain grinned. 'All right!' He held up his hands. 'Prickly, aren't we, Jana? Believe me, there was no criticism intended.' He hesitated. 'Actually, I was wondering whether we could find a meal somewhere in town. I've just discovered that dinner in this crazy hospital is served at five o'clock. We've missed it again.'

'I've arranged to have dinner with Barry,' Jana said curtly. What was it about this man that left her feeling like a gauche schoolgirl?

Iain looked thoughtfully down at her. 'That'll be nice.'

'Yes, it will be.' She stood up abruptly.

'Well, don't worry about me,' he said resignedly. 'No doubt there'll be a plate of sandwiches in the kitchen.'

'I'm not sure there will be tonight,' Jana said maliciously, laughing up at his martyred expression. 'I think Cook's worried about mice.'

He strode over and held the door open. 'Go on,' he ordered. 'Go and carouse with your boyfriend. Don't worry about me.' He smiled down into Jana's bespectacled green eyes and the laughter in his face made her catch her breath. 'If it comes to the crunch I know where there's still half a drum of strawberry ice-cream.'

Barry was waiting at the hospital entrance. Jana walked towards him, trying to suppress the niggle of guilt she felt at leaving the hospital. It was more than that, she acknowledged to herself. Faced with a choice of a three-course meal with Barry or eating strawberry ice-cream in the back room of the children's ward with Iain. . .

She shook herself angrily. She was being daft.

Her father had been such a one as Iain Carisbrook, laughing at life as it threw up one obstacle after another. His debts weren't serious and neither was the fact that his wife was worn out before she was thirty and his children often went hungry.

'Life's not a joke,' she told herself quietly. She climbed into the car beside Barry, smiling up at him and finding reassurance in his look of concern.

'Tired, my love?'

'Mmm,' she murmured. She wished suddenly that she could tell him about Sophie and Nick and the problems of her day, but as the wish entered her head she rejected it. Even if she were free to talk about her patients to Barry, she knew he would hate to hear 'medical talk'. When they were together they talked about him. He started the engine and the car moved out of the hospital grounds.

'Let's go down to the beach,' Jana said suddenly. She had been trapped inside for the last few days with hardly a break. All of a sudden she was desperate to be outside.

Barry looked startled. 'I've booked at the hotel,' he said. 'They're expecting us.'

'We could drop in on the way and let them know. Why don't we buy some fish and chips and go down the beach to eat them?' Suddenly the idea was irresistible.

Barry shook his head, looking down at his immaculate trousers, crisp shirt and tie. 'I'm hardly dressed for the beach,' he protested. 'And neither are you. The salt would mark the leather of these shoes.'

'You could always take them off,' Jana suggested.

'I'd look ridiculous.' He negotiated the corner of the main street and pulled up outside the hotel. 'Besides, how could you possibly want fish and chips when you can have steak followed by apple pie?'

There was no more to be said. Jana sighed and allowed herself to be ushered into the hotel.

Two hours later, having heard all of Barry's news for the last few days, Jana's time out was over and she was dropped off again outside the hospital. Barry leaned over and kissed her lightly on the brow.

'Two more days until Christmas, my love. Will I see you again before then?'

'I'm not sure,' she answered truthfully. 'I really can't leave Iain in charge. It's not fair when he's working as a volunteer.'

Barry nodded. 'It's good of him to give you this help,' he agreed. 'Make sure you tell him I appreciate it.'

'I will,' Jana agreed, knowing she would do no such thing. Already she knew Iain well enough to guess his reaction. 'Goodnight, Barry.' She returned his perfunctory kiss and climbed out of the car, trying to suppress her feeling of relief. Why was she feeling like this? A week ago she had been so sure that she was doing the right thing.

The fire engines were on their way down as she entered the hospital and she turned to watch the first one come into the hospital yard. The men would be bone-weary. For five days now they had been up on the ridge and there was still no easing of the situation.

Everyone was hoping for a change in the weather. A shift in the hot north wind would drive the fire back on itself. The wind was blasting across the hospital forecourt, hot and dry. There would be no relief in the immediate future.

Iain was already in Casualty, making preparations.

'Did you get any dinner?' she asked penitently.

'Yes, thank you.'

'Pink ice-cream?'

He grinned and relented. 'Nope,' he told her. 'Cook was still in the kitchen when I went to get my sandwiches, and took pity on me. She whipped me up an omelette.'

'Your mouse-like activities have been forgiven?'

'I told her it was all your idea,' he said blandly, and Jana choked.

'How about you?' he continued, ignoring her laughter. 'Did you get some fresh air and exercise?'

Jana shook her head. 'Barry wanted a hotel meal.'

'You sat in the hotel on a night like this? You're mad.' His face furrowed into a frown of concern. 'When did you last get any exercise, Dr Reiss?'

Jana shrugged. 'I hardly see that it's any of your concern, Dr Carisbrook,' she said quellingly.

Iain looked at her curiously but said nothing. The first of the men came through the entrance and their conversation ended.

Tonight there were no major problems. The men were weary and quieter than the previous night. The good-natured banter was missing and Jana

realised that for most of them now the fire had just
become hard slog. Their constant vigilance meant
that the town was safe, but the little town was
becoming complacent in its safety and the effort of
the volunteers had lost some of its glamour.

Charlie, the fire chief, came in with the last of the
engines, checking on the injuries sustained by his
men. Jana introduced him to Iain and the fire chief
gripped his hand warmly in welcome.

'The town's grateful,' he told Iain warmly. 'Our
Dr Reiss works too hard. Your help is appreciated.'

'So what about you getting some help too,
Charlie?' Jana interrupted. 'You can't keep this
pace up. You'll kill yourself.'

'I'm going in to the caravan park tomorrow to call
for volunteers among the tourists,' he said, shrug-
ging off her concern. 'It's not just me. All the boys
have had enough and it's the tourists' skin they're
protecting as well as the townspeople's. Besides,' he
told her, 'I'm sick to death of the whingeing we're
getting about the road blocks. I'd like a few of them
to see what's happening up there.'

Jana nodded. Anything that would give these
tired men a break would be welcome.

'Are you getting some sleep?' she asked him.

'Enough,' he told her roughly. 'I'll go to bed
when the wind changes and stay there for a week.'

There was nothing more Jana or Iain could do.
Iain returned to where he had been working when
Jana had called him over and Jana turned her
attention to bathing the chief's eyes.

'Let's hope it's soon,' she told him as she worked.
'I think we've all had about enough.'

By nine-thirty they were finished. As Jana finished writing up her notes for the night, Iain disappeared.

'I'll just do a last ward-check.' Fifteen minutes later he was back.

'All quiet,' he told her.

Jana smiled absently and stood up. She winced as her legs screamed a protest. The strain of the last few days was catching up with her. Iain saw her grimace.

'You need some exercise, Dr Reiss.'

'It's the last thing I need,' Jana said firmly. 'I need my bed.'

Iain shook his head. 'You haven't had any exercise for days. Come on, let's go for a walk.'

'We can't. Not both of us.'

'Yes, we can,' Iain said firmly. 'I've just been talking to Sister. With her help I've mapped a walk from here down to the beach and back. I've promised not to stray one metre from our proposed route and if she needs us she'll send a car. Now stop quibbling, Dr Reiss, and do what the doctor tells you.'

'Yes, sir.'

They walked in silence for a while. The roads were deserted. Most people were behind closed doors making last-minute preparations for the coming Christmas festivities. Jana was acutely aware of the presence of this big man at her side. She ventured a look at him and found that his eyes were on hers. She looked away, her colour mounting.

'It's Christmas Eve tomorrow,' Jana said, trying

to break the loaded silence. They were nearing the end of the road and crossing to the beach. 'I can't believe it's come so fast. When I was a child it used to take forever.'

'But it was worth the wait,' Iain smiled. 'Christmas has never been the same since Santa disappeared from my life. There's nothing more wonderful than not knowing what Christmas has in store for you.'

'Or if it has anything,' Jana said drily.

He looked at her oddly. 'Do you mean now, or in your childhood?'

Jana bit her lip. 'Christmas at home was a bit unpredictable,' she admitted. 'Sometimes we had to cope with disappointments.' One Christmas their mother had packed the children off to the local hall for a meal with a welfare agency, but Jana wasn't going to admit that.

He was still watching her. Jana flushed. Why did she have this unnerving feeling that this man could read her thoughts? She bent down and took off her shoes.

'I'm going for a paddle,' she said firmly. Leaving her shoes on the grass at the edge of the sand, she ran lightly down to where the waves swept in, tongues of white foam edging the black of the sea.

The beach down from the hospital was around the headland from the town and was totally deserted. The sand was still warm from the heat of the day and, in contrast, the water was ice-cold. Jana gasped as it surged around her ankles. She looked back up the beach. Iain was bending to remove his shoes and roll up his trousers. His figure was a shadow in the dark. She watched as he approached, his features gradually becoming clearer as he grew nearer.

'The sting-rays come in to feed at night,' she warned him. 'Take care.'

'So why are you paddling?'

'They won't sting me,' she said confidently. 'I caught one once when I was fishing and I cut my line. They've let me alone ever since.'

Iain laughed. Striding into the water, he grabbed Jana's hand. Turning seaward, he held their joined hands up in the air. 'I'm with her,' he yelled.

They strolled on through the shallows. Iain made no move to relinquish her hand. Jana tugged to release herself but his grip tightened.

'No fear,' he said determinedly. 'For the sake of the sting-rays, we're a team. They get me and we go down together.'

Jana gave up the effort. The moon, still shrouded in a film of smoke, sent weak rays across the water. She kicked out a spray of water in front of her, enjoying the sheer physical effort of pushing her feet through the shallow water.

'Do you fish?' Iain asked.

'I used to,' she replied. 'I was never very serious. In fact, after I caught the sting-ray I stopped baiting my line.'

'You stopped baiting your line,' he said blankly.

'Well, I didn't really want to catch anything,' Jana explained. 'If I come down to the beach and sit and stare at the sea for hours on end, people look at me sideways. In a small community it's a bit difficult for me to practise medicine if people have doubts about my sanity. But if I sit here with a fishing rod, then my staring out to sea is considered normal. People stop and chat, ask me about the fish, commiserate with my bad luck and go on their way. It's lovely.'

'But you've stopped doing it?'

'Yes.'

'Because of Barry?'

'He doesn't like the beach much,' Jana admitted.

'Jana, what the hell do you see in him?'

This time Jana's tug on her hand was insistent, and she was released. She walked ahead. She kicked out at the water again, this time with anger. The bottom of her skirt was soaking, but she didn't care.

'You know, if you loved him you could defend him,' Iain said conversationally. 'The man's a worthy, pompous bore and you haven't even got the certainty to deny it.'

'I do deny it,' Jana said stiffly. 'You don't know anything about him.'

'I know he took you to the hotel on a stifling night when the only decent place to be was outside,' Iain said. 'And I know that he doesn't like the beach. Would he do this? Would he get his toes chock-full of sand and walk beside the girl he loves in a place where huge manta rays might strike at any minute?'

Jana caught her breath at what he was saying. Surely he didn't. . .

'Jana Reiss, you're ignoring the issue,' Iain said softly. 'I think it's time you woke up.'

Still silence. Iain reached down, scooped up a handful of water and directed it firmly at the back of Jana's neck. The shock of cold water hitting her skin made her gasp. She wheeled round to face him.

'How dare you?' she yelled. 'Leave me alone.'

'Or what?' he goaded.

Jana took a deep breath, glaring at the man in front of her. His piercing eyes mocked her defiantly.

Deliberately she brought her foot back and kicked with all her strength. A huge spray of water came up and hit Iain full in the face. Jana took a step back, gasping with shock at her action.

For a drawn out moment there was silence between them. Then Iain's dripping face broke into a grin of unholy joy.

'So it's war, is it, sweetheart?' he said softly. He edged around until he was between Jana and the safety of the shore.

Jana walked towards him, summoning defiance.

'Let me past,' she demanded as he moved to intercept her. 'This is childish. I'm going back to the hospital.'

'But I'm wetter than you are,' Iain protested. 'It wouldn't be fair to leave it as it is.' He reached out and removed her glasses, carefully placing them in his sodden shirt pocket. Then, before Jana could make a move to defend herself, she was seized and swung strongly up into his arms. Once secure, Iain strode purposefully out into the waves.

'What are you doing?' Jana's voice was a squeak. The water was up to Iain's waist. 'Put me down.'

He looked down into her indignant face, his eyes alight with laughter.

'Anything you say, Dr Reiss.' He lifted her high above the waves, waited until the next breaker foamed towards them and heaved her skilfully into its path.

* * *

Jana emerged, choking and spluttering. Her tightly coiled hair had loosened and strands of soaking curls lay streaming around her face. A piece of seaweed hung crazily down over her eyes. She pulled it away as she struggled to find her feet.

'You...you...' Words failed her. She pushed her way towards the big, laughing man.

'You did tell me to put you down,' he said virtuously.

For answer she sent up a shower of spray, soaking the parts of him that weren't already saturated. He answered in kind and for the next few minutes the two figures were lost in a fury of splashing.

Jana was torn between anger and laughter. She pelted the water as if her life depended on it, almost as if she was afraid to stop and let this laughing man near.

The water didn't stop him. Still splashing, he drew nearer until he finally reached out and grasped her.

'Enough. Enough,' he ordered. 'I know when I'm beaten.'

'You're not beaten,' she retorted. 'You're not even repentant.'

'I am,' he said in an injured tone. 'I'm really sorry I'm wet.'

Jana choked. 'And what about me?' she demanded.

Grasping her hands, he held her back at arm's length. His eyes raked her, her slight figure revealed in stark clarity by her clinging clothes, her soft blouse almost transparent with wetness and her normally severe hairstyle in disarray.

'No,' he said thoughtfully, 'I'm not sorry you're wet.'

Jana made to pull away, but his grip tightened.

'Jana, what is this game that you're playing?' he said softly. 'You're too much of a woman to marry Barry Fitzsimmons. Look at you,' he demanded. 'My God, if I had a woman like you and hadn't spent any time with you for days do you think I'd be taking you to a hotel for a quiet meal with a hundred other people in the same room?' His voice rose to goaded anger. 'Did he bother to kiss you goodnight, Jana? Or was it a peck, suitable for use every morning and evening for the next sixty years? Do you know what it's like to be kissed?'

Jana made a tiny sound of protest, a whimper of fright. It caught him. He put a hand up to force her to meet his eyes.

'Don't worry, my love,' he said softly. 'I won't hurt you. I'll never hurt you.'

For a long moment he stood, staring down at the girl in his arms. Then, slowly, his mouth lowered on to hers.

For a moment Jana held herself rigid, shock riding in waves through her body. His hands came down, pulling her soaking body into his, holding her hard against him. His mouth found her lips and softly kissed.

Between their bodies there was nothing. Their clothes might not have existed. The soft contours of Jana's breasts were held hard against Iain's chest. She could feel the rhythmic pounding of his heart, and she could feel her own response.

Her struggles died away. She had never known

anything like this. The feel of his lips on hers, his
body against hers, drove away every thought, every
vestige of resistance. She felt her body lift and
respond. Far away, in her head, her consciousness
melted and disappeared to be replaced by waves of
pure joy. Her lips slowly parted, welcoming, wanting the gentle exploration of his tongue.

Endlessly they stayed, locked together, the waves
crashing around them in tireless motion. Sometimes
a wave, bigger than usual, crashed hard against
them, forcing them to move to hold their footing.
Their bodies moved in perfect synchronisation,
unable to part.

Iain finally was the one to break away. Holding
her face softly between his hands, he moved back
so he could see her eyes in the faint moonlight. His
voice, when he spoke, was husky with emotion and
suddenly unsure. For the first time since Jana had
met him, the laughter had gone.

'Now tell me again that you're going to marry
Barry Fitzsimmons.' With surprise, Jana recognised
the undercurrent of anger in his voice. She met his
look with wonder.

'I. . . I don't know.'

'You don't know what?'

'Please. . .' She pulled away from him and fended
him off with her hands. 'Iain, I don't want this.'

'You don't want what? You don't want a man?'

'I've got a man,' she said helplessly. 'I've got
Barry.'

Iain laughed scornfully. 'No,' he said harshly.
'You've got a bank balance and a hot-water bottle.
Does that make a man?'

'That's unfair.'

'Is it?' He reached over and seized her, pulling her hard back against him. 'You know what your body's telling you, Jana Reiss. Listen!'

This time the kiss was not gentle. His mouth enveloped hers, forcing her lips apart. His tongue demanded entrance. His hands searched for and found the separation of her blouse and soaking skirt. While one hand held the small of her back, allowing no escape, the other came around to cup her rounded breasts, teasing each nipple in turn, demanding a response.

The hands moved lower, pulling her thighs in to feel the urgency of his manhood, forcing her to acknowledge his desire.

Then they were somehow out of the shallows, on to the drier sand. Jana was no longer in control. Her body was moving of its own volition. As Iain pulled her down on to the sand she sank with him, unable to find the will to fight.

His kisses deepened, and Jana found herself responding with a fire she hadn't known her body was capable of. Her mouth moved to his, her tongue making an investigation of its own. As his hands moved against her thighs she felt her body arch in pleasure and desire. From a long way off she heard herself moan, in passion and pleasure.

Finally Iain pulled himself up, to hold himself at arm's length above her.

'You do want me, Dr Reiss. Admit it.' The laughter was back in his voice.

Jana put a finger up and traced the contours of his face. 'Iain. . .'

'Yes, my love?'

She shook her head, lost in a confusion of whirling emotion. He smiled down at her.

'We'd better get back,' he said regretfully. 'I told Sister we'd be half an hour and we've been considerably longer. Besides, if we stay here. . .' He didn't finish, but both knew what he was saying. Their soaked clothing lay between them, keeping their last vestige of control.

He stood up, reaching to pull her after him. 'Come on, my love. I don't want Sister sending a car to find us in this state.'

Jana looked down at herself, and then across at Iain. 'Whoops,' she said ruefully. Her voice sounded strange, unfamiliar.

'Whoops is right,' Iain said sagely. 'Now then, my lovely one, it's time for another dip.'

'Another one!'

He grinned. 'We can explain being soaked by a crazy impulse to have a swim. I'm darned if I can think of a reason why we're coated with sand from head to foot.' He tugged on her hand. 'Come on, or I'll have to use previous tactics.'

Jana came.

The walk back to the hospital was done in silence. Jana was too stunned to speak, still trying to come to terms with her emotions. What was this man doing to her? Iain held her hand lightly and seemed to be content with her silence.

As they neared the hospital Jana fought for her tongue.

'We can get into our flats from the back,' she said. She motioned to a path behind the hospital.

'I see,' Iain said. 'You've crept in this way before, Dr Reiss. After a small-hours tryst with the worthy Barry, no doubt.'

Jana stifled a giggle, and forced herself to speak stiffly.

'Goodnight,' she said formally. Iain's flat was on the other side of the hospital to hers.

'It doesn't have to be, you know,' Iain said gently.

'Yes, it does.' Unhappiness was in Jana's voice and Iain looked at her for a long moment.

'So be it,' he said at last. He leaned forward, tilted her chin with his fingers and kissed her lightly on the lips. Then he reached into his pocket and retrieved the salt-stained spectacles, resting them gently back on her nose. 'Here are your defences, my love,' he said softly. 'Guard them well.'

He was gone, striding swiftly over the grass. Jana was left staring after him, her safe, secure little world in tattered ribbons around her.

CHAPTER FOUR

CHRISTMAS EVE. Jana was awake before dawn, lying staring into the lessening dark.

Despite the emotional turmoil of the night before, she had slept almost as soon as she put her head on the pillow, driven to it by sheer exhaustion. Now her body's desperate need for sleep was satisfied. The emotions she had fallen asleep with returned, intensified by the solitude of dawn.

What was she doing? Falling in love with Iain Carisbrook, a man who two days ago she hadn't known existed?

Who was he? She knew nothing about him. Nothing. Dr Howard would be back in a few days and Iain would be free to move on. He was a man with no ties. . .

He was like her father. The thought hit her and cemented into certainty. The laughing eyes that she so mistrusted were the same. She thought back to the last time she had seen her father, when she was fifteen.

He had just heard of another 'golden opportunity', three days' drive away in the Northern Territory. There was little food in the house and Jana was the eldest of four, but her father had picked her mother up, swung her round and kissed her goodbye.

'You'll be right,' he had said confidently. He had

looked down and winked at his eldest daughter. 'Jana'll look after you.' Then he was gone. They had never heard from him again.

Mary Reiss had not depended on Jana. She had insisted that her daughter stay at school, though Jana had taken as many casual jobs as she could find while a scholarship helped put her through medicine.

Now Jana was no longer dependent on her mother, and could at last help to put the younger ones through school and university. For the first time for twenty years, Mary Reiss had been able to stop taking in other people's washing. Occasionally on her last few visits home, Jana had seen glimpses of the mother she thought she remembered from when she was tiny, a woman who was again free from overwhelming burdens and able to enjoy life just a little.

It gave Jana joy to see it, and she wasn't going to risk losing it. She couldn't. She had talked it over seriously with Barry and she knew she would have his support in continuing to help the younger ones. Barry took his responsibilities very seriously.

And here came Iain Carisbrook of the laughing eyes and dangerous smile, threatening to blast away all the security she had worked for.

Iain... She said his name softly to herself, her eyes closing as if in pain. The thought of his lips, his hands on her, made her stir restlessly against the soft linen. It was as if her body was searching, aching for what he was offering. She bit her lip, a tear trickling unchecked down her cheek. Life was so damned unfair.

Perhaps for herself she could take the risk, allow herself to fall deeply and irrevocably in love as her mother had done so disastrously thirty years before. But there were still the younger ones. Jana's brother had two years to go before finishing his engineering course, and behind him were the two girls.

Perhaps Iain was dependable too, she told herself. Perhaps she was being unfair.

She shook her head. Perhaps he was. And perhaps he wasn't. If she allowed herself to go any further it would be too late. Already she had been disloyal to Barry. The thought of last night brought colour sweeping over her. That she, the cool, sensible Jana Reiss could have allowed herself to be so carried away was unthinkable.

There was only one course of action open to her and the thought of what she must do left her feeling cold and forlorn. She climbed out of bed, trying to check the tears which were now flowing freely. She ran the shower and stood under the streaming water until she was sure that she had herself under control, that she had the strength to do what she had to.

She altered the pattern of her ward-round, knowing that Iain would probably be up and moving through the hospital wards as well. He had admitted his own patients yesterday and had assumed responsibility for those who were nominally under the care of Dr Howard.

Sophie Lanzo was in Jana's thoughts as she worked her way through the wards. Was she still in pain? she wondered. She shook her head, trying to shake the fog of depression and sadness welling within her. It was Christmas Eve, but the excitement and joy of Christmas seemed like a forgotten dream.

Her thoughts were broken by Iain entering the corridor. He looked totally confident and at ease, his face creasing into a smile of welcome as he saw her.

'Good morning, Dr Reiss. Have you got the sand out of your crevices?'

Jana bit her lip, refusing to respond to the intimacy of either his smile or his words. If she met his eyes she was caught. It wasn't fair that he was so good-looking, that just the sound of his voice could do such things to her.

Behind Iain was the open door of the children's ward from which he had just emerged.

'Good morning, Dr Carisbrook,' Jana said quietly, looking intently at a spot on the wall over his left shoulder. Taking a deep breath, she went on. 'I'd like to apologise for my behaviour last night. I was tired and overwrought, and perhaps I led you to make incorrect assumptions.'

Having said what she wanted to say, she ventured to look at him. The smile had faded. He was watching her with puzzlement and something else. Concern?

She didn't care. She looked away again towards the door of the children's ward and caught the eye of the nurse standing in the doorway.

'I'm on my way, Sister,' she called, breaking the feeling that there was just she and Iain in the corridor. Defiantly she moved forward and Iain stepped aside to let her past.

'What's wrong, my love?' he asked quietly.

Jana shook her head. 'There was something wrong last night,' she said with finality. 'This morning I've come to my senses.' She looked up at the nurse. 'Good morning, Sister,' she said, trying to assume a note of efficiency and dismissal of the man beside her. 'What have you got for me this morning?'

The day was endless. Jana worked in a haze of misery, trying to blot out Iain's presence, the sound of his laughter and the knowledge that he was watching her, wondering.

During Outpatients she could hear him, and as they emerged from their twin consulting-rooms they occasionally met. Worse was when the phone rang and it was Iain, wanting to know a brand name for a generic drug or a prescription quantity. To each of his queries she responded with rigid formality.

Her head ached. She tried to shrug off her feelings of fatigue and lethargy. It was as if she was working in a room filled with fog. Jana blamed it on the oppressive heat, but knew that not all the blame could be laid at its door.

The heat was certainly oppressive. Jana wondered how Charlie was going with his recruitment of tourists for firefighting duties. She wished him luck.

If only she could order the tourists off the beach, her workload would be cut in half. The temperature at midday was forty-two and still the beach was packed. In the mornings and late afternoons the beach was lovely, but at noon the sun was scorching and no amount of sunscreen could protect exposed skin. Outpatients consisted of a constant stream of sunburn victims, some a mass of blisters and vomiting with pain. Two were in so much pain that Jana had to admit them to hospital.

There was more than enough work for both doctors for Jana to be able to legitimately avoid Iain. As the day progressed, however, so did the level of tension within Jana. She found herself listening for the sound of him, watching for him to appear.

Barry phoned towards evening and she accepted gratefully his suggestion that they meet again for dinner. Once more they ate at the hotel, a meal during which Jana was preoccupied and silent.

'What's the matter?' Barry asked her as they finished their meal. Jana looked up at him with a guilty start. She hadn't heard a word he had been saying for the last ten minutes.

'I'm sorry,' she apologised. 'I'm just overtired, I guess.'

He nodded. 'This new doctor not pulling his weight?'

Jana flushed. 'That's unfair,' she said. 'There's a lot he can't do because he doesn't know the hospital or the routine, but he's doing all he can. And he is only working as a volunteer.'

Barry nodded thoughtfully. 'You think he's good?'

'Very good,' Jana said quietly.

'How would you feel if the board offered him a permanent job?'

Jana's eyes, wide with shock, flew to Barry's face. 'What. . .? What do you mean?'

Barry leaned back complacently, enjoying her

surprise. 'Frank Howard doesn't want to stay here,' he said. 'The board's known that for a while now. There's been general dissatisfaction with the level of commitment he gives to the town.' He looked in approval across to Jana. 'Especially compared with what you put in, my dear.'

Jana ignored the compliment. 'So?' she prodded.

'Well.' Barry took a last sip of his tea and eyed the empty cup regretfully. 'The chairman of the board dropped in to the shop this morning and asked whether we shouldn't offer this young man the job.'

Jana smiled in spite of herself. 'Barry, when you speak like this you sound about a hundred. Iain Carisbrook is probably older than you.'

Barry smiled benignly across the table. 'Well,' he said expansively, 'what I lack in years I make up for in experience.'

Jana choked into her cup of tea, but managed to turn her splutters into a convincing cough.

'Well?' Barry asked. 'What do you think? It would give the board considerable pleasure to write to Frank Howard and give him notice.'

It would give Jana pleasure too. Frank Howard was lazy and bordering on incompetent. The town had put up with him because there was no choice. Now, though. . .

There was still no choice. She shook her head. 'Iain wouldn't want to stay here,' she said.

'We can only ask,' Barry said decisively. 'Ask him tonight. Or I will, if you like.' He hesitated, considering. 'Perhaps it would be better coming from a member of the board.'

'I'll do it,' Jana said hurriedly. Her mind froze at the thought. What if he accepted?

He wouldn't. Surely he wouldn't travel all the way from England to settle in a place such as Carrabookna.

But if he did? The thought filled her with panic. For a moment she considered telling Barry that the man was incompetent. She couldn't. If Iain could be persuaded to stay, then Carrabookna would be the richer. And Jana? Safely married to Barry but having to watch Iain live and work in the town, to work beside him, to perhaps watch him fall in love and marry someone else. . .

She stood up and said, in a voice not quite steady, 'I'll have to get back now, Barry. The fire engines will be coming down soon.'

They walked out together, each looking almost instinctively up at the mountains as they came into the open. The dull orange glow still showed through the smoke-filled dusk.

'It's time we got a wind change,' Barry said worriedly.

Jana nodded, trying to regain some composure. 'The men have had enough,' she said quietly. 'And I hate to think what the forest will be like when it's over.'

'Or how our cash registers will be,' Barry said drily. 'Christmas usually brings hundreds of visitors into the town. Those trapped here are running out of money and we aren't getting replacements.'

Jana bit her lip. The state of Barry's cash register was the last of her concerns at the moment.

The work of attending to exhausted firefighters

was becoming almost routine, Jana thought, as she searched for an elusive piece of debris in a man's eye an hour later. She welcomed the steady flow of work. Engrossed in the needs of these weary men she could ignore the turmoil in her mind, even block out her overpowering awareness of Iain's presence treating a patient in the next cubicle.

She located the carbon particle triumphantly. It was tiny but had been causing the man misery for the last few hours.

'It's scratched the eye,' she told him. 'I've got it out but it'll feel as if it's still in there for a day or so. I'd like you away from the ridge tomorrow. It's going to be sore enough without filling it with smoke again.'

'They need every man they can get,' the firefighter protested.

'There'll be enough to manage without you being a martyr,' she told her patient severely.

'Well, if you say so, Doc.' He grinned ruefully at her. 'I'll feel a bit guilty having Christmas dinner down here while the blokes are still up on the ridge.'

'Perhaps there'll be a wind change in the night,' Jana said optimistically. 'Wouldn't it be great to wake up to an easterly gale?'

'It's on my Santa list,' the man agreed.

'Well, I hope you've been good,' Jana smiled. Finished, she straightened and looked around. This man was the last for the night.

'Where's Charlie?' The thought suddenly occurred to her that she hadn't seen the fire chief that night. He always dropped in to check on his men.

'I haven't seen him.' Jana's patient looked up, frowning in concentration. 'I thought he must have come down on an earlier engine.'

Jana shook her head. 'If he'd come down earlier he'd have been in, or at least rung to find out what the injuries were for the day.' She turned to the sister at the desk. 'Ring his home,' she said, frowning in sudden anxiety.

He wasn't there. The nurse put the phone down, her face creasing in worry.

'I've upset his wife,' she confessed. 'She thought he'd be here.'

The others in Casualty had been listening in. Jana hesitated, unsure as to what course of action to take and, as she tried to get her thoughts in order, Iain walked over and picked up the phone.

'I'll ring through to the police station,' he said. 'They'll have a radio link back up to the ridge.'

Twenty minutes later, when the police called back to the hospital, no one had left. The men who had been treated were lingering, waiting for the phone to ring or for Charlie to walk in. Jana sat at the desk and worried. The thought of the tired face of the elderly fire chief rose before her. She knew he loved his job, but the responsibility of the last few days should surely have been shouldered by a younger man.

Iain answered the phone when it finally rang. After listening for a couple of moments he replaced the receiver and turned back to the room full of waiting people.

'He's not with the team on the ridge, but he hasn't come down. The police have checked every driver.'

There was a long silence in the room. Finally a man spoke up, his voice hesitant.

'I don't suppose he would have gone out along the goat track?'

'The goat track?' Iain voiced the query.

'It's a rough track leading back from the ridge.' The man frowned in concentration. 'The chief was saying at lunch that if this wind didn't change by morning we'd have to start back burning along there. He wanted to know if it was clear. It's been unused since logging was stopped in the national park.'

'And he might have gone along to check?'

'Yeah.' The man's voice firmed into certainty. 'Yeah, he might have. He had Bruce Hogg's little four-wheel-drive truck this morning. It's smaller than the department vehicles, and easier to turn on the narrow tracks. You could ring Bruce and see whether he's returned it.'

Iain proffered the phone to the man. 'You do it.'

The truck hadn't been returned. Jana felt herself go cold as the implications of the news hit.

'What's the state of the fire along the goat track?' she asked quietly. 'Is it threatening?'

'No.' The men shook their heads decisively and Jana let her breath out in a sigh of relief. Instinctively she turned to Iain.

'I'll ring back through to the police. Someone will check it,' he said, his voice authoritative and sure. He turned back to address the men. 'There's nothing we can do now except wait for news,' he said. 'Why don't you take yourselves down to the pub? We'll ring through as soon as we hear anything. And if he turns up here having spent the afternoon Christmas shopping we'll send him on down to you with a flea in his ear.'

The men smiled and went out. Their smiles were perfunctory, however. They knew their chief, and they knew that something was badly wrong.

With the cleaning up finished the nurses also left. Jana and Iain were left alone in the deserted Casualty area.

'Why don't you go to bed?' Iain suggested, looking over at Jana's tense face. 'I'll stay here until we hear and I'll call you if I need you. Chances are he's just had a breakdown.'

'The truck will have a radio in it,' Jana said shortly. 'They wouldn't have it up on the ridge if it didn't.'

Iain was silent.

'There's still no use in our both staying up,' he said finally. 'Go to bed, Jana.'

She shook her head stubbornly. 'I wouldn't sleep. You go.'

He smiled faintly. 'I wouldn't sleep either.'

Jana looked at him for a long moment, unsure. She couldn't stay here with him. 'I'll go to my office and get some more paperwork done,' she said briefly.

He nodded. 'That's a good way to spend Christmas Eve, Dr Reiss. Ploughing through paperwork, waiting to hear of the fate of a friend and avoiding the man you're going to marry.'

Jana gasped. 'I'm not going to marry you!' she said, as her breath returned.

Iain raised his eyebrows in polite enquiry. He said nothing.

'I don't even know you,' Jana said angrily. 'You're being ridiculous.'

'Am I?' he said softly. 'I don't know you, Jana, but I know what I felt last night.' His hands came up and gripped her shoulders. 'I know what I feel now. I don't know your age in years and months. I don't know whether you sleep in curlers or whether you eat spinach, but. . .' He hesitated and looked down into her face. 'I know that I love you.'

Jana made an angry gesture of denial. 'How can you love me?' she demanded. 'It's crazy.'

'How can I not?' he smiled. 'And how can you not love me. This thing between us. . .' He hesitated. 'Look, OK, it's crazy, but it's there. It's happened whether we like it or not.'

'Oh, yes? And how many women has it happened with before me?' She flung the question at him as if it was a poisoned barb.

His face darkened. The lean contours of his face went still.

'Jana, I'm not going to answer that,' he said quietly. 'If you're asking whether you're the first and only woman I've ever looked at then I'll tell you that I'm thirty-two and you're being ridiculous. If you're asking me to tell you that you can trust me, though, then there's nothing I can say. I know how I feel and what I'm offering. It's up to you to find the courage to trust, to know that this is something that has never happened before and will never happen again.'

Jana said nothing. She couldn't. Her voice wouldn't operate. Finally Iain broke the long silence between them.

'Tell me, Jana, what does Barry offer that is so irresistible?' Iain's voice was harsh and insistent. 'Do you love him?' He gripped her shoulders hard. His smile faded. 'If you tell me you love him, that this thing that I'm feeling is how you feel about Barry, then I'll get out of your life. Can you honestly tell me that?'

'Barry cares for me,' Jana said disjointedly. 'Neither of us believes in romantic love. All it creates is misery, and mismatching. Barry will be a reliable, kind husband and help me support my family...'

'Your family?'

'My mother, my brother and sisters.'

'And I wouldn't?' Iain asked quietly.

'I don't know.' It was a cry of pain. She broke from him and turned away. 'They depend on me, you see, my family. My father left us.' She took a deep breath. 'My father loved us, or he said he did. He made us laugh and he kissed my mother and could make her smile even when she was hungry, but still he left us. That's romantic love.'

'And it's not for you?'

'No.' Jana was crying now, tears slipping helplessly between her fingers. 'Iain, I don't know what's happening to me. I've never felt like this before.' She took a deep breath and turned to face him. 'All

I know is that it's the same thing that happened to my mother and I don't want it.'

'You don't want me?'

She shook her head. 'No, Iain. I don't want you.'

He was silent for a minute, watching the bowed head before him. Finally he reached out and touched her hair lightly.

'In a few days Dr Howard will be back and you'll never have to see me again,' he said quietly. 'Will that make you happy? Will it, Jana?'

She looked up. He was smiling tenderly down at her and her breath caught on a sob. He reached down to hold her but she pulled back.

'Please Iain... No.' There was something else she had to say, though, and it might as well be now.

'Iain, you don't have to go,' she said abruptly, still standing back from him.

His eyes looked a question.

'The board wants me to offer you a job,' she said hurriedly. 'Dr Howard's only here temporarily and the board are desperate to find a replacement. They asked me to offer you the job.'

His face was still. 'Do you want me to stay?' he asked finally.

'No.' It was a cry from the heart. Despite himself Iain smiled.

'And yet, I could be happy here,' he told her. 'I love the bush and the sea. I've never been happy in city medicine, and this is the sort of place I dreamed of all the time I practised in London. I could do enough surgery to keep my hand in and the hospital's efficient and well-run. And I get on exceptionally well with my medical colleague.'

'If you mean me, you do not,' Jana said harshly. 'You spend your time treating life as a joke. Medicine's a serious profession.'

'And it's wrong to laugh?' Iain asked. 'I could teach you a lot, Jana Reiss.'

'I don't want to learn,' Jana said desperately. 'Iain, you can't stay.' Her voice was almost a wail.

He eyed her, consideringly. 'I'll have to think about it,' he said finally. 'It's a very interesting offer.'

Jana closed her eyes. 'I'm not staying to listen to this,' she said. 'I'll be in my office.' She walked out of the room, aware of his eyes following her through the door.

It was like a cat-and-mouse game, she thought savagely, sitting behind the paperwork at her desk. It was as if he was playing with her. Somehow he held her by an invisible thread, and could play with her emotions as if they were visible to all.

Jana stared down at the work in front of her, her pen idle in her hand. Anything she did tonight she would have to repeat tomorrow. She wondered where Iain had gone to wait, and shoved the thought aside with fury. What Iain Carisbrook did was no concern of hers and never would be. Marriage! Surely it was another of his jokes, and a sick one at that? She put her head down on her arms and closed her eyes.

She was asleep when the knock on her door finally came. She started guiltily and looked at her watch. Two a.m.

'Yes,' she called.

A nurse put her head around the door. 'Dr Carisbrook asked me to fetch you,' she said. 'They've found Charlie. They're bringing him down now.'

'What's wrong?' Jana's voice was sharp with anxiety. Charlie had been a friend ever since Jana had arrived in this town.

'They're not sure. They found him semi-conscious on the track beside his truck.'

Jana bit her lip. It could be any of a number of things.

Iain was back in Casualty and one glance told Jana that there was little she had to do now besides wait. Iain was ready for any eventuality. An impressive array of equipment stood ready. As she went to wash, Jana sent up a silent prayer that they'd need none of it. Even as she sent it up, she acknowledged to herself the futility of the hope. She had just finished drying her hands when a fast-moving vehicle turned into the hospital yard, its brakes screeching.

Charlie was conscious as they wheeled him in to casualty, his eyes glazed with pain. He managed a weak smile at Jana. On his other side Iain was already cutting away clothing, baring his arm for a drip. As the arm was bared he handed the scissors over to Sister, who moved with practised precision. By the colour of Charlie's skin there was no time for careful undressing.

'Tell me where it hurts, Charlie?' Jana bent over him, trying to focus his attention on her. Behind her the nurses were wheeling the trolley with the ECG machine into position.

'My chest. . .' It was a pain-racked whisper. 'Feels as if it's being crushed. In my arms, my neck. . .' His voice tailed off.

Jana gave a sharp order for morphine. She reached to start attaching the wires for an ECG.

'It's my heart?' The whisper started again.

'I think so,' Jana told him. She took his hand and held it firm, signalling the sister to keep attaching the wires. 'We're just giving you something for the pain. It'll ease soon.'

He shook his head, a weak tear trickling down his rough cheek.

'I'm dying. I can feel it.'

Jana shook her head. 'Charlie, let's fight this,' she said. 'You can do it.'

'You fight it for me,' Charlie said. His voice was a thread from a long way away. Jana had to bend her head to hear what he was saying. 'I'm too tired.' He closed his eyes.

Jana stared down at him. 'Charlie!' Her voice rose in shock. 'Iain!'

Iain let the drip fall from his fingers and started urgently, automatically, attaching the leads of the monitor. Jana was already shoving her fists down on to Charlie's chest. She came down hard, pounding, fighting to restore the rhythm in the failing heart.

'One, two, three, four. . .' She started counting, her mind blanking every thought other than the rhythm. Iain manoeuvred the leads of the monitor around her pumping hands and flicked the switch. Jana glanced briefly over at the tiny screen, keeping her rhythm as she did so. There was nothing there. The heart was floppy and lifeless.

'One, two, three, four...'

Beside her Iain injected intravenous adrenalin, then reached swiftly for the mask and bag. With the mask over his face, Charlie's chest started to respond as air was pumped in.

'One, two, three, four... One, two, three, four.' Jana was putting all her strength into what she was doing. Sweat was pouring down her white face. Where was her professional detachment? she wondered savagely, blinking back the tears that threatened to cloud her vision. 'One, two, three, four.'

She bit her lip and kept pumping. Over and over. At Charlie's head Iain operated the bag, his eyes not leaving the screen, desperately searching for some flicker of activity that meant the heart might respond to their efforts.

For fifteen minutes or more they worked. Around them were the men who had brought Charlie in, the nurses, and finally his wife, supported by her daughters, weeping with fear.

It was no use. Finally Iain reached out and held Jana's hands still.

'Enough,' he said quietly. 'Let him go.'

Jana caught her breath on a sob. She looked down at the man who had been her friend and quietly reached forward to touch his face.

'Goodbye, Charlie,' she said softly. Then she turned around to tell his wife that he was dead.

An hour later, having walked Charlie's still stunned wife and daughters to their car, Jana returned to Casualty to find Iain waiting for her. The rest of the people involved in the drama of the last couple of hours had dispersed. As she walked inside, Iain put his hands on her shoulders, kissing her lightly on the hair. Jana had no strength left in her to fight.

'You do take this job to heart,' Iain said quietly, looking down into her grief filled eyes.

'Charlie was my friend,' she said simply. She looked up wonderingly into the tired blue eyes above her. 'Besides, I didn't hear your customary laughter, Dr Carisbrook.'

'I only met him once,' Iain said. 'I would have liked the chance to know him better.'

The words were simply said, but Jana, searching his face, knew them for the truth. Looking up at him, she also knew another truth. This man had integrity and kindness. This man she could trust with her life.

'Jana. . .'

'No.' She broke away from his hold. 'Iain, please. No more. I can't take any more.' She broke on a sub and turned and fled.

CHAPTER FIVE

JANA woke late to the phone's insistent ring. The sun was already streaming into her bedroom window. She groped for consciousness as her hand searched for the phone beside her bed.

'Hello.' Her voice was still blurred with sleep.

'Merry Christmas, my dear.' It was Barry.

Christmas. Jana rolled over and looked at the clock. Eight o'clock. There was so much to do. . .

'Are you there?' Barry's voice sharpened.

'Yes. . . Yes, sorry, Barry.' She caught herself. 'Merry Christmas.' She hesitated. 'I'm sorry. We had a bad night last night. Charlie Simpkin died.'

'I know,' Barry said steadily. Of course he would, Jana thought bitterly. There was little in this town that Barry missed. 'He's going to be a great loss to the community,' he continued solemnly. 'A great loss.'

'And besides that, we'll miss him,' Jana said quietly. She sat up in bed. 'Thank you for calling, Barry. If I'm going to get to your place for lunch I have to go now. The hospital's full.'

'I'll pick you up at twelve.' Tragedy shelved, Barry's jovial voice returned. 'Merry Christmas,' he repeated.

Jana dressed slowly. She pulled on her normal serviceable skirt and white blouse, then stood looking at herself for a long time in the mirror. Was this how she would look for the rest of her life?

On top of her wardrobe was a box, her mother's Christmas gift to her twelve months before. She pulled it down and lifted the lid. It was a brilliant crimson dress, with shoestring shoulder-straps, a clinging bodice and a full circular skirt sweeping out from the waist. Around the hem of the skirt was a wide border of white reindeers, Santa Clauses, bells and holly. It was a totally frivolous dress, meant only for Christmas Day. Jana had thought her mother crazy to make it for her. She had worn it the previous Christmas to appease her mother's feelings and then had shoved it away. Now, in sudden decision she pulled off her skirt and blouse, replacing them with the dress.

It felt strange. She stared into the mirror at her unaccustomedly bare shoulders. It looked wrong.

Tentatively she put her hand up and removed her glasses. She really only needed them for reading. Then she pulled out the clips holding her knot of hair severely in place. Black curls cascaded on to her shoulders. Her green eyes stared back from the mirror in her pale face. The red dress fell around her in soft folds, accentuating the curves of her figure. Jana took a deep breath, slipped on some white sandals, then walked quickly out of her apartment before she could change her mind. After all, it was Christmas.

She did a slow ward-round. The hospital was already full of visitors—the normal ten a.m. start for visiting time had been waived for Christmas Day. Beds were littered with layers of wrapping paper and ribbons, and the normal crisp efficiency of early morning in the hospital was non-existent.

Iain was nowhere to be seen. As Jana approached each ward her heart stilled, expecting him to be there, and as she left she was certain that he would be in the next room.

When she reached the children's ward she opened the door expectantly. It took her several moments to ascertain that Iain was not there. It seemed as if most of Carrabookna was. The Christmas tree in the centre of the ward was surrounded by a mountain of discarded wrapping paper and sick children, parents, brothers and sisters, aunts, grandpas and second cousins twice removed were turning the ward into a huge party.

She made her way from bed to bed with difficulty, admiring train sets, building blocks and new dolls as she went. By the time she reached the far end of the ward she had quite a collection of gifts herself, presented to 'Dr Jana' by the children. They loved her dress, and their pleasure in it made her almost feel comfortable with her new image.

There was still no sign of Iain.

He had to be somewhere. He couldn't have walked out because she had offended him.

She caught herself. Still she was aligning him with her father. The thought came to her with sudden crystal clarity, making her stop dead in the corridor as she left the children's ward. She had loved her father and he had left. She loved Iain and therefore she expected him to leave.

She loved Iain. . . The words went round and round in her mind, making her head ache with confusion. Love. What was it?

She closed her eyes and took a grip on herself.

She was tired and emotionally overwrought, she told herself savagely. Charlie's death the night before had shocked and upset her. She was in no condition to make any emotional decisions.

Her last patient for the morning was Ben McKenzie. He was old and dying slowly of cancer. A garrulous, belligerent man all his life, he had been made even more so by his illness, and he refused to co-operate with anyone trying to help. He had to be held down to be washed and had been known to hurl plates of food at the ward-maid if the food didn't take his fancy. With no family, and after six months of illness, he was almost totally isolated.

Jana took a deep breath before entering the old man's single room. She was used to his abuse, but this morning it was all she could do to make herself open the door. Be cheerful, she told herself grimly. Don't let him upset you this morning. She pushed open the door and discovered Iain, perched on the end of the bed.

He looked up as she entered, the remembered smile lurking behind his eyes.

'Well, well, well. Here's our Dr Reiss,' he told the old man. 'At least, I think it's our Dr Reiss.' He stood up, his face alight with admiration and approval. 'Wow!' He turned back to the old man. 'I suppose we have to forgive her for being late when she comes in looking like this.'

To Jana's amazement Ben's face creased into a grin. For a moment she was stunned into silence.

'Merry Christmas,' she finally made herself say. She looked down at the tray in front of Ben. There was a chess set, obviously new, with a sheet of wrapping paper on the bed-cover denoting it as a Christmas gift. A game was well under way. 'Am I disturbing something?' she asked weakly.

'Not at all,' Iain said expansively. 'Just try and put Ben off his game, will you, and give me a chance?'

The frail old man gave a throaty chuckle and Jana smiled in delight.

'I wouldn't dream of it,' she told them. She turned to Ben. 'Dr Carisbrook could do with being taken down a peg or two,' she told him firmly. 'Feel free to wipe him off the board. I'll leave you to it.' She motioned to the chart at the end of the bed. 'If you're not too devastated when you finally lose,' she asked Iain, 'could you check Ben's chart?'

Iain nodded. 'Actually,' he said, 'Ben and I have just been discussing a change of doctor.'

Jana raised her eyebrows and waited. To her surprise it was Ben himself who spoke.

'This young feller wants to learn how to play decent chess,' he explained. 'If he treats me instead of you we could keep a permanent game going.' He hesitated. 'Not that I'm ungrateful to you, girl,' he added. 'I wouldn't want to hurt your feelings.'

This, from a man who the previous morning had called her a 'bloody quack'. Jana took a deep breath, fighting for a straight face. Then the implications of Ben's words sank home and the desire to laugh faded as if it had never been. Her eyes flew to Iain's face.

'Does this mean you're staying?'

Iain was seated on the bed again, concentrating

on an obviously troublesome pawn, but at her query he looked up.

'Why, yes, Dr Reiss. It does mean that I'm staying. I had a long think about it last night and decided that this place has everything that I've been looking for.' His eyes met hers, challengingly. 'Everything.'

There was a long silence. Ben turned his attention to the board and it was he who finally broke the stillness.

'You know, young feller, I shouldn't give you hints but because it's Christmas I'll tell you. If you move that pawn, you're going to get done.'

Jana walked out and left them to it.

Iain found her an hour later when he came to see how Outpatients was faring. It was quiet. Jana had seen one cut knee from a new skateboard and one toddler who'd swallowed a building block, but the usual queue of patients was missing. The population of Carrabookna was obviously too busy trying out Christmas presents to be worried about getting sick.

'Finished already?' he said lightly. 'Sorry. I got engrossed in the game.'

'I don't mind,' she said steadily. 'It was a joy to see Ben actually smiling. What on earth blessed you with the insight to give him a chess set?'

He tapped his forehead. 'Pure genius.' Then, at her look of incredulity, he laughed and relented. 'Actually, I've been asking all the older locals who've come my way if they knew anything he was interested in. One of the firefighters said his dad used to play chess with him.'

Jana shook her head. 'Thank you for your care,' she said quietly. 'He's been troubling me.'

'I know.'

Jana flushed. He was watching her steadily, his eyes sending their own message.

'What did you mean back there?' she asked, forcing the question out. She turned to face away from the watchful eyes. 'Iain, you can't stay here.'

'I can stay,' he said firmly. 'I've been offered a job by the board and I intend to accept.'

'But it wouldn't work.'

'Why not?' He rose and put his hands on her bare shoulders. Her body stiffened at his touch. 'Why not, my lovely Jana? Because you can't relax when I'm here? Because you can't pretend you're an emotionless woman when I'm around? Because you can't marry Barry if I stay?'

Jana gasped and pulled away. 'Don't be ridiculous.' She turned to face him. 'Of course I can marry Barry. Who do you think you are, judging me and my relationships?'

'I'm the man who loves you,' Iain said calmly. He made no move to touch her again and she stood glaring at him. 'I'm the man who loves you before he knows you, before he's decided whether it's sensible or not.' He hesitated and then held out his hands. 'Jana, I don't want you because you'll make me a suitable wife, or because you make great sponge cakes or because we make a great medical team. Or. . .' He hesitated, his eyes resting on her face, his look a caress. 'Or because you're the most beautiful woman I've ever known. I want you only because I want you. I trust you only because I trust you and I love you only because I love you.'

Jana shook her head helplessly. 'You're crazy. It doesn't make sense.'

'So you keep saying,' he said gently. He reached for her. Jana was caught, held by, lost in the depths of tenderness in his eyes. She took a hesitant step to take his hands but stopped as the silence around them was broken. Footsteps and the sound of Barry's voice in the corridor announced that they were no longer alone.

He came in accompanied by one of the nurses, bearing a vast box of chocolates.

'There you are.' He frowned, suddenly taking in the different appearance of his intended. 'What on earth are you wearing?'

Jana smiled self-consciously and touched her dress. 'My Christmas dress. Do you like it?'

'It's a bit juvenile,' he said shortly. 'It's not the sort of thing a woman in your position should wear.' Then he shrugged and smiled. 'Never mind. It's Christmas.' He kissed Jana soundly on the cheek. 'Are you ready, my dear? Mother's just put the vegetables on.'

Jana cast a look at Iain, then nodded. 'I'm ready,' she said quietly.

'I've just got to drop these off to the children's ward,' Barry said jovially, gesturing towards the chocolates he was holding. He held out his arm to Jana. 'Coming with me while I play Santa Claus?'

Jana looked at the chocolates with dismay. The ward had been awash with sweets since early this morning. Any more and she'd have children making themselves ill.

'You know, Barry, the children have had an awful lot,' she said gently. 'Every organisation in the town has contributed something to the children's ward for Christmas. I know who'd appreciate it a lot more.'

'Who?' His voice was suspicious.

'The old people in the nursing home.' She tucked her hand persuasively into his arm. 'You know, there are people there who aren't going to have a visitor today. Your chocolates would be really appreciated.'

'Well. . .' He looked down, reluctant to lose the vision of himself as Santa Claus. 'If you say so.' He thrust the box at the nurse who had brought him to Casualty. 'You deliver them,' he said uninterestedly. Then he turned to Iain. 'Did Jana give you our offer?' The chocolates forgotten, he was off on another tack.

'If you mean the job offer, yes, she did,' Iain replied. 'Thank you, I intend to take it.'

Barry beamed, his good humour restored. 'Well.' He rubbed his hands. 'That's excellent.' Another thought occurred to him. 'What are you doing now?' he demanded.

'Now?' Iain looked a query.

'Now. Are you eating in the hospital?'

'I suppose so,' Iain said slowly. 'I hadn't thought. . .'

'Come and have your Christmas dinner with us,' Barry said expansively. 'Mother's got more than enough. She'll be delighted to meet you.'

Iain's eyes met Jana's. She opened her mouth to speak but he forestalled her.

'Thank you.' He smiled. 'I'd love to.'

It was the longest meal Jana had ever sat through. The formal dining-room was stifling, with every window firmly shut.

'I can't bear the smell of smoke,' Mrs Fitzsimmons explained. 'It's everywhere in this town. It's even in Barry's clothes when he comes home. Besides, with the north wind the dust gets on to everything.'

Jana thought longingly of her mother, her brother and her sisters. Christmas at home, now money wasn't quite as tight, was something to save for and savour. They would be settled at the table and chairs under the big old gum tree in the backyard eating crayfish, cold hams and salads, with champagne stored in a bucket of crushed ice under the table. There would still be the pudding, their only concession to the traditional meal, but it would be served with lashings of ice-cream.

Here there was hot vegetable soup, with a dry sherry to accompany it. A vast turkey, far too much for them even to make an impression on, was brought to the table to be attacked ceremoniously by Barry with a carving knife. Barry heaped their plates, then divided the tureens of vegetables fairly into four, pumpkin, turnip, cauliflower, peas and huge, soggy roast potatoes.

Jana waded through as much as she could manage, grateful only for the fact that Barry's constant flow of small talk enabled her to keep silent, her attention fixed firmly on her dinner rather than on the gently mocking eyes of the big, fair-haired man at the end of the table.

'What's the matter, my love?' Barry asked solicitously as his mother cleared the plates. 'Saving room for pudding?'

Jana nodded, her heart sinking as she saw the size of the pudding.

'Do we have to watch for sixpences?' Iain smiled, and Barry shook his head decisively.

'We would have put them in if children were coming, wouldn't we, Mother.'

Jana took a deep breath, took a sip of the seemingly endless supply of horrible sherry and started on her pudding.

The phone rang as the teapot was brought in, signalling the end of the meal. Jana looked up hopefully. She almost wanted an emergency. Barry answered it and handed it over to Iain. 'The hospital,' he said shortly.

Iain stood and took the receiver, listening intently. He replaced it and turned to Jana.

'One of the drips in the children's ward has packed up,' he told her. 'I'll go back.'

Jana stood up, pushing her chair back. 'I'll go.'

Iain shook his head. 'My patient,' he said, smiling. His eyes held a sardonic gleam. 'You enjoy the festivities,' he told her. 'I'll ring if I need you.'

They did the dishes together, with Barry washing, Jana drying and Mrs Fitzsimmons anxiously examining her precious china for damage before she packed it away again for next year.

'I'm off to have a nap now,' the older woman announced as the last precious piece disappeared from view. 'Why don't you two young things go for a walk and get yourselves an appetite for tea?' Clearly she wanted her house to herself again.

Barry smiled benignly down at Jana. 'Would you like to?' he asked. 'Or would you prefer to sit quietly and listen to some Christmas music?'

All Jana wanted to do was to get out of the stuffy little house. The heat was overpowering.

Outside the wind was blowing strongly, the air laden with dust and smoke. Jana looked upward dubiously. The sun was completely hidden.

'That's cloud cover,' she said slowly. 'It's too thick for smoke. Do you think we could be in for a weather change?'

Barry looked up as well and shook his head. 'Who knows?' he said ponderously. 'With our luck the north wind will blow for another fortnight and we'll miss the entire summer tourist season.'

Jana frowned in distaste. Barry's attitude to the fire was entirely commercial.

They walked down the road to the inlet where boats were moored on the scores of little wooden jetties. The inlet was deserted. The town was sleeping off its combined Christmas pudding.

'I didn't get you a gift,' Barry said finally. He hesitated. 'Actually,' he admitted, 'this fire has interfered with my plans in more ways than one.'

'Oh?'

'I was going to ask you to marry me,' Barry said. 'I had it all planned, but then the fire came through and I couldn't get to Melbourne to buy the ring.'

'Can't you ask me to marry you before getting the ring?' Jana asked, smiling.

'I can't do that,' Barry exclaimed, shocked. 'It wouldn't be right.'

'It wouldn't be right.' The words hung in the air between them.

Jana took a deep breath. Three days ago her future had seemed absolutely settled. Now her world had been torn into a tangle of conflicting emotions. All she knew, for certain, was that she could no longer enter an emotionless marriage with Barry. Not with Iain mocking from the sidelines. Gently she told the man at her side that his question should not be asked.

To her surprise, Barry seemed neither hurt nor, after the first moments, unduly disappointed.

'It's not as if you're breaking off an engagement,' he said, clearly relieved that things hadn't gone so far. 'Mother will be upset.'

'Mother will be upset.' The words resounded round and round in Jana's head, making her feel almost giddy with relief. Barry had planned to marry her as the 'sensible thing to do'.

'I'm not sure,' Jana said finally. 'I don't think she relishes the thought of another woman in her house.'

Barry nodded. 'I'm lucky to have her,' he said gravely. He turned to face her. 'If I didn't have her to look after me I'd be a lot more upset at your decision, my dear.'

'Why?' Jana asked curiously.

'Well, a man needs a woman to look after him,'

Barry said seriously. 'And it has to be said that Mother's getting on.'

'Oh, I'm sure there are plenty of years of service left in your mother yet,' Jana assured him, trying to suppress her inward laughter and relief. 'And you can rest assured that she'll always get the very best of medical attention.'

He grasped her hands gratefully. 'I'm sure she will,' he said. 'And, even if we can't be man and wife, as pharmacist and doctor I'll always value our professional relationship.'

Jana agreed gravely and they turned to walk back to the house.

Mrs Fitzsimmons was out on the front porch waiting for them, clearly annoyed at having been woken from her nap. 'Dr Carisbrook is on the phone,' she said curtly to Jana.

Jana walked inside swiftly to take the call. What she wanted now was an excuse to leave.

Iain gave her one, but when she knew what it was she would have preferred to stay and sit through Mrs Fitzsimmons' afternoon tea.

'Jana?' Iain's voice was curt and to the point. 'Nick Lanzo's just rung. Sophie's collapsed. The ambulance is bringing her in now. Can you come?'

CHAPTER SIX

JANA spent the drive back to the hospital trying to get her mind back into working order. Regardless of whether it was a tumour or a cyst, if Sophie had collapsed in pain then they would surely have to perform exploratory surgery. If Sophie would let them. . .

Whatever it was, the last thing Sophie needed now was a doctor whose mind was not a hundred per cent on her job. Jana shook her head bleakly. Sophie hadn't even had her Christmas before this thing had overtaken her.

The ambulance arrived at the hospital just before her. Iain was standing at the entrance, white-coated and ready. He came forward and was reaching to open the vehicle doors as the ambulance drew to a halt.

Jana parked her car and followed the trolley and its attendants in to the hospital. Sophie was lying in a crouched position, sobbing with fright and pain. At her side walked Nick, white and shocked and stumbling in his fear.

As Iain supervised, the orderlies wheeled Sophie straight into Theatre. A nurse led Nick away. His terror was palpable in the little room and he was very close to collapsing himself. As he left, supported by the nurse, Iain drew back the cover from the distraught woman and together he and Jana cut away the loose frock she was wearing.

As the soft folds fell away they both stared in amazement and disbelief. A strong contraction was holding Sophie in its grip.

Iain put his stethoscope to the tight, hard belly and listened. His face broke into a wide grin and he transferred the instrument to Jana's ears. Jana listened, first with disbelief and then with growing joy and acceptance. She heard what Iain had heard. From deep within Sophie's swollen, contracting belly came the strong heartbeat of a healthy child waiting to be born.

'It's definitely a tumour,' Iain said, almost under his breath. His voice was filled with wonder. 'A growth of new tissue. Sophie has the fastest-growing tumour known to man. A child.'

Jana closed her eyes. The build-up of emotions over the past few days surfaced in a flood of relief and joy. Tears poured down her cheeks and she let them go unchecked.

As the next contraction passed Iain went to the head of the bed and took Sophie's hands tightly in his. Her eyes were wild with fear and pain, and her body was rocking from side to side.

'Sophie.' He raised his voice, trying to force her to listen. 'Sophie!'

Sophie caught her breath on a sob and ceased her rolling, held by Iain's voice.

'Sophie, you have to stop throwing yourself about.' His voice gentled as he knew he had her attention. 'Sophie, you haven't got cancer. You have a baby in there, Sophie. There is absolutely nothing wrong with you. The pain you are feeling is a baby trying to be born.'

There was absolute silence in the little theatre. Jana's tears still flowed. As she looked at Iain's strong hands grasping Sophie's, reassuring her and giving her strength, she felt her own fears dissolve, her own uncertainties disappear. The miracles of life and death and love. . . She had known them all in the last twenty-four hours. The miracle of love. . .

'A baby. . .' Sophie's voice was a terrified whisper. Then she was caught again as the next contraction took hold. This time, however, she didn't roll. She returned the grip of Iain's hands and held on as if she was drowning. Jana wiped the back of her hand impatiently across her eyes and moved to check dilation, but there was no need. The head was already crowning.

She looked up to the nurse standing in shocked amazement beside her.

'Bring Mr Lanzo back,' she managed to say, her voice breaking with sheer happiness. 'Fast.'

One minute later Nick Lanzo walked back into the theatre just in time to see his perfect little daughter enter the world.

Half an hour later Sophie was wheeled out of Theatre, still weak and shocked but gently cradling her precious bundle against her breast. Nick walked beside her, his chest expanded by at least a third in the last half-hour. They were stunned, they were exhausted and they were parents.

Iain and Jana cleared their equipment and washed silently. So much had happened in the last few hours that Jana had trouble taking it in.

'Sophie must have been in labour for two days,' Jana said slowly as they finished at the sinks. 'She must have been going through hell.'

Iain smiled. 'I think she'll vote it worthwhile now,' he said. 'I've never seen two prouder parents.'

Jana shook her head. 'I still can't believe it.' The sound of an infant's soft cry emanating from the nearby ward made her smile. There was nothing unreal about the newest Lanzo. 'Why on earth didn't she suspect?'

'I guess after twenty years of trying it wouldn't even have entered her mind,' Iain replied slowly. 'And when she was so frightened of cancer she just put two and two together and made fourteen.'

Jana nodded. That, and the fact that Sophie was big to begin with. . .

'I suppose you realise that we've missed tea again,' Iain said morosely, and Jana laughed. With a shock she heard the sound of her own laughter. It was light and free.

'I don't intend to eat for a week,' she admitted. 'However, I know where there's an excellent supply of cold turkey. I'm sure Mrs Fitzsimmons would be more than happy to feed you again.'

'Are you going back there tonight?' Iain asked, and Jana shook her head, smiling.

'Did Barry ask you to marry him?'

'Did you think he would?'

Iain pursed his lips. 'He's the sort of chap who'd plan things ahead,' he said consideringly. 'I imagine he'd consider it a waste to give you both a Christmas present and an engagement present when he could easily combine the two.'

Jana bit her lip, trying to suppress laughter.

'I didn't get either,' she said, attempting to sound disappointed. 'He couldn't get the engagement ring because of the fires, so he couldn't ask me to marry him. It wouldn't be proper.'

Iain looked up suspiciously. 'You're kidding.'

'I'm not.'

'The man's a fool.'

Jana said nothing.

'Jana, you can't still consider marrying him.'

'No,' Jana admitted honestly. 'I can't.' She finished drying her hands and looked at her watch. There was still an hour or so to go before the firefighters finished for the day.

'I'm going for a swim,' she said decisively. 'You're on your own, Dr Carisbrook.'

The wind had changed. As Jana walked out of the hospital entrance she felt it immediately. The searing heat had faded; in its place was a cool evening breeze. It was blowing from the sea, taking the smoke away from the town. For the first time in a week Jana could take a lungful of air without smelling the fires.

That's my second miracle for the day, she said to herself. The Lanzo baby and now this. The fire would be blown back on to burnt country, and burn itself out. In a day or two the roads would be clear and the town would revert to normal.

Normal? She turned the word over in her mind as she walked. Her world was no longer normal. Somehow, in the last few days it had been irrevocably changed.

The beach was a long, deserted stretch of sand. The sun was low on the horizon and the coolness of the breeze was balm after the heat of the last few days. Jana had her swimsuit on under her dress, a bikini consisting of two scant slips of white satin. She slipped off her dress and ran full tilt into the welcoming surf.

For ten minutes she let the waves pound her, then she swam strongly out past the breakers and turned to float on her back, enjoying the gentle swell of the sea. She didn't move, letting her tired body and mind absorb the quiet and the peace.

She was just starting to think that perhaps she should return to shore when her calm was shattered. A body surfaced directly under her, upsetting her balance and causing her to tilt under the water.

She emerged, coughing and spluttering, to find Iain laughing, treading water beside her.

'You don't take much care,' he said mockingly. 'I might have been a shark.'

'Instead of a doctor running out on his responsibilities,' she said severely. 'Who's looking after the hospital?'

'I told Sister where to find us,' he said in an injured tone. 'We discussed the matter at length and finally decided that the local basketball coach has a megaphone.'

Jana choked again at the idea of Sister standing on the shore hollering through a megaphone.

'You've got no sense of responsibility,' she told him.

'I thought we'd had that out.' They were still treading water, their faces inches apart. Jana was achingly aware of his body, naked apart from a brief swimming costume, tanned, muscled, and altogether too close. 'I'm a totally responsible person. To win you I'll take on four mothers, fifteen brothers, seventy-six sisters and two dogs. No cats, though,' he said firmly. 'Cats make me sneeze.'

Jana laughed. She turned and swam strongly through the swell to the anchored buoy at the end of the beach. Her body was alight with joy and love. Behind her Iain followed, stroke for stroke, matching her perfect rhythm. Finally she reached the rim of the buoy. Holding its edge, she turned her head to watch Iain's strong body come up to her. His bare chest brushed the soft skin of her back as he reached to enfold her body and gain a hold on the buoy.

'Are you proposing?' She tried to sound surprised, but it didn't quite come off. Her body was alight to his touch.

He turned her gently to face him. His eyes met hers, warm with love. 'Yes,' he said simply.

'Without a ring?' she teased him softly. 'You should be ashamed.'

With one swift movement he was gone, and Jana watched his lithe, brown body diving deep beneath her, through the brilliant green of the sea. A minute passed and then another, before his head again broke the surface. In his hand he held a huge frond of seaweed.

'Hold that,' he demanded, depositing the slimy brown plant unceremoniously around her shoulders. He hauled himself up on to the buoy, pulled off three strands and tied them into a knot. Two minutes later he reached down and grasped the laughing Jana, pulling her streaming body up beside him on to the buoy.

'There.'

In his hand lay a plaited ring of weed, thick and slimy but still, indisputably, a ring. He took her left hand and slid the ungainly ring on to her third finger.

'Never let it be said that I don't do things properly,' he said seriously. He reached and tilted Jana's chin, forcing her to meet his eyes. 'Jana Reiss, merry Christmas and will you marry me?'

Jana met his eyes, her own reflecting the love, the trust and the sureness that she saw there. She had known this man for less than a week and yet she knew that she would trust him with her life. He was her life.

'I'll marry you,' she whispered. And then, as he took her in his arms and the rest of the words were lost to the softness of his kiss, her final words rested with contentment in her mind.

'You are my most perfect Christmas miracle.'

THE REAL CHRISTMAS MESSAGE

Sharon Kendrick

CHAPTER ONE

'I WONDER if he'll be home in time for Christmas?'

'Who?' asked Lara absently—she was unloading a last box of water for injections from a large cardboard container.

Dr Cunningham smiled at her from behind the old-fashioned spectacles he always wore. 'Why, Nick, of course. You remember Nick, don't you?'

Twenty ampoules of H_2O almost hit the deck. Remember him? No woman who had met Nick Cunningham for a tenth of a second would be likely to forget him, she thought. But then of course—she hadn't been a woman when she'd met him. Just a girl.

'Yes, I remember him,' she replied. 'Vaguely.'

Just who did she think she was kidding? Sometimes she felt that she could have taken an exam on the subject of Nick Cunningham, she remembered him so well!

It was as bright and as clear as yesterday... Christmas Eve, seven years ago...

She had been fifteen. And fat.

Nick had been years older, of course—almost twenty-four. The whole town knew that he'd recently qualified as a doctor—following in his father's footsteps. Rumours abounded in small towns, but one of the most enduring that festive season was that Nick Cunningham was coming home for Christmas.

Every female under forty had held her breath, wondering if he would attend the Christmas Eve dance. Lara could still recall it: the collective sigh like the cooing of a hundred wood pigeons as he'd walked into the hall.

It had been her first dance and the hall had looked magnificent. The sight of the pink and silver balloons and the garlands of laurel leaves had more than made up for the fact that finding something suitable to wear had proved a Herculean task, and that in the end she'd resembled a pink blancmange. But at least the heavy golden hair had come up trumps as usual, gleaming in a thick curtain to her shoulders. And her mother had allowed her the faintest smear of blue eye-shadow, which made her dancing eyes look impossibly blue.

And when the paper cloths covering the buffet supper on the trestle tables were removed, there was a murmur of appreciation. What food! Lara moved forward, to pile heaps of chicken drumsticks and sausage rolls and French bread and cheese on to her plate.

And just at that moment, Nick Cunningham had walked in wearing a dark overcoat, snow sprinkled on to the black hair, and she was unable to touch a morsel.

She had tried not to stare at him—others were not succeeding quite so well!—but he was hard to miss. He was the tallest man in the room, and the most elegant—and whoever had invented the suit would have been delighted to see it worn by Nick Cunningham.

He stood talking to his father for most of the time, but their conversation was interrupted time and time again by a constant stream of young women, eager to meet him.

And then the last dance was announced. Couples began drifting on to the dance-floor. Lara knew that at least four girls refused offers in the hope that *he* would be the one to ask them. Feeling gloomy, she started to move towards the lemon squash.

There was a tap on her shoulder, and a deep voice was saying, 'Would you like to dance?' and she had found herself looking up into the most handsome face she had ever seen outside the movies.

Was she dreaming? She blinked to find him still looking down at her expectantly.

'I—I'd love to,' she stammered.

The disc jockey put on 'I'm Dreaming of a White Christmas' by Bing Crosby, and he took her into his arms.

It defied all description. She would nurse the memory for years, like a special friend, reliving it time and time again. Recalling dreamily the light touch of his hands on her waist. The elusive, wonderful masculine scent of him. The smiling way he had bent to talk to her.

In the few minutes it took for the famous crooner to croon out the most famous Christmas song in the world, he managed to coax a hesitant life-story out of her. That she lived with her parents in Stonebridge, that she had an older brother who was hoping to go to university.

'And what do you want to do, when...' There was a slight pause.

She was sure that he had been going to say 'when you grow up', but instead he said 'when you leave school'.

She frowned. 'Oh—be a nurse. Or a teacher—I'm not sure.'

His eyes twinkled. 'Be a nurse,' he said. 'You've got a beautiful smile. You'd be a good nurse!'

Had he really said that?

The dance ended, he excused himself, and Lara wandered out to the washroom in a happy daze, her cheeks flushed, her blue eyes sparkling.

She heard only the tail-end of the conversation.

'Fancy dancing with fat Lara King!'

'Did you see her dress? She must have used two pairs of curtains to make it!'

'Thank goodness she didn't step on the poor man's foot—she'd have broken it!'

Their giggles drowned out the sound of her retreating footsteps. She found her shawl and her friend Joan MacCormack, and they walked home, Lara strangely silently.

But she never forgot Nick Cunningham, or the dance, or the things those girls had said, and the following morning she had refused sugar in her coffee, and a second slice of toast, and the sweet shop missed seeing her cheery face on the way home from school every day.

She did a year's nannying in between leaving school and starting her nurse training. She also lost three stones in weight. Her parents retired and moved up north, but Stonebridge was *her* home, and last year, after her hospital staffing experience, she had come back to Stonebridge to work for old Dr Cunningham.

She had answered the advertisement in the *Nursing Times*, not really thinking about who the GP asking for a practice nurse might be. After all, Stonebridge was a medium-sized town with nearly eighteen thousand patients—and there were more than eight doctors practising there.

None the less, Lara was surprised and delighted to find that Dr Cunningham was the doctor in question—even more so when she got the job. And if she was perfectly honest with herself, she knew that part of her delight lay in the possibility of seeing Nick again, wondering what he would think of the young woman who was no longer a fat, gauche schoolgirl, but a qualified nurse who was slim, fit and confident.

But her girlish hopes quickly faded, and her memory of Nick grew tarnished, when she realised with a pang that he had little time for his father. His visits were few, and fleeting—apparently—for he had never once called at the surgery in the year she'd worked there. . .

Her blue eyes clouded over at the thought, as she neatly folded up the empty cardboard box.

Dr Cunningham looked at her fondly. 'A penny for them, my dear? You looked miles away—and why so pensive?'

Lara liked and respected her boss immensely. It simply didn't occur to her not to say the first thing which came into her head.

'I was thinking that Nick doesn't come to see you very often.'

Dr Cunningham signed the last of the prescriptions she had placed before him with a flourish. 'Oh—Nick's far too busy a young man to spend all his time trotting to Stonebridge and back. He's doing surgery, you know! Busy men, surgeons!'

She knew that all right. She also knew that Dr Cunningham's own dreams lived on vicariously through his son.

John Cunningham had himself cherished hopes of becoming a surgeon. At school he had excelled, winning the prestigious Forman science cup. There were great hopes for the tall young man with the slight stoop.

And then a man named Adolf Hitler had invaded Poland, and, along with the lives destroyed in the second great war which followed, lay the dreams of John Cunningham.

By the time he returned from fighting, his burning ambition had left him. He was older, wiser, and a great deal sadder. He took up his deferred place at medical school, but the many years of training needed for surgery now seemed an insurmountable obstacle, and instead he opted for general practice.

Eventually he married, and his son Nick instead proved to be his finest achievement, especially when his mother succumbed to and died from influenza when he was still a boy.

It was no wonder, thought Lara as she ticked the last box of ampoules off on the pharmacy list, that he was so proud of his son's achievements. It was just a pity the son couldn't spend a little more time at home.

It was a busy morning. Dr Cunningham was a single-handed practitioner and Lara wasn't just his practice nurse, but his receptionist and his secretary all rolled into one!

In the morning she booked patients in for the first surgery of the day, answered the phone, and took requests for repeat prescriptions. After surgery, on some days she gave injections, or took blood-pressure readings. Then she—rather slowly—typed up the hospital referrals. She'd started going to night-school to improve her typing, and since then it had progressed from the faltering two-fingered variety to something fast approaching forty words a minute!

The trouble with a doctor's surgery, she had thought more than once, was that there were *always* interruptions—which meant that inevitably you never had as much time as you thought you did.

Lara had returned from visiting a mother with her new baby at home, and was collecting together the cards for the afternoon surgery when the phone rang. Dr Cunningham was out on an emergency visit, and he was due to start surgery in ten minutes, and, what was more, Mrs Morgan was bound to complain loudly and bitterly if she was kept waiting!

Please don't let it be a visit, she prayed, as she picked up the phone.

'Hello?'

She almost dropped the receiver. She hadn't heard the voice for seven years, and it had only spoken a few words to her, but those words were engraved on her memory as boldly as if they had been written in letters of fire—and just as memorable was the voice that had spoken them.

'Hello?' The voice repeated, sounding puzzled. 'Is that Dr Cunningham's surgery?'

'Y-yes,' stammered Lara, making a huge effort to pull herself together. 'This is Dr Cunningham's surgery—how may I help you?'

'Who's that?' The voice sounded interested.

'This is Lara.' She drew in a deep breath. 'Lara King—the practice nurse and receptionist. Who's speaking, please?' She felt such a fraud as she asked the question, but imagine his horror if she'd suddenly said, 'Hello, Nick.'

'This is Nick—Dr Cunningham's son. Is he there?'

'I'm sorry, no. I'm afraid he's out on a visit. Can I ask him to ring you?'

There was a pause. 'No, I've got to go out now. Will you give him a message for me?'

'Certainly.'

'Just tell him that I'll be home, would you? I'll be home for Christmas.'

It was a pity that a whooping cough epidemic should coincide with the return of the prodigal son, thought Lara, a touch bitterly, as she pushed the wire trolley round the brightly lit supermarket. And poor Dr Cunningham had been rushed off his feet—it wasn't good at his age. So what alternative did she have but to offer to do the shopping for him?

She put a packet of figs into the already loaded trolley and added one of dates for good measure. Dr Cunningham had invited her to join them for

Christmas lunch—and then promptly asked if she'd mind cooking it!

'Would you mind, my dear?' he had asked tentatively. 'He's worked for so many Christmases, and so have I. I'd like to make this one to remember.'

Lara would have found the request difficult to resist anyway, but, coupled with the fact that she still had a ridiculously strong schoolgirlish crush on the man in question... Her smile was huge as she nodded her agreement.

Days began to be ticked off on the calendar.

On the twentieth of December, a baby almost died from the whooping cough and had to be admitted to the hospital as an emergency.

'Baby Rawlins is touch and go,' said Dr Cunningham, his face grave.

Mrs Rawlins' husband was being flown home from his RAF base the following morning.

'I'll go and sit with his wife at the hospital,' promised Lara.

Dr Cunningham's eyes shone. 'You're a good girl, Lara,' he said.

'Nonsense,' she said briskly, and began to button up her gabardine.

On the twenty-first, young Alicia le Saux was rushed to hospital with appendicitis and Mrs Donaldson discovered that she was pregnant. Lara was in surgery with Dr Cunningham when he announced the result of the urine test.

'It's positive,' he said gruffly. 'You're going to have a baby.'

Lara had to provide wads of tissues for the woman to dry her eyes and blow her nose. At the end of surgery Dr Cunningham found a bottle of port waiting for him on the reception desk. The Donaldsons had been trying for a baby for over ten years.

On the twenty-second, a woman of twenty-four was recalled because her cervical smear showed that there had been pre-cancerous changes.

On the twenty-third there was a succession of sore throats, and so many parents who were anxious about the whooping cough brought their children in with non-existent 'sniffles' that Lara thought she would scream.

On the twenty-fourth, old Mr Parker finally died, after a long and debilitating illness. And Nick Cunningham arrived.

He had not been expected so early. Surgery had finished at midday, and Lara had offered to help make the house presentable. Dr Cunningham had a cleaner, but it was the *little* touches which made a house home, especially at Christmas, and Lara bustled around hanging holly, buying a tree to decorate with all the baubles which they'd fished out of the attic. She could see that Dr Cunningham was getting quite unusually excited.

She was standing on a chair, positioning the voile-clad fairy on the top of the tree, when she heard the distant peal of a doorbell. She imagined it to be a patient, or a neighbour, but then she heard exclamations of obvious joy, and she knew that it was Nick.

It was not how she had planned it to be, their reunion. She had spent the afternoon in the kitchen, preparing a beef wellington and making batch after batch of mince pies. Consequently, the heavy golden hair was drawn back in a severe ponytail, her un-made-up face was pink and shiny, and there was a smear of pastry on one cheek. Her jeans were faded and old, and a button of the old shirt she wore had come undone near the waist, showing a glimpse of summer-brown midriff.

She turned round just as he walked into the room, a few large flakes of snow glittering on the coal-black wavy hair, just as they had all those years ago. He was less tall than she remembered, but still a head above his father, and the hair now had the odd streak of silver-grey at the temples. The face too, was older, but even more handsome, if that were possible—the lines around the blue-grey eyes showed a new maturity.

He stood, framed in the oak doorway, staring at her, an unsure expression flitting across the craggy features.

And then he smiled, and it was like the sun coming out. 'Hello,' he said. 'You must be...'

Her welcoming expression froze for a split second. 'I'm Lara King,' she replied calmly. 'Your father's nurse. We spoke on the phone.'

The smile widened. 'Yes, of course. Pleased to meet you, Lara.'

She climbed down from the chair, moving a piece of tinsel away from the back of it, hoping that he wouldn't notice her high colour.

Of course he wouldn't remember her—why the hell should he? They hadn't even been introduced, had they? And everyone said she didn't look like the same girl any more. A three-minute dance with a fat and blushing schoolgirl nearly seven years ago hardly merited the description of something he would never forget, now did it?

Her smile had about a quarter of its usual radiance, but she managed a pretty fair imitation of it, and was about to speak when there was some commotion just behind him.

In came Dr Cunningham, and behind him a woman.

The woman moved elegantly into the room, taking in the scene of the young girl by the Christmas tree standing gazing wide-eyed at the dark doctor on whose arm she now laid an authoritative beige kid glove.

To Lara, she seemed the *palest* woman she had ever seen. Pale blonde hair and pale pink lips and nails. Pale grey eyes. Even her clothes were pale. A beige coat of the softest leather, with cuffs and collar in some pale fur. Lara chewed on her lip just a little — fancy having the nerve to wear fur in this day and age!

The woman was speaking now; she had a low, American drawl. 'Cat got your tongue, Nick? Aren't you going to introduce me?'

For the briefest moment he actually looked uncertain, something which somehow surprised Lara, then came that smile again.

'This is Lara King, my father's nurse. Lara, this is Annabel Hummerstone — my fiancée.'

CHAPTER TWO

THIS wasn't how it was supposed to happen at all, thought Lara, as she moved forward automatically to shake the immaculately manicured hand, from which the glove had now been removed to reveal a huge, sparkling diamond solitaire ring.

She made polite small talk, but as soon as she could she excused herself and left, heading off home on her rusty old bicycle, refusing all offers of a lift from both Cunningham doctors, and sure she saw a smile of relief on the face of the stunningly beautiful Annabel.

She spent Christmas Eve in the pub, with some friends she'd known since schooldays, and they piled out at midnight, singing and laughing and jostling as the bells from the church in the square began to chime. Lara slipped in quietly at the back for midnight mass and offered up a prayer that she wouldn't be so selfish as to spend the festive season wishing above all else that Nick Cunningham hadn't come home with a fiancée.

On the twenty-fifth, she arrived at Dr Cunningham's house to find herself greeted by Nick, and her cheeks went pink.

'Where is everyone?' she asked.

'Annabel's still in bed.' Lara tried very hard not to wince. 'And my father's taken the dogs out. You're nice and early.'

'I'm cooking lunch,' she said defensively.

He grinned. 'Not yet, you're not! Come and have a glass of champagne.'

'Isn't it too early?' she protested, not sure if she wanted to spend any more time alone with him than was absolutely necessary.

'Nonsense! It's Christmas. And, what's more, you're not cooking the lunch like some Dickensian character—you're going to get some help!'

They drank some champagne but Dr Cunningham still didn't come back from walking the dogs and Annabel didn't emerge from upstairs, and when eventually she did she didn't look best pleased to find Lara chopping up sage for the stuffing and Nick companionably making a festive cross in each of the Brussels sprouts.

She raised a quizzical eyebrow and flopped into the nearest chair. 'Someone get me some black coffee, quick!' she groaned. 'I'm hopeless in the mornings.'

But not too hopeless to make your face up immaculately, thought Lara as she filled up the kettle, and immediately felt ashamed of the thought.

Annabel was clearly someone who was used to people doing things for her. She also giggled a lot. Lara found herself wondering what on earth Nick saw in her, and then silently told herself not to be so naïve. It was perfectly obvious what he saw in her. The combination of a mane of blonde hair down her back, legs up to her armpits, and a perfectly featured face. What man wouldn't like her?

Dr Cunningham returned, and they all adjourned

to the sitting-room for a drink. 'Let's hope things will be quiet enough so that at least we can eat our lunch in peace.' He smiled. 'Still, the patients don't usually bother me unnecessarily on Christmas Day.'

Annabel threw up her hands in horror. 'Don't tell me you're actually *working*?' she asked.

Lara thought that she made it sound like an infectious disease!

'Dad's very old-fashioned,' explained Nick. 'He doesn't trust anyone else to take care of his patients—though if it were me I'd join on to a rota system with the health centre here in town. That way you'd only be on call every fourth night and weekend, instead of every night.'

'Every night?' squeaked Annabel.

'It isn't as bad as it sounds,' remonstrated Dr Cunningham gently. 'If you educate your patients properly, then they learn to only call you in the case of a *real* emergency. It's when they don't get any degree of continuity that they feel nervous and stop trusting their doctors—and that's when they call you out for niggling sore throats.'

'It needn't be like that, Dad—being on a rota doesn't preclude educating your patients, you know!' Nick looked at his father affectionately.

'Well, anyway,' Dr Cunningham put his empty glass down on the small side-table, 'you've no need to concern yourself about a general practioner's burdens—as a surgeon your on-call duties will be arduous but infrequent—and they'll be mapped out for you.'

'But Nick is——' pouted Annabel, when Nick interrupted her.

'I think we've talked enough shop for one meal.' His tone was light, but Lara thought that there was an unmistakable warning in it, and that the blue-grey eyes had turned distinctly chilly. She wondered what Annabel had been about to say.

Dr Cunningham turned to Annabel. 'Nick's right—too much shop can be tedious—his mother used to say exactly the same thing! Are you connected with medicine, Annabel?'

Annabel gave a tinkly laugh. 'Oh, no—not me! Nothing so noble! I'm one of that rare breed, I'm ashamed to admit. I act.'

Dr Cunningham beamed. 'An actress? My dear, how splendid! What have you done?' His eyes grew dreamy. 'More a Celia than an Ophelia, am I right? Less of a Cleopatra, and more of a Katharine, am I correct?'

'What?' Annabel looked at him blankly.

'Shakespeare, darling,' interposed Nick hastily. 'Annabel's not exactly into Shakespeare, Dad. More into soap-powder commercials, actually. She's a model, really.'

'I am *not*! Nicky, sweetheart—you know that isn't true!'

I can't stand a minute more of this, thought Lara fiercely. What on earth was he doing with such a lightweight, feather-brained, beautiful dolt as this one? What a waste.

She stood up. 'I'd better go and baste the turkey, and see about the spuds,' she said.

'What talents,' trilled Annabel. 'I can't even boil an egg!'

Well, bully for you, thought Lara as she headed for the door.

Nick had got to his feet. 'Shall I come and help you, Lara?'

'No,' she answered hastily. 'Too many cooks and all that...' The last thing she wanted was to be marooned in the kitchen with him, cooking a meal together, wishing that he'd come here on his own, seen her, and fallen in love. And you're too old for fairy-stories, she told herself fiercely, as she added butter and sugar to the carrots *julienne*.

To her surprise, despite her preoccupations, the lunch was a great success, and Nick proposed a toast to the chef.

'Tell me, are you sure you aren't a professional cook?' he asked, the blue-grey eyes twinkling in a way which she wished she didn't find quite so devastatingly attractive. 'What are you like as a nurse?'

'She's better,' said Dr Cunningham instantly. 'I don't know what I'd do without Lara.'

You'd rely on your son more, thought Lara. He'd have to come to see you more often. She wanted to concentrate on his bad points; she didn't *want* to like him. There was no point.

'I could never be a nurse,' grimaced Annabel. 'All that blood and gore!'

No one challenged her, and Nick stood up to begin clearing away the plates when the phone rang.

John Cunningham answered it, and they heard a series of delighted responses. When eventually he put the receiver down, he turned to Lara with a wide smile.

'Baby Rawlins is in the clear,' he declared, looking as if he'd just won the jackpot.

Lara saw Nick looking interested. 'Baby Rawlins had a bad attack of whooping cough,' she explained. 'I expect you know there's been a bad epidemic recently.'

'Oh, surgeons never know about things like that!' interposed Dr Cunningham jovially.

'Your father admitted him on the twentieth,' continued Lara.

'They've discharged him home for Christmas Day,' smiled Dr Cunningham. 'His father's home, and they're all together.' He brushed his eye with the back of his hand. 'I said I'd pop over, just to see him settled. Would you mind? Can the pudding wait, Lara?'

What a superb doctor he was, she thought fondly. 'Of course it can wait,' she smiled. 'Do you want me to come with you?'

He shook his head. 'If you're here, it means I don't have to put the phone over to the answering service.'

After he'd gone, there was a moment or two of awkward silence, broken only by the clattering of cutlery on china as Nick continued to clear the dishes away. Lara wondered idly if he was a true 'new man' or whether it was just that Annabel was so lazy that he'd got used to doing all the chores!

The phone started to ring again, and Lara moved to answer it.

'Is it always as busy as this?' complained Annabel, and Nick grinned conspiratorially at Lara.

'Busy?' he exclaimed. 'This is quiet!'

Lara began to take details. The call disturbed her, and yet she couldn't put a finger on why. She opened her mouth to form more questions to ask the patient, when they were cut off. The woman had been calling from a phone box.

She frowned as she replaced the handset.

'What's up?' asked Nick.

She shook her head. 'Something. Nothing. I don't know.'

'Need a second opinion?' he suggested gently.

She looked at him gratefully. 'It was such a vague history. A woman with "funny" pains in her stomach.'

'And Dad can go and see her when he gets back. What's the problem?'

'He's likely to spend ages with the Rawlins baby.'

'Then bleep him,' said Nick.

She shook her head. 'He's trained me only to bleep him if it's urgent. And it doesn't sound urgent. And yet...'

'And yet you've got a hunch?' he ventured.

'Exactly,' she agreed.

'Then you've got to bleep him,' said Nick.

'I know.'

But Dr Cunningham didn't answer his bleep, and Lara began to grow restless. She eventually got through to the Rawlins family on the phone, to be told that he'd only just left. And they lived on the periphery of the practice area. Miles away.

Nick saw her glance at her watch for the fortieth time. 'What do you want to do?' he asked.

'What can I do?' she asked desperately. 'She isn't

on the phone, and I certainly can't call an ambulance on a hunch. I guess I'll just have to wait until
your father gets back.'

Nick stared at her. 'Get your coat,' he said
decisively.

'What's going on?' demanded Annabel
petulantly.

'Lara and I are going to see the patient,' he
explained.

'But you're not... I mean, you can't...'
stumbled Lara.

'I'm not her doctor, it's true,' he agreed.
'Although I've done locums for Dad in the past. I'll
just come along for the ride. We'll go in and see
how she is. If it's a false alarm, fine. But if you need
a doctor—for whatever reason—then I'm there.'

His calm assurances warmed her and she smiled.
'Thanks,' she said, and then turned to the grumpy-
looking Annabel.

'I've switched the phone back over to the answering service. Could you explain to Dr Cunningham
where we've gone?' she asked. 'Tell him I'll ring if
we need him.'

'OK,' muttered Annabel sulkily.

They drove there in Nick's car, towards the centre
of the town where the patient lived in a tall tene-
ment block—a shabby building from the sixties
which looked anachronistic next to the new dual
carriageway which it overlooked.

They had to take the stairs to the sixth floor—the
lift had long ago been vandalised. The stair-well was
strewn with Coke cans and chip wrappings, and
there was the rank odour of sweat and urine.

Ginny Chambers, the patient, opened the door on the second ring, a huge, ungainly girl of about twenty with a flaccid, pale face who managed an attempt at a smile when she saw them.

Lara smiled. 'Hello,' she said. 'We haven't met before. I'm Lara King—the practice nurse, and this is Dr Cunningham's son, who's also a doctor. Dr Cunningham has been delayed on an emergency, and I was a little bit worried about you, so we thought we'd just pop over to see how you are.' You're a fool, Lara King, she thought to herself. This girl looks fine. You've panicked, and goodness knows what Dr Cunningham Junior will now think of your professional judgement.

'Come in,' said the girl.

Lara and Nick entered the flat, which was sparsely furnished, though surprisingly clean.

'Now, then, Ginny,' asked Lara briskly, 'have you still got the pains you described?'

'Well, Nurse—they come and go——' The girl faltered for a second and suddenly there was the most astonishing transformation as sweat broke out on her already pale face, and she clutched her abdomen with a kind of primitive desperation.

Lara recognised well enough the signs of true, severe pain—and this girl had it. She caught hold of her arm, but Nick was there, too.

'How long have you been having these pains?' he asked urgently.

'Since last night,' she gasped.

'And are they getting worse?'

'I—yes!' The fervent exclamation was gasped out.

'We're going to help you on to the bed,' he said gently. 'I'm going to examine you.'

The girl nodded numbly.

Lara was impressed with his rapid examination, but it was all academic since the diagnosis was immediately apparent to both of them. He raised his dark head and looked at Lara questioningly. She nodded.

He spoke very kindly to Ginny. 'Did you have no idea at all that you were going to have a baby, my dear?'

The young but slightly vacant eyes stared back at him uncomprehendingly. 'A baby?' she asked. 'A baby?' And then another tight contraction forced her knees to buckle up to her chest.

'Shall I run out to use the phone for an ambulance?' asked Lara.

Nick shook his head. 'It's too late for that. This baby's on its way.' He turned back to Ginny. 'Nurse and I are going to help you have your baby—and I want you to try to do what we ask you. Do you understand?'

'Yes,' answered the girl, and Lara looked at her in amazement, wondering at her simple compliance.

She had read about things like this, of course, in women's magazines, but part of her had always been slightly sceptical—and yet from the expressions that had crossed the girl's face she honestly believed that she had been completely ignorant of her pregnancy.

'What have you got in your bag?' asked Nick.

Lara swiftly perused the contents. 'Forceps, clamps, sutures if you need them. Pethidine.'

'Can you boil some water up to sterilise the forceps?'

'Sure.'

'And see if you can find a hot-water bottle and clean towels—we'll need something warm to wrap the baby in. Once the water's on, could you scout around outside—get one of the neighbours to call an ambulance? She'll need to go in afterwards.'

Lara nodded and set to work. The minutes flew by, and the forceps were standing by ready only just in time.

The girl's cries sounded loud in the small room.

'We're nearly there,' said Lara. 'Try and breathe like me.' She began to make light puffing noises, but the girl had her eyes closed and didn't hear.

'I can see the head,' cried Nick, and gripped the girl's hand. 'I want you to wait until I tell you, and then to give a huge push. Do you understand?'

He looked up at Lara, sweat beading his brow. 'Is the ambulance on its way?'

'Someone's calling one.'

'Good.' He turned back to Ginny. 'Now, push!' he commanded. 'Really push—there's a good girl.'

Four pushes and the baby was out. Lara caught him while Nick clamped the cord and cut it, and then they swathed him in a warm towel. The infant let out a lusty cry as Lara hooked some mucus from his mouth.

'It's a boy!' she cried delightedly. 'Ginny—you've got a beautiful baby boy!'

They placed the baby into the mother's arms, straight on to the breast, and stood grinning happily at one another.

'You were great,' he said softly.

'So were you,' she answered shyly. 'Thanks.'

Nick had just finished washing his hands, and Lara was tidying Ginny up when there was a loud knock at the door.

'Ambulance!' shouted a voice.

Nick opened the door. 'Too late!' he joked.

One of the men came in and looked around. 'Strewth!' he exclaimed.

After the ambulancemen had left with mother and child, Nick and Lara stood in the dingy flat, unsure what to do next.

'A Christmas baby,' Nick said, in a voice of soft wonderment. 'Didn't you always long to deliver a Christmas baby? Or perhaps you have. . .?'

'No, never,' she said quietly. 'You were very good. I didn't think that surgeons were usually so obstetrically efficient?'

For a moment he looked evasive, and then he smiled. 'I had a brilliant assistant, didn't I?'

Their gaze held and locked, the blue-grey eyes seeming to ask a question. She felt magnetised by the power of his presence, the effect of being in his company as heartrendingly electrifying as it had been to a young girl of fifteen.

Eventually, he spoke. 'I've been meaning to ask you, it's been puzzling me since yesterday. There's something very familiar about you. . . Have we — met before?'

'We met at a Christmas dance seven years ago. We had the last dance.'

'That's it. . .of course!' he exclaimed. 'You were. . .'

'I was very fat,' she said bluntly.

He frowned. 'I was going to say that you were the girl with the beautiful smile.'

Which was what he'd said at the time. Had he really remembered that? She wanted to believe so, and yet the sudden intimate course which the conversation had taken unsettled her. She liked him too much. He made her feel vulnerable, and what was more he already had a fiancée.

'We'd better be going,' she said abruptly. 'Your father and Annabel will be wondering what has happened to us.'

He looked a little taken aback, as if puzzled by the sharpness in her voice.

On the way back to the car she cleared her throat. 'I wonder if you'd mind dropping me off at my place? I'm not feeling so good. . .'

Perhaps he detected the lie, for he tried to dissuade her. 'Oh, do come back.' He grinned. 'I'll even flame the Christmas pudding for you!'

He had no right to be this nice, she thought savagely. Didn't he realise how attractive he was? Didn't it occur to him that he might be making her fall in love with him? Was he really so innocent of his own attraction?

'No, honestly—I'd like to go home,' she repeated.

She saw him give a puzzled frown as he started the engine, as if he couldn't understand her sudden belligerent attitude.

'Where do you live?' he asked.

'Fourteen Cranmore Gardens. It's——'

'I know where it is.'

They drove in silence in an atmosphere which had suddenly grown uncomfortable, and the journey seemed to take a lifetime. She wished that it would just be over, and that she could get out of his car, and away.

He stopped the car in the dark street directly outside her house.

'Thanks for the lift,' she said conventionally, and put her hand out to open the door, but his words stopped her.

'Just a minute,' he said. 'I get the feeling that I'm being punished for something, that maybe I've done something to offend you, and I don't know what it is. Is it because I didn't recognise you yesterday?'

There was a note of solicitude in the deep voice which she strove to ignore, an eagerness to amend things which she fiercely blotted out. No, it wasn't because you didn't recognise me, she wanted to cry out. I'm glad you didn't recognise me, because I look nothing like the girl you danced with. I didn't want you to turn up with your beautiful sleek fiancée, someone who is going to spend the rest of her life with you, someone whom I can't even like.

That was what she wanted to say, but of course she couldn't and the words which spilled out of her mouth were true, too—but a poor substitute for what was really troubling her.

Her voice was trembling. 'I'll tell you why I'm angry, if you like. I'm angry because I see your father, an old man whose son is his life. And how often do you bother to visit him? Answer me that! You're all he's got—you ought to remember that——' She stopped in mid-flow, suddenly aware that she had said too much. She saw that his face had gone white in the gloomy light of the car interior, that the muscles around his mouth had tightened.

'I'm grateful to you for your outstanding honesty,' he said in a chilly voice. 'And I'm sorry if you think that I've failed in my filial duty.'

She pushed the car door open, close to tears, regretting her behaviour and yet seeing no way to rectify what had happened.

'I'm sorry——' she cried, and, half running, she stumbled up the path to her house, only too aware that he sat there for what must have been several minutes before he started the engine up and drove away.

CHAPTER THREE

LARA didn't see Nick again. When the surgery reopened after the Christmas break he had left to go back to work. Dr Cunningham was his usual charming, easygoing self, and so she assumed that Nick hadn't told him that his nurse had vehemently attacked his son, about something which was nothing at all to do with her.

She almost thought of writing him a letter to apologise, but then abandoned the idea. What on earth could she say? She certainly couldn't tell him her real reasons for her totally unjustified anger. Rarely had she felt more ashamed of anything in her life.

January was, as usual, one of the busiest months. Not only were their chronic bronchitics succumbing to chest infections, but they also found that those with a predisposition towards depression often became ill during the winter months. There was also a massive demand for influenza vaccinations, and Lara was kept very busy.

One morning in February, the phone at Reception rang.

'Hello,' said a deep voice.

'Nick!' she said instantly, before she could stop herself.

He sounded amused. 'Very good! Can you recognise everyone like that, or just errant sons?'

314

Ouch! His teasing tone was letting her off the hook, but he deserved an apology. She took a deep breath. 'Nick, about what I——' She fumbled and cleared her throat. 'I had no right to say what I did, and I'm sorry.'

'It's forgotten, Lara,' he replied gently. 'Is Dad there?'

The conversation should have made her feel better, but it didn't. Renewed contact with him started her thinking about him, about how much she liked him. I hope Annabel realises how lucky she is, she thought, as she slammed another load of instruments into the steriliser.

Dr Cunningham called her in to chaperon him while he did a vaginal examination, and after the patient had left and Lara had tidied away she turned casually to her boss.

'Nick was on the phone, then?' she asked conversationally.

He beamed. 'Yes, indeed! Coming down again this weekend—can't think what's got into the boy!'

She looked up. 'Again?' she queried.

There was obvious pleasure in the old man's voice. 'Yes, he's been coming to see me just about every other weekend, whenever he's not on call, in fact. That's a bad sign, wouldn't you say, Lara? Must think I'm on my last legs or something!'

'Nonsense!' protested Lara. 'You're as fit as a flea!'

So he'd been visiting his father, had he? Could her words to him have had anything to do with it? And she wondered what Annabel thought of coming to dull old Stonebridge every weekend!

February continued into March. Sticky buds appeared on the trees, birds rediscovered their voices and pale daffodils waved in splendour in the chilly March wind, when the inexplicable and the unexpected happened.

Lara was paid a visit early one morning by Sergeant Grimes from Stonebridge Police Station to tell her that Dr Cunningham had died in his sleep.

For a minute she just stared, mouth open, too stunned to speak. 'But he can't have... I mean, he was fine yesterday...' She had heard the denials a million times from patients, words which seemed to come from nowhere.

The policeman had obviously heard them too, for he looked at her with compassion. 'Why don't you sit down, miss?' he said gruffly. 'I'll make you a cup of tea.'

She was sensible enough to allow him to do so, and sensible enough to drink it, observing objectively as she did so that he had loaded it with sugar for shock.

She felt better afterwards. 'I'll have to go down to the surgery anyway,' she told him, practical as ever. 'Most people won't have heard. The FPC will have to tell me what to do.' She looked at him distractedly. 'They'll know what to do.'

'Can I give you a lift, miss?' he asked.

'Yes, please.'

At the surgery she was informed that a locum doctor could not be sent until the following day, but that doctors from the health centre would see all urgent cases; the rest would have to be rescheduled.

Organising this took all the morning, and Lara

stood in Reception, leaning over the counter composing a carefully worded notice to pin to the door.

She didn't hear the sound of footsteps until they were close behind her and she glanced up, startled to see Nick beside her.

The grief and the anguish evident on his face suddenly brought home to her what had happened. His loss, and her own. All morning she had worked non-stop, suppressing her own feelings while she sorted out the patients, but the sight of Nick opened the floodgates.

'Nick,' she mouthed soundlessly. 'I'm so——' But she couldn't even finish the sentence because the tears had started, pouring down her cheeks, unquenchable. He took a handkerchief from his pocket and started wiping them away with infinite care, and when she still cried he pulled her into his arms, her head on his shoulders, letting her cry her heart out.

And when eventually there were no tears left she became aware that she had soaked his shirt, and she pulled away, embarrassed.

'I—I'm sorry,' she stammered. 'It came as such a shock. Do they know why it happened?'

He shook his head. 'There'll have to be a post-mortem, of course. I suspect it's just one of those things. Don't most doctors and nurses say that it's the best way to go—in your sleep?'

'I don't know,' she replied, in a small voice.

He looked at her closely. 'This has been a terrible shock for you, too. Get your coat and I'll take you home.'

'But I can't—there's. . .' She gestured in the direction of the door.

'Put that notice up. I'll come back when I've given you a lift, to reallocate any of the afternoon cases which turn up. Come on, now.'

His calmness and his presence of mind were astonishing. Lara felt as though she had been hit over the head with a sledgehammer. It was her first contact with death on a personal level, and perhaps he suspected this, for he helped her on with her coat as if she were a small child.

Outside her house he turned to her. 'Do you have any brandy?' he asked.

She nodded. 'Some.'

'You should have one,' he said firmly. 'Just one, though. Then eat something. The locum will be there tomorrow. The funeral will be on Friday. I'd like you to come from the house. With me. Would you do that? I think that's what Dad would have wanted.'

She turned her troubled eyes to meet his. 'Yes, of course I will. I'd be honoured.' She swallowed, trying to keep the quaver of emotion from her voice. 'He meant a good deal to me.'

'I know.'

She said nothing more; she didn't trust herself not to break down again. She just mumbled her farewells, and he said that he would ring her about the arrangements.

The next few days passed in a strange kind of daze for Lara, though she functioned well enough to continue working with a locum GP named Tony

Elliott, who had been appointed until Dr Cunningham's replacement could be found.

The day of the funeral was grey and blustery, as only a March day could be. Lara walked to the house, deep in thought, her hands in the pockets of her jacket, the cold wind stinging her cheeks dark pink.

There were flowers everywhere, and she travelled to the church in the car with Nick, aware that something was not quite right.

'But where's Annabel?' she asked, after a moment.

'Annabel's not coming,' he replied shortly as he held the door open for her.

She had never been to a funeral before, and she found it very moving—the church packed full to bursting, the hymns lustily sung—a celebration of a worthy life.

Nick asked her to go back with him afterwards, and she found herself helping to pass plates of food and drink around, to murmur her responses to the wistful statements spoken by the guests.

She scarcely realised that the room had begun to empty, until at last only she remained. She watched as Nick emptied an ashtray into the fire.

'I'd better be going,' she said.

He turned, and she saw how pale and strained he looked. Why wasn't Annabel here with him, she thought indignantly, comforting him and helping him—now—when he needed it?

'No, don't go yet!' He must have realised that his tone sounded curt, for he smiled. 'Please! I want to talk to you.'

And suddenly, to her horror and chagrin, she began to cry, as bitterly as she had done once before, only this time her tears were not the natural signs of grief, but of guilt.

He looked startled, then concerned. 'Lara!' He moved quickly towards her, as if afraid that she might faint. 'Please don't upset yourself.'

She shook her head, as if trying to deny the thoughts, so that the heavy gold hair came loose from its ponytail, and swung like a shimmering halo around her head. 'How could I have said those things to you?' she sobbed. 'How could I?'

He looked puzzled. 'Things? What things?'

The sobs meant that her words came out in jerky little gasps. 'Accusing you of being a bad son! Telling you that you never came to visit him. It was none of my business, and I shouldn't have done it. And now he's dead.'

He sat her down gently on the chair. 'But I'm glad you said it, Lara. Don't you see? I'm glad.'

The bluebell-coloured eyes took on an almost luminous quality as they stared back at him uncomprehendingly. 'But why?'

He gave her a sad smile. 'Because everything you said was true. I *had* been avoiding Dad, and your words brought me to my senses. They meant that I was able to make my peace with him, to be reconciled with him before he died.' He saw her still puzzled frown. 'Let me fetch you a glass of wine. And can't you take that jacket off? You're far too young to wear black.'

He helped her off with the jacket and settled her

in the chair in front of the fire with a glass of wine, then stood by the mantelpiece, watching her.

'You know that Dad always wanted to be a surgeon?' he asked, and she nodded. 'And that when he came back from the war he was too old to start the long training?' There was a pause, and a glimmer of memory flickered in the blue-grey eyes. 'When I got to medical school, Dad made no secret of the fact that he wanted me to carry on where he had left off, and for a long time I went along with it. I did well in my surgical shadows, and my house jobs. Surgery is a popular speciality, and I suppose that I revelled in the fact that it came so easily to me.' He took a sip from his own wine.

'But the funny thing was that I wasn't particularly *happy*, and it took me ages to discover exactly why.' He gave a wry smile. 'It was so simple really. You see, the truth was that I didn't particularly enjoy surgery—I found that its horizons were rigid and limiting. And so, much to the dismay of my superiors, I gave it up—just over three years ago now, but. . .' He hesitated.

'But what?' she prompted.

He sighed. 'There just didn't seem to be a right time to tell Dad. I felt I'd failed him badly. I suppose that subconsciously evasion was preferable to confrontation, and that's why my visits grew fewer and fewer, although, in my defence, I was also very busy. Your words shocked me into action.'

'You told your father?'

He nodded. 'At first he was disappointed, naturally. But in the end he saw for himself that I was happy in my new field.' His voice grew soft. 'We became very close during the past few months, and I have you to thank for that, Lara.'

She blinked at the compliment, coming on top of the unexpected revelations.

'And you've not been doing surgery for three years?' she asked.

He nodded again. 'I wanted to talk to you mainly to find out what your plans are.'

To this she had given some thought. 'I'd like to stay in Stonebridge. It all depends on how I get on with the new doctor.'

His eyes twinkled. 'Do you think you could get on with me?'

She didn't understand. 'I don't get your drift.'

He relaxed and smiled then, the first happy smile she had seen on his face all day. 'Do you think you'd like to work with me?'

'You?'

He decided to put her out of her misery. 'Yes, me! Haven't you wondered what I've been doing for the last three years if I haven't been doing surgery? I've been doing my general practice vocational training scheme.'

'You mean you're going to apply for the job?'

'I have done. It's mine! How do you feel about having me for a boss, Lara? I'm the new GP!'

CHAPTER FOUR

LARA stared at him blankly, still confused. 'Wh-what are you talking about?'

He grinned. 'Do I have to spell it out for you in words of one syllable? I'm taking over Dad's post. I applied for the job, and got it. So now will you answer my original question, and tell me whether you think you'll be able to work with me?'

'I—I don't see why not,' she faltered. And then thought of something else. 'You mean that you're coming to live here?'

'Lock, stock, and barrel.'

She frowned. 'But what about Annabel? Doesn't she mind?' She remembered all her little digs about Stonebridge being 'the back of beyond' and 'a one-horse town'.

The blue-grey eyes clouded over, so that they looked like the angry sky which preceded a storm. 'It's over between Annabel and me.'

'Oh.' Her lips framed the word which could have been a question, but one which she didn't dare ask.

'I haven't seen her since after Christmas.'

'Oh,' she said again.

And that was all he said on the subject of Annabel, but she guessed from the curt way he spoke that he didn't want to talk about it, and there was quite enough to talk about on the subject of general practice without having to resort to discussing their private lives.

For it soon became clear that Nick intended to make sweeping changes. He called her in after morning surgery one day.

In those first few weeks she had noticed the deepened furrows which had appeared on his brow gradually begin to lessen. She knew that the sadness would take a long time to go, but that the first sharp pain of bereavement had gone. For herself, she had missed Dr Cunningham dreadfully at first, but now she could hardly imagine a time when Nick hadn't been there. Life went on, they said, and how true it was.

'Hi.' He smiled. 'Do you think we deserve some coffee, and is there time?'

'Yes, to both questions,' she replied. 'There are no extras and I've had the machine on for ten minutes!'

She disappeared, to return with a tray of fresh, steaming coffee, china cups, cream, and some Belgian biscuits. He received his cup with a great show of pleasure.

'This is the life,' he sighed. 'Are you always so civilised, or are you just trying to sweeten me up?'

No need to do that, she thought, bending the glossy golden cap of her head over the sugar bowl.

'Your father thought that, as we had so little time to drink coffee, when we did we might as well do it in style!'

Nick's face grew thoughtful. 'I'm proposing to make some changes, and I want to know if you'll object.'

She put her cup down. 'Such as?'

He drew out a sheet of paper from the drawer of his desk. 'Basically, I'd like to expand. It seems a pity to waste my surgical experience, and I'd thought of doing minor ops at the cottage hospital— I could do day cases, and it would free some much-needed beds.'

Lara nodded cautiously. 'Sounds good.'

He leaned back in the chair, his eyes narrowed. 'I'd need you to assist me, of course—but that means that you'd need to be freed from your commitment at the desk.' He leaned forward again. 'To be honest, Lara, I think that as a trained nurse you're wasted answering the phone. I could employ a receptionist to do that. Her typing would probably be faster, too!'

'Well, no one would argue with that,' she answered with a smile. 'Any more plans, while you're about it?'

His enthusiasm was catching, she thought, as his whole face lit up.

'I've got hundreds!' he exclaimed. 'I'd like to start a series of clinics—regular sessions for the relevant patients at the same time every week. That's better for the patient because it allows them to plan ahead, and better for us, because it frees surgery time.'

'What kind of clinics?'

'A baby clinic, for a start. Babies can be weighed, their progress assessed. They can be inoculated, and their mothers can talk over any problems or queries they might have. We devote one of the empty rooms to it, paint it up brightly and fill it with toys—make it somewhere that the children like to visit, so that hopefully we can try and prevent them building up unnecessary fears about coming to the doctor's.'

She laughed at this. 'You're being very ambitious!'

Now it was his turn to look cautious. 'Too ambitious, do you think?'

She shook her head. 'Not at all—I think you'll give people in Stonebridge something to think about. What else have you planned?'

'I'd like a diabetic and a hypertension clinic. That's fairly straightforward, but I'd like to incorporate education into these clinics. Maybe give them small talks, backed up with hand-outs on common problems which arise when you have one of these conditions. I'd also. . .' He paused here.

'What?'

'I think we're going to have to computerise.' He waited for her reaction.

She poured herself another cup of coffee. 'Oh.'

'You're against the idea?'

'It's not that I'm a Luddite—I just hope that having a computer won't make the practice impersonal.'

'Meaning?'

'Oh, just that I hope we don't forget to look at the patients when they come in, and not at the computer screen.'

'You speak for yourself!' he teased.

One more thing struck her. 'But surely,' she said, serious now, 'what you're proposing is far too much for one man alone?'

He fixed her in the full glory of his dazzling stare.

'I'm not ruling out taking on another partner in the future. Would you object to that?'

She wondered why he was deferring to her quite so much. Even Dr Cunningham had not been quite so deferential. Surely, if she didn't like what he was proposing, then she'd leave and he'd just get another nurse?

'It's bound to change the nature of the practice, if you stop being single-handed,' she ventured.

'But the nature has changed anyway, Lara,' he said gently. 'Inevitably, when my father died and I took over, the practice changed.'

She could not believe how easily they worked together. Mutual respect for the other's abilities seemed to make for superb communication between them. Lara had wondered how the reality of general practice would seem to him once the excitement of a new challenge had worn off. She had feared that the full import of what he had given up would hit him, and that the lure of surgery would prove to be irresistible. But she was wrong. He adapted to the many facets of general practice as if he had been born to it — which in a way, she supposed, he had!

One of the things Lara found so exciting about general practice was that you could never predict what kind of day you would have, how busy it would be, how serious, or how trivial, or both. When each patient walked through the door, you had no idea whether he had a life-threatening disease or some relatively minor ailment.

'It's so different from hospital medicine,' Nick said to her one morning, after a particularly varied surgery. 'There, you feel as though you're in a zoo—with all the patients neatly diagnosed and labelled for you. In practice, it's like walking through the jungle—you never know what you're going to come across next!'

Sometimes the patient had nothing organically wrong with them, just a need to talk their problems over with somebody, with no one other than the doctor to turn to.

Nick had his theories on this, too. 'It's such a secular world now, Lara. I often think that the doctor has taken the place of the priest as a listener, in many cases.'

'Don't let the vicar hear you say that!'

The smile lifted the corners of his mouth. 'Oh, we've had quite a debate on it already—over a glass of whisky and a plate of sandwiches. Perhaps you'd like to join us next time?'

'Perhaps,' she replied non-committally, turning away to dry her hands on the paper towel. She didn't know what she had expected, but it certainly hadn't been an invitation to spend the evening with him and the vicar!

And what had she expected? she mused, as she shopped for groceries on the way home. Just because he was no longer engaged, it didn't mean for a minute that he would ask her out. Why should he? Just because she was near and she was available, it didn't mean anything to him. Men like Nick didn't need proximity as a reason to date someone. And there were loads more girls in Stonebridge more attractive than she.

Look at Debby Rees, the glamorous air hostess from the other side of town. She was far more his type than a small-town nurse nearly ten years his junior.

Or Major Roberts' daughter, Elspeth—horsey and bouncy and very eligible. Lara knew that he had dined there because he had told her. She had seen him grimacing one morning, and had asked him what was wrong.

'I was given a portion of chicken last night which tasted like a piece of warm rubber!'

'And where was that?' she had asked casually.

'Over at the Hall. They had a party.'

They had a party. Not that she'd heard about it—but then she wouldn't have done, would she? She just had to accept that he moved in different circles, lived in a different world from the one she inhabited. Much though she might detest class barriers, and much though the world might protest that they did not exist, this she knew not to be true. She was Lara King, whose father had worked at the bottle factory all his life, and had saved up to retire to his birthplace up north—to a tiny ex-pit cottage. While Nick was the doctor's son, which in a small place like Stonebridge carried some clout. He had had every advantage given to him that life could offer.

But he didn't have a mother, a small voice reminded her. And you do him a disservice if you think he's a snob.

No, she had to admit—he was no snob. But Elspeth Roberts was, and so was her mother. They weren't patients of the practice, but they had called by one day to hand-deliver an invitation to Nick. They had looked through the slim young practice nurse with the sparkling blue eyes, and hair the colour of ripened corn, as if she had been invisible, and had demanded to speak to Nick.

Nick had made them wait, and when he had finally appeared had been charm itself, full of abject apologies, but Lara could discern no outright show of affection for the Major's young daughter. Or maybe that was just wishful thinking.

Perhaps he was still carrying a torch for Annabel. He never mentioned her, and the one time he had an angry look had turned his eyes to flint. If Annabel had jilted him, then perhaps he was still in love with her.

And yet Lara was sure that she didn't imagine his gentleness and his affection towards her, which was quite different from the manner he adopted with the new receptionist, Janice.

Could it be that he felt paternal towards her, as his father had done? That he felt in some way responsible for her well-being?

And what if he did? That didn't mean he was going to scoop her up in his arms, did it? No. He liked her; and she was his nurse, and that was as far as it went.

She was assisting him in his room one afternoon, waiting for the next patient, and watching as the dark head bent over the prescription pad. He looked up to find her watching.

'You see?' he said. 'When we get our computer— all these repeat prescriptions will be done automatically. . .'

She held her hands up. 'I know! And it will make us a birthday cake and throw a party while it's at it!'

'Sarcastic!' he grinned. 'So when is it?'

'What?'

'Your birthday?'

'It's on the twenty-eighth—Wednesday week. How did you know it was soon?'

He grinned. 'Easy. You projected it on to your joke about the computer. What are you doing for it?'

She grew flustered. It was on a Wednesday, so there wasn't time to visit her parents. She had supposed that she would go out with a group of her friends. 'Well—er—nothing,' she said. 'I hadn't really given it much thought.'

The question came out of the blue. 'Can I take you out for dinner?'

It was a simple enough request, and one which she'd secretly been hoping for for ages, yet when it came she was so flabbergasted that she was lost for words.

'Of course—if you'd rather not——' he began.

'No,' she said hastily. 'That would be lovely,' and could say no more because the patient came in, carrying a baby.

Nick looked down at the card. 'Come in, Mrs Chambers.' He smiled.

The large girl plumped herself in a chair, holding the baby close to her chest, and smiled.

'It's miss, Doctor. I'm not married.'

Nick looked momentarily confused. 'I'm so sorry,' he said. 'It's just that. . .'

The girl laughed uproariously. 'That's all right, Doctor—no offence taken!'

The baby had a bad cold and had not been feeding properly.

'You're feeding him yourself?' asked Nick.

'Oh, yes, Doctor. I don't think I'm organised enough to get those bottles clean. Breast feeding's so easy! And cheap, too!'

Nick smiled as he placed the stethoscope carefully on the infant's chest. 'It certainly is.'

As he listened to the history, told falteringly by the mother, Lara could see him frown once or twice in concentration, as if he was trying to recall something. Eventually he put his pen down on the blotter.

'You seem very familiar to me, Miss Chambers. Have you been in to see me before?'

·The girl threw back her head and laughed heartily. 'Lord, no, Doctor! You was at me house, remember? On the night my Nicholas was born.'

Nick looked up at Lara, who nodded at him, a smile dimpling her cheeks.

'Am I being dense, Nurse King? Or is this the baby that you and I delivered on Christmas Day?'

Instinctively her eyes grew soft. She nodded. 'It is.'

He gave a chuckle of delight. 'He's a bonny little fellow!' There was a silence of infinitesimal length. 'What did you say his name was?'

'It's Nicholas, Doctor!'

'After St Nicholas, of course?'

Ginny chortled once more. 'Who? Why, no, Doctor—I called him after you!'

They sat chuckling together for a long time after she'd gone.

CHAPTER FIVE

THERE had been times enough in the past when Lara had wondered if nursing was the best job in the world. Dark, rainy Saturday mornings in the depths of winter when she had struggled in on her bicycle for an early surgery while most of the world snoozed. Then, she had been sure that she was in the wrong job.

Or, at party time, when her friends had been splashing out on the best and most expensive party dresses, while she had had to run something up on the sewing machine—nurses' salaries being notoriously bad!—she had wished that she had been a secretary or a computer programmer.

But now, when this exciting yet alarming new precedent had been set—of her *boss* actually asking her out for dinner—she was glad enough of the demands of nursing which left little room for analysing just what his motives were. About whether he saw her as an attractive woman, or just as an employee—his nurse. There was certainly nothing in his behaviour towards her which indicated otherwise. She hadn't suddenly looked up across the clinic room to find him gazing at her longingly. She was more likely to find him gazing longingly at a lab. result, to discover whether his first tenuous diagnosis had been proved correct!

That was the trouble with working with someone,

she mused. You knew them very well, but in a particular way. Professionally. Usually, when you met someone at a party or through friends, you knew pretty soon whether they liked you or vice versa, but she wasn't at all sure what Nick thought of her. Oh, she knew that he liked working with her—you could always tell *that*—and she knew that he liked her as a person. But more than that? Who could tell?

If only he had given her an intimate, smouldering look which would tell her that he found her irresistibly attractive. Perhaps this was a duty dinner, one such as his father might have taken her to—but on her *birthday*? Surely there was more to it than that? But how awful if she had built it all up and it was nothing...

She dropped the cusco into a silver bowl and began to wash her hands. Her birthday was eight days away—she would just have to be patient and wait.

The surgery now seemed permanently tinged with the new dynamism which Nick had injected. The diabetic and hypertension clinics were full to bursting and, as he had predicted, proved very popular.

So did her talks, especially at the diabetic clinic. They always had a group discussion afterwards, and Nick remarked one day that it was a kind of group therapy.

'We tend to forget that diabetics have to face a lot of common problems,' he said. 'And, by discussing them among themselves, not only do they feel less isolated, but they can also help one another with ideas and suggestions. It's especially good for the newly diagnosed ones.'

'A bit like Weight Watchers?' she suggested.

The stormy eyes took on the hue of a summer evening sky when he smiled.

'And what do you know about Weight Watchers?' he queried.

She blushed. 'You forget—I was once fat.'

The lingering glance he gave her was less professional than usual, she thought, or was she reading something into it that she just wanted to find there?

'It's hard to believe,' he murmured, and looked as though he was about to say more when the intercom on his desk buzzed. 'Excuse me,' he said, and pressed the button on the box. 'Yes, Janice?'

Janice's disconnected voice came piping through. 'I've got an extra here, Dr Cunningham. A young lady named Avril Waters. She's very insistent that she see you today.'

Nick glanced at his wristwatch with a rueful sigh. He was already running late, thought Lara, and she knew that his visits were piling up. Avril had been in the year above her at school. She wondered what she wanted.

'Ask her to come down, will you, Janice?' he asked.

Lara turned to him when he had clicked the intercom off.

'Perhaps I'd better go,' she ventured. 'I know Avril—she might be embarrassed to talk to you in front of me.'

'Do you know her well?'

She shrugged. 'Not particularly. She was in the

year above me at school—and I see her around from time to time. It's a small town. . .'

He nodded. 'Exactly. It's a problem in small towns. I find it difficult to relax with patients— however much I might like them as people. And in a small town half the people in it are likely to *be* my patients.' He smiled. 'Why don't we ask Avril if she'd mind your staying? After all, she must know that your profession binds you to confidence. And if I have to examine her, then I'll need you to chaperon me anyway.'

'OK.'

There was a tap on the door.

'Come!' called Nick.

Lara thought that Avril looked pale and worried and didn't even appear to recognise the slender nurse who stood at the elbow of the doctor. She sat down in the chair which Nick indicated.

He leaned forward on his desk. 'Now then, Avril,' he asked gently. 'What seems to be the problem?'

For an answer, the girl broke into sobbing tears. Lara was at her side immediately, pressing a tissue into her hand, a comforting arm around her shoulders. Avril looked up for a moment.

'Hello, Lara,' she sniffed.

'Do you want me to leave?' asked Lara softly, but the girl shook her head.

'What's the problem, Avril?' repeated Nick gently.

Avril's reply came out in broken whispers. 'I. . . I've found a lump, Doctor.'

Nick nodded. 'A lump where?'

'In. . .in my breast, Doctor.'

Oh, no, thought Lara, but her expression remained unchanged, and she gave the girl another squeeze around the shoulders.

'Left or right breast?'

'Right.'

Nick went through a whole list of questions, and his air of calm seemed to settle the patient.

'And you first noticed the lump—when?'

'Just. . .just last week. I wanted to come to you then, but I was too frightened; eventually my boyfriend made me. . .' She began to cry again.

'Sshh.' Nick made a comforting sound. 'I'd like to examine you now, if you don't mind.'

Avril nodded and got up on to the couch, but Lara had to help her remove her top and her bra, her hands were shaking so much.

Nick examined her thoroughly, both breasts, abdomen and lymph glands, and then listened to her chest with his stethoscope, then, when she had finished dressing he spoke to her.

'I'm going to refer you to the specialist at the hospital for biopsy. I'd like that done as quickly as possible.'

Avril's face was white. 'Is it. . . I mean, can you tell if it's. . .' Her voice faltered away into nothing.

'Malignant?'

She nodded.

He put his pen on the desk and looked at her carefully. 'I can't give you a diagnosis until the biopsy has been done. Conjecture is useless at this point. Why don't we wait and see what the test shows?'

She looked like someone in a trance. 'Will I be in hospital for very long?'

'Just overnight,' he answered. 'The biopsy is a short, straightforward procedure. The only reason you have to stay in is because you'll have a light general anaesthetic.' He waited. 'Is there anything else you'd like to ask me?'

'I... No.' She stood up. 'Thank you, Doctor.'

It was strange how they always said that, thought Lara. She had known people be told that they would be lucky to see the year out, yet they always said 'thank you, Doctor', as politely as a small child at a party.

'I'll ring the consultant myself tomorrow, and he'll send you an appointment. If you're worried, or if you want anything that you don't understand explained—then I'm always here to talk to. OK?'

Her anxiety was evident in her eyes, thought Lara.

'Yes, Doctor.'

Nick and Lara sat for a moment in silence after she'd gone, and then she stood up and shut the door.

'You know, don't you?' she asked in a low voice.

The stormy eyes scrutinised her. 'Know what, Lara?'

Her fear had become anger, and she directed it against him. 'Oh, don't be so obtuse, Nick!' she cried. 'You're an experienced surgeon, aren't you? You must have been able to tell whether or not the lump was malignant.'

There was a very long pause. 'As I told her,' he

said deliberately, 'I can't give a diagnosis until the biopsy has been done.'

'But you do know, don't you?' she persisted.

'I think so. Yes.'

'It's malignant, isn't it?'

'Yes.'

She briefly covered her eyes with her hands, desperation making her voice raw. 'Then why didn't you tell her? Why give her false hope? Why——?'

'No, Lara.' His voice was stern; she had never heard it sound quite like that before, and it silenced her. 'I *can't* give a diagnosis on palpation alone. I just can't and you know that. It isn't reliable enough, and if I were wrong. . .'

'But——'

'And what would you have me do? What can I possibly do tonight? Why fill her with more fear than she already has?' His face was full of compassion. 'I know that she's your friend, that you're the same age. I know that it frightens you. But cancer isn't the dirty word it was even a decade ago. It's not a death sentence any more. You of all people should know that, Lara.'

Her eyes filled with tears. 'I know. It's just. . .'

'What do you want me to say?'

She looked at him with helpless appeal in her face, and he was on his feet in a moment, supporting her, her arms around her, but it was not simply comfort that he gave.

'What?' he whispered.

'I don't know.' But she did know. She didn't want his words, and perhaps he guessed as she thought it, for he bent his head to kiss her. Unexpected, and yet entirely predictable; they kissed with a kind of pounding feverishness which was more than mere attraction and desire—for a moment it obliterated all thoughts of life, and death—and they drew away from each other, stunned by the sheer intensity of their embrace.

'That shouldn't have happened,' he said, at last.

'No,' she agreed shakily.

'I meant—not here.'

'No.'

'But I wanted to, Lara.' He paused. 'So much.'

She met his eyes, unafraid now. 'So did I.'

He smiled then. 'Pretty unprofessional.'

She nodded. 'I'd say so.'

'How long do I have to wait for this birthday of yours?'

'It's on Wednesday.'

'Keep those kisses on ice until then?'

She gulped. 'I certainly will.'

And it was perhaps fortuitous that Janice chose that moment to rap sharply on the surgery door with a heap of letters for him to sign, and Lara set off to find her gabardine.

CHAPTER SIX

LARA rode home on the rusty pushbike, singing loudly, tunelessly and triumphantly—not caring who heard her. The words were all mismatched snatches of songs from well-known musicals, and the common theme which ran through them all was love.

He *must* care, she thought as she carefully wheeled the bike into the small hall of her house. A man didn't kiss you like that if he was merely taking you out platonically—two colleagues simply passing a pleasant evening together. Come to think of it, she couldn't remember ever having been kissed like *that* before. But perhaps that had something to do with the way she felt about him. Perhaps kisses could only be that stupendous if you fancied like mad the man who was kissing you.

She sighed. 'Keep those kisses on ice.' He had actually said that! She kicked off the sensible sturdy black shoes and lay back on the sofa, too dazed to even consider making herself her customary cup of coffee.

Then she thought of Avril Waters, and her heart plummeted. How would she be feeling tonight—knowing that she would be admitted into hospital within the next few days, imagining the worst? Oh, please be wrong, Nick, prayed Lara silently. But she knew from the expression in his eyes, from the quiet resignation in his voice, that he would not be wrong, save by a miracle.

She put the half-drunk cup of coffee back down on the tray. 'You can't take it on board,' he had once said, and he was perfectly right. But how difficult not to. To have to maintain a calm and unruffled composure, when inside you just wanted to kick something. That was one of the most difficult things about nursing—you were expected to be so damned *capable*.

But presently her mood lifted again, and she thought about what he'd said: that cancer was no longer a death sentence. She knew that, and owed it to her patients to actually believe in it. She must stop feeling sorry for herself, and just hope that, if Avril's breast lump *was* malignant, it had been caught early enough to be treated successfully.

But that night, for the first time in ages, she examined her own breasts very carefully before putting the light out.

Next day there wasn't time to analyse whether or not the atmosphere of camaraderie between Nick and herself had been strained by the intimacy of a kiss in his surgery, because she scarcely saw him all day. She spent almost the whole morning checking blood-pressures in the clinic, and it was a particularly negative clinic, since every single patient seemed to have a legitimate problem.

Nick came into the staff-room at lunchtime to find her scowling at her salad sandwich.

He grinned. 'Shall I go out and come in again?'

She coloured prettily and could have kicked herself—it wasn't really very cool to blush in this day and age, now, was it? 'Sorry,' she mumbled, putting the sandwich back on the plate. 'I'm just fed up with human nature!'

'A common complaint,' he agreed sagely. 'Care to share the cause of your disillusionment?'

'I am fed up,' she stressed vehemently, 'with telling people to give up smoking. I tell them it makes their blood-pressure shoot up. They know it does and yet they still do it. Why?'

He shrugged. 'Stress. It's a condition of our affluent society. We eat too much. We drink too much. We burn ourselves in the sun. We don't exercise enough; instead we drive everywhere and let our cars belch out lead which poisons the atmosphere. We——'

'Don't,' she shuddered. 'I wanted comfort, not a Job's comforter.' She saw him raise an eyebrow and managed a smile. 'Just ignore me — I'm having a bad day.' She took another bite of her sandwich and briefly her blue eyes danced with amusement. 'I ride a pushbike anyway — so at least I'm not poisoning the atmosphere!'

He was looking at her with a definite glint of appraisal in his eyes. 'About tomorrow——' he began, when Janice walked in, a package in her hands which smelt irresistibly tantalising, and which, when she opened it, revealed huge, fat, greasy chips. Nick pounced on them immediately.

'Tut, tut!' he said. 'Very bad for you, Janice — all that fat and cholesterol,' and with that he popped one of the largest into his mouth and Lara burst out laughing.

'Hypocrite!' she giggled, and took one herself when Janice offered her the package.

She left the staff-room soon afterwards, and didn't see him for the rest of the afternoon, but when she went next to her in-tray there was an envelope on the top in his writing, and she ripped it open to find a note inside, which read,

Dear Birthday Girl,
    I'll pick you up tomorrow evening at seven-thirty. Chip shop suit you?
                                    Nick.

She laughed and tucked the note inside her uniform dress. All those crazy old clichés were coming into their own now, she thought. Walking on air? She was floating!

She spent one of the most studious evenings of her entire life, for no exam revision had ever received quite so much joyous attention as the choice of what she should wear to go out with Nick. Smart or casual? Trousers, dress or skirt? If she went over the top, he might be embarrassed, but how awful if she dressed down and he was wearing a suit—oh, *what* to wear?

She rang her friend Joan.

'What shall I wear?' she wailed.

'Wear the red,' suggested Joan.

'It's too short!'

'What about the black?'

'It's too clingy!'

There was a sigh. 'Well, what about your blue velvet? That always looks good.'

'And you don't think it's too dated?' asked Lara anxiously.

'It's classic,' said Joan patiently. 'Not dated.'

She tried it on. In fact, *it* seemed a bit too short and too clingy. She rang Joan again.

'I don't want to look like a tart!'

Joan chuckled. 'What is it with you? I'll tell you what, Lara—why don't you play safe and wear your nurse's uniform? I mean, he likes you in that, and if he gets called to a case then you can accompany him with decorum!'

'Shut up!'

A glittery brooch was dragged out of her jewellery box and dusted vigorously, sheer tights found, matching shoes and handbag. She painted her toenails, used a face-mask and spent so long pummelling an imaginary spot of cellulite on her hips that she looked all pink and blotchy and was terrified it wouldn't go.

Lara King, you're worse than any schoolgirl, she chided herself, but laced her bedtime cocoa with brandy all the same, and was gratified, yet surprised, when she fell sound asleep before midnight.

Next morning, a clutch of cards lay on the hall mat. One from her parents, with some Marks & Spencer gift vouchers inside. Another from her brother, hurriedly scrawled, with a postscript, 'Present to follow—sorry, but I'm stony broke!' What else is new? thought Lara with amusement.

There were several others, one from Joan, a couple more from other schoolfriends, and a lavish but rather sickly quilted satin one from Tim Burton, whom she had been out with a long time ago, and who had pursued her from a distance ever since.

Nothing from Nick. But then again, he was buying her dinner. She mustn't be greedy!

The day was erratic. Lara was just finishing weighing a baby when there was an enormous commotion in the waiting-room. An old alcoholic patient who had been with the practice for years suddenly began having a severe convulsion. Nick raced down from his surgery, Lara from the clinic room to help him. Together they held him steady while Nick somehow managed to inject some Diazepam. Janice pulled screens around them, and shepherded the other waiting patients into a far corner of the room.

The ambulance had just taken him away, when Nick was called out to a patient who was suffering from chest pains.

By four o'clock things were beginning to wind down.

'So much for getting the chance to eat some of that cake you brought in,' said Janice wistfully, eyeing the extravagant whorls of cream studded with cherries.

'Oh, take it home with you,' said Lara gaily. 'I shan't eat any of it now.' I don't want to spoil my appetite, she thought happily.

'Thanks,' said Janice. 'My kids will love it!'

Lara knocked off promptly at five, cycling home as fast as if there were a strong wind behind her. She had drunk her coffee and was just running a bath when the phone rang.

It was Nick, and he sounded distinctly uncomfortable. 'Lara?'

'Yes?'

'Look—I'm so sorry, but I'm not going to be able to make it tonight. I know it's unforgivably short notice, but I'm. . .' There was a muffled kind of noise in the background, and she thought that she heard him say 'in a *minute*', and then he came back on again, sounding ill at ease. 'I'm terribly sorry, Lara,' he said, in a softer voice. 'I'll explain when I see you tomorrow.'

For a second she felt let-down and thoroughly insecure; she couldn't remember feeling that way since she had been a fat teenager and people had snorted with derision when she passed. He didn't like her. He didn't really want to go out with her.

But then a voice of common sense reasserted itself. Don't be foolish, it called to her—this is Nick Cunningham we're talking about; your boss, your colleague. The man you admire. The man you trust. He's said he'll explain. So give him the benefit of the doubt.

Her trusting heart won. 'That's OK,' she said in a low voice.

'Goodbye, Lara. Happy birthday.'

'Goodbye.'

But the phone was returned to its cradle with indecent haste, and immediately the self-doubts re-emerged. Why sound so mysterious and ill at ease? Why hadn't he explained his sudden change of plans there and then, on the phone?

The doorbell pealed noisily, and she jumped, flinging the door open to find a grinning Joan there, who immediately burst into song.

'Happy birthday to you! Happy...' She stopped. 'What's the matter with you?'

These things always sounded worse when you explained them to other people, Lara thought.

'Nick can't make it,' she mumbled.

Joan raised one eyebrow sceptically. 'Can't *make* it? Why? Is he ill?'

Lara squirmed. 'I—yes, no...he didn't say.'

'He didn't *say*?' asked Joan incredulously.

'Oh, for goodness' sake,' said Lara crossly. 'Will you stop repeating everything?'

Joan took no notice whatsoever. 'What do you mean, he didn't say? Has he lost his powers of speech?'

Lara pulled Joan inside and shut the door. 'He said he'd explain when he saw me.'

'Good of him!'

'Oh, don't Joan—I'm sure he's got a perfectly good excuse.'

'Hmm. You're far too soft, Lara—it won't get you anywhere.' She smiled. 'Oh, well—if you've been stood up...'

'I have *not* been stood up.'

'Sorry!' Joan amended hastily. 'As your escort has been "unavoidably detained"—you may as well put the ruddy blue velvet on, and we'll hit the town together.'

Joan was her oldest and dearest friend, but Lara was bitterly disappointed about Nick and the last thing in the world she felt like doing was going out.

'I don't think so...' she started to protest, but Joan was extremely difficult to refuse, and within ten minutes Lara was zipping up the back of her dress.

They had a drink at a pub, sitting outside in a pretty garden filled with terracotta tubs of flowers, and it was there that they decided to throw caution and their bank manager's better opinion of them to the wind, and eat in the Trattoria Donato, Stonebridge's one Italian restaurant. It was a slightly old-fashioned place, full of Chianti bottles and plastic grapes hanging from the ceiling, and huge Technicolor posters of Roma, Firenze and Napoli, together with the mandatory garrulous and flirtatious waiters who always, as Joan pointed out, made you feel slightly glamorous.

Joan ordered uninhibitedly, Lara less so.

'I'll have the *spaghetti alla vongole* to start—followed by the *pollo soppresso*,' said Joan. 'Lara?'

'Parma ham and melon, followed by the lemon chicken, please,' smiled Lara, handing the menu back.

They ordered wine, and the waiter poured them a huge glassful each.

'Melon! Lemon chicken with no spuds! I don't know why you're being so careful,' complained Joan. 'After all—it *is* your birthday.'

Lara shook her head. 'If you've ever had a weight problem, it's there for life. I always have to watch it.'

'Could have fooled me,' muttered Joan.

The wine, the good food and the convivial atmosphere made both girls feel irresistibly mellow, and Joan had almost persuaded Lara to share the *zabaglione* with her when Lara froze, a glass of wine halfway to her lips.

'Oh, my God,' she whispered.

'What is it?' hissed Joan.

Lara was white. 'Don't look now. It's him.'

Joan didn't have to be a contortionist to half wriggle round in her chair to see what Lara was talking about, and she turned back again, her eyes soft with sympathy.

Lara felt sick, but her ringside seat forced her to watch Nick being ushered to a table with a woman who was so stunning that every man in the restaurant paused to give her a second glance. She was no stranger to Lara. Who could forget pale blonde hair which cascaded over narrow shoulders, pale lips and pale eyes—or clothes in animal skin—furs and soft leathers which probably cost more than Lara's entire monthly pay cheque? Lara shut her eyes briefly. No—who could possibly forget Annabel Hummerstone?

But how *could* he? How could he stand her up on her birthday—to take his ex-fiancée out? Had he been playing games with her all along? Or was Annabel's hold over him just too strong to resist? She felt as though she'd been kicked in the teeth.

Joan was looking at her anxiously. 'Are you all right?' she whispered.

'Not really,' she said wanly. 'But don't worry—I'm not going to make a scene. Let's just get the bill and get out of here.'

Lara was praying that he wouldn't see them, and they almost managed it, right through having to refuse the waiter's offer of a liqueur on the house. For one awful moment she thought that they might be going to sing 'Happy Birthday' to her.

She edged out of the diner-filled room, taking a circuitous route which completely bypassed his table. The waiter was just helping her on with her stole when she turned very slightly, the honey-blonde hair swinging silkily to her shoulders, and found herself staring directly at Nick.

He looked wretched—guilt written all over his damnably handsome face, and he half rose to his feet, as though he was about to come over to her.

Well, he could keep his fumbling excuses—she didn't want to know. Bad enough to be stood up for another woman, without having to be confronted with the evidence of it quite so publicly. Nick Cunningham ought to learn to make his mind up about exactly what it was he wanted.

Deliberately she turned her back on him.

'Come on, Joan,' she instructed. 'Let's go.'

CHAPTER SEVEN

'LET ME in!'

'Go away!'

The knocking resumed. 'I'm not going anywhere until you let me talk to you.'

'Then you'll have a long wait!' Lara wiped another treacherous tear away. The damage was done. He had his feather-brained Annabel, and he'd hurt her badly—so what was he doing outside her house at midnight, trying to rub salt into the wound?

She took a deep breath as she realised that the knocking had finally stopped. She leaned back against the front door and shut her eyes, when a soft voice through the letterbox made her jump.

'I came straight here from the restaurant,' he said.

'Well, hip, hip, hooray! I'm surprised that you could drag yourself away,' she nearly sobbed.

She heard a loud sigh. 'I just want you to hear my side of it,' he said reasonably. 'So won't you let me in and listen?'

Lara knew that she was weakening. Oh, *why* was she so soft? 'And what if I refuse?'

'Then I'll kick the bloody door down!' His reasonableness seemed to have evaporated into thin air!

With that she pulled the door open and glared at

him. 'Do that and I'll have you done for criminal damage!'

He walked in past her, the stormy eyes looking decidedly more stormy than usual. 'The police never prosecute domestic disputes—you should know that!'

But that's only if they're cohabiting, she nearly squeaked, and hastily put a block on it—that was a subject she most certainly didn't want to discuss with him at the moment.

He was glowering at her so darkly that anyone would think *she* was in the wrong, and she drew her shoulders back and gave him a frosty smile.

'Where's your fiancée?' she sniped sarcastically. 'Sitting in the car?'

'She is *not* my fiancée!' he thundered.

'Really?' she snapped. 'Then how would you classify her? She must be pretty important for you to stand me up and take her out instead, or perhaps it isn't really like that—perhaps I'm imagining that it ever happened?' Now why had she said that? The whole plan, which she had discussed with Joan on the way home from the restaurant, was that she would be calm and collected when she saw him, that she would not give his ego an extra boost by showing him how much he had hurt her.

Suddenly he looked tired. 'Look,' he said. 'I've had one hell of an evening...'

'I'll bet you have!' Now she was sounding like a fishwife.

He regarded her steadily. 'Just hear me out, will you?'

'If you insist,' she said moodily, turning away from him, but he caught her by the shoulders.

'Don't,' he said, in a ridiculously gentle voice. 'Don't turn away. Listen to what I have to say.'

She backed away—his touch was causing her body to send crazy, dizzy sensations back to her brain which wildly conflicted with her thoughts about him.

'You must know how much I've been looking forward to this evening. . .'

She started to scowl but he held his hand up before she could reply. 'Don't, Lara,' he said. 'Don't keep making flippant responses. Answer me honestly—did you know that I was really looking forward to taking you out tonight?'

'I've really no idea,' she said haughtily.

'Did you?' he persisted.

'I suppose so,' she answered sulkily.

'I've been keyed up about it all week.' For a second, his face lit up so that he looked almost boyish, but then he frowned again. 'Perhaps I should have talked to you about all this before,' he mused. 'But it didn't really seem appropriate at work. Look——' He paused and stared at her very hard. 'Annabel didn't take the break-up of our engagement particularly well, even though the relationship had been in the doldrums for a long time. She's used to getting what she wants—and she wanted me. It was a classic case of "hell hath no fury". . .except that I tried very hard not to hurt her, and I had hoped that she would see that fundamentally we were unsuited, and that we would be happier apart.' He pushed a lock of the jet hair off his forehead.

'And of course,' he continued, 'she has always blamed you for the bust-up of the relationship.'

Lara's blue eyes were like saucers. 'Me?' she squeaked. 'Why on earth should she think that?'

He stared at her incredulously, then shook his head. 'I don't think we'll go into that at the moment. Suffice it to say that she has been ringing me repeatedly since I came to live down here, pleading with me to give it another go. I kept saying no. I couldn't see the point, and by then. . .' He shook his head again and appeared to change his mind. 'On Thursday, when she rang, I told her that I was taking you out for your birthday, and could we please call it a day? She hung up, which she'd never done before, and I thought that was the last of it. But of course, it wasn't. When I arrived home last evening after surgery, she was there, wild with temper—I'd never seen her quite like that before. She intimated that she could and would ruin our evening in a spectacular way unless I took her out. She also. . .' He paused, and looked at her questioningly.

Lara had softened considerably—it was obvious that he was telling the truth; she only had to look at the consternation and concern written in his eyes to see that. 'What?' she asked.

'She also said that if I would spend the evening with her and at the end of it could honestly tell her that I didn't want her—in any way—she would leave me alone for good.'

Lara turned away again. 'So?'

'It seemed too good an opportunity to miss — peace from the constant harrassment. And so I agreed. But, Lara,' the stormy eyes were deadly serious now, 'she pulled every trick in the book this evening to try to get me to want her back, but nothing worked. Nothing.'

She gave a hollow little laugh. 'Oh, really?'

But he had stepped towards her, had lifted her downcast chin with the tenderest of touches.

'You can't see it, can you?' he asked softly. 'You just can't see it.'

She looked at him in bewilderment. What on earth was he talking about?

'She's very beautiful, yes, but she's not what I want. She doesn't have stars in her eyes, and cheeks like roses, and the softest heart in the world. Because she's not you, Lara — and it's you I want, you I need. You. . .'

And suddenly all her good resolutions had gone the way of good resolutions the world over, and she was in his arms, kissing him, being kissed, laughing and sniffing, all at the same time.

They somehow found themselves on the sofa, and the bodice of her blue velvet dress had managed to slip over one shoulder, revealing an expanse of soft, creamy white skin which Nick seemed to enjoy kissing over and over again. Her legs were feeling like jelly when he suddenly pushed himself away from her, the black hair delectably ruffled, and grinned.

'I think I'd better get going,' he murmured. 'Before things get out of hand.'

'Who cares if they do?' she sighed.

He laughed. '*I* do. And I get a funny feeling that not only would the whole town rise up in arms against me, but that my father is somewhere up in the great blue yonder, telling me to damn well treat you properly!'

'Oh, very well,' she said, wrapping her arms around him.

'Perhaps one more kiss?' he suggested.

Just one more kiss nearly proved their undoing, but at last they stood on the doorstep saying goodbye.

'Do you like picnics?' he whispered.

'Mmm. I love them,' she murmured back. 'Why?'

'Because I'm providing one for us tomorrow. I'll pick you up after work. Sweet dreams.'

Sweet dreams indeed! And the sweetest of all those dreams had but one irresistible protagonist—Nick Cunningham.

As he had promised, there were picnics—lots of them. They drove to the sea, to a forest, and, once, took a ferry to Boulogne—and on that occasion jettisoned the meal they had brought with them, to eat instead in a tiny seafood restaurant, ordering mussels and cold white wine in their execrably bad French.

But there were indoor feasts too, and trips to the theatre. And games of Scrabble. And films.

And one Saturday afternoon he took her to bed and made love to her.

She was very much in love with him, and she found it a little strange, to work so closely with a man she loved. She was so determined to act circumspectly that at times she was more distant with him than she had been before they went out!

She spoke to him about it one night.

'Do you find it odd, working with me?'

'A little,' he admitted, turning on to his back and stretching his arms. 'Oh, I've been out with people I've worked with before, but it's never. . .' His voice tailed off and the blue-grey eyes regarded her thoughtfully.

She knew that she was fishing. 'Never what?' she prompted, her heart in her mouth.

He leaned over and kissed her softly. 'It's never been as serious as this,' he whispered.

She didn't dare to hope that he loved her as much as she loved him, but although he behaved as though he did he had never actually said so.

How silly and conventional I am, thought Lara one morning as she prepared for her diabetic clinic. It was how people behaved that mattered, not what they said. Nick treated her with passion, and with gentleness. She had the best of everything. The words 'I love you' often seemed to be used to excuse the most appalling behaviour—so why was she setting so much store by them?

Avril Waters' results came back from the hospital—it was as Nick had suspected and feared: the lump was malignant. The consultant had sent a letter. Nick read it and looked up.

'He decided against a radical mastectomy,' he told Lara. 'In view of her age, and the fact that she caught it early, he did a lumpectomy. There has been no involvement of the lymph glands, so things are looking good. She's going to have radium treatment around the site of the lump, so she'll be feeling pretty poorly. Perhaps you could pop round and see her?'

'I will,' said Lara, heaving a huge sigh of relief that the diagnosis had been made early enough to prevent the far more traumatic mastectomy.

When she visited Avril at home, she was amazed at her cheerfulness.

'You look wonderful!' she exclaimed.

Avril grinned. 'I'm just so relieved that I'm still intact. Well, almost!' Abruptly, she halted. 'I'm living positively. That's what they told me I must do. I've had cancer, and that's a fact of life. I doubt whether a day will go by without my remembering that, but it's something I must come to terms with. Can you understand that, Lara?'

'Perfectly,' answered Lara quietly. 'But it's just an illness. Like living with diabetes, or asthma.' She remembered Nick's words to her. 'The fact that you talk about it is good. Cancer is just a word, and the sooner we start regarding it that way, the better off we'll be. And your prognosis is very good.'

'Yes, it is. Is it true I'll get sick with the radiotherapy?'

Lara nodded. 'Most probably.'

'Will you come and visit me?'

'Just try and stop me!'

She told Nick about it later.

'She's being so brave. . . I don't know whether I'd be quite so cheerful.'

He shook his head. 'You don't know what reserves of strength you have until you're called upon to use them—or else how would young boys get up the courage to go off and fight wars?'

'Young boys don't think about it,' she argued. 'Youth thinks it's indestructible—it's the older men who have to do the soul-searching.'

There was a long silence, and then he spoke.

'I love you, Lara. Will you marry me?'

He said it in exactly the same kind of way as he might have asked her if she'd like a glass of wine, so that she blinked and stared at him.

'What did you say?'

'I said, I love you, and I asked if you'd marry me?'

Her blue eyes were like saucers, and then she smiled with a shy delight. 'Oh, Nick, darling—of course I'll marry you.'

There was a good deal of scrambling as they both left their respective chairs and met somewhere in the middle of the room, consumed with breathless kisses and hugs.

He closed his eyes tight. 'I've been wanting to ask you for weeks, but I didn't want you to think me fickle—leaping straight from one engagement into another.'

'Oh, Nick,' she sighed. 'I could think you many things, but never fickle.'

He lifted a strand of the corn-gold hair and let it fall over her shoulder. 'Like what?' he queried.

'Oh—stubborn, single-minded. . .'

'Shut up,' he muttered, and kissed her. 'Shall I tell you something crazy?'

'What?' she murmured, her head against his shoulder.

'Do you know when I first knew that I wanted to marry you?'

She shook her head.

'Last Christmas Eve. You were hanging the fairy on the tree. You were wearing old jeans. . .'

'I looked *awful*!' she protested.

'You looked beautiful!' He kissed her again. 'You weren't wearing a scrap of make-up, and there was a great big smudge of flour, just here. . .' He touched her cheek. 'But there was something so soft, and wholesome, and warm and welcoming, and I knew then. I thought—that's the woman I could spend the rest of my life with. That's the woman I'd like to be the mother of my children.'

She gave a very wide smile. 'How many children?'

He grinned. 'Would four do you?'

'Five at least!'

'Seriously?'

'Absolutely.' She felt as though her heart would burst with happiness.

'You are an amazing woman, Lara King. When shall we get married?'

She knew without having to think about it. 'What about at Christmas? That's when we met.' Her eyes shone. 'And there's always something special about Christmas.'

CHAPTER EIGHT

LIFE was just *peachy*.

Lara had everything she'd ever wanted, and more. Every morning when she woke up, it felt like Christmas.

The town buzzed with the news that the pretty young nurse and the dark, dashing doctor were engaged to be married.

'Oh, it's just like reading one of those romantic novels,' cooed one of the patients.

Love was fine, and work was fine. Nick's reputation as a good and caring doctor grew daily, and he was brilliant with children. One morning Lara watched as he played with a baby while doing a six-month check, pulling faces and making funny noises to the obvious delight of both the infant and its mother.

'I've never known a man so besotted with children!' she teased, after they'd left.

For a second he looked bashful. 'I know. I think it's because I'm an only one—big families always made me feel very envious when I was a boy. And——' There was a short pause. 'Well, Annabel didn't want children.'

She was secure enough in his love now not to feel jealous when he spoke of Annabel. 'And did that contribute to the relationship's splitting up?' she asked quietly.

362

'I suppose it did.' He smiled. 'That's enough talk about the past. Would you like to go shopping before evening surgery?'

She was exhausted, and had been hoping for a nap in front of the fire. 'Must we? What for?'

His look was one of studied innocence. 'I thought you might like to choose an engagement ring. . .'

She was on her feet in seconds. 'Give me five minutes, and I'll be ready!'

When they got back she showed Janice the ruby surrounded by seed pearls.

'It's beautiful, Lara,' sighed Janice wistfully. 'He's so kind, and considerate—and so good-looking, too! You're very lucky.'

'I know I am.' She couldn't believe just how lucky she was. Sometimes she was afraid—that it was all so perfect. That it couldn't possibly last.

Janice extracted another chocolate biscuit from the packet. 'And when's the wedding?'

'On Christmas Eve.'

Janice was in raptures. 'A Christmas wedding— how romantic! But you haven't got much time.'

Indeed she didn't. They were already at the end of October, and she still hadn't bought a dress. Christmas seemed such a long way away.

But November was a different matter—and, as the days ticked on towards the end of the month, the wedding began to take shape. It was to take place at Stonebridge. They booked the church and ordered a cake. Lara bought a simple silk dress and tulle veil in softest ivory. The florist promised her an arrangement of lilies of breathtaking simplicity.

She took Nick home to meet her parents and they loved him.

And, as the wedding plans were made, Christmas itself finally began to claim its magical hold. Lara and Janice decorated the surgery from top to bottom.

'Don't go *too* mad,' said Nick, as he handed over his contribution towards the decorations.

'Of course we won't,' agreed Lara, winking broadly at Janice.

Several of their regular patients even stayed on after surgery to help them!

'Do be careful of your back, Mr Peters,' urged Lara anxiously, as the old soldier stretched up to pin yet another paper chain to the wall.

'Stop fussing, girl,' he answered testily. 'Haven't had so much fun in years!'

And neither have I, thought Lara, as she wiped away a tear of laughter from the corner of her eye.

Ginny Chambers brought the baby in—Lara couldn't help but think of him as 'their' baby, since they had delivered him in such unusual circumstances! She thought that the ungainly young woman seemed quieter than usual.

'How's Nicky?' she asked, as the rosy-cheeked youngster lunged for her cap.

'Oh, he's fine,' she answered lethargically.

Lara looked at her closely. 'Just as important—how's his mum?'

The young woman shrugged. 'It's not easy being on your own, but at Christmas it's even worse. Everyone seems part of something, except me.'

'I can see that,' said Lara thoughtfully. 'Let me

see what I can do.' Surely there must be some way of arranging for lonely people to get together on Christmas Day? There were so many of them. She would talk to Nick about it.

But her good intentions were left by the wayside in view of what happened next. . .

Nick held a drinks party at his house. Lara had spent days dreading it, going hot then cold at the thought of what to wear, and how she'd get through an evening's small talk with people who petrified her.

He had caterers in to do the food—fancy finger-food—impossibly small sandwiches of smoked salmon, and tiny tarts with asparagus nestling on sour cream.

Lara wore the blue velvet and spent a long time being kissed by Nick before the guests arrived, while he assured her that she was the most exquisite-looking creature he'd ever seen.

'And you're sure that this dress is OK?' she asked him anxiously.

There was a roguish twinkle in his eye. 'I think I prefer you without anything on at all,' he murmured, moving in to kiss her once more, when a loud peal on the doorbell halted them.

'Behave!' she whispered.

In the end, her fears proved groundless. As Nick's fiancée she was welcomed into the circle immediately, and her natural charm soon disarmed even Major Roberts' crusty wife, even though she had held out great hopes of landing Nick for her daughter, Elspeth!

By nine o'clock the party was in full swing, with

no one looking as though they planned to leave, and Nick had begun to walk across the room towards Lara when, to his surprise, he saw her glass of champagne slip from her hand, falling as if in slow motion to the ground and bouncing harmlessly off the carpet. Several people turned to stare.

'Butterfingers. . .' he teased, when he saw her face, white and drawn, and without warning she suddenly gasped, bent double, and collapsed to the floor.

He was at her side in seconds, brushing her hair from her face, which was sweating profusely. Her eyelids fluttered open.

'Oh, Nick. . .' The gasp faded into nothing as she clutched at her stomach convulsively.

He picked her up immediately and carried her out of the room, taking her straight to his study and lying her on the examining couch there.

By now she was doubled up and groaning.

He spoke quietly. 'I know it hurts, darling—but can you point to where the pain is?'

She managed to point a finger at the place where the stabbing intensity of the pain threatened to cut her in two.

He swiftly examined her. 'You've got rebound and guarding—acute abdominal pain, my darling. I think it might be appendicitis. I'm going to have to take you into hospital.'

Through the mists of her agony, she heard his words, some still rational corner of her brain wondering how he could be so certain, and then remembering that for many years he had been a surgeon.

Later, she would vaguely recall him carrying her

out to his car, of people milling around in the hall, their faces bewildered and concerned. Of the drive to the hospital she remembered nothing.

Like a faraway dream she saw white-coated figures. Doctors—how many of them were there? Probing and pressing down on her abdomen until she thought that she would die. And then more figures, only this time they wore green. A smiling face above a mask, and something black and heavy being placed over her mouth and nose. A sickly, sweet smell. And then, mercifully, oblivion.

'Hello, darling.'

The mists cleared and she opened her eyes to find him sitting beside her. 'Oh, Nick,' she breathed, and gently, gingerly, he took her into his arms.

'Nick. . .' Her voice was hoarse.

'Darling girl.' His voice had a choking sound to it. 'You had us scared for a minute there.' He carefully moved her back against the pillows.

She gripped his hand. 'What was it? What happened?'

'You've had an operation. You had a ruptured ovarian cyst—we thought it was appendicitis at first. They took you to Theatre last night as soon as we got here. And you're going to be fine. The gynaecologists tell me you've got the constitution of an ox!'

'Charming!' she said weakly.

He gave her an enormous smile. 'That's better! You've got to rest, oh—and there's just one thing. . .'

'Mmm?' she was beginning to feel sleepy.

'You'll have to stay in for about a week, and you'll feel a bit tottery after that—so. . .' He hesitated a little.

'What?'

'The doctors think we ought to postpone the wedding—just until the New Year, when you'll be fully recovered. Do you mind very much?'

'Mind?' She smiled. 'Nick Cunningham, when I do marry you, I want to enjoy not only the ceremony, but the honeymoon as well!'

'Oh, you will, my darling,' he promised. 'You will.'

Her week in hospital flew by. Nick visited her every day—often twice or three times!

'I'm not going anywhere,' she scolded him, but he held her hand very tightly. 'The nurses are complaining that you're becoming part of the fixtures and fittings!'

'Let them complain!' he muttered.

The day before she was due to go home, the ward sister buzzed up to her bed, smoothing the counterpane and plumping up the pillows.

'Mr Stedman is here to see you,' she told her.

Lara was surprised. The consultant did his two ward-rounds on Monday and Thursday.

'I'm honoured, aren't I?' she asked the sister.

The ward sister suddenly became very busy. 'Yes, yes,' she said hurriedly. 'You are.' She drew the curtains around the bed, and at that moment, Mr Stedman appeared and sat on the edge of Lara's bed. Lara thought that his smile appeared heavy, and laden.

'Hello, Lara. How are you feeling today?'

'I'm fine.' She nodded, looking at him quizzically, because instinctively she felt that her post-operative state was not why he was here. His juniors could assess that for him. Her heart started beating very quickly.

'Your operation went very well,' he began. 'And you're healing up very nicely...' He paused. 'It's just that during the operation...'

She looked up quickly, every nerve-ending suddenly alert. And then she saw it. It was written on his face, in his eyes; it had been there, too, on the ward sister's face. Pity.

'Go on, Doctor,' she said, in a low voice.

And, with growing disbelief, she began to take in every word that he uttered.

CHAPTER NINE

NICK stared at her incredulously. '*What* did you say?'

'I can't marry you,' she repeated quietly.

His look of astonishment quickly changed to one of concern. 'Darling, no one's rushing you—you're still recovering from your operation.'

She clenched her fists behind her back, digging her nails in until she could feel pain, steeling herself for the strength she needed now. She moved a step back, as if trying to physically increase the distance between them. He was being so understanding, and that was the last thing she needed. She didn't want him to be understanding; she wanted him to rant and rave, to dislike her.

'Don't misunderstand me, Nick, please. I just don't want to marry you. Not now. Not next week. Not ever.'

He sighed. 'Lara, sweetheart—I think you're a little bit depressed. You've been like a different person since you came home. But it's common to feel low when you've been ill. . .'

'No!' The protest came out as a shout which startled them both. 'I'm trying to do this as best I can, but it's not easy. I'm trying to tell you that it's over between us, Nick.' Her voice faltered. 'I'm sorry.'

He studied her with a clinical detachment for a moment. 'Why?'

She had thought about this, had anticipated this query. She had ready the one answer which would guarantee his departure from her life for good. She looked down, afraid that the lie would show in her eyes. 'Because I don't love you any more.'

'I see.' He spoke in a tone she didn't recognise, one that he had never used with her before, and she looked up to find that his face was no longer the one she knew so well, that it had become a mask, concealing—what?

She spoke quickly, terrified that if she didn't get it all out, that it might be too late, and that she would change her mind. 'I'm signed off work until January anyway, so I shan't be leaving you in the lurch. I'm going to go up to my parents'. I think—I think that you ought to advertise my job——'

But she wasn't sure whether he'd heard her last words, for he had walked out, slamming the door of her house so furiously that for a minute she was afraid it had been wrenched off its hinges.

That same day she packed and took a train up north to her parents. The journey was an agony in itself, for the carriage was filled with people going home for Christmas. Fired by the festive spirit, they joked and laughed, complete strangers conversing with each other. All except Lara. She sat very still, and silent, staring out of the window at a passing landscape which remained a blur.

She was still weak after the operation, and she used this to try to quell her parents' obvious anxiety when they saw her white face, with the panda-like shadows beneath her eyes. Explaining that the engagement was off was harder.

'We weren't as compatible as we first thought,' she said. 'It's just one of those things.'

Her mother looked unconvinced, and Lara couldn't miss the glance that passed between her parents.

She felt like a stranger in their home, too miserable to be able to join in with the Christmas build-up. But at least she had not grown up there — she knew no one, and she saw no one, did not have to endure questions about why the marriage was off.

The build-up to Christmas continued.

On the twentieth she went Christmas shopping with her mother, trying to summon up a degree of enthusiasm for the task.

On the twenty-first she hung paper-chains in the sitting-room and cried over an old film.

On the twenty-second her brother came home. She loved Daniel dearly, but when he heard about the broken romance he upset her by saying that she was too young to be serious.

On the twenty-third, the whole family went to a carol service, and it took every ounce of self-control that she possessed not to break down in the church, as she listened to every poignant word.

On the night before Christmas she was in the house alone. Her brother had walked up to the pub, her parents were meeting old friends and going on afterwards to midnight mass. None of them had offered to take her with them, and frankly she wasn't surprised — she was no fit company for anyone.

She wrapped her few presents. Switched the TV on, and then off again—and did the same with the radio. Made herself some tea and sat in the armchair to drink it.

She thought of last Christmas, when she had turned round to see Nick standing there, snowflakes on the jet-black hair. A large tear welled up and splashed into the teacup. She put the cup down and wiped the tear away angrily.

In the corner of the small sitting-room, the Christmas tree glittered and glimmered, the fairy-lights twinkling and causing the tinsel to sparkle magically. She shut her eyes tightly, and another tear squeezed out.

How silent it was tonight. Silent night. Holy night. She remembered the story that her mother would read to her each Christmas Eve.

Twas the night before Christmas, when all through the house,
Not a creature was stirring, not even a mouse.

But then she heard the creak of the gate, and she hastily scrubbed at her eyes with a handkerchief. Her brother back, probably—maybe to persuade her to join him at the pub.

The doorbell rang, and she looked up. Trust Daniel! He'd forgotten his key! Pinning a bright smile to her face, she got up and opened the door.

He stood there, like her most enduring memory of him—with soft, new snowflakes peppering the dark waves of his hair; and just for a second she knew an almost overwhelming urge to hurl herself into his arms, to know the warmth and comfort she had so often found there. Her bright, false smile switched to one of dismay.

'What on earth are you doing here?' she cried.

He walked straight past her into the sitting-room without being asked. 'Coming to talk to you, of course.' He sounded quite matter-of-fact, as though he were about to discuss a patient with her, and she knew for certain that she would be unable to keep up the charade, that he had to leave, and quickly.

'My parents will be back any minute,' she lied.

He shook his head. 'Nice try—except that I telephoned first, and they agreed to let me see you alone.'

Her mouth fell open. 'There's nothing to talk about, Nick.' She spoke with a kind of quiet desperation.

'Oh, I think so, Lara. I think we have a lot to talk about.'

She shook her head. 'It's over,' she whispered.

He moved closer, the blue-grey eyes compelling her to gaze into their depths, and she found herself powerless to do otherwise. She was drowning in the intensity of his stare.

'Tell me again, Lara. Tell me that you don't love me any more, and I'll never bother you again.'

She licked her lips. 'I——' She opened her mouth to form the words, but no sound came out.

'Tell me,' he urged.

She shook her head violently, as if trying to rid herself of some demon, and then she burst into tears.

She was in his arms in seconds, he was stroking her hair, and murmuring, 'It's all right,' over and over again, until he had almost convinced her that it would be, until she remembered—that nothing would ever be all right again. She made as if to move, but the power of his embrace was too strong.

'Now kiss me,' he whispered, and she found herself complying, raising her face to his, waiting for and wanting the touch of his mouth, the heat of his breath. The kiss went on and on until neither had breath left, and when it finished they stood, inches apart, fear on her face, triumph on his.

'You're a liar, Lara!' His voice was exultant. 'I know you too well. You *do* love me, you know you do—you could never have kissed me like that if you didn't.'

'Go away,' she said desperately. 'Go away! I can't marry you!'

'Why not?' The question rang out on the still air.

A sob erupted from her throat. 'Because I can't give you the babies you want so much! I'm infertile, Nick—that's why I can't marry you.'

His expression didn't change. She had been expecting her words to provoke some reaction but his face remained implacable, his voice calm as he spoke.

'But you didn't think you should tell me? You didn't think I had a right to know?'

'And what would you have done?' Her voice rose. 'You want children, and I can't give them to you. One of the reasons you split up with Annabel was because she didn't want children. You *told* me that.'

'Oh, for God's sake!' he exploded. 'There were a hundred reasons why we split up—the main one being that I didn't love her.'

She shook her head. 'It's no good, Nick. I'm setting you free.'

The expression on his face was fierce as he turned to reply. 'I see. And do I get no say in the matter? What if I don't want this so-called freedom?'

She was near to tears now. 'Oh, maybe at the moment you don't think you do—but in five years, ten years—what then? Then you'll wish that you'd let me finish it. My infertility will always be there— a barrier between us!'

His eyes were bright as he held her gaze again. 'I want to marry you, Lara.'

'No!' she cried, wondering how he could bear to prolong the torture. 'If you marry me now, it will be for the wrong reasons. Because you pity me, the way Mr Stedman and Sister pitied me, and I couldn't live with that. I——'

He held his hand up. 'Look at my face, Lara— there's no pity there. Just love. I love you. I've always loved you. Not just the colour of your eyes, or your hair, or the way you wrinkle your nose when you laugh—it goes deeper than that. I love the essential you, the woman that you are. The whole package. I didn't choose to fall in love with you; I just did. A fact of life. And there are no guarantees in this life—no one ever guaranteed we'd have children.' He smiled. 'When two people fall in love, of course they talk about having children. I would have liked my own children, but not at such a cost— not if having them would mean that I'd lose the woman I love. . .'

'Oh, Nick. . .' She had started to cry, and he

pulled her tenderly towards him. 'I just didn't want to deny——'

He placed his finger over her lips. 'Shush, now. You deny me nothing. Come here.' He sat down on the squashy old sofa and pulled her on to his lap, kissing her over and over again, until her tears had dried.

'What made you come?' she whispered eventually.

His eyes were serious. 'Your behaviour just seemed so inexplicably out of character. I thought about what you'd said—"I can't marry you"—and that made me suspicious. You only told me that you no longer loved me when I pressed you, and that didn't ring true, but I was so angry at the time that I didn't stop to analyse it. When I started thinking about it afterwards, I pinpointed the change to when you had the operation. I suspected then what you've confirmed today and I knew that I had to come and confront you.' He ran his hands lingeringly over her breasts. 'I'm off for the next two days, and when I go back I'm taking you with me, understood?'

'Yes, Nick,' she said meekly.

'And listen.' His voice was very, very gentle. 'Later we may want to foster, or adopt—there are thousands of children just crying out for a decent home—and we could give them one. But maybe we won't want to do that—our work may provide fulfilment alone. God knows, the patients have missed you these last weeks, and so have I. Now I can't imagine working without your help, your support, your tender smile.'

She nodded, each word that he spoke as precious

as gold-dust, illuminating every dark corner of her mind, so that finally she began to peep into some glorious, glittering future which they would share together.

She tried to explain. 'It being Christmas somehow made it worse. All those carols. Everywhere I turned I seemed to be confronted with images of babies, and Christmas is all about birth, and I thought—I'll never have a baby of my own.'

But he was shaking his head. 'No, my darling. Christmas isn't just about a baby—that baby is the symbol for the real Christmas message, which is love. Love is the enduring human quality. It's love that lifts us, love that separates us from the beasts in the field. Precious, beautiful love. And we have it, Lara—we have so much of it.'

Whether it was the tree lights, or her imagination, she didn't know, but the room seemed incandescent with radiance, and when she looked up at him her eyes were bright with unshed tears.

And then he took her by the hand, across the room, and pulled open the front door.

'What?' she whispered.

'Listen,' he said softly, and they stood perfectly still, listening to the twelve chimes of midnight mass ringing out for Christmas Day, splendid and soaring as they pealed across the valley.

'Happy Christmas, Lara.'

'Happy Christmas, Nick.'

They stood in silence for a while, not feeling the cold, and she knew a moment of complete and blissful fulfilment.

As she leaned her head against his chest, her

attention was suddenly caught by a bright star that sparkled and spangled in the dark sky, and she was reminded of another star which had hovered over the baby, the symbol of love, almost two thousand years earlier.

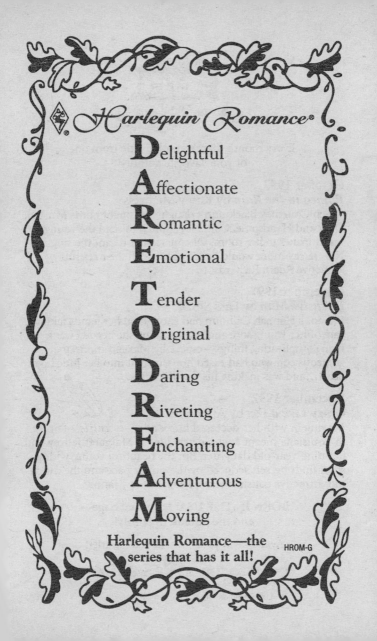

Harlequin Romance®

Delightful

Affectionate

Romantic

Emotional

Tender

Original

Daring

Riveting

Enchanting

Adventurous

Moving

Harlequin Romance—the
series that has it all!

HROM-G

Every month there's another title from one
of your favorite authors!

October 1997
Romeo in the Rain by Kasey Michaels
When Courtney Blackmun's daughter brought home Mr. Tall,
Dark and Handsome, Courtney wanted to send the young
matchmaker to her room! Of course, that meant the single
New Jersey mom would be left alone with the irresistibly
attractive Adam Richardson....

November 1997
Intrusive Man by Lass Small
Indiana's Hannah Calhoun had enough on her hands taking
care of her young son, and the last thing she needed was a
man complicating things—especially Max Simmons, the
gorgeous cop who had eased himself right into her little boy's
heart…and was making his way into hers.

December 1997
Crazy Like a Fox by Anne Stuart
Moving in with her deceased husband's—*eccentric*—family
in Louisiana meant a whole new life for Margaret Jaffrey and
her nine-year-old daughter. But the beautiful young widow
soon finds herself seduced by the slower pace and the much-
too-attractive cousin-in-law, Peter Andrew Jaffrey....

**BORN IN THE USA: Love, marriage—
and the pursuit of family!**

Available at your favorite retail outlet!

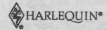 

WELCOME TO *Love Inspired* ™

A brand-new series of contemporary inspirational love stories.

Join men and women as they learn valuable lessons about facing the challenges of today's world and about life, love and faith.

Look for:

Christmas Rose
by Lacey Springer

A Matter of Trust
by Cheryl Wolverton

The Wedding Quilt
by Lenora Worth

Available in retail outlets
in November 1997.

**LIFT YOUR SPIRITS AND GLADDEN YOUR
HEART with *Love Inspired* ™!**

Steeple
Hill™

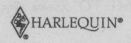

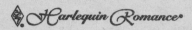
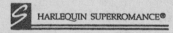

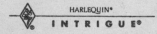